PEOPLE OF
CAHOKIA

MORNING STAR:
Star Path

PEOPLE OF
CAHOKIA

MORNING STAR:

Star Path

W. Michael Gear and
Kathleen O'Neal Gear

A TOM DOHERTY ASSOCIATES BOOK · NEW YORK

STAR PATH

Copyright © 2019 by W. Michael Gear and Kathleen O'Neal Gear

Maps, timeline, art, and ornaments by Ellisa Mitchell.

A Forge Book
Published by Tom Doherty Associates
175 Fifth Avenue
New York, NY 10010

www.tor-forge.com

Forge® is a registered trademark of Macmillan Publishing Group, LLC.

The Library of Congress Cataloging-in-Publication Data is available upon request.

ISBN 978-1-250-17615-8 (hardcover)
ISBN 978-1-250-17636-3 (ebook)

Our books may be purchased in bulk for promotional, educational, or business use. Please contact your local bookseller or the Macmillan Corporate and Premium Sales Department at 1-800-221-7945, extension 5442, or by email at MacmillanSpecialMarkets@macmillan.com.

First Edition: June 2019

Printed in the United States of America

10 9 8 7 6 5 4 3 2 1

To Robert Porter

For

All those years of support

Thanks, Bob.

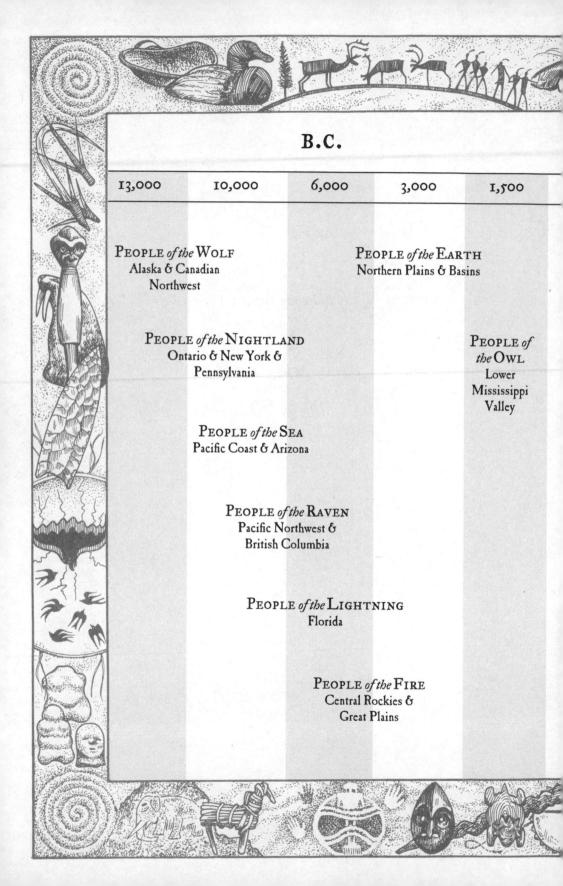

B.C.

13,000	10,000	6,000	3,000	1,500

PEOPLE *of the* WOLF
Alaska & Canadian
Northwest

PEOPLE *of the* EARTH
Northern Plains & Basins

PEOPLE *of the* NIGHTLAND
Ontario & New York &
Pennsylvania

PEOPLE *of*
the OWL
Lower
Mississippi
Valley

PEOPLE *of the* SEA
Pacific Coast & Arizona

PEOPLE *of the* RAVEN
Pacific Northwest &
British Columbia

PEOPLE *of the* LIGHTNING
Florida

PEOPLE *of the* FIRE
Central Rockies &
Great Plains

A.D.

0	200	1,000	1,100	1,300	1,400

PEOPLE *of the* LAKES
East-Central Woodlands
& Great Lakes

PEOPLE *of the*
WEEPING EYE
Mississippi Valley
& Tennessee

PEOPLE *of the* MASKS
Ontario & Upstate New York

PEOPLE *of the*
THUNDER
Alabama & Mississippi

PEOPLE *of the* RIVER
Mississippi Valley

PEOPLE *of the* MORNING STAR
SUN BORN
MOON HUNT
STAR PATH
Central Mississippi Valley

PEOPLE *of the*
LONGHOUSE
New York
& New England

PEOPLE *of the* SILENCE
Southwest Anasazi

The
DAWN
COUNTRY

PEOPLE *of the* MOON
Northwest New Mexico
& Southwest Colorado

The
BROKEN
LAND

PEOPLE *of the* MIST
Chesapeake Bay

PEOPLE
of the
BLACK
SUN

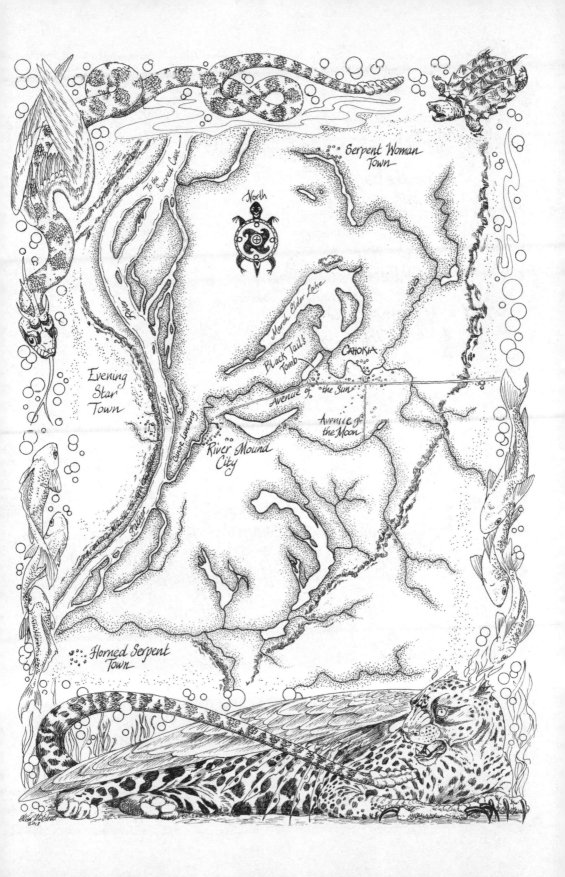

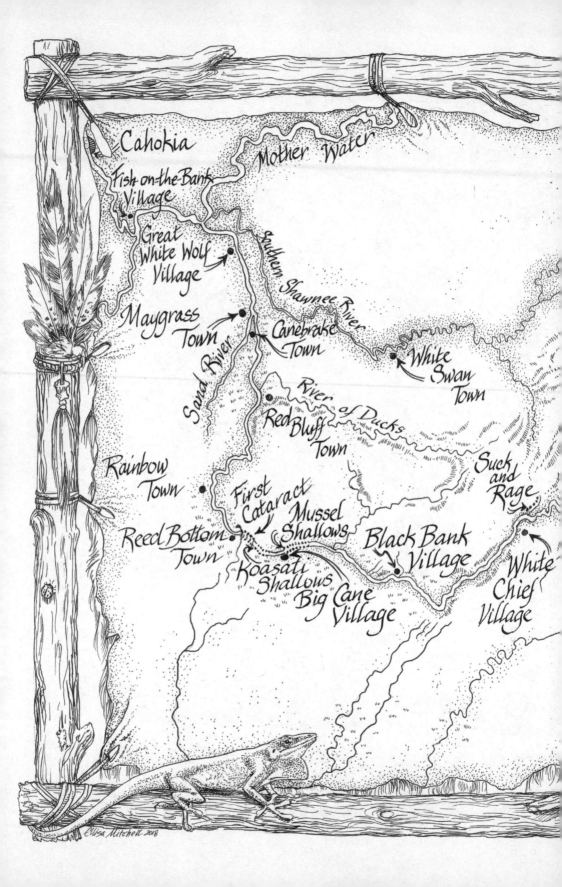

Chestnut
Place Village

Beautiful
River

Joara

Wide

Cane
Town

Fast River

Cofitachequi

Canyon
Town

the Tenasee
River Valley

PEOPLE OF
CAHOKIA

MORNING STAR:
Star Path

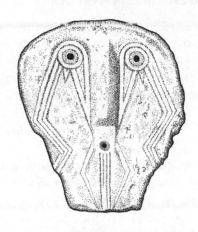

Prologue

*A*s I stare down at the young woman, I am delighted by what I see. She's just turned sixteen, finished her first woman's moon, and has passed from girl to womanhood. She came to me still wearing her skirt tied with a prominent virgin's knot.

Not that she came willingly, of course. Her father's lineage abducted the girl from her mother's village. Muskogee are matrilineal, so while the girl might have been the man's daughter, she was merely the product of his ejaculation. Not of his clan or lineage, and hence, not his family. Essentially his, but not his. Perfect for a sacrifice. Didn't really cost him anything but a little emotional distress.

Which is nothing compared to his and his lineage's much more parochial desire to influence the scales of justice on their behalf. Seems the man's uncle, a man he adored, had gotten into a little trouble with the local orata, or village chief. Something about a murder.

Frowned on, you see.

But in the convoluted way the Muskogee think, a word from me to the orata would set everything straight. Place the guilty cur beyond the pale of local retribution. Hence the offer of the girl.

To me.

And who am I?

Some call me a witch. The Muskogee have given me the name Lightning Shell, for the mask I wear. It covers the horribly scarred left side of my face.

I am as puzzled by that scar as anyone. One should remember getting burned *like that. Must have been terribly painful. But I have no memory of it. As I have no memory of so many things since that day in the river.*

As I stare down at the girl, her eyes fix on the beautifully flaked long chert knife I hold. She is tied to one of the polished center posts that hold my roof up. It's a heavy piece of black locust, driven deep into the ground. She can't pull it up no matter how hard she struggles. The wad of cloth in her mouth will dampen her screams.

Which disappoints me, but I do have to make some concessions to the town's folk. The way they fear me already is almost irrational.

I reach down with the blade and sever the rope holding her skirt up. As it slides down her young hips, her eyes widen and she shrieks into the cloth.

Like my ancestors, I, too, have come to Cofitachequi after a setback.

When the first Cahokian expedition crossed the Blue Mountains and followed the ancient trails into the east, they found a rich and fertile land. The Muskogee peoples who lived in small villages along the waterways called their country Kofitachake. Kofita means to scoop out, excavate, or dig out. Chake means shallow waters.

My people, as they so often do, butchered the pronunciation and called it Cofitachequi: Ko feeta check ee.

The Cahokians came to Cofitachequi a little more than a generation ago led by War Leader Moon Blade, a Four Winds Clansman in line for the high chair at Horned Serpent House. I was just a boy back then, but I remember the uproar. Cahokia had almost broken out in open warfare. Something about the work levy needed to flatten out and grade the Great Plaza. At the time Moon Blade, resisting the levy, was threatening to march Horned Serpent Town's warriors on the Morning Star House.

Blue Heron, who was a young beauty at the time, had outmaneuvered Horned Serpent Town's clan matron, and Moon Blade was sent east by order of the Morning Star himself. Not that it was called exile—nor was Moon Blade's departure from Cahokia anything less than a pageant; Moon Blade left at the head of nearly a thousand warriors and commanded a flotilla consisting of five hundred canoes.

The journey down the Father Water, up the Mother Water to the Tenasee, thence east and across the Blue Mountains to the coastal plain of Cofitachequi had taken nearly nine months.

The various tribes along the Tenasee would never forget. They paid for the army's passage in stolen food stores, enforced labor, and when they resisted, in blood. Entire villages were left destitute.

Once east of the mountains, Moon Blade's disciplined warriors had made short work of the petty Muskogean chiefs. Being used to scuffling among themselves, the Muskogee—barely masters of the organized raid—had no chance. Disciplined Cahokian squadrons were able to surround and defeat them with little effort. The local chiefs and war leaders found themselves hanged in squares; their people were then taken captive and turned into work details.

Nor was dissent a problem. Again, the key word is "petty." So great was the animosity between the various local factions that the previously abused among them rarely hesitated to turn on their former chiefs when called upon to aid the Cahokians.

Moon Blade was a man of many talents, not to mention charisma. And he had learned from the fine art of politics. After his arrival and conquest, he set about building his chieftainship. Adopted the local term Mikko, *or high chief. Nor was he averse to women, seeing as he married a woman from each of the major Muskogean lineages. Eleven women in all. And he promptly went about siring children from them.*

In a sense, Moon Blade grew the colony into an organic blend of Muskogean and Cahokian. They worship the notion of Morning Star but don't play chunkey with the same passion. Build palace-topped mounds but keep their old beliefs in the ancestral Spirits.

Unlike Moon Blade, I have no idea how I got here. Seriously, no memory at all. One heartbeat I was underwater choking Night Shadow Star. The next, it's half a year later and I am here with a horrible scar ruining the left side of my face, and wearing a shell mask.

The night I appeared to them, lightning struck one of their sacred charnel houses. As it burned down to coals and charred bones, I came walking out of the smoke and flames, my shell mask on my face.

After an entrance like that, is there any reason they shouldn't consider me a Powerful sorcerer and witch?

There are times when the simplicity of human belief leaves me stunned.

Beyond the walls of my mound-top temple, lightning laces the storm-torn sky like tortured worms of light. Wind gusts shake the walls, cause the leaping flames in my central fire to twist and curl.

The girl screams again, her eyes glistening with fear.

She is a pretty thing. I trace the tip of my knife around her round breasts, tease the tips of her nipples with the knife's point to make them stand erect.

She throws herself against the bindings, tears leaking down her cheeks.

Lightning flashes again. White and blinding, it is close. Followed by the head-splitting crack of thunder, as if it were breaking the world.

"It's all right," I tell her, knowing a Muskogee girl can't understand a word of what I say in Cahokian. "I need to see the future. And to do that, I need your blood."

Her scream is so violent it puffs her cheeks around the cloth gag in her mouth.

A terrible staccato of thunder bangs and booms, violent belts of rain pelt down from the storm.

As a blinding stab of lightning—my Spirit Power—turns the clouds white, I make my first slice up from above her thick black pubic hair to just below her sternum.

As her entrails spill out, I see the pattern. Watch as they slither, fold, and spill.

The lightning's blinding flashes enable me to see across the distance. The shape of my sister's face is molded by the ropy knot of intestines.

"So," I whisper, "you think you are coming for me? Oh, my beautiful love, you have no idea."

I shall be ready.

Ever so ready.

One

He is waiting for you." Piasa's words sounded so crystal clear in the night. They snapped Night Shadow Star out of a deep sleep. The Spirit Beast's mouth might have been but a finger's width from her ear.

She blinked in the darkness, her thoughts unusually sharp after being roused from such a deep slumber.

Images flashed. The memories like second sight. Given the intensity and clarity of their details, she might have just stepped from Matron Columella's burning palace in Evening Star Town. What she'd seen inside the blazing inferno haunted her: blood everywhere—a scarlet intensity as it soaked into the woven mat covering the floor.

And there, laid out in a bizarre pattern, were pieces of Lace's body. The tiny bits of arm, leg, head, and torso had been hacked from the fetus Lace had carried inside her. Each of the parts had been placed just so to create a partial circle—the beginnings of a portal that her brother believed would have allowed the Powers of the Underworld to flow upward into the Sky World.

In the middle of the carnage, staring at her with gleaming and predatory eyes, a smile of anticipation on his bloody lips, stood her brother, Walking Smoke. Blood smeared his naked skin, partially obscuring where it had been painted in magical designs. The long chipped-stone ceremonial knife was held as if to mimic his straining and erect penis.

Walking Smoke had indicated that partial circle of body parts on the floor. "The sacred opening, like that wonderful sheath of yours, Sister.

The passage of life through which Piasa's souls will emerge in order to consume my body."

He had believed that. Thought that through ritual he could call Piasa's Spirit from the Underworld, that he could trap the Underwater Panther's essence inside his own flesh as Black Tail had first done with the Morning Star.

Memories. Just memories.

Night Shadow Star stared up at the dark ceiling above her bed and re-played the events of that terrible day. She'd managed to defeat Walking Smoke. At Piasa's whispered command, she had accompanied her brother as he fled the burning palace. Lured Walking Smoke out onto the river and distracted him. She had loathed every moment of it. The first time her brother had raped her had been so hideous, so terrible, that she'd de-nied herself the memory—buried it so deeply down between her souls it had taken Piasa and Horned Serpent's Underworld Power to make her re-call. Had that day started it all? Her violation, first by the newly reincar-nated Morning Star, and then, within mere hands of time, by a jealous Walking Smoke? Was that the moment that forever set the three of them on this path that would end in the destruction of one or more of them?

That day on the river she'd sought to end it all, stripped, offered her-self to Walking Smoke once their canoe was well out in the Father Water's current. She could almost feel her brother's chilled body as he crawled on top of her. Rain was beating down in a hard and pounding cadence. She had heaved violently at his touch. In the last instant before he had driven himself into her, she had capsized the canoe.

In the icy river's depths, Night Shadow Star had struggled, his hands clasped tight on her throat . . .

"He knows you are coming."

Piasa flickered at the edge of Night Shadow Star's vision, a flash of glow-ing blue light in the darkness of her room. It no longer bothered her that no one else saw the Spirit Beast or heard its voice when it spoke to her. Most of her family and associates had taken for granted that she was possessed. That the creature owned her souls and used her for its own purposes.

"It's up to me to destroy him," she said aloud as she stared at the dark-ness of her sleeping quarters. "The three of us, Morning Star, me, and Walking Smoke, we're caught in a terrible triangle. Brothers and sister, torn between Sky and Underworld Power, locked in a combat of posses-sion, jealousy, and incest."

Piasa hissed his agreement. She caught flickers of his movement among the shadows as he darted between her storage boxes.

"Lady?" Fire Cat's voice asked from her doorway. "Did you say some-thing?"

"Piasa says that Walking Smoke knows I'm coming."

Fire Cat stepped in, seated himself at the foot of her bed. Bound to her by oath, he was in his early thirties, muscular. In the dark she couldn't see his pink, healing scars.

"How can he? Some agent of his? A spy who sent word? Even then, he's half a world away."

"He can feel the Power. Can feel me."

"Your family line is tangled in Power like a flock of birds in a net." He paused, and she could imagine his smile. Then he said, "That or madness."

"Is there a difference?"

"Lady, I no longer know. I have trouble accepting that your other brother, Chunkey Boy, really plays host to the souls of the Morning Star. After our journey to the Underworld, he taunted me. Told me outright that he was manipulating me for his own ends."

"Is it really so hard for you to believe that Morning Star is the resurrected god?"

"I don't waste my time questioning. I have other more pressing concerns."

"The journey to Cofitachequi? The knowledge that Walking Smoke knows I'm coming?"

"That's for later. My immediate concern, along with the preparations for the journey, is that you turned away two runners yesterday. One from Clan Matron Rising Flame, and the other from your betrothed."

"Don't call Spotted Wrist my betrothed."

"Your clan matron has ordered you to marry him."

She felt the tightening in her chest, the fear that Fire Cat might be right. That somehow, some way, Rising Flame and Spotted Wrist would manage to force her to marry before she could escape downriver. It would be done through trickery, some threat. A manipulation that made her choose between two intolerable situations.

"There are whispers." She reached out in the darkness, laid her fingers on his knee. Felt his instant reaction, as if a charge had run through his muscles. Her own body quickened at the contact, brief as it was. This small intimacy was all that she would allow herself.

"Whispers?" he asked somewhat hoarsely.

"That we spend every spare moment with our loins locked together. That their spies can't prove it? I think that drives them half mad."

He was silent for a time, thinking—no doubt as she was—about the bargain she'd struck with Piasa. Saving her world had come at a price. She might love this former enemy and slave of hers more than life itself, but the choice had been Fire Cat, or her city. Trained to rule, she'd chosen her people over the man she loved.

"Lady, we have mere days before the canoes, provisions, and warriors will be assembled to take us east. Rising Flame and Spotted Wrist will have to move quickly. Spotted Wrist needs your name and standing to solidify his position. If he marries you, he joins the most powerful family in the city. That you have spurned him for so long has become an affront. People are talking about it. Makes him look weak, undesirable. For the Hero of the North, that must burn like cactus thorns in an open wound."

"He is placing as many of his people as he can in our expedition. Fire Claw has been replaced by Squadron First Blood Talon and his picked men. All veterans from the Red Wing campaign. I would hope that you won't let them provoke you."

"I have made my peace with what happened at Red Wing Town. How they dealt with my family. Power was at work. Shaping me. I shall not let them use my weaknesses against you."

And people wonder why I love this man?

"Once again, Fire Cat, we are being tested. I have dreamed of you and me, alone in the forest, on a small farmstead. Just the two of us and our children. Living by ourselves, growing our own food." A pause. "We are so happy."

"I know that dream."

"If we do this, if we destroy Walking Smoke, Piasa says there may be a way for us. A chance that the dream might become a reality."

She saw his head lower, as if considering very carefully. "You would do that? Leave your life here? Become nameless, a dirt farmer without fine dresses, without servants and porters?"

"Are you happy, Fire Cat?"

"Only to serve you, Lady."

"As long as I am Lady Night Shadow Star, they will be trying to marry me off to someone I cannot abide. As long as I am that woman, I remain a tool that Piasa can use for his purposes. Maybe if I were nameless, clanless, and worthless to them, they would let me be free."

"It is a wonderful dream, isn't it?"

She heard Piasa's mocking laughter coming from the corner of the room.

The Spirit Beast's sibilant whisper carried in the night: *"The most insidious deceit comes from the lies you tell yourself."* A pause. *"In the meantime, be careful. They will try to use the Red Wing against you."*

"What?" Fire Cat asked, recognizing the way she tensed.

"Piasa. He says they will try to use you against me. It's something they are plotting. Whatever happens, you must promise me that you won't play into their hands."

Two

The new Clan Keeper, Spotted Wrist, appeared like an avenging eagle as he strode through the palisade gate that opened onto the Morning Star's high mound-top courtyard. Hard to think of him otherwise given the splays of feathers radiating from each shoulder, the feathered cape hanging down past his knees.

The first thought in Blue Heron's head was: *This ought to be fun!*

Blue Heron had spent most of that morning socializing with the various nobles and ambassadors who'd gathered in the high courtyard before the Morning Star's towering palace. All had dressed in their best, their faces painted, and they had outfitted themselves in finery. She might have been "demoted" from her position as Clan Keeper, but Blue Heron had prudently maintained her spy network. People still feared and respected her.

The way Spotted Wrist made his entry and strode through the crowded courtyard you'd have thought he was the living god. In his early fifties, the Hero of the North was a solid man. Muscular. In addition to the gaudy eagle-wing splays at his shoulders, a bloodred apron hung to a point between his knees. The long cloak—crafted out of a thousand painted bunting breasts—swung behind him with every step. His blocky face was filled with purpose, a tension in the set of his wide mouth and hard eyes.

At his heels followed ten of his handpicked warriors under the able command of Blood Talon—the legendary squadron first and Spotted

Wrist's most trusted friend. Each of the warriors was dressed in wood-and-leather armor, every surface polished so that it shone in the morning sun. Hardened leather helmets capped their heads, and beaded forelocks swung on their foreheads. As they marched, they clasped their feather-studded arm guards against their chests; grim expressions gave them a ferocious look.

When Clan Keeper Spotted Wrist passed the massive World Tree pole that thrust up into the morning sky, he let his fingers slip across the lightning-riven wood, carved as it was with scenes from the Morning Star's life in the Beginning Times. The towering post was crafted from a giant bald cypress trunk floated up from the south.

Where she sat, her back to the Morning Star's palace wall, old Blue Heron bit her tongue—not that she had a lot of teeth left to give the action much emphasis. In her fifties now, she wore her gray hair in a tight bun at the back of her head. Until four months ago, she had been the Four Winds Clan Keeper, a position she'd held for ten more years than she had fingers and toes to count. To be supplanted by a swaggering, over-feathered spoonbill of a man like Spotted Wrist grated with the same irritating intensity that wet sand did when lodged in the delicate folds of one's private parts.

As the new Keeper approached, War Leader Five Fists emerged from Morning Star's palace, taking his place before the beautifully carved double doors.

The lop-jawed and gnarled warrior remained in charge of the living god's security—a position to which he was particularly suited given he had the same disposition as an old boar grizzly with a toothache. Morning sunlight slanted across the palisade walls to illuminate the man's weather-beaten face with its dislocated jaw. His skin, aged to dark walnut and deeply lined, made his clan tattoos illegible.

Blue Heron growled to herself as she forced her tired bones to stand. After all, she was an elder in the Morning Star House, of the Sky Moiety, of the Four Winds Clan. Sister to the Lady Wind—who served as the "great sky," or *tonka'tzi*, the ruler of secular Cahokia. Blue Heron's nephew, Chunkey Boy, had surrendered his body as a host for the Morning Star's reincarnated spirit.

Just because Blue Heron had been deposed from her position as Clan Keeper was no reason she shouldn't act like the noble she was.

Around her, the Earth Clans chiefs and matrons paused. All lowered their heads, placed fingers to their foreheads in a gesture of respect.

Spotted Wrist nodded in reply, his sharp eyes catching on Blue Heron's as she stood, back stiff, arms crossed, her gaze burning into his like obsidian fire.

Something flickered behind his eyes; she thought it the sort of look the renowned war leader would have given his enemies across a battle-field. He had to resent her. Of all the humans in Cahokia she *knew* the extent of his failures.

Blue Heron baited the man with a mocking grin and tapped her fore-head in a flouting gesture that smacked of disrespect.

Spotted Wrist glared daggers at her.

Before the palace doors, Five Fists bowed and gestured that the Keeper precede him. Notably, however, Five Fists stepped between Spotted Wrist and his honor guard as they entered the great palace. An affront that turned Squadron First Blood Talon's expression black and angry. She could see the warriors, bristling, shuffling, controlling their anger as they filed through the double doors.

Following them inside the palace, Blue Heron blinked, then shuttled her way along the wall to the right, passing the opulently furnished sleep-ing benches, covered as they were with the finest of textiles, furs, and blankets. Packed beneath were magnificently carved and inlaid wooden storage boxes, large jars, intricately woven baskets, and the greatest con-centration of accumulated wealth in the known world.

Well, at least north of the Gulf. Who knew about the Maya and those other people down south?

Blue Heron, by virtue of her rank, displaced old Kills Four, chief of the Snapping Turtle Clan of the Earth Moiety. She smiled as she indi-cated his place. Kills Four graciously rose and retreated to the second rank of seated people where he in turn displaced a lower-ranked chief from one of the Deer Clan lineages. That chain would follow its links down to some lesser noble who'd be forced outside.

Blue Heron seated herself, nodding to old friends, acquaintances, and enemies. She could see the curiosity in their eyes as they gazed back and forth between her and Spotted Wrist.

The new Clan Keeper had stopped just short of the great central fire. It shot flames and occasional sparks toward the high roof and illuminated the great room filled with painted and ornately attired occupants.

Young Rising Flame—high clan matron of the Four Winds Clan—stood to one side and gave Spotted Wrist a nod to acknowledge the new Keeper's arrival. Rising Flame, young, athletic, and in her twenties, re-mained a controversial figure as the recently appointed Four Winds Clan matron. She'd gained the position through Morning Star's intercession—a fact that still rankled in each and every one of the Four Winds ruling Houses.

No one, however, denied the living god.

One of the boys who guarded the eternal fire tossed another log onto the flames. Bright tongues of fire cast light that leaped and flickered on the ornamented walls, glinted off polished copper reliefs, caressed brightly colored wood carvings and statuary. It bathed the faces of the nobles and foreign dignitaries who were all seated, awaiting the Morning Star's entry.

And he came. Emerging from his rooms in the palace's rear as if from a cocoon. An eagle-wing splay spread wide behind his shoulders, and a quetzal-feather cloak—gift of the distant Itza—hung from his shoulders. The spotless white apron at his waist dropped to a point between his legs; scalp bundles decorated its front flap. Layers of beaded necklaces surrounded his throat, and a polished arrow-split-cloud headpiece with a soul bundle was pinned to his tightly wound hair. His face had been carefully painted black with a white forked-eye design around each eye. Shell masks covered his ears.

Here was the reincarnated god, walking among them in human form. People immediately knelt or prostrated themselves, depending on their rank.

Blue Heron merely bowed until her forehead touched the intricately woven matting upon which she sat.

The Morning Star—born of First Man and Old-Woman-Who-Never-Dies—along with his twin brother, the Wild One, had helped to destroy the monsters and establish the laws of Creation in the Beginning Times. Then his Spirit rose to join *Hunga Ahuito,* the two-headed eagle who ruled the realms of the Sky World.

There he had stayed until two generations ago. That was when the Spiritual essence of the hero had been called down from the Sky World and reincarnated into a human body that had once belonged to Chief Black Tail. Upon the death of Black Tail's body, Morning Star had again been resurrected in the body of Blue Heron's nephew: Chunkey Boy. Even if she looked hard, she could barely see the likeness of her hellion of a nephew in the being who now seated himself on the raised dais behind the fire.

"Arise!" Morning Star called. A pause. Then he added, "Thank you for coming, Clan Keeper. I was delighted to accede to your request for an audience."

Blue Heron sucked her lips in and clamped her jaws tight. It would be foolishness to allow even the hint of a smile to betray her anticipation.

Spotted Wrist, the Hero of the North, the man who had defeated the heretics in Red Wing Town and pacified the northern forests, threw his head back. He clasped his arms behind him, and said, "Lord, I have asked Clan Matron Rising Flame to attend, for the problem involves her as well. It is the order of the clan matron that Lady Night Shadow Star join me in marriage. As leader of her clan, Rising Flame has the authority to demand that the marriage take place now. Before Night Shadow Star leaves for the east. I have been patient, but Night Shadow Star has ignored me and the orders of her clan. Told me that while she cannot cancel the clan matron's—"

"And you expect me to influence Night Shadow Star on your behalf?"

"Lord, a simple decree on your part would—"

"What news do you have for me regarding the theft of the Koroa copper, Clan Keeper?" The Morning Star's eyes narrowed, the tone of his voice as cutting as an obsidian blade.

Blue Heron went giddy with delight.

Spotted Wrist stiffened at the change of subject. Seemed to be searching for words, shot a surprised look at Rising Flame, who in turn was blinking her confusion.

Blue Heron fought to keep from giggling. Fool that Spotted Wrist was, he'd never seen it coming.

"What Koroa copper?" Rising Flame asked.

"The *stolen* Koroa copper," Morning Star said with exaggerated patience.

Spotted Wrist cleared his throat. "The search for the culprit is proceeding as we speak, Lord. I have my men looking everywhere. If necessary, we will turn all of Cahokia upside down."

At the words, Blue Heron cocked her eyebrow. Brilliant at war, Spotted Wrist thought in terms of brute force. He still hadn't figured out that being Clan Keeper required different skills. Granted, in the days following Rising Flame's appointment, Spotted Wrist's reputation—not to mention his veteran warriors—had been instrumental in restoring order throughout the city. The various ruling Houses had teetered on the verge of war when it seemed the Morning Star might have died. Spotted Wrist's loyal squadrons squelched any such foolish notion on the part of the high chiefs and the matrons.

"Lord?" Rising Flame asked. "I have been in Serpent Woman Town for the past five days. While I may have heard vague rumors about this copper theft, I am unfamiliar with the details. Perhaps the Keeper could enlighten me?"

Blue Heron smothered a snort of delight, turned her eyes back to Spotted Wrist.

"The Koroa are a people who live on the Father Water's west bank way down in the south. They occupy swampy land just north of the Gulf," Spotted Wrist told the matron. "Eight days ago, a Koroa embassy was received by *Tonka'tzi* Wind in the Council House. They came with a wealth of conch shell, yaupon leaves, hanging moss, purple and red dyes made of snails, and batches of feathers from spoonbill, parakeet, white heron, and swans. Additionally, they offered a young woman as a bride to the Morning Star."

Spotted Wrist, warrior to the end, kept his back straight and stood at full attention. "They proposed an alliance. One that would be of strategic advantage to us as it would give us a firm ally on the Tunica's southern border. In return the Morning Star gifted the Koroa chief with two plates of thin-beaten copper. Good sheets, perfect for placing on a wooden mold to be pressed into a relief."

"And it was stolen?" Rising Flame asked, her serious face slightly pinched.

"From the middle of their camp, Matron. Down at the canoe landing below River Mounds City. Seeking redress and the return of their property, the Koroa immediately stormed their way into High Chief War Duck's palace. While they made the nature of the theft known to the chief through signs and river pidgin, they weren't able to communicate all the details. It took a while for War Duck to get a message to *Tonka'tzi* Wind. By the time the Great Sky could get a translator to River Mounds City, it was the middle of the following day."

Spotted Wrist made a pained face. "Suffice it to say that by that time, the situation had deteriorated, angry accusations being traded by all parties involved."

Blue Heron had heard all of this before, witnessed most of the proceedings in Wind's Council House.

"It seems," Spotted Wrist said, "that it was probably a single thief. The Koroa were awakened as the thief was sneaking away into the night and said that the man had a bird's head."

"A bird's head?" Rising Flame asked.

Morning Star, on his elevated chair, had adopted a subtle smile, his dark gaze evaluative as it fixed on Spotted Wrist.

"We think it was some sort of feathered headdress, Matron." Spotted Wrist broke his pose just long enough to wave away a pesky fly. "That, and a dog may or may not have been involved."

"A dog? The canoe landing is infested with the mongrels."

"Yes, Matron. All the Koroa can confirm is that a big dog was slurping up the contents of their stewpot when the theft took place."

The first tingle of premonition ran down Blue Heron's spine.

Oh, no.

She straightened, grinding the few teeth left in her jaws.

"The Koroa who awakened," Spotted Wrist continued, "raised an alarm. In the ensuing confusion, packs were overturned, people stepped on. Lots of shouting and thrashing about. Both thief and dog were seen disappearing in the direction of the warehouse district."

"And you've made no progress in finding the copper or the culprit?" Morning Star asked softly from his raised dais.

"I have men searching all over the city, Lord," Spotted Wrist insisted, his face grim. "I have an agent stationed every hundred paces at the canoe landing. They inspect every vessel that leaves. Those two pieces of copper would be worth a fortune in the south. The word is out that any Trader who accepts them, no matter what story he's told, he'll hang in a square."

Blue Heron swallowed down her suddenly tight throat. The struggle to keep her expression bland remained ever more difficult.

"That's all you've got?" Rising Flame demanded. "Keeper, this isn't the theft of some wooden statue out of a dirt farmer's shrine. This was a major embassy. The potential of brokering an alliance in the far south. Beyond the Tunica—"

"Matron, with respect." Spotted Wrist inclined his head. "It's a small chieftainship. A smattering of outlying villages around a single town with a couple of mounds and a palisade. Most of it lies in swamp. I had the recorders look it up. The fact that the copper was stolen out of the Koroa camp, from under their very noses, while they were camped in the midst of Traders from over half the known world, doesn't reflect on us."

"What would you tell the Koroa, Clan Keeper?" Morning Star asked softly. "That it's their problem?"

Spotted Wrist shrugged. "Lord, we're doing all we can. That's the important thing. The Koroa can see that we're searching every house, temple, and shrine in Cahokia."

"And that's all you have?" Rising Flame asked. "Just a bird-headed man, and maybe a dog, in the middle of the night?"

"And they might not even be the culprits." Spotted Wrist shot her a placating glance. Then he hesitated. "There's one other peculiarity that came out after my warriors started asking around in the surrounding camps. It doesn't make much sense."

Blue Heron was aware that Morning Star's attention was now fixed fully on her, his gaze probing, almost conspiratorial. What was *that* all about? She'd been the center of the living god's attention before. It never boded well.

She almost missed it when Spotted Wrist said, "It's confusing. Just like everything relating to the theft. Something about passing gas."

"Really?" Rising Flame asked emotionlessly. "We're dealing with a major diplomatic incident, and you bring up breaking wind?"

"One of the Traders in a nearby camp heard the bird-headed thief shouting as he ran away. The man insists the thief was yelling, 'Come on farts!' over and over as he ran."

Oh, no. Blue Heron's stomach dropped. She knotted her jaws, desperate to keep her face straight.

On his dais, Morning Star was watching her with those knowing eyes; what might have been a flicker of amusement tightened his lips.

He turned his attention to Spotted Wrist, saying, "Orchestrate your own marriage, Clan Keeper. I would think a man of your capabilities could handle such a simple chore. But in the meantime, you would best be served recovering the Koroa copper."

Then the living god's gaze settled on Blue Heron, burning in its intensity, as if in warning. She tried to swallow, but it was as if a plum pit was stuck in her throat.

Three

Squadron First Blood Talon winced as he and the Hero of the North's honor guard followed the new Keeper into his palace. For two decades now, Blood Talon had been one of Spotted Wrist's most trusted commanders, confidants, and friends. But ever since their army's triumphant return from the conquest of the north, Spotted Wrist hadn't been the same.

Always cunning and politically astute, these days Spotted Wrist was like a different man—and it wasn't subtle. In the past, the war leader had often spoken in jest: "After as hard as I've worked, when the Spirits and Power finally give me my just due, it will probably mean they wish to destroy me."

Blood Talon now wondered if his friend's words hadn't been prophetic.

Storming into the palace—and out of sight of the passing crowds of gawking dirt farmers, Traders, and vendors—Spotted Wrist turned on his retinue, finger thrusting like a spear.

"Pus-rotted gods, can you believe that?" The man's eyes burned. "I am chastised, embarrassed like a child, over a couple of sheets of copper stolen from some distant swamp rats' camp?"

"War Leader," Nutcracker, the squadron second, said hastily, "we're doing everything we can."

Spotted Wrist fumed, stomped his foot. "I am *humiliated*. And in front of those fawning Earth Clans chiefs. Not to mention the embassies from half the world! Why? Because that arrogant young woman treats me like some low-born suitor, I might be as good as a dirt farmer in her eyes. One of these unwashed, incomprehensible rabble who've flocked to Cahokia. I am *Spotted Wrist*! I've been taking care of her since she was an infant swaddled in cattail down."

"War Leader"—Blood Talon took his stand, back to the door—"she has special standing with the reincarnated Morning Star. The word is that she's possessed by the spirit of Piasa, that the Underworld and the living god—"

"I know the rumors, pus take them, and I know Night Shadow Star. She's always been impetuous. Never had to face the consequences of her actions. I spent half my time when she was a girl keeping her and her uncontrolled brothers from facing the consequences. I wouldn't be in this position if her father were still alive. Red Warrior Tenkiller wouldn't stand for it."

Spotted Wrist's face puckered, as if he'd just remembered something. "Thought she was finally becoming a woman instead of a spoiled little wild weasel. When they reincarnated the Morning Star into Chunkey Boy's body something happened. She passed her woman's moon and married Three Falls. Was taking her place in the leadership. At least until he was killed up north.

"Figured she'd have cut that Red Wing we sent her into little pieces. By rain and hail, he sure wasn't much when we tossed his sorry carcass into that canoe and sent him downriver.

"No," Spotted Wrist mused. "And now he's her lap dog. Her slave. And she dotes on him."

Nutcracker muttered, "Half the city thinks he's serving her as more than a slave. Rumor is that he's just as adept with his shaft as he is on the chunkey court or in combat. If he's half as good under the covers as his reputation, you may have to poison him after you finally marry the woman."

The frown deepened on Spotted Wrist's forehead. "Wouldn't be the first time a woman's given up everything for a tingle in her sheath. Word was that she and Makes Three . . ."

As his commander hesitated, Blood Talon saw the man's change of expression. "Yes, War Leader? I know that look."

Spotted Wrist slapped a fist into his palm. "If she's as beguiled by the Red Wing as she was by Three Falls, it would destroy her in the event that anything happened to her bed toy."

"You mean like last time, she'd fall apart." Blood Talon remembered the way Night Shadow Star had grieved for her dead husband. The woman had lost her souls to the Underworld. So great was her grief that she'd become totally listless.

"She'd have agreed to anything," Spotted Wrist whispered. "It broke her will."

Nutcracker asked, "So if something should happen to the Red Wing?"

"That's not even difficult." Blood Talon grinned. "A well-placed arrow? Shot from ambush? Say, in the middle of a crowd? Who'd know?"

"Maybe have someone anonymous, one of our warriors, dressed as a . . . a dirt farmer," Nutcracker said. "You know, just hand Fire Cat a cup of soup laced with water hemlock. I've seen how the people adore him. The stories they tell have made him into a walking legend. People offer him food and drink all the time."

"Water hemlock's a terrible way to die," Blood Talon added. "If Night Shadow Star calls old Rides-the-Lightning, he'll know which poison it was."

Nutcracker lifted his hands, looking innocent. "They'd never know who did it. Just a face in the crowd."

Spotted Wrist added, "It's not like the Red Wing doesn't have enemies. I've heard that the Natchez and the Quiz Quiz, not to mention some of the other Houses, bear him ill will."

"Or one of us could sneak in and smack his brains out in the middle of the night. Set up an ambush, something that would draw him out of her palace . . ."

Spotted Wrist narrowed his gaze. "It can't look like an assassination. She'd know we were behind it."

Nutcracker crossed his arms. "We'd do it in a manner that couldn't be traced back to us."

"She'd know. Believe me."

"Then it has to look like an accident," Blood Talon told them. "A drowning. A slip or fall. Something."

Nutcracker made a face. "Have to get close for that. When have we ever had the chance?" He glanced at Spotted Wrist. "Lord, if you could make some plan? Get her to accompany you out away from the city? Perhaps find some pretext to get her to journey with you to the Moon Temple over east? The lunar maximum is coming up, after all."

"Once out of town we would have to separate her from him," Blood Talon said. "He's always with her. Can't have her witness us breaking his neck."

"We don't have time," Spotted Wrist said. "She leaves in three days. I need him dead now."

"Poison," Nutcracker insisted. "Concentrated essence of acorn leechings mixed with boiled nightshade and poison ivy leaves. It just shuts the body down."

"I'd rather kill him outright. Face to face. But how do we manage that?" Blood Talon asked. "It's not like I can just walk up to him and challenge him to combat."

Spotted Wrist straightened, a gleam coming to his eyes. "Why not?"

"Well, War Leader, it would be pretty obvious, don't you think? You said it can't be traced back to us. Night Shadow Star is going to be pretty certain who's behind it if I'm standing over his dead body while I'm wiping his blood and brains off my war club."

"Who said it had to be combat?" Spotted Wrist arched an eyebrow. "No, it's a friendly bout. Just sparring for practice. After all, you're in charge of the squadron accompanying the Cofitachequi expedition. Just a routine training match, a way to feel out his worth and skill prior to the coming trip. But somehow it goes wrong."

Nutcracker was grinning. "And accidents do happen."

"Do you think it would be that easy?" Blood Talon felt his blood begin to race. "He's supposed to be the greatest warrior in Cahokia if you believe the stories told in the Great Plaza."

Spotted Wrist waved it away. "Stories are like penises. They grow in the telling. So, the Red Wing killed a bunch of Itza warriors? Me, I've never seen an Itza fight. We were up north, doing real fighting. And I'd put Blood Talon up against anyone in the whole of Cahokia when it came to the club and shield. Think, Nutcracker. Who, among all the warriors you know, is better?"

Nutcracker lifted an eyebrow.

"That's right." Spotted Wrist stepped up, placed a hand on Blood Talon's shoulder. "Now, you really can make it look like an accident, can't you?"

"Absolutely, War Leader. I'll be horrified. Brokenhearted. On my knees on the point of tears when she comes rushing up. And, oh so sorry. I'll offer to kill myself."

"No need to go that far." A pause. "But I will have to exile you. Make a show of your punishment. Some demonstration of my rage and displeasure. You understand that, don't you?"

Blood Talon broke out in laughter. "What of it? You'll be married and have Lady Night Shadow Star's title. I'll be headed off in charge of the expedition within days anyway. By the time I return in glory from Cofitachequi, who will remember a dead slave?"

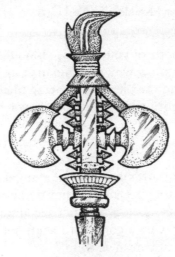

Four

The last of his clan and lineage, Fire Cat was in his early thirties. Once he had been the most renowned warrior on the upper Father Water, war chief of Red Wing Town, and son of Clan Matron Dancing Sky. Now Fire Cat, his mother, and two sisters were slaves. Conquered and captured by War Chief Spotted Wrist.

Weapon in hand, he faced one of the men who had planned and carried out his downfall.

That knowledge burned within Fire Cat as he leaped and swung his copper-bitted war club. What was supposed to be an impromptu sparring match now felt as if it had a sinister purpose.

Squadron First Blood Talon had arrived at Night Shadow Star's palace that morning accompanied by five of his most respected warriors. Said that since they would be traveling together on such a long and dangerous journey, perhaps they might train. Get the feel of each other's mettle.

Always anxious to hone his skill, Fire Cat had agreed. From the first trading of blows, this had been anything but a friendly bout. Fire Cat could see it in his opponent's eyes, in the viciousness of his attack.

Nor was that fact lost on the watching warriors as the two combatants circled and clashed in the small yard before Night Shadow Star's mound-top palace.

Blood Talon caught Fire Cat's blow on his shield, the impact making a loud crack. Fire Cat felt the sting of it through the handle of his war club.

"I enjoyed taking both of your wives," Blood Talon remarked as he backpedaled. "Now I know why they moaned as I drove my shaft into them. They'd never had the pleasure of being filled by a real man."

Fire Cat feinted, fighting his rage. Somehow he managed to keep his head. Strangled the urge to charge, to beat this man down, to hammer his way through the shield and smash the brains from Blood Talon's head.

"Your children were difficult. They screamed and bawled like deer fawns as we cut them apart. Alive. So they'd know true pain and terror. But my warriors took turns shooting their seed into your little daughters. Wanted them to know what a good hard shaft felt like. A kindness, you know, since they would be dead so soon."

Fire Cat barely checked a mad rush at the man.

From the cunning smile on Blood Talon's face, the squadron first was hoping for just that. Which meant he had a plan, some way of turning that reckless charge into a trap. Was it something to do with the watching warriors? So far, they had done nothing to intercede, just stood, faces stiff and eyes hot with anticipation.

I hate this man.

Fire Cat's body ached with the need to kill. Under Spotted Wrist's command, Blood Talon had directed the sack of Red Wing Town. Nor did Fire Cat doubt the man's boast that he'd led the gang rape of False Dawn and New Fall Moon before they were given in slavery to some forest chieftain. Spotted Wrist's goal had been to erase every last vestige of Red Wing heresy. Wipe it clean from the face of the earth.

They expect me to travel all the way to Cofitachequi in his company? If I kill him now . . .

From the way Blood Talon attacked, struck, and parried, he must have shared Fire Cat's dislike. Every fiber of Fire Cat's being tingled with the comprehension that something deeper was at play here.

He wants me to lose control.

Fire Cat leaped right. Landed. His balance perfect, he darted left as Blood Talon's backhanded strike whistled through the air where Fire Cat had been but an instant before.

Fire Cat twisted right, and back, his club held before him in perfect form.

Blood Talon no longer had breath for taunts, the first flickers of doubt behind his eyes.

In unison, they crashed together, smashing shields, war clubs clashing as they struggled to throw the other off balance. Blood Talon broke first, retreating, seeking some advantage.

Fire Cat held back, biding his time. Blood Talon, if he had any fault, was weakest on the attack. A slight desire to rush his offense and over-power rather than finesse a killing blow.

But who is the sacrifice? Me? Or him?

Both men crouched, panting, each trying to anticipate his opponent's next move. Sweat beaded on their skin. Trickled from beneath the wood-and-leather armor that encased their chests and shoulders. Arm guards protected their forearms. Heavy leather helmets covered their heads. A crowd had gathered below the flat mound top where they sparred. The watching warriors were looking nervous now, as if whatever was supposed to happen had gone awry.

If I am killed, Night Shadow Star will accede to Spotted Wrist's demand that she marry him. If I kill him? Who stands to gain?

The morning sun pierced the last of the clouds that had hung low over Cahokia. Days of cold drizzle had finally ceased and reluctantly sur-rendered to a misty steam that rose where the sun warmed the sides of the mound.

Replaying the man's moves, it came to Fire Cat that Blood Talon, while excellent at defense, did follow a peculiar pattern. Yes, that just might be the key.

"You've been played. Who wants you dead? What do they gain?" Fire Cat asked.

"Just sparring," Blood Talon said past tight lips. "Wanted to know what sort you were before my back was turned."

"Figured it out yet?"

"Pretty much." Blood Talon charged forward, shield up, head down, as if to barrel his way right through Fire Cat. Again the shields clashed. Fire Cat skipped sideways, away from Blood Talon's wicked right swing; the war club hissed as it cut air where Fire Cat's head had been.

Had it connected, it would have caved in Fire Cat's helmet, skull, and brains.

Fire Cat leaped, slashed with his club, danced to one side, and whipped the club in a backhanded strike. Blood Talon parried, ducked right, and used all the strength in his body in an attempt to knock Fire Cat's shield to the side with an uppercut. The club head blurred up from between the man's knees with serpent-like speed.

Fire Cat barely managed to tilt his shield in time: the blow skipped off the battered surface. Momentum carried the war club high through its arc.

Fire Cat saw it in Blood Talon's eyes: the stark realization of his mistake, that the squadron first was defenseless, the knowledge that he was a mere heartbeat away from death.

Fire Cat was already swinging, using his excellent control to stop the keen copper edge just as it touched Blood Talon's exposed neck. Then he let the war club settle onto the man's armored shoulder, all the while staring into his opponent's startled eyes.

I could have severed his neck.

A tiny measure of revenge for what had happened to his family and people at Red Wing Town.

Even better, the reality was right there in Blood Talon's eyes. He'd not only failed at what he'd come to accomplish, but knew that had Fire Cat played for keeps, he'd be dying on the very ground he stood upon.

The watching warriors were whispering back and forth, wary and disbelieving eyes on Fire Cat. One, the squadron second, Nutcracker, was shaking his head, as if trying to convince himself of what he'd just witnessed.

"Pus and blood!" Blood Talon cried, stepping back, lowering his shield and war club. Panic filled his eyes as he gasped for breath. A violent loathing lurked there, backed by a froth of resentment and disgust.

"Let me guess. Accidents happen in training. You'd approach my lady looking remarkably contrite. 'Sorry, Lady Night Shadow Star, my club slipped.' Or maybe, 'Apologies, Lady, but he stepped right into my blow before I could check my swing. So sorry. It wasn't supposed to end this way.'"

"Think you're pretty smart, don't you, slave?" Blood Talon's rising anger had him on the point of trembling. "We know you for what you are. You just got lucky." He sneered the word: "Hero."

"Combat is always a gamble, Squadron First. You never know how clever or fast or tenacious your opponent is going to be."

"No, you don't," Blood Talon admitted reluctantly as he gasped for breath. "Today is yours. It won't always be."

And with that, the squadron first inclined his head in deadly promise. As he did, his beaded forelock bobbed where it hung down from under the brim of his war helmet. Turning, he gestured for the others to follow, waving away their questions and mutters of disappointment as they headed for the stairs.

Why, in Piasa's name, would a lauded squadron first ask for a "training" match? Especially given Fire Cat's reputation as a warrior?

But then, Spotted Wrist and his warriors never saw me fight the Itza. All they've heard are the wild stories.

Fire Cat watched the squadron first and his men pass between the guardian posts where Piasa stood to the right, Horned Serpent to the left. Then they descended the wooden steps that led down to the avenue below. There the crowd of pilgrims, Traders, and dirt farmers parted, all calling out, talking among themselves and pointing as Blood Talon and his warriors shoved them out of the way.

Behind Fire Cat, Night Shadow Star's palace rose high, the plastered walls white, the steep wedge of thatched roof grayed by winter storms. From the veranda a full view of the Great Plaza could be had, as well as of the Avenue of the Sun, which served as the major east-west thoroughfare that bisected the city of Cahokia.

Immediately to the east rose the Morning Star's Great Mound with its south-facing walled terrace upon which the Council House was built. The Morning Star's palace dominated the heights above the Council House and was reached through a grand staircase that led up the mound's southern face to the gated compound with its soaring thatch-roofed temple and World Tree pole.

Fire Cat squinted, seeing the lone figure up in the high bastion. Something glinted in the morning light, the reflection from a polished copper headdress. Couldn't be anyone else but Morning Star. Not up there.

So, is Chunkey Boy part of this?

Impostor he might be, but he always played a deep game.

Finally catching his breath, Fire Cat began releasing the ties that secured his armor. Fingers of fatigue began to rob his muscles of agility as the thrill of battle drained. Without a doubt, Blood Talon was one of the finest warriors Fire Cat had ever faced. It would have been the perfect assassination. This morning, he'd won by the narrowest of margins.

Piss and spit, I hate Cahokian politics.

Letting his cuirass fall, Fire Cat walked to the southwest corner of the mound to look down on the Avenue of the Sun. A flood of people, like a relentless mixing stream of ants, traveled the great avenue. From the west and River Mounds City came Traders, dirt farmers, stone workers, and gangs of men bearing great wooden logs. Others staggered along under high-piled stacks of firewood to feed the city's voracious need. People with baskets hanging from tumplines that held corn, goosefoot seed, bread, fabrics, dried fish, smoked meats, feathers, pottery, and goods of every kind passed below.

Among them were the foreign Traders bearing shells from the Gulf, yaupon tea, dyes, southern fabrics, northern copper, furs, and exotic foods and spices. Obsidian was imported from the far mountains in the west as were large sheets of mica from the highlands in the distant east. Stone for carving came from the four corners of the Cahokian world.

From all directions came parched corn, saplings for construction, blanks of milky gray chert for flaking, hardwood planks, quarters of venison, split cane for construction, and just about every other resource.

Cahokia flourished on sacred Trade.

Fire Cat rubbed the back of his neck, shivered as the first of the chill ate through his sweaty skin and reminded him that it was still early in the year and winter was just running the end of its course.

He looked east, down the long Avenue of the Sun toward River Mounds City, the river, and the canoe landing. Under orders from Morning Star, eight large canoes were resting on the dirty sand just above the river's lapping water. Provisions were being collected and stored in a warehouse on the levee.

We have only days before we're supposed to leave.

Fire Cat shivered again, noticed that the crowd was still staring up at him. Many of them pointing. He made a face, went back, collected his armor, and started for the veranda.

Of course people stared at him. He'd wrested the city back from Thirteen Sacred Jaguar, saved it for the Morning Star when he fought Itza warriors on this very mound. He'd won a fortune when he played the Natchez lord, Swirling Cloud, in a game of chunkey. More recently he was known for having gone to the Underworld to rescue Morning Star's soul.

All of which he'd Trade at a moment's notice for the chance to slip away to a forest farmstead with Night Shadow Star and live like a regular human being.

He climbed up on the veranda, surprised to see Night Shadow Star, her form partially obscured by shadow where she leaned in the doorway, a straight-handled cup in her hand. She watched him with her large, otherworldly eyes, lips pursed, long black hair tumbling down her back like a wave.

"That was no friendly match," she noted.

"You saw? He was trying to kill me."

"Curious, isn't it?" Her gaze had gone distant, as if she were hearing Piasa's Spirit voice whisper in her ear.

What was it about her? Not just her eerie possession by the Powers of the Underworld, but the whole of her. Beautiful, frightening, somehow fragile, and so terribly profound and knowing. She'd told him on occasion that Piasa allowed her glimpses of the future, that some terrible challenge awaited her on their journey to Cofitachequi. As if facing Walking Smoke wasn't frightening enough.

"I wasn't sure you'd let him live," she noted as she made way for his entry. "I heard his boasts. He served Spotted Wrist at Red Wing Town."

"Blood Talon is one of Spotted Wrist's most cherished squadron leaders and friends. Killing him might complicate your relationship with your future husband." He laid his armor and club down.

"It was an attempt to break me." She shot him a knowing look. "The hope was that your death would leave me bereft. That in my pain and grief I'd agree to anything. They think my feeling for you fuels my refusal to marry Spotted Wrist."

He accepted the cup of tea from her. For a moment he stared into her eyes, then said, "Power plays us as it will, Lady. We both know that its uses for us change with the moment. For now it needs us to travel to Cofitachequi. Should that change?" He shrugged. "The Powers of the Underworld might discover a need to put you in that man's bed."

He noted the tightening behind her eyes, the recognition of the truth behind his words.

"For everything there is a price. If there were a way that you and I . . ."

She chuckled at her foolishness. "I might as well wish the sky were orange and that fish could fly."

He sipped the tea she had given him, letting the smoky taste run over his dry tongue. This was black drink, brewed from the yaupon holly leaf and imported from the distant south along the Gulf's coastal plain. The leaves were roasted until slightly charred, boiled to a froth, and allowed to steep for several hands of time. That she shared it with him was a sign of their bond.

I would do anything to make the sky orange and fish fly.

He smiled wistfully and handed the cup back to her. Hard to believe that he had killed her husband, that she had hated him enough once to have Spotted Wrist promise to capture him alive so that she could torture him to death.

"Spotted Wrist is getting desperate. He's running out of time. He wants that marriage before we leave for Cofitachequi."

"That he does." She turned, leading the way across the intricately woven floor mat to the main fire. A pot of hominy bubbled there, as did a thick stew of duck and turtle meat seasoned with dried squash blossoms.

On the sleeping benches to the rear, Green Stick, Winter Leaf, and Clay String were working on Night Shadow Star's clothing, making sure it was ready to be packed in a long wooden box that would fit between the gunwales of one of the large Trade canoes. She was, after all, a Cahokian Lady of the first family of the Morning Star lineage. From formal ceremonial feasts with high chiefs along the river to hunkering in the canoe during snowstorms, she needed to be dressed accordingly.

The manner in which the Cofitachequi expedition was being planned left Fire Cat longing for the days when he was in charge of organizing war parties. Provisioning and supply were so simple in comparison to this major expedition. Not to mention the ritual aspects.

Across the Great Plaza, the old Earth Clans shaman, Rides-the-Lightning, had been conducting rituals for the last two weeks to ensure success.

And now, Blood Talon—who would be in charge of the expedition's military escort—had just tried to kill him?

"Worse than that, Fire Cat," Night Shadow Star whispered, "now that he knows you can best him in combat, he'll come at you sideways, when you least expect it."

Five

Seven Skull Shield leaned his head back as he filled his lungs and sang, *"A woman so fine, I couldn't believe she was mine. When I grasped her nipples, they turned hard as stones. Just the touch alone was enough to shake me to my bones."*

"Pus and mud," Elder Crawfish, the old shell carver, moaned as he made a face. "I liked it better when he was running for his life."

Elder Crawfish was a Deer Clan man, one of the finest shell carvers in the city. His work was Traded and owned by the wealthiest chiefs on the river. Even the Morning Star wore his pieces. The small shop was packed in among the warehouses a little north of the River House palace mounds and plaza. Years back, Elder Crawfish had chosen that location for its proximity both to the canoe landing and the constant flow of Traders bearing freshwater clam and mussel shell from the rivers as well as saltwater specimens from the distant Gulf down south. Not to mention that Elder Crawfish's reputation and artistry brought premium profits for his family's beads, engraving, and finely shaped shell for inlay and decoration.

Seven Skull Shield often came here just to sit and pass the time. Well, and because the shell carvers were some of the few people graced with an appreciation for not only his unique singing voice, but also his dazzling lyrics. Not everybody could sing like Seven Skull Shield.

"I couldn't believe my eyes as she parted her thighs. My shaft, it hardened

and rose, and a tingle ran clear to my toes!" Seven Skull Shield belted out the verses, eyes closed as he crooned to the split-cane roof overhead.

A loud sigh came from where Meander worked a bow drill to perforate a whelk-shell bead. Then the man said, "I think I've finally figured out what he sounds like. That must be the kind of noise a buffalo bull makes when it's eaten too much prickly pear cactus and has a violent bellyache."

Seven Skull Shield interrupted his song just long enough to shoot a sidelong look and say, "As if you've ever seen a bull buffalo. They've been hunted out everywhere within ten days' hard travel of Cahokia."

"Saw a calf a couple of times," Bent Cane, the youngest son, said. "Traders bring them through on occasion. Trade them off for the novelty of it."

"They get paid handsomely for them, too," Right Fist replied. "High Chief War Duck Traded a sheet of fine copper for a buffalo calf last fall." He shook his head sadly. "That was just before River House had its Power broken. You remember that night? When someone tried to assassinate Matron Round Pot? When the sacred fire got put out?"

"Bad doings, that," Meander agreed.

Seven Skull Shield glanced warily at his dog, Farts, who lay by the door. The big-boned beast was ugly, its coat brindle brown with black accent. Word was it was descended of pack dogs from the far Shining Mountains in the west. It looked like it, having a blocklike head, heavily muscled jaws, and odd eyes—one blue, the other brown. The beast was chewing on a clamshell. The scratching and grinding of the dog's teeth on the shell sent a quiver up Seven Skull Shield's backbone.

Yes, he remembered the night the fire had been extinguished in River House's palace. And he was thankful that dogs couldn't talk. Farts had been right in the middle of it.

To change the subject, he drew breath and sang, *"My shaft hard as wood, and feeling so good, I dropped 'tween her knees, lest she think me a tease."*

"Was there a reason, specifically, that you chose to come torture us today?" Elder Crawfish illustrated his point by waving an abrading stone. "I mean, couldn't you have wandered up to the Morning Star's palace? Driven them half mad with your bellowing?"

"See, we're back to sick buffalo again," Right Fist reminded as he used a finely flaked chert burin to carefully incise the interior of a large clamshell. When finished it would be a gorget. He was in the process of outlining the legs of Cosmic Spider: a Spirit Being from the Beginning Times. She had not only brought fire from the sun to earth, but also carried souls across the sky to the Land of Dead in the Sky World.

"Actually, I'm here in celebration," Seven Skull Shield told them. "I had a rather busy night."

Images of Willow Blossom's body writhing beneath his remained as clear as if but mere moments had passed. To enjoy a woman like that . . . Ah, the pure ecstasy of it.

"Lying low again, huh?" Meander asked dryly. He wet his drill tip in the pot of water beside him, then dipped it in the finely screened sand. He rotated it until the tip was covered with grit. Replacing it in the hole he was drilling, he began sawing the bow drill back and forth.

"Let's just say it took a while for my charm to work its magic." Seven Skull Shield polished the backs of his nails on his shirt and studied them in the half-light shining through the door. "You see, that's the thing about most husbands. They don't care for their wives. Take the poor women for granted. I mean, what would you think was more important? A basket full of basswood rope or a nubile, hot-blooded young woman whose loins were bursting with the need to be filled?"

He smiled. "Not to mention those large dark eyes. Depthless. Like pools. The sort that just melt a man."

"Basswood rope?" Two Fish, the cousin, asked as he entered with a sumac basket full of olivella shells Traded up from the Gulf. "You don't mean surly old Robin Feather, do you? He specializes in rope and cord. Basswood's the best. He's married to that young Panther Clan woman that every man in the neighborhood . . ."

Two Fish stopped short, as if slapped. "Oh, spit and piss! Willow Blossom? Her? *You got her?*"

"Blood and thunder, man," Elder Crawfish sputtered. "Robin Feather killed his last wife for philandering with that Natchez Trader a couple of years ago. If he figures out that you've been sticking that oversized pole of yours in that sassy young wife of his? He'll gut you for it."

"Who's Robin Feather? Never heard of him," Seven Skull Shield lied mildly, assuming an expression of absolute innocence.

Meander, always the canniest of the lot, wasn't buying it. In awe he whispered, "She's beautiful. What man in River City hasn't wondered . . . you know. What it would be like."

Two Fish placed his basket on the ground before the central fire. "Not that I'd ever fall prey to such a sad state myself, but half the men I know, when they're lying with their wives, they're making believe they're with Willow Blossom."

Every eye in the place was on Seven Skull Shield as he sighed wearily and shook his head. "Now I have to go see this woman. Just so I know who you're talking about. But no, it wasn't her that I was with last night.

I was in Evening Star Town. Across the river. Dallied with a cute young thing from Hawk Clan whose husband was out hunting in the forests off to the west."

"Liar," Two Fish growled. Pointing to the basket of olivella shells, he added, "I was down at the landing at dawn to barter for these with a Tunica Trader. Cross-river traffic was slow. I didn't see you getting out of any canoe."

"This is a common problem with you shell workers." Seven Skull Shield waved a dismissive hand. "You spend all your time squinting down at what's a hand's width in front of your nose while you're doing all that fine carving. Makes your eyes bad for seeing long distance, like to where I was paying off old Rag Hand for paddling me across the river at first light."

"Spit in a bucket," Elder Crawfish said in wonder. "Willow Blossom? Of all the women in the world? You never cease to amaze us. It's always something. Like the time Keeper Blue Heron dragged you out of here. Or the time Tula were hunting you, or when the Quiz Quiz wanted you dead. If Robin Feather, of all men, finds out you've—"

"I tell you, it wasn't her." Seven Skull Shield gave the man an innocent smile. He could feel a cold sweat breaking out on his lower back. What in the name of Old-Woman-Who-Never-Dies had possessed him to mention basswood rope? And who'd have thought that lunk-headed Two Fish would be the one to put it together?

Two Fish looked puzzled. "That Willow Blossom, she could have any man she wanted. Probably even High Chief War Duck if she'd so much as bat an eye at him. Why would she choose to share that magnificent body with some bit of walking vermin like Seven Skull Shield?"

Because she was lonely, neglected, and wondering if everything exciting in life was now lost to her.

Seven Skull Shield threw his head back, belting out, *"I lowered myself onto her chest, and slipped in my best. Using all of her might, she clamped round it tight. She had such a squeeze it made my heart wheeze."*

"A heart can't wheeze. That's lungs, you fool."

"Okay, how about, *'It made my blood freeze.'*"

"I've heard geese with better voices. It would help if you could carry a tune." Right Fist scooped a pile of scrap shell into a pot and set it on the fire to bake. Within moments the onion-rank smell of cooking shell filled the air. After it cooled, the calcined shell would be ground up and sold to potters for temper to use in their thin-walled ceramics.

But now Seven Skull Shield had a problem: They knew about Willow Blossom. How in the name of the Underworld Spirits was he going to handle this? Not that the shell carvers were the worst of the gossips along the waterfront, but if this ever got back to Robin Feather?

Seven Skull Shield wasn't all that concerned about himself. He'd been dodging jealous husbands for years. And sure, Robin Feather would try to take him from behind, striking from the shadows, but it was Willow Blossom he was worried about.

He had come to like the young woman over the month it had taken to slowly wear down her resistance. In a lot of ways she reminded him of Wooden Doll when she was younger, more innocent and vulnerable. He hadn't been this infatuated in years. Willow Blossom's sense of humor, her quick wit, and the way she looked at him with that sparkle in her large dark eyes just made him happy.

Though she hadn't meant to, she'd charmed him last night. Part of it was her surprise at their first joining under the blanket. Old Robin Feather must have put as much enthusiasm into coupling with his wife as he did when he was braiding rope. Or maybe less. Any woman who gasped, twitched, wiggled as she had and kept repeating, "I never knew, I never knew," afterward was speaking volumes about the men in her life.

She'd been a quick student after that. By the time Seven Skull Shield had slipped away under the cover of first light, she'd pitched herself wholeheartedly and with total abandon into an exciting new exploration of all the ways a man and a woman could conjure lightning in their loins.

Made him wonder how she was going to react the next time Robin Feather climbed on top of her.

The Willow Blossom Seven Skull Shield had come to know was probably canny enough to play dumb again.

"The fair young lass, she grabbed onto my ass. Her nails they dug deep, at the pain I did weep."

"We could throw something at him," Right Fist noted.

"Naw," Meander said. "Kind of nice to have him around again. Ever since he got famous and stopped dropping by, we've been lacking in entertainment."

"Not to mention the reminder of how good our lives are when he's away in Morning Star Town rubbing elbows with the high and mighty." Bent Cane stooped and began sorting through the olivella shells.

"So, what's the real story?" Elder Crawfish asked. "How did that Spotted Wrist really manage to outfox old Blue Heron and get the Keeper's position?"

The change in subject took Seven Skull Shield by surprise. Grateful that they were no longer thinking about Willow Blossom, he told them, "Four Winds Clan politics is like being trapped in a big basket of snakes. It was that new matron."

"Rising Flame?"

"That's her. And a vicious little sheath she is, too."

"Maybe you ought to try and charm that one."

"I have standards," Seven Skull Shield replied. "But don't count Blue Heron out just yet. Spotted Wrist might be the Hero of the North, and might have everyone's gratitude and thanks for dealing with the heretics up at Red Wing Town, but he's in a game he can't win."

"How's that?" Right Fist asked.

"I'll lay you a wager: A basket full of polished whelk shell says that Blue Heron is Clan Keeper again by next fall."

Elder Crawfish lifted a graying eyebrow. "And when you lose, where will you come up with enough Trade to barter for a basket of whelk shell?"

"Watch it, Elder," Meander cautioned. "This is Seven Skull Shield. He didn't specify what size basket. And people weave some really small baskets, some barely big enough to cover the tip of a little finger."

Seven Skull Shield laughed hard enough that Farts looked up from the floor, his one-blue-and-one-brown gaze quizzical. "A basket that size." He pointed at the olivella basket.

"Which brings me back to my initial question. Where would you get that much wealth?" Elder Crawfish used a knobby finger to emphasize his point.

"I won't need it, my friends." Seven Skull Shield grinned. "Blue Heron has a secret weapon."

"A pot full of water hemlock?" Right Fist wondered. "Those Four Winds Houses like poison when it comes to disposing of a rival."

"She doesn't need poison. She has me."

"You?" Meander asked.

"By the time Spotted Wrist figures out he's been blindsided, Blue Heron will not only be Keeper again, but all of Cahokia will be begging for her to do so."

"And you think—"

"*Seven Skull Shield!*" an angry voice bellowed from somewhere the other side of the hemp warehouse next door. "Where is that lying, thieving, two-footed bit of shit!"

"Sounds angry," Elder Crawfish mused.

Seven Skull Shield cocked his head. Something about the voice was familiar.

Two Fish leaned his head out the door, peered, and glanced back inside. "Robin Feather. I just saw him pass between the hemp warehouse and the potter's workshop. He's got a war club. And by spit, he looks really, really mad."

"Dear friends," Seven Skull Shield said, already on his feet. "If you will excuse me, it just hit me that I have some pressing business down in Horned Serpent Town."

On the way out the door he nudged his oversized and ungainly mongrel of a dog. "Come on, Farts. No sense in lingering when there's opportunity at hand."

As Seven Skull Shield slipped carefully around the hemp warehouse to get behind Robin Feather's fury, he heard the man bellow, "When I find that stinking weasel and that cheating woman, I'm gonna knock their brains out and leave them for the maggots to chew!"

Seven Skull Shield sighed. If Robin Feather was searching for Willow Blossom, she must have managed an escape. He figured he knew where she would have hidden. On his way out of River Mounds he'd have to make a quick stop to be sure that she was safely out of the way. If nothing else, he'd have to broker a deal with Crazy Frog to get her out of the city and someplace beyond Robin Feather's reach.

"You know, Farts," he told the dog, "that man simply has no sense of humor."

Six

War Leader, I fought one of the hardest fights I've ever fought," Blood Talon declared. Burning with humiliation, he stood in front of the war chief's fire. Clan Keeper Spotted Wrist sat perched on his litter atop a clay dais on the other side of the flames. The Hero of the North had his chin resting on his palm, his elbow braced on a propped knee.

Spotted Wrist was of Red Night's lineage, and he was in line for the high chief's seat up at North Star House in Serpent Woman Town should anything happen to High Chief Wolverine. Spotted Wrist was close to fifty, and his temples had begun to gray; lines now deeply incised his weather-blackened face and obscured his Four Winds tattoos. But nothing through the years had dimmed his hard black eyes or the strength in his angular jaw.

He looked every bit of what he was: a most capable military commander and a force to be reckoned with.

The palace, just east of the Morning Star's great mound, was new, its walls still pale with fresh plaster, and the ceiling had barely begun to darken with soot. It stood on a low mound that had once belonged to Lady Lace, sister of Night Shadow Star and daughter of Red Warrior Tenkiller. After Lace's abduction, the old palace had been burned, ritually cleansed, and a layer of earth had been added to cover the whole. Then the new palace had been built, ready just in time for Spotted Wrist to claim it as his just due for the conquest of Red Wing Town.

Blood Talon stared anxiously around the interior, noting the shields,

bows, carvings, and other wealth that had been hung from the walls—
trophies taken during Spotted Wrist's glorious career. Present, too, were
the occasional skulls, all polished and painted, as well as incised and
decorated arm and leg bones from various adversaries Spotted Wrist
had defeated in battle.

"What do you think?" Spotted Wrist turned his attention to Nutcracker. The squadron second was tall, in his early thirties, with long
black hair and a deeply scarred left cheek.

"Blood Talon fought brilliantly, Keeper." Nutcracker lifted expressive
hands, palms out. "The Red Wing was like a dancer, every move smooth
and perfect. Watching that fight, it was a thing of beauty. I wouldn't have
believed that any man alive was better than Blood Talon when it came
to single combat with the club."

"But he bested you!" Spotted Wrist turned his head back toward Blood
Talon.

"It had to be some sort of magic, War Leader. Maybe Underworld
Power. Something dark that that woman cast on me."

He could feel Nutcracker's questioning sidelong glance. In his own
defense, he demanded, "How else do you explain it? He shouldn't have
known I was in earnest. We started, each of us pulling our blows, sparring, just like I told him we'd be. When I had him at the right tempo, I
used a feint, swung fast and hard for the side of his head. The blow should
have caved in his helmet and skull, but somehow he managed to dodge it.

"Thought I had him off balance, so I pressed the attack. Hard. Figured he'd be overwhelmed. He just parried, ducked, and skipped away
each time."

"So, he knew?"

"Of course, War Leader. Nothing else explains it. I tried goading him,
told him what we did to his wives and children. Threw it right in his face.
You could see it, he wanted to kill me. Hated me from down between his
souls. We fought for blood and bone."

"And yet he didn't kill you?" Spotted Wrist mused, his eyes now on
the fire, as if he were seeking some answer there.

Nutcracker said, "Keeper, the Red Wing laid the blade of his club
against Blood Talon's neck as softly as a songbird would alight on a limb.
Like nothing I'd ever seen."

"We dismissed the stories about him," Blood Talon said in irritation.
"All those impossible tales of his battle against the Itza, that he fought in
the Underworld for Morning Star, that he singlehandedly saved Cahokia
on the chunkey court. What were we to think? I was with those who
captured him that night in his own palace. I carried his weeping body
down to the canoes that night. *That* was not the man I faced today."

"We caught him by surprise that night," Nutcracker reminded. "Got him in his bed. Asleep."

"I think it was magic," Blood Talon insisted. Down in the heart of his bones, he absolutely burned with rage and shame. It had been such a simple assignment. Kill the Red Wing and make it look like an accident.

Yet here he stood after one of the hardest fights he'd been in since he was a youth in training.

Across the fire, Spotted Wrist's eyes were hardening, the War Leader lost in thought. In the end, he slapped a hand to his muscular thigh, declaring, "What is it with her? I did everything for her. Took Red Wing Town for her. Covered for her when she got in trouble with those wild-weasel brothers of hers. And now she throws it in my face. She chooses that Red Wing filth over me?"

Blood Talon kept his mouth shut, having learned over the years to let his commander vent. He glanced sidelong at Nutcracker, seeing his old friend's remarkably blank and empty-eyed expression. Smart man. Never give so much as a hint of amusement or emotion when the war leader was in this mood.

"I could just take her," Spotted Wrist snapped. "Walk over there with a half dozen men, pick her up, and carry her off to the Four Winds Clan House. Have Rising Flame declare us married. It would all be over. Nice and neat."

Blood Talon did his best to mimic Nutcracker's empty expression. He'd already failed once today. Of course, the Red Wing would have no chance against that many warriors. There would be injuries, but they'd surround Fire Cat and take him down before anyone got killed.

"I'd do it in a heartbeat if I thought I could get away with it," Spotted Wrist growled. "No one would blame me, either. It's Morning Star. He's the problem. Him and his missing copper. Who in Piasa's name are the Koroa anyway? Some bunch of swamp-footed barbarians with mud between their toes. Probably have moss growing in their armpits. As if it's my problem they can't keep an eye on their own possessions."

He shot a hard look at Blood Talon. "Any progress finding that accursed copper?"

"No, War Leader."

"You will address me as Clan Keeper."

"Yes, Clan Keeper."

"And you should have seen old Blue Heron. She mocks me. Looks so rotted smug. I'd love nothing better than to hear that dried-out old skull of hers crack under a solid blow from my club."

"Maybe you could enlist the dwarf?" Nutcracker asked carefully. "The one who spies for Lady Columella over in Evening Star House."

"Name's Flat Stone Pipe. Shares Columella's bed, too, I'm told," Blood Talon added, relieved to no longer be the center of attention.

"How do you think that works?" Spotted Wrist asked absently, his attention back on the fire.

"A little bit of this, a little bit of that?" Blood Talon suggested.

"Night Shadow Star has turned me into a mockery." Spotted Wrist's gaze was burning as hot as the fire he stared into. "Was she there this morning? Did she seem worried that the Red Wing was in a fight for his life? A woman usually can't help herself when the man she loves is in danger. Did you see that?"

Blood Talon glanced at Nutcracker, who said, "I think she watched from inside her palace, Keeper. All I saw was a shadow standing back from the doorway."

"Well, there's that. At least she's not giggly-girl-silly-in-love-with-him to the point she'd throw herself in the middle of a fight to save him."

"Word is that after her possession by Piasa, she's aged beyond her years," Blood Talon said.

Spotted Wrist stroked his chin. "She's not the child I remember, that's for sure. And all the more beguiling because of it. You see it, don't you? The reason why I've got to have this marriage? No other woman in all of Cahokia, not even the *tonka'tzi*, is as renowned, respected, or beloved by the people. Everyone knows she stands toe-to-toe with the Morning Star. He treats her as his equal. There is no greater prize in the entire world."

Blood Talon bit his lip, forcing his face to remain blank, thinking, *That is why she can spurn you, old friend. Because in the end, she's more Powerful, with more authority and prestige than any woman you've ever known.*

And he was supposed to travel halfway across the world with her after trying to murder her lover?

A cold shiver found its way down Blood Talon's back. But perhaps there might be a way to bring the entire expedition to a halt. Buy them all time.

"War Lea . . . Clan Keeper, I have an idea."

Seven

The canoe landing below River Mounds City was bustling in the cold morning air. It might have been above freezing—but just barely. Night Shadow Star could see her breath frosting before her as she and Fire Cat walked down through the Traders' camps. At their passing, people stopped, staring, some dropping to their knees. The Cahokians looked at her worshipfully; the foreigners gawked.

Of course they would. Outside of Morning Star himself, she and Fire Cat were probably the most famous people in Cahokia. People looked at her as if she were a breathing legend and Fire Cat as if he were one of the heroes of the Beginning Times walking among them. While she'd been raised with a sense of privilege as a daughter of the highest-ranking family in the city, she still hadn't grown used to this new worship reflected in the people's eyes.

She nodded at the hawkers who'd come early to claim the best spots for Trade. This time of year, the traffic was down, the canoe landing handling nothing like the volume of Trade it saw in summer—and especially in fall after the harvest. But for hardy Traders, at this time of the year the best bargains could be had for firewood, corn, and dried meats when larders where almost emptied of winter stores.

Nevertheless the narrow strip of beach bustled with a different kind of activity, driven by the approaching departure of her Cofitachequi expedition. An entire squadron was camped just the other side of the large

Trade canoes that had been assembled. Smoke from the warriors' fires hung in a low pall and added to the day's haze.

The big canoes, wide enough for people to sit three abreast, had a predatory look where they lay in ranks, high prows carved in effigies. Boxes were already stacked in piles around them.

"That's a lot of people and supplies just to go kill one man," Fire Cat granted as he stepped up beside her. "It will be like a moving city."

"Matron Rising Flame, *Tonka'tzi* Wind, and Spotted Wrist have handled the organization. Each has his or her own agenda."

"Trying to transport that many people by canoe? All those nobles? Their staffs and households? Not to mention the squadron of warriors? We'll be lucky if we make the mouth of the Mother Water within a moon. And that's normally just a two-day journey. This is a disaster in the making."

"Too many leaders and too many different ideas about what we're about. As if any of the subchiefs are going to take orders. My guess, Red Wing? This expedition is going to tear itself apart within a week. We'll be lucky if the different nobles aren't fighting among themselves by the time we make the first camp down below The Chains."

"You and I think a lot alike," Fire Cat told her. "The notion that Blood Talon is going to follow your orders? After you humiliated Spotted Wrist and I shamed him before his men? I expect him to ignore you starting the moment we shove off from shore."

She glanced across the lead-gray surface of the Father Water to Evening Star Town. The mound-top buildings dominated the high bluff. Matron Columella's new palace could just be seen where its wedge-shaped roof rose against the sky. The thatch was only slightly grayed by the winter.

Hard to believe it had been less than a year since the palace had burned, and that just out there, in mid-river, was where she'd capsized the canoe with Walking Smoke.

"*So close that day. Only to have the lightning save him,*" Piasa whispered in her ear.

"All I saw was the blinding flash," she answered, remembering the white light that had flared behind her closed eyes. Walking Smoke had been in the process of strangling her. Fool that he was, his clamped hands had kept her from sucking water into her lungs. In trying to kill her, he'd saved her life.

"Lady?" Fire Cat asked, giving her a questioning sidelong glance.

"You were there that day. Paddling after us. You said the lightning hit all around you."

He instantly understood. "I don't think I've ever been as terrified. Four bolts, all blasting down from the storm. One from each of the directions. I was left stunned."

"It leaves us with a question."

"Which is?"

"Were the Thunderbirds trying to save Walking Smoke? Or did they only strike because Piasa had placed himself within their reach?"

"I don't think we'll ever know," Fire Cat told her. "The war between the Sky World and Underworld goes back to the Beginning Times. Of all the Spirit creatures, only Horned Serpent has the Power to fly up from the Underworld into the Sky World like he does in early summer through fall. Piasa, the Tie Snakes, they're forever locked in the Underworld. A few creatures, like ducks and cormorants, water beetles, and some of the other insects, can travel between the worlds with impunity."

"We'll be traveling on the rivers. Vulnerable. Floating on that narrow margin between the sky and the depths."

Fire Cat turned his attention to where porters were carrying baskets of corn to the warehouse where provisions for the expedition were being stockpiled. It was a low-walled, plastered structure with a thatch roof that stood just slightly down from the cluster of buildings.

In the morning the corn would be poured into large seed jars, their lids sealed with pine sap. The sticky resin served two purposes, keeping out water and discouraging insects and vermin. The jars would in turn be packed into the heavy canoes.

The last of the equipment, baggage, and Trade goods would be loaded, and the day after tomorrow, the great Trade canoes would be launched. It seemed like an eternity, and just a fleeting moment away.

"Makes you wonder."

"How's that?" she asked.

"Walking Smoke is evil. He's a twisted, tortured, bloodthirsty, and murderous soul bent on inflicting suffering and misery on everyone around him. Why would any form of Power align itself with him?"

"I'm not sure that align is the right word." She frowned, her attention on the scattered guards who watched over the row of heavy canoes. Spotted Wrist's men. A fact that left her with a bitter taste in her mouth. "Like us, Walking Smoke is serving some purpose." She chuckled dryly. "Perhaps as the lure to entice this expedition to the east? Maybe to get us in close where Walking Smoke can kill us, thereby depriving the Underwater Panther of two of his most valued tools in this world."

"You and me?" Fire Cat made a face, tucking his blanket tighter around his shoulders and exhaling a frosty breath. "Lovely thought."

"Power plays an intricate game. Maybe that's why Morning Star favors and supports our leaving. Ultimately, he and I are opponents. He is a

Sky Being. I serve an Underworld lord. Currently we are uneasy allies. One of these days, events will place us in conflict."

"Sky and Underworld. Opposites crossed," Fire Cat whispered. "No place on earth has politics as twisted and perverse as Cahokia with its Houses, Power, and clans."

She gestured at the grounded flotilla. "With that many warriors and people—assuming any of them make it that far—perhaps you and I should just conquer Cofitachequi and set ourselves up as rulers. After all, we're forced to take an army and half of Cahokia with us despite my objections."

"I would take one of those smaller canoes. That little one over there. Looks like it's crafted from bald cypress. I'd place you in it, shove off, and head south. Find some quiet glade in the forest far from any town, chiefs, gods, lords, or politics and spend the rest of my days with you, farming, hunting, and watching you smile."

His words warmed her as she noticed the canoe he mentioned. Nice thought, but the vessel was much too small to be trusted for a long river journey. "I want a bigger canoe. But Red Wing, Piasa was serious. If we do this thing, destroy Walking Smoke, win this one for the Underworld, it may well be the price of our freedom. Never forget that."

"You trust Piasa?"

"The beast has no reason to lie. I am his to do with as he wishes. His souls are inside me." She touched her breastbone. "Right in here. He hears my thoughts, knows my wants."

"And uses you for whatever purpose he wishes."

She stared at the line of waiting canoes, the river's water lapping at their sterns. The day after tomorrow, they would push off with over five hundred warriors, Traders, recorders, translators, a couple of priests, and the retinue of nobles Rising Flame, Spotted Wrist, and *Tonka'tzi* Wind insisted upon.

Many of those nobles were being exiled, removed from Cahokia for having supported the wrong Houses in the chaos that resulted from Morning Star's near death last fall. Rising Flame and Spotted Wrist were solidifying their hold on the Four Winds Clan, carefully having chosen which individuals to "honor" with the chance to build a new colony on the other side of the world. It was a time-honored tradition, one her own relatives had used over the years to dispose of potential rivals and troublemakers.

Now she found herself in charge of the whole unwieldy mess. "I don't like it. I'm saddled with angry and scheming nobles who are stewing in their resentment and a small horde of administrators, not to mention Blood Talon."

But Fire Cat seemed oblivious, stepping over to stare at a long and beautifully crafted canoe, also made of bald cypress. The smooth lines, polished wood, and narrow beam made the craft a thing of beauty. "How about this one?"

"And head south? Try and find that farmstead in the forest?"

"We can dream, can't we?" He glanced at her. "We both know that this entire expedition is defeated before the first paddle is even dipped in the river."

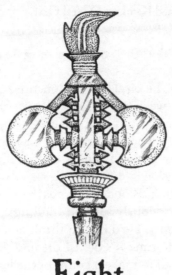

Eight

Blood Talon, through years of hard training, had toughened his body. Despite the frost that coated the thatch roofs, the ramada poles, and frozen ground, and the fact that he was dressed only in a war shirt with a split-feather turkey cape over his shoulders, the squadron leader barely shivered.

In the darkness he moved like a wraith through the packed buildings in River Mounds City. From long practice he made his way through the deep shadows cast by the warehouses. Somewhere in the distance an owl hooted. Maybe up at one of Old-Woman-Who-Never-Dies' temples. Being messengers from the Dead in the Sky World, owls were known to frequent such places of Underworld Power. He didn't know why. That was a question for the priests.

The warehouse sat slightly down the slope, isolated from the rest of the buildings. The closest ramadas along the riverfront were dark. Thankfully the cloud cover acted to obscure Blood Talon's dark-clad form and the pack that rested on his back.

Two guards stood before the warehouse; both paced back and forth, shivering, sometimes stamping their feet and blowing into their hands. These were men from his squadron. Trained.

"You will keep these supplies safe," Blood Talon had told them. "Neither of you will leave sight of this door. It's the only way in or out of the warehouse."

Handpicked, they would do exactly as told.

Which left Blood Talon the challenge of making it to the rear of the warehouse undetected.

Moving like a ghost, he circled wide, ensured that he could keep the bulk of the building between himself and the guards. Had to skirt around a couple of Traders' camps, but he managed to slip up to the back of the warehouse. The sturdy wooden box he'd placed there that afternoon remained. Carefully he tipped it on its end. He had tested it earlier to ensure it would take his weight.

Climbing onto the box, Blood Talon reached up, pulled loose shocks of thatch from their previously severed bindings. Of all the challenges, that had been the hardest. He'd had to think up an excuse for why he'd had to spend a finger of time inside. In the end, he'd offered the explanation that someone had to make a count of the large seed jars to ensure the food ration had been delivered as promised.

Nutcracker had remained outside with the guards, all the while using a plate-sized slab of sandstone to grate away at a hickory pole he insisted he was turning into a chunkey lance. With the guards holding the wood, the rasping of the sandstone was to cover any sound that might betray Blood Talon's activities as he cut the cords that held bundles of thatch into shocks.

Perched atop his box, he was delighted that all it took was a hard push to collapse the thatch. The broken shocks disintegrated under his hands, falling in scatters into the warehouse.

When he had the hole large enough, Blood Talon bunched, leaped, and braced himself atop the mud-plastered wall. He eased a leg over, squeezed between the split-pole beam and wall, and lowered himself into the darkness. Balancing on the heavy seed jars he'd placed for the purpose, he stepped down.

The fallen thatch he raked together with his fingers until he had a pile. Then, one by one, he tilted the seed jars, spilling their contents onto the ground.

From his pack he removed the jar of hickory oil, sprinkled it liberally on the thatch, and then onto the nearest spill of corn. The thick-walled clay jar, he lifted from the bottom of his pack and unwound from an insulating wrapping of dogbane cloth. The thing was hot enough to sear his callused fingers. Nevertheless, he finally managed to undo the stopper and pour hot coals onto the oily thatch.

He bent, blew on the glowing coals, and watched the flames leap to life. As they began to greedily devour the thatch, Blood Talon climbed up, hoisted himself out into the night, and eased down onto his box. He carefully replaced it on its side again.

As he stole away into the night, he turned to see the fire's red glow reflected around the edges of the hole. By the time the guards out front realized what was happening, the roof would be engulfed. Any proof that someone had started the fire would be long turned to ashes.

Nine

In the first light of dawn, Blue Heron hitched her way up the steps that led to the Council House Gate on the southern terrace of the Morning Star's great mound. She should have had her porters carry her litter up the wide staircase, but the thought of them climbing the frosted steps, perhaps slipping and falling, had sent a deeper shiver through her than the cold and damp morning air.

She'd take her own chances, thank you.

Blue Heron might no longer be the Four Winds Clan Keeper, but somehow, despite all the commotion, upset, and chaos that had been unleashed by near civil war when Morning Star temporarily lost his soul to the Underworld, she'd managed to hold on to her palace where it stood in the western shadow of the Morning Star's great mound.

She had also kept her spy ring.

Not that she had the political clout that she used to, but she had something just as important: wealth and status.

In addition, many of her spies had been with her for years. Her network of informants was so deeply ingrained in Cahokian society that for many, passing along information was just the way it was. Since they were in the habit, she wasn't about to do anything to discourage them.

Therefore, when a runner had arrived a couple of fingers before first light, she'd been among the first to learn that the precious corn stores had burned. Her agent—one of Crazy Frog's people—had no clue as to who the culprit was.

Her best guess: Spotted Wrist.

He had the most to gain by delaying the expedition's departure for distant Cofitachequi since his ploy to murder Fire Cat had spectacularly failed.

Unless she could weasel someone into Spotted Wrist's hive of close-knit warriors, the new Clan Keeper's culpability was going to remain speculative. At least for the moment. In the end these things generally came to light provided that she put enough effort into ferreting out the truth.

She hesitated at the top of the steps and nodded to the two bundled and shivering guards at the Council Gate. Took the moment to catch her breath and massaged her hip where it throbbed. The joint hadn't fully healed since she was abused by the Quiz Quiz who'd taken her hostage last fall. One of the barbarians had beaten her so badly it was a miracle that her souls had stayed with her body.

Bad business, that. If she'd had her way, an army would have been sent downriver to burn the vermin out of their lands, towns, and fields. Rising Flame and Wind had vetoed the idea, having hanged the leaders in a square to be tortured to death and sent the rest of the rank-and-file warriors packing in disgrace.

Lavender hung above the bluffs on the eastern horizon and shaded into deep purple in the west. The image was of a bruised sky: ominous and a presentiment of trouble to come.

Below her—beyond the clutter of litters, porters, and awaiting embassies—the Great Plaza was stirring to life. Traders, craftsmen, and vendors of all kinds had braved the darkness and chill to arrive early for the best spots to set up their stalls. Or in the case of the poor, just to throw out a blanket upon which to place their wares, food, and other Trade.

Frost had turned the Morning Star's perfectly groomed chunkey courts hoar-covered and pale in the morning light. Ice crystals shimmered on the beaten grass, and the central World Tree pole looked like a giant spear where it rose in the center of the Great Plaza.

As far as she could see, the city was emerging from the night in a patchwork of farmsteads cluttered around mound groups with their raised temples and palaces. A haze of brown smoke, like a blanket, hung low over the city, fed by a thousand morning cook fires as people warmed themselves and heated breakfast. So thick was it this morning that she could barely make out Black Tail's tomb at the bend in the Avenue of the Sun. Beyond that, River Mounds City, the Father Water, and Evening Star Town were obscured.

Walking through the gate, she plodded to the Council House where it stood on the west side of the courtyard. News of the burned warehouse would spread like wildfire. So far as Blue Heron knew, it would only be her, her sister Wind, and Five Fists, the Morning Star's head of security, who had been alerted. And they only knew because she'd sent Dancing Sky to alert Five Fists and dispatched Soft Moon to appraise Wind of the situation while Smooth Pebble made a quick breakfast and helped Blue Heron get dressed.

Entering the Council House door, she was pleased to find a fire had been kindled and was crackling its way up to a roaring blaze.

Tonka'tzi Wind stood before the fire, her hands offered to the heat. A thoughtful look possessed her age-lined face as she stared into the leaping flames. She'd wrapped her hair tightly into a bun at the back, pinning it with polished copper feathers that caught the light in bronze splendor. A fabulous spoonbill-feather cloak hung from her shoulders.

"Good morning, sister," Blue Heron greeted as she stepped over to the fire and mimicked Wind's posture as she basked in the fire's warmth.

"There's no chance that this is a mistake? The food stocks are really burned?"

"Crazy Frog's not exactly the most trusted of my sources. If it were something with a political angle, like information that would compromise a competitor of his or High Chief War Duck's, I'd have my doubts. In this case, he wanted me to know first, expecting, correctly, that I'm going to reward him for the privilege."

"The Morning Star is going to be mightily displeased. Think there's a way we can discover who did it? Prove it?"

"Proof? No. We both know who had the most to gain by this."

Wind smiled wistfully, her narrowed eyes gleaming in the reflected firelight. "Spotted Wrist will argue that it could have been any of the Houses or clans, that not all of the nobles 'honored' by the chance to carve colonies out of the eastern wilderness are happy about the prospect."

"Of course he will," Five Fists agreed from the door as he entered the Council Room. The old warrior had a thick bear-hide cloak over his shoulders; the warm war shirt he wore fell to just above his knees, and tall trail moccasins shod his feet. One of the warriors who'd accompanied him down from the Morning Star's palace closed the door, ensuring they'd be left in private.

"Good morning, *Tonka'tzi*," he greeted Wind. Then nodded at Blue Heron. "And to you, Keeper.'

"Not these days, but I appreciate the gesture," Blue Heron replied.

Five Fists grinned, the effect anything but reassuring given his offset jaw. "Mark it up to habit. In this room we know who has Cahokia's best interests at heart."

"You were the one who got Rising Flame declared matron," Wind reminded.

Five Fists shot her a look. "The living god plays his own game. I only follow orders. For his own purposes, or perhaps for the needs of Power, he has made his choice. But our immediate problem is the burning of the expedition's food. This will set the departure back several weeks. Require additional levies on the Earth Clans, necessitate that they surrender more of their dwindling winter reserves. And worse, they'll have to confiscate additional food stocks from the dirt farmers in their districts. Supplies are already tight in many areas in the city. It will stir unrest."

"As if we haven't had enough as it is," Wind mused.

Blue Heron gave Five Fists a meaningful glance. "Pick your unrest. We need to get the discontents out of here. The longer they're here, the more trouble they're going to brew up."

Five Fists' lips twitched with distaste. "*Tonka'tzi,* how soon could you replace the burned corn? Get the expedition out on the water? Even if they were short a couple of weeks' worth of ration?"

"Five days?"

"Make it three."

"Can't. Cahokia's a big place. It'll take a day to send the runners out. Two days—assuming every chief complies immediately—to gather the sacks of corn, and at least two days for the outlying areas to pack it all down to the canoe landing."

Five Fists made a face; it did nothing for his already unpleasant features. "I will explain the situation to the living god. If Morning Star so inclines, I will dispatch a couple squadrons of warriors to hurry the Houses along, and perhaps to knock some heads in the process."

Blue Heron pulled at the wattle under her chin. "I think I can have the expedition on the water in two days."

"How?" Wind looked startled. "You been holding something out on us?"

Blue Heron arched a challenging eyebrow at Five Fists. "I need your promise. You'll give your word. Both of you. If I get this done, you'll back me up. I'm going to have to go way out on a limb . . . one that could be cut off behind me."

"What limb?" Five Fists couldn't hide his skepticism. "If you're asking us to get you reinstated as Clan Keeper, that's out of our hands. That's up to Matron Rising Flame."

"I'm well aware of where the authority lies in that regard. No, I need you to swear on your souls that if I can fill the expedition's granary in two days, you'll see that every last kernel of corn, every last sack of dried squash, every nut down to the last hull, is repaid, in addition to another tenth portion in payment for the loan."

Wind and Five Fists glanced back and forth suspiciously.

"Just who are we borrowing this from?" Wind asked. "I know for a fact that you don't have enough stocked away in your granary to cover that much."

"I don't, but Columella does. It'll empty the Evening House granaries, leave her destitute if we renege on the deal."

"And she'll do this?" Five Fists asked warily.

"She might," Blue Heron replied. "If I ask her. But I'm not asking until I have both of your promises that she'll not only have every morsel replaced, but another one portion in ten thrown in for her trouble. And it will be delivered to her warehouses within ten days."

Five Fists had a distasteful scowl on his face. Wind had crossed her arms, staring thoughtfully at the fire.

"That's just a single day's delay," Wind finally said. "Might have been that much of a postponement even if the storehouse hadn't burned."

"The added benefit is that it keeps Spotted Wrist off balance. He thinks he's gained at least a week to finally figure out how to force Lady Night Shadow Star to marry him."

Wind gave Blue Heron a crafty wink. "You have my word. All the food returned, and one part in ten more as payment."

"Mine, too," Five Fists agreed. "Even if I have to send warriors to seize it from anyone foolish enough to try and evade the levy."

"Then I need a batch of your best porters and a warrior escort," Blue Heron told them. "The sooner I get to Evening Star Town, the faster I can talk Matron Columella into this."

"What are you going to promise her?" Wind asked.

"Absolutely anything she wants." She gave Five Fists a cunning smile. "I'd offer her my life as a guarantee, but that might be too much of a temptation for you. You could cripple Evening Star House on the one hand, and finally get me permanently out of your hair on the other."

Five Fists gave her his crooked-jawed smile. It came off as anything but nice. "You're right, Keeper. Don't tempt fate. Now, get going. I'll have two tens of warriors ready at the foot of the stairs by the time you can hobble down to your litter."

Blue Heron sighed, wishing she'd dressed in warmer clothing. Something told her it was going to be a cold day.

And then there was the problem of what Columella would say. Blue Heron had placed herself and everything she had in jeopardy. By refusing, Columella could cut her off and send her tumbling to a fateful crash.

Ten

The problem with Robin Feather was that he was a rather wealthy man. The rope spinner had a well-deserved reputation for being a genius when it came to rope, cord, and string. Not only did he Trade for the finest fiber that Traders carried up and down the river, he had a sense for his materials. Could judge quality by sight and feel and knew all the secrets of spinning the material into remarkably strong end products. His ropes—a mere two-thirds the thickness of his closest competitors'—could lift the heaviest of loads. They were used for the erection of World Tree poles, to secure rafts of logs, and for hoisting ridgepoles to the highest of temples and palaces.

Being in such demand, such fine ropes brought Robin Feather the richest in Trade. This he bargained off in turn for the best fiber he could get, but the surplus he dutifully handed over to his lineage. They, in turn, gave to the local Panther Clan chief, and he, to High Chief War Duck, who along with his sister, Round Pot, ruled River Mounds House for the Four Winds Clan.

That was a lot of clout.

What made the situation intolerable was that the rope maker obsessed over his possessions—especially his young and most attractive wife. No sooner had he discovered Willow Blossom's indiscretion than he began calling in favors to not only find her, but the rascal Seven Skull Shield who'd cuckolded him.

The word was already out by the time Seven Skull Shield had arrived at the "Goosefoot Woman's" house on the south end of River Mounds City where it overlooked the marshlands and river.

Willow Blossom had looked up from where she crouched on the floor, covered only by the blanket she'd grabbed in her haste as she fled Robin Feather's house. "He'll kill us! What are we going to do?"

While Willow Blossom hadn't exactly greeted Seven Skull Shield with outright joy—could he blame her when she in turn blamed him for her current mess?—he gave her a wry grin. "Me? I'd say good ol' Robin Feather ruined it long before I did. If he'd worshiped you the way you deserved, you'd have never looked twice at the likes of me."

She watched him with curiously keen eyes. A shadow of a smile flickered at the corners of her lips. For an instant, he almost took it as predatory. Then she was in his arms, pressing that marvelous body against his.

He sniffed, adding, "As good as the old woman's baking goosefoot-seed bread smells, you can't stay here forever. He knows you Trade for the old woman's bread. He's got his whole lineage out searching for you, and it'll be half of the local Panther Clan by nightfall." He pushed her back, offered her his hand. "Come on. Let's get you out of here and to someplace safe."

"Why should I trust you?"

"Because I'm here. Because I like you. Because I'm the only friend you've got who can't be bought, bribed, or bullied into helping your husband find and murder you. Or because I'm going to get a real thrill out of whisking you out of his miserable life and seeing that you end up happy. Pick one."

She'd warily taken his hand, her dark eyes fixing on his with a curious intensity, which was how she and Seven Skull Shield ended up where they were, sharing blankets around a small fire in a camp butted up next to War Leader Spotted Wrist's squadron on the canoe landing. Right out in open sight. Packed in among the people who'd assembled to leave with the Cofitachequi expedition. A place where Robin Feather's Panther Clan kin would least suspect his runaway wife to be.

"You do have something better than this in mind, don't you?" she'd asked after a round of passionate lovemaking.

As the morning broke and the sky turned lavender in hopes of dawn, Seven Skull Shield disentangled himself from Willow Blossom's warm and inviting body.

"You do, don't you?" she repeated, pulling him down close again. "Don't make me get up. It's too cold." Her breath frosted where it floated up from the blankets he'd stolen the day before.

Not that they'd had a good night's sleep. First had come the coupling. It had taxed Willow Blossom mightily to keep the little yips of ecstasy from arousing the nearby warriors. No sooner had they drifted off in each other's arms than shouts brought them awake to watch the food stores burn as fire consumed the warehouse.

The assertion had been repeated among the warriors that someone had left a hickory-oil lamp burning in the warehouse, that it must have tipped or fallen to cause the fire.

Seven Skull Shield had finally fallen asleep thinking that was ridiculous. But, hey, it wasn't his warehouse full of corn.

Now, in the purple light of dawn, the idea seemed even more ludicrous. As did the notion of getting out of a warm bed filled with Willow Blossom.

"I do. But first, we have to keep from being caught. And you're right, there's no sense in rushing into trouble on a cold morning like this."

He'd just settled himself against her back and wound his arms around her, her supple bottom teasing his shaft into awareness of the proximity of her willing sheath, when a low voice from the warriors' camp ordered, "On your feet. Pack your gear in your bedding. No shields, just war clubs. One day's worth of cornmeal and your water bladders. We're going on a raid for the squadron first."

"A raid?" one of the sleepy warriors protested. "In Cahokia? Who are we going to fight? Dirt farmers?"

"It's a grab. Come on. The war leader wants his bride. We're going to get her for him. Oh, and by the way, you can kill the Red Wing when he tries to stop us. Now, shake your skinny butt out of those blankets, sweetheart. We got work to do."

Any hint of romance had gone cold, Seven Skull Shield feeling the growing dread.

"Willow Blossom?"

"Hmm?"

"Get up. Someone needs our help."

"Who?"

"A woman who treated me kindly once."

"That's half of Cahokia."

"No, this is a very special woman. Let's go. And even better, you're going to ride all the way to Morning Star Town on a litter borne by the fastest runners we can hire."

"Now that's an improvement," she murmured. "I've never ridden on a litter before."

Eleven

Ever since that unsettling purple sky had dawned, Fire Cat had been on edge. In anticipation, he'd dressed in his armor first thing, his club hanging from his belt along with a long copper stiletto. His bow, arrows, shield, and spare war club were tied in a bundle beside the door, ready for any eventuality.

He could feel the threat, hanging low like the clouds that continued to darken the city. In less than a week, the whole of Cahokia would be totally rapt in its celebration of the spring equinox. At the great observatory, the Sky priests were counting down the fingers of time, aligning the phases of the moon and the moving stars in the constant quest to read the will of Power.

Not that he and Night Shadow Star would be around to see it. By the Blessed sunrise that marked the event, they were supposed to be past the confluence and headed up the Mother Water for the Tenasee. Or that had been the plan before the supplies were burned.

He grinned to himself. Betrayal always came with a sense of building excitement, and he and Night Shadow Star were about to execute the biggest betrayal of all.

He sniffed the odor of cooking yellow lotus mixed with mashed acorn and cornmeal. Half a turkey carcass rested on skewers beside the fire. Green Stick and Clay String fussed over the two small packs laid out on one of the sleeping benches.

The large box containing all of Night Shadow Star's wardrobes and clothing had been retired to the storage area behind the back wall. To Fire Cat's way of thinking, the single ornately carved box of Trade and two smaller packs made a great deal more sense.

But then, nothing about the new plan left him any more thrilled than the old plan had.

Under his breath, he whispered, "I live to serve." And, of course, to love. What Power commanded, he would do his best to ensure that the outcome would be a success. Whatever it took.

Outside, shafts of sunlight had finally managed to poke through holes in the cloud cover. Not that it helped much to cut the damp chill.

Night Shadow Star emerged from her rooms in the back, walked over to the fire, and crouched, hands extended. She wore a thick and warm dogbane-thread shirt beneath a beaver-fur cloak. Her hair was done in a simple bun and held in place with wooden skewers. The only hint of ostentation was in the small carved wooden box tied above her bun. The delicately engraved wood depicted Cosmic Spider and was inset with pearls for eyes and bits of polished shell. Fire Cat had no idea what it contained, but it had been a gift from Rides-the-Lightning.

She looked pensive, her large eyes seeing into a distance far beyond the glowing coals in the fire pit.

She had to be worried about what was coming, about their change of plans. The information that the expedition's food stores had been burned was just the latest complication, and, if anything, had spurred her to an even greater resolve.

"Lady?" he asked, walking over to crouch beside her.

Green Stick and Clay String seemed to be waiting, unsure of what to do next.

"One last thing, Red Wing," Night Shadow Star told him. "After that, we're going to have to move fast."

"I don't understand. Is this something Piasa told you?"

A fleeting shadow of a smile flickered and died on her lips. "When I was a girl I always knew I was going to be a prize. No secret in that, really. What I didn't know was that I would also be a weapon. To be a prize and weapon at the same time, that is an interesting dilemma. While half the world is trying to claim me, they are but obstacles trying to keep me from fulfilling my purpose as a weapon."

"You mean killing your brother."

She nodded. "I'm a gaming piece. Cast onto the blanket like a bone die in one game, while other dice are cast in an attempt to win me in another. There are so many levels to the game it is hard to know which side I'm playing on at any given moment."

"We're taking a risk, you know. Changing the game in midthrow. You heard *Tonka'tzi* Wind's messenger. Two days until they can replace the burned supplies. Spotted Wrist won't be expecting that."

"If Columella agrees to empty her granaries."

"There is that."

She shot him a conspiratorial look. "The best way to ruin someone's game is to take the pieces off the hide. Doing so throws all the schemes into chaos. Changes the rules. Especially if it's done in a way that no one expects."

"Just like in war, my lady."

"Do you think this is any different?"

"It's all strategy and tactics."

"Yes, it is," she mused, gaze lost in the fire again.

Footsteps could be heard pounding up the steps. One of the warriors who had been guarding her stairs appeared and dropped to his knees in the doorway. He touched his forehead to the matting and announced, "A man and woman are here to see you, Lady. It's that thief, Seven Skull Shield. The woman I do not know."

"The final die has been cast, and we know which markings are now faceup," Night Shadow Star whispered, and aloud, said, "Send them up."

"Yes, Lady." The guard leaped up, wheeled, and trotted out to the top of the stairs, calling, "Lady Night Shadow Star will see you now."

"You were expecting this?" Fire Cat asked.

Night Shadow Star shrugged. "I wasn't sure who it would be. Piasa wasn't specific."

"So, he knows we're changing the plan?"

"My master knows a great many things." She sighed. "He just doesn't know how they will end."

"But he doesn't object to what we're doing?"

"On the contrary, he tells me that there is no other way for us."

"Why doesn't that reassure me?"

Fire Cat turned to see the burly thief accompanied by his miserable brindle dog as he topped the stairs and strode between the Piasa and Horned Serpent guardian posts. He was dressed in his usual coarsely spun hunting shirt; a blanket woven of strips of twisted rabbit fur was wrapped around his shoulders and was held tight before him. The woman who followed a half-step behind was young and remarkably endowed, with tangled and disheveled black hair. Her wide eyes and awed expression—not to mention her half-panicked gait—reminded him of a fawn ready to bolt after entering a panther's lair.

Seven Skull Shield had a grim look on his gnarled face as he half-heartedly tapped fingers to his forehead in a token gesture of respect and bulled his way into the room. The dog, to Fire Cat's disgust, peed on the doorframe and went sniffing for the stewpot.

"Lady," Seven Skull Shield blurted, "you're in trouble. Hard on my heels is a pack of Spotted Wrist's warriors. Their orders are to dispose of the Red Wing and carry you off to the Four Winds Clan House where Spotted Wrist is waiting. Like it or not, you're going to be married within another couple of fingers of time. Figured I'd give you as much warning as I could."

Night Shadow Star and Fire Cat rose together.

Seven Skull Shield kicked the raw-boned dog away from the stewpot, then gave the dazzled young woman a reassuring grin. She was staring slack-jawed at the wealth piled around the palace. Winnings from Fire Cat's chunkey victory over a Natchez champion.

Night Shadow Star stepped up to the thief, placed her hands on his shoulders in a gesture Fire Cat found way too familiar. "I need you to do something for me."

"Of course, Lady."

"After I have gone, I need you to go to the Morning Star. Tell him that I have chosen my own way to deal with the problem in the east. Tell him: I'll do it one way, or another. He will understand."

"Me? Just wander in and tell him, huh?"

"My things are at your disposal. You had best dress the part. If anyone tries to stop you, tell them you are my agent."

Seven Skull Shield frowned slightly, shot her a narrow-eyed and suspicious look, then laughed at himself. "For you? Of course."

The pretty young woman was looking covetously at the palace furnishings. Now her startled gaze fixed on Night Shadow Star as if she just realized who she was.

Night Shadow Star told the thief, "By doing this, you are placing yourself at great risk. You know that, don't you? This changes everything for you. In ways you can barely comprehend."

Seven Skull Shield shrugged. "Lady, since way back when, you've treated me fair. Taken my side and made a place for me when you didn't have to. I was there last time they made you marry a man you didn't want to. Thought I'd give you a fair warning, so I didn't have to watch you go through that again."

She smiled up at him. "Then we'll be on our way." To Fire Cat she said, "Get the packs. Call the porters up for the Trade box. Our work here is done."

Fire Cat stepped over and lifted his and her packs from the sleeping bench, a curious gaze fixed on Seven Skull Shield the whole time. "How much time do we have?"

"They were organizing their party when Willow Blossom and I left the canoe landing. They'll be coming, probably at a dog trot. Which reminds me. I hired a litter to bring me here. Got it from Crazy Frog with a promise I'd give his men a sack of something worth a small fortune if they'd run in teams to get me here fastest. Lady, if you wouldn't mind?" Seven Skull Shield's eyes drifted to the exotic pottery, the engraved wood boxes, and the extravagant wealth hanging from the walls.

"I'll see to it myself," she told him. "Crazy Frog's porters are waiting at the bottom of the stairs?"

"They are."

She took her pack from Fire Cat and grabbed up a small sack that contained copper bracelets. "Green Stick, you, Clay String, and Winter Leaf keep the palace in order. I'm leaving Seven Skull Shield in charge while I'm gone. You are to obey his every order. Any disobedience, and he may discipline you any way he chooses."

"Lady?" Fire Cat and Green Stick cried in shocked unison. Leave the thief in charge of her palace? What kind of lunacy was that? Even Seven Skull Shield, never one to show surprise, gaped in disbelief.

She told Seven Skull Shield, "You might want to keep that knowledge secret. Use this palace as a place of refuge. I think your coming days are going to be dangerous enough."

Seven Skull Shield grinned, looked over at the horrified household staff, and said, "It'll be waiting here, safe and sound, when you get back, Lady. On my promise."

Fire Cat slung his pack over his shoulder and scooped up his bundled weapons where they lay beside the door. The porters had entered for the Trade box.

Night Shadow Star ignored them, turning to the still-stunned Seven Skull Shield. "My master tells me that Power hasn't decided what to do with you. I am asked to find out. If you had a choice, would you prefer to die after being betrayed by a woman you love, or because you were caught while pulling off the most audacious theft of your career?"

Fire Cat watched Seven Skull Shield's expression turn cunning. "Given a chance, Lady, I will always place my life in jeopardy over a beautiful woman."

Fire Cat choked a deep-seated growl as Seven Skull Shield took Night Shadow Star's hand and raised it to his cheek in a brazen but tender gesture.

She laughed, eyes flashing with amusement. "You know my heart belongs to another. I wish you well, thief. Perhaps the ways of Power will allow us to meet again. In the meantime, be smart. You will need all your wits to survive what's coming."

With that she headed for the door, not looking back.

Fire Cat, still unsettled by it all, called, "Thanks for the warning, thief." Then, he paused. "You and I . . . well, we didn't start so well. Know that you have my gratitude for everything you did for her, for me." He bowed his head, touching fingertips to his forehead in a gesture of true respect.

He, too, refused to look back as he passed through the door. All the while he was wondering if he'd ever see Night Shadow Star's palace again.

Behind him, he heard Green Stick's cry of, "She left *you* in charge? Of us?"

Clay String was bellowing, "Get that dog away from the stew!"

Under his breath, Fire Cat muttered, "Thief, something tells me you've never been tested the way you're about to be tested. May Power help you."

Then he was past the guardian posts and headed down the stairs to where Night Shadow Star dickered with the porters loitering around Crazy Frog's ornate litter.

Twelve

She's gone? What do you mean, she's gone?" Spotted Wrist thundered. Little drops of flying spittle made Blood Talon flinch. He fought the urge to reach out and push the war leader back, out of his face.

Around them, the great room in the Four Winds Clan House had gone deathly silent. People were watching, various expressions of amusement, unease, and surprise mixed with a couple of downright smiles.

The fire burned brightly, pots of food bubbling. The scent of roasted venison, turkey, quail, and fish hinted at the extravagance of the anticipated wedding feast.

Clan Matron Rising Flame—dressed in her finest with white swan feather splays at each shoulder, a brilliantly dyed red skirt on her hips, and an eagle-feather cloak hanging over her shoulders—stood with her gilded-cedar staff of office. The copper-arrow headdress on her tightly wound hair gleamed like liquid blood in the great fire's light. No hint of amusement reflected from her dark and angry eyes.

"Did you search her palace?" Spotted Wrist demanded, his right hand spinning the thick leather arm guard on his left arm—a sign of frustrated embarrassment that Blood Talon had seen but rarely over the years.

"I myself went through her palace, War Lea . . . er, Clan Keeper. I had warriors posted on all sides. There was no way she could have escaped. As soon as I determined that she wasn't in her palace, I sent warriors in all directions. Some to her aunt Blue Heron's, some to the Morning Star's palace, others to see if she might be at Rides-the-Lightning's or perhaps the Sky Watchers' or the Surveyors' society, even to the Record Keepers' society house, and the Women's house. She wasn't in any of those places. No one even reported seeing her after she returned from the canoe landing yesterday."

"What did her servants say?"

"That she left this morning." Blood Talon fought to keep his face straight. "They, uh . . . Well, one of them, a big man, almost seemed amused. Made me want to take a war club to his smug face. He assured me that the lady had left just after dawn in company of the Red Wing, but he hadn't a clue as to where she'd been headed."

Spotted Wrist's face worked, the corners of his lips quivering. He twisted his arm guard back and forth so hard that Blood Talon wondered if it would chafe his commander's skin.

"I *won't* have this! Go! Now, Squadron First. You take your men and you *find* that woman if you have to pick her up out of the Morning Star's bed and bring her to me."

Blood Talon bent his head low, smacking a fist to his forehead in submissive obedience. "Yes, War Lead . . . Clan Keeper. Right away, Lord."

Spinning on his heel, he winced as Spotted Wrist angrily kicked one of the stewpots, shattering the ceramic and blasting hot liquid to hiss in the fire and spatter on the matting.

I pity Night Shadow Star. Something tells me her wedding night is going to be most unpleasant.

Thirteen

The fire in Columella's palace burned hot and fierce, which not only illuminated the great room's interior but came as a welcome relief to Blue Heron's chilled limbs. While she'd had a blanket wrapped tightly around her as the porters bore her down the Avenue of the Sun to the canoe landing, the chill had slowly eaten its way into her bones.

Pus and blood! Would summer never come?

As she'd been taken across the river in a Trader's canoe, the few rays of sunshine had vanished, thick black clouds blowing down from the northwest. By the time her litter and porters had been ferried across, the first flakes of snow had begun drifting and twisting down from the leaden sky.

She could smell the strength of it. This was going to be one of those miserable, sodden storms. And it came at the absolute worst time. Somehow she had to get the expedition resupplied in two days.

Everything now depended upon her relationship with Matron Columella—a woman who had once plotted to destroy Blue Heron. And whose relatives Blue Heron had managed to exile to distant colonies over the years.

"This is a surprise," Columella announced as she stepped out from her personal quarters in the rear of the palace. "Wouldn't have expected you. Or, perhaps I should. Let me guess. The burning of the Cofitachequi expedition's food warehouse wasn't an accident. You're here trying to figure out who the guilty party was."

Columella wore a white skirt woven of fine dogbane thread, its hem accented by black Four Winds spirals. Tall moccasins crafted from soft fawnskin rose to her knees. A quilted goose-down cape hung over her shoulders, and a simple hair bun was held in place with polished bone skewers.

"I wouldn't be much of a Keeper if I didn't know who burned the warehouse and why." Blue Heron clapped her hands before her, happy that feeling had been restored by the roaring fire. "Had to be Spotted Wrist. Oh, not him personally, but one of his trusted warriors. And the reason? To keep Night Shadow Star in town long enough that he can get her to the Clan House and safely married. Once the union is consummated, she can run off to the end of the earth for all he cares."

Columella pursed her lips, climbed up onto the litter atop the clay dais across the fire. "Then your presence here is something of a puzzle. What can I do for you?"

Blue Heron indicated the clay dais where it rose waist-high from the floor. "Flat Stone Pipe in there? If so, he can come out and be comfortable. Matron, you and I are beyond trying to cut each other's throats and battling for prominence. Back when we did, it proved to be a senseless game that cost us both more than we could afford to lose."

"Yes, it did, didn't it?" Columella smiled wistfully. "I appreciate your candor. Flat Stone Pipe, however, isn't here. Had I known you were coming, I would have seen to it that he was on hand. I think he's over in River Mounds City keeping an eye on War Duck and Round Pot. Ever since that debacle when their eternal fire was snuffed last fall, they've been struggling to keep their hold on the high chair. Too many cousins are sparring to take them down. Three Fingers, second cousin I think, is up to his eyebrows in intrigue."

"It's been nice, actually, to have them at each other's throats rather than causing mischief. I, however, am here with a proposition. And yes, it's about the burned warehouse. It was full of food, corn mostly, that was supposed to keep the expedition fed as it winds its way south and east to Cofitachequi. For a variety of political reasons, Wind, Five Fists, and I need to have those people gone. Day after tomorrow at the latest. For that, I need corn, beans, and squash. A lot of it."

"Meaning everything in my warehouses?"

"How clever you are. You could be a House matron." Blue Heron shot her a conspiratorial smile. "I owe you, and I take my debts seriously. In return for your food stocks, we, meaning Five Fists and Wind and me, promise to replace every last kernel as soon as we possibly can, even if that means stripping some of the other Houses. And in addition? We'll give you a tenth part more."

"What makes you think the other Houses will allow themselves to be stripped? Let alone see Evening Star House end up with a tenth part more?"

"I think Morning Star will order it."

"But you're not sure?"

"Since when is anything sure with Morning Star? But here's my hunch: He always plays a deep game. He wants Night Shadow Star to make it to Cofitachequi. They're in that together somehow. Beyond that, he has me pitted against Rising Flame and Spotted Wrist in some kind of competition that I don't completely understand, but I've played the game long enough to know that it's for keeps. Beyond that, Wind is fully committed to getting that bunch on the river and gone, especially the dissidents. So is Five Fists, who knows how close we came to civil war last fall. And he really despises Spotted Wrist."

"You were never really one of his favorites either, as I recall."

"This is Five Fists we're talking about. He doesn't have favorites. He and I have always tolerated each other. Respected each other. Not that that stopped him from taking me prisoner, nor would it have kept him from dutifully hanging me in a square if the Morning Star ever commanded it."

"I've had my own troubles, you know. Ever since that vile and twisted Walking Smoke burned my palace, half of my House has been plotting to overthrow me. War Duck and Round Pot are not the only ones who have been staggered by unfortunate events in the past couple of years. But for Flat Stone Pipe, Two Moons would have built a strong enough coalition to have me retired to a farmstead somewhere out west."

"I'm aware."

"Then you are also aware that I raised eyebrows in this House by supporting you and Wind during the Council last year. That fed a lot of suspicion that I was a Morning Star House lackey. People say I've lost my nerve, and I've surrendered my House and my values to become your creature."

Blue Heron ground the few teeth she had left. "We both know better than that."

"They don't."

"Evening Star House's ultimate goals are best served by sending that expedition downriver."

"If I give you the food, it will seem like I'm playing your game for you." Columella arched an eyebrow. "And, like you say, the game is ultimately to unseat Spotted Wrist, isn't it? Get your position back as Keeper?"

"I won't lie to you about that."

"Then, what's the truth about this Koroa copper that has everyone's balls in a knot? You steal it to make Spotted Wrist look bad?"

"I did not."

"Of course not. Word was there was a dog named Farts involved."

"I wouldn't know about that."

"So, *you* didn't steal the copper, but we know who did. Did the thief do it at your suggestion?"

"I give you my word of honor, I had no part in the planning, execution, or even any knowledge of what happened to that gods-rotted copper."

Columella narrowed an eye. "Old friend, I have to tell you, I fear getting involved in your games. I need a couple of months to quell the unrest here on this side of the river without stirring up more trouble for myself."

"You're not going to like it if Spotted Wrist and Rising Flame turn their attention your way. And they will."

"Let me think." Columella took a deep breath, mulling things, her lips moving.

Blue Heron wasn't sure if Columella really needed all the time she took to think it through, or if she just stalled as a way to inflict a subtle form of torture. Finally, Columella said, "All right. I'll empty our warehouses. Resupply the expedition, but I want two-tenths part in addition."

Blue Heron felt her heart skip. How was she supposed to sell that to Wind or Five Fists? Especially when it was the end of winter when all of spring lay before the city and most of the granaries were empty? Could she do it? Could Wind?

"A tenth part and a half."

"Done." Columella slapped a hand to her thigh. "And Blue Heron, if you don't come through with this, we're both in trouble. You understand that, don't you?"

Fourteen

The way Seven Skull Shield saw it, he'd just been given a dream and a nightmare. The precariousness of his current situation had really been brought home as he tried to accommodate that squadron first, Blood Talon. The man had arrived shortly after Night Shadow Star and Fire Cat's departure. Given that he was at the head of a party of armed warriors, and in a pissy mood, and declaring he came at the order of the Four Winds Clan Keeper, it wasn't like Seven Skull Shield could tell the man to go stick his finger up a dark and nasty place in his posterior.

So, accompanied by four warriors, Blood Talon had searched the palace, making a mess and getting even further riled as it became apparent that no great Cahokian lady was hiding under one of the sleeping benches or in one of the cooking pots.

Seven Skull Shield had immediately decided he didn't like the squadron first. And he'd had to temper his better judgment, which was to wait until the two-footed maggot was faced the other way and whack him in the head with a club. Given the need to appear helpful in proving that Night Shadow Star wasn't in her palace, it had really hurt to be polite, sound reasonable, and acquiesce.

Somehow, the knowledge that twenty-some warriors surrounded the palace kept him from acting on his impulses. Therefore, he'd pasted on his honest face, kept Farts from peeing on the man's leg, and gladly explained that he had no idea where Night Shadow Star was. Then he'd maintained his polite veneer while the man searched, and poked, and prodded in places that would have enraged Night Shadow Star's propriety.

Sometimes he even amazed himself.

Seven Skull Shield had kept his mouth shut as the warriors withdrew, irritated and mumbling among themselves. Then he'd clapped his hands and looked again at the palace to which he'd been entrusted.

What in seven shades of shit did he know about a palace, let alone Night Shadow Star's? Palaces were for robbing, not running.

When it came to Green Stick, Clay String, and Winter Leaf, the way they looked at him was the same as if some giant bug had just crawled in their door.

Willow Blossom, however, was still in a state of wonderment. After Night Shadow Star's departure, Willow Blossom had collapsed, loose-limbed, onto one of the sleeping platforms, whispering, "That was really her. I'm in *her* palace. No one will believe this."

Willow Blossom had told Seven Skull Shield that she was a Panther Clan woman from somewhere up beyond the eastern bluffs. Said her parents had raised her in a small mound group out by the Moon Mound in the prairie lands a day's hard travel east on the Avenue of the Sun. There they kept an eye on the local dirt farmers and laborers who worked for the moon priests.

She'd considered a marriage to Robin Feather as a step up in wealth and status—if not happiness and wedded bliss. Now she gawked at the finery that surrounded her. Something feral gleamed behind her eyes, an eagerness in her expression.

"Most of this," Seven Skull Shield told her, "was winnings from when Fire Cat beat that Natchez, Swirling Cloud. I hear it was a remarkable game. Each player wagered his life on the outcome. All of Cahokia bet against Fire Cat. In the end, the Red Wing won all this and more. First thing he did, though? He clubbed Swirling Cloud in the head, and then he cut it off the man's still-twitching body. That's Swirling Cloud's skull up there. The polished one painted red."

She followed his finger to where the Natchez's skull grinned down from up by the center pole.

"Who is this woman?" Green Stick demanded, stepping forward. "What's this all about? Why would our lady trust you, of all people?"

"As to Willow Blossom, she's a friend of mine. She's going to stay here for a while because it's safe." Seven Skull Shield spread his hands wide. "Listen, Night Shadow Star caught me by as much surprise as she did the rest of you. So, here's the thing: I don't want to get in your way. Do what you normally do. Cook and all that. Keep the fire going, get wood, water."

"And what are you doing?"

"I have my own affairs to attend to." He made a face, glancing out the door. "She really thinks they'll let me in to give Morning Star her message?"

And will it put me in special danger when I do it?

That sent a shiver up his back. He'd never enjoyed Four Winds politics. Especially since he was more or less expendable in the eyes of the various two-footed serpents who struggled for supremacy among the privileged elite. After all, what was one shiftless and clanless thief compared to lords, chiefs, matrons, and war leaders?

"You mean that?" Willow Blossom asked. "You're really going up there? Face to face with the living god?"

"I've been there before. Granted, it was with the Keeper." Still, it left him feeling unusually wary.

"I thought that was a lie to impress me."

"Oh, he lies all right," Clay String muttered where he was trying to shoo Farts away from the food bowls. Long threads of drool were spindling off the dog's jowls. "Just not about the impossible things. You should have seen him passing himself off as a noble when our lady had to marry that despicable Itza."

"Didn't think she needed to marry another pile of walking vomit like Spotted Wrist."

"He's a great man," Winter Leaf shot back from where she was folding some of the blankets that Blood Talon had tossed about in his search.

"Explain what's so great about him?" Seven Skull Shield asked as he paced along the walls, looking at stacks of boxes, jars, and overstuffed baskets. "Compared to Fire Cat, he's a bit of walking puke. All this, these are the Red Wing's winnings from the chunkey court, and Night Shadow Star gave away the rest of it. Only the Morning Star has more wealth in the whole world."

"And Night Shadow Star leaves the most notorious thief in Cahokia in charge of it?" Green Stick wondered. "How does that work?"

A very good question, and one Seven Skull Shield was asking himself.

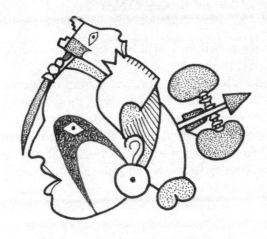

Fifteen

Snow fell in thick sheets. At times Fire Cat could barely see farther than he could have thrown a rock. And then a shift in the wind would leave a hole, as if parting a veil in the dancing and falling flakes. At those times he could see clear across the Father Water to where gangs of men and women slipped and slid their way down the path from Evening Star Town to pile basket after basket of corn into the waiting Trade canoes.

As soon as one was full, it was paddled across the river where waiting warriors and laborers carried the baskets and sacks to shelter. The ash-stained sands of the canoe landing were now a slushy mess. People slopping back and forth.

"Who would have believed it?" Night Shadow Star asked from beneath a snow-encrusted hood.

"Word is that Clan Keeper Blue Heron herself is overseeing the operation," Crazy Frog told her.

After the return of his litter, the noted gambler had insisted on accompanying them down to the canoe landing. The nondescript man wore a bark hat that kept his head and shoulders protected. A thick cloak hung from his shoulders for warmth.

"She's no longer Keeper," Fire Cat noted.

"Hard not to call her that." Crazy Frog pulled his blanket tighter. "You really want to leave in this?"

"Sooner is better," Night Shadow Star told him. "It's just snow. And a late winter storm at that. It will be melted in a couple of days, and by then we'll be past the confluence."

"Cofitachequi's a long way to travel. Lot of dangers, and not just the wild tribes. The river will try and do everything it can to kill you."

The gambler reached into his bag, offering a small stone carving to Night Shadow Star. She lifted it, and Fire Cat saw it was in the shape of a fox. Carved from jasper, it had been finished by a master, the beast's cunning expression artfully worked into the stone.

"You get in trouble on the Tenasee, Lady, you hunt down a Trader called The River Fox. There's no one better when it comes to the Tenasee. He's—"

"Winder?" Fire Cat interrupted in surprise. "But he's the one behind all that Surveyors' Bundle trouble that—"

"Who can blame a man for a little trouble?" Crazy Frog shrugged, and tilted his bark hat, which allowed a smattering of flakes to land on his shoulder. "That business with the Keeper and Seven Skull Shield last fall, that wasn't personal. It was a hired job. Winder lives by the Power of Trade. If you give him that token, tell him it's from me, he'll get you to Cofitachequi if there's any human way possible."

Fire Cat was filling his lungs to object when Night Shadow Star cut him off, saying, "Your kindness is deeply appreciated. On many levels. If we find need, I shall be sure to hire him as a guide."

"Lady," Crazy Frog said with a slight bow.

She laid a hand on the gambler's arm, adding, "I also know how you have served Fire Cat and me in the past. It will not be forgotten." From her bag she extracted a shell gorget carved in the shape of an open square and depicting four overlaying sides.

This she handed to Crazy Frog, adding, "Should you find yourself in need, present this to either of my aunts. Both Wind and Blue Heron will recognize it and your claim. That gorget was a gift from my first husband. They will do what they can to assist you."

Crazy Frog spared her a stunned look, bowed deeply, and touched his forehead in respect. "I am honored, Lady."

Fire Cat shot the man a wary look. This, after all, was Crazy Frog. He had fingers in half of the dirty dealings on the canoe landing—not to mention that he almost lived in War Duck's pocket, had been in the middle of last fall's excitement over the Surveyors' Bundle, and played all sides against the others. In that fiasco, a party of Quiz Quiz had stolen the sacred Bundle containing the Surveyors' Society's instruments, the ones they used to lay out angles, measure, and parcel land. People had died, and Cahokia had almost come apart at the seams.

The man had also—through his knowledge of chunkey—played a role in analyzing Fire Cat's game so that he could win that vaunted match against Swirling Cloud.

Fire Cat sighed, grinned. What matter? Chances were slim that either he or Night Shadow Star would see Cahokia again.

"Now these Traders," Crazy Frog said, leading them down to the waiting canoe. "They're Yuchi. From Big Cane Town down on the Great Bend of the Tenasee. I know them. Good people."

In the falling snow, the canoe, called *Red Reed*, didn't look nearly as elegant as it had the last time they'd seen it. Snow clumped on the gunwales and seats, mounded on the packs and box they'd had delivered. But the four men and one woman stood waiting, hoods protecting their heads and shoulders from the thick white flakes.

White Mat, in his thirties, was the leader. Like all river Traders, the man had wide shoulders, muscular arms, and a dark-tanned face.

Shedding Bird, a year younger, had a slightly larger nose than his brother, and kept his hair longer. He grinned at Night Shadow Star in a shy sort of way.

Mixed Shell and Made Man hailed from the same village, both tough-looking, strapping, and sharing that squint-eyed expression that came from years on the water.

The woman, Made Man's wife, was in her midtwenties; she had been named Half Root. She stood with a cocked hip and studied Night Shadow Star with a saucy air of disregard and superiority.

"These are very important people to me," Crazy Frog told the Yuchi. "I would take it as a personal favor if you took special care of them."

"We promised to get them as far as Big Cane Town at the bottom of the Mussel Shallows cataract," White Mat replied. "Until then, we'll treat them right."

"A canoe's no palace, Lady," Half Root said, her skeptical gaze still on Night Shadow Star. "We can't be stopping and camping all the time."

"We're aware," Night Shadow Star told her, a slight smile to her lips. Then her eyes went vacant—a look that told Fire Cat that Piasa was whispering in her ear.

"We can make a fair distance today if we get on the river now," Fire Cat said in an effort to distract them from Night Shadow Star's vacant gaze. They'd see a lot of it, but later, once they were on the river. He dropped his weapons and chunkey gear inside the polished bald cypress hull.

To Crazy Frog, he offered his hand. "Thank you. If I run into any outstanding players, I'll send them your way."

"Watch your release," Crazy Frog reminded. "You have a habit of rushing it. Let the stone kiss the ground."

"I won't forget."

Fire Cat helped Night Shadow Star into the canoe, watched her wipe the snow from one of the central benches and seat herself.

Bending his back with the rest, Fire Cat helped shove the hull from the sand, watched as the Traders nimbly leaped into the canoe, grabbing up paddles.

Fire Cat slipped over the side, settling himself beside Night Shadow Star and reaching for one of the paddles.

"You going to help?" Mixed Shell asked, approving.

"We'll get there faster," Fire Cat told him. Then he took a look back as the canoe slid out into the current.

Through the falling snow, River Mounds City could barely be made out above the canoe landing—a ghostly outline of buildings that faded into encompassing white. The effect was almost magical.

The bustle around the expedition, an arrow-shot's distance upstream from them, seemed surreal. Snow-clotted figures like ants in line, trudging to and from the canoes, transferring baskets of corn.

"Spotted Wrist is going to be furious," Night Shadow Star observed. "He thinks he's still got days."

"They'll have that expedition on the river by tomorrow," Fire Cat decided. "Wind and Five Fists want them gone."

"Can they catch us?" Night Shadow Star asked.

As if such a statement was an absurdity, White Mat laughed. "Lady, if that bunch can catch *Red Reed*, we'll suck toads and river slime."

"*Red Reed*? How did you come up with the name?"

"Ever flick a floating reed with your finger?" Made Man asked. "It almost squirts across the water. The difference is in the bow, sharp, like a knife. Lot of work goes into shaping a proper Trade canoe. This one was crafted down south by the Tunica for river work. Took us years to accumulate the Trade needed to obtain *Red Reed*."

"Worth it, though. You'll see," Half Root told him from her position in the rear. She was stroking just as vigorously as the rest of them.

Night Shadow Star was staring off into the snow, as if she could see some pattern in the falling sheets of white. Her mouth pinched, frown lines deepening in her forehead.

After a time, she said, "Nothing will be the same from here on. My master says he's going to try and kill us now."

"What? Who?" White Mat asked warily.

"Walking Smoke," she said cryptically. "He's going to try and use Power against us. He knows if we make it to Cofitachequi, everything he's built will be destroyed."

Sixteen

Turned out that getting into the Morning Star's great mound complex wasn't the hard part. Lady Night Shadow Star had given him free use of her palace and its assets. This included not only the finest of noble dress, warm robes, furs, and jewelry, but the ability to choose from a couple of Four Winds Clan staffs of office.

While Green Stick, Winter Leaf, and Clay String wailed at the impropriety of it, Seven Skull Shield was able to dress himself like a noble, paint his face, and brandish a staff of office like it was a grass flail.

The hard part was leaving Farts behind. He and the dog had shared some of the most outlandish adventures.

"This time, you stay behind, my friend," he told the panting and drooling dog. Bending down on one knee, he mussed the canine's floppy ears, only to wince at the fetid breath issuing from the beast's mouth.

Farts watched him with his odd blue-and-brown eyes, the big tail slashing back and forth, knocking a water jar from one of the benches to spill on the matting.

"You don't mean to leave that . . . that *thing* here?" Winter Leaf asked shrilly.

"Well, if he goes along, I'm not making it past the guards at the bottom of the stairs, right? What Four Winds noble do you know who goes everywhere with a big Spirit dog like this one? So, keep him here. Keep him out of trouble. Willow Blossom, you know Farts, don't let him out."

"What if he has to go?" she asked. "You saw how much water he drank."

"That was my cooking water," Winter Leaf told him through gritted teeth.

"Well, don't leave it just sitting unattended on the floor like that."

"I have to throw what's left out now."

"Oh, come on. You're going to boil it, right? Surely a little dog spit doesn't affect the taste."

Winter Leaf had her fists clenched at her sides, her body literally shaking. "This is impossible! What did we ever do to the lady to deserve this?"

"Must have been something good," Seven Skull Shield told her as he climbed to his feet. "She wouldn't turn a place like this over to just any old thief. She wanted someone outstanding."

He stepped to the door, setting it aside, and waved for Farts to stay. "I mean it, don't let him out."

And with that, Seven Skull Shield set the door back in place behind him.

He peered out through the falling snow. Cahokia was oddly silent, the only sound the soft shishing patter of flakes as they landed on the accumulation.

Seven Skull Shield plodded across the yard, nodded to the snow-capped guardian statues. For once neither Piasa nor Horned Serpent looked very dangerous, their heads mounded in soft white caps of snow. Made them almost look cuddly.

The stairs leading down to the avenue were treacherous. He picked his way one step at a time, feeling the first chill as it ate into the gaps in his clothing. The fine scarlet shirt he'd found in a box was too small.

"That was her first husband's!" Green Stick had cried in dismay. "You can't wear that!"

The garment was the only appropriate raiment that came close to fitting. As if Makes Three would care. He'd been dead for years now, his soul disposed of in the Underworld by Fire Cat before Spotted Wrist's army had paid Red Wing Town a reprisal visit.

At the base of the stairs, Seven Skull Shield slopped his way through the wet snow to the Avenue of the Sun, then along the Great Mound's base to the snow-cold guards and miserable porters. The latter stood, stamped, batted the snow from their soaked clothing, and shivered as they awaited their masters.

"I bear a message from the Lady Night Shadow Star for the Morning Star," Seven Skull Shield announced with a flourish and lifted his staff as if it were an invincible weapon.

"Go on," the guard told him. "Watch out for the steps, had one bad fall already tonight. Bear Clan chief from down south. Got lucky, just broke his leg."

Seven Skull Shield tested each step, climbing carefully. At the Council House Gate he repeated his claim, was admitted to the Council House courtyard. The climb up the Great Staircase to the Morning Star's rarefied domain actually unnerved him as wind pasted snow against his clothing and sought to topple him off the slippery and snow-packed wooden steps.

At Morning Star's palisade gate, the guard, snow-caked and shivering, took one look at the staff and waved him through.

Here and there people huddled in the high courtyard. Snow stuck to one side of the World Tree pole, its top lost in the dark and swirling flakes.

Before entering the palace, Seven Skull Shield hesitated at the great double doors. Little tufts of snow clung to the deeply engraved image of Morning Star.

Did he really want to do this? He could just turn around, head back to the warmth and safety of Night Shadow Star's palace. Bury himself in Willow Blossom's soft and welcoming body. Then, in the morning, he could wander the short distance up the avenue to Blue Heron's palace and ask her what to do.

Nerves weren't one of his normal responses. He'd sneaked into countless palaces, stolen from some of the most dangerous people in Cahokia, and brazenly courted disaster since he was a snot-nosed kid. But this was different. Sure, he'd been seated across from the living god a time or two, but always in the company of Blue Heron or at the invitation of Night Shadow Star.

This time he'd be going in alone. Literally into the god's lair. Not as an observer, but as one of the players. Not to mention one who stood right out front. This time he wasn't working from the shadows, nor was there a safe line of retreat. It was him, alone, in a world he didn't really like, let alone fully understand.

What if they don't like Night Shadow Star's message? Wouldn't be the first time it got taken out on the messenger.

If only she hadn't trusted him.

Seven Skull Shield made a face, hated the roiling in his stomach—full as it was with Night Shadow Star's food—and with a sigh, pushed open the door and slipped into the warmth.

He took a moment, caught his bearings.

Lots of nobles, of course. Many seated, sharing food from large wooden platters. The women were perfectly dressed, hair done, pale shell necklaces at their throats, and faces painted. The same with the men.

Just this side of the fire sat Matron Rising Flame, her hands gesturing as she discussed something with Spotted Wrist. Some of the other no-bles were people Seven Skull Shield could only place by their clan insig-nia. Warriors stood in ranks along each wall, watching the proceedings with bored eyes.

Across the fire, Morning Star reclined on his litter while a pretty young woman dressed in fine fabrics, her hair piled high and pinned, plucked meat from a turkey thigh and plopped it into his mouth.

And here came Five Fists. The lop-jawed old warrior pinned Seven Skull Shield with hard eyes as he crossed the intricately woven matting. He stopped before Seven Skull Shield and fixed on the staff.

"I know you." The old warrior grinned; crooked as his jaw was, it didn't come off as friendly. "Tow rope. That thief we were sent after. Blue Heron's . . . what? Spy? Confidant?" A pause. "Thieves aren't welcome here. Bad choice if you were thinking of lifting wealth from anyone, let alone the living god. And you'd better have a most convincing explana-tion for why you are carrying Makes Three's staff."

"Listen, I don't want to be here any more than you want me here. Lady Night Shadow Star sent me with a message for the Morning Star. The staff was to get me past the guards."

"What message?"

"She said to tell Morning Star that she's chosen her own way to deal with the problem in the east. One way or another. And that Morning Star would understand. So, if you'll just go tell—"

"What problem?"

"She didn't tell me. She had that spooky look like she gets when Piasa is talking to her."

"Why didn't she come to tell the living god herself?"

"She's gone."

"Where?"

"Didn't tell me. So there, you know. I've done my duty. That being the case, I'll be more than happy to leave your high and exalted com-pany and remove any temptation you might have to—"

"War Leader?" Morning Star's voice carried across the room, silenc-ing the conversations. "Who comes?"

Seven Skull Shield made a face as he felt that knot in his stomach begin to turn runny.

Five Fists answered, "The thief, Seven Skull Shield, Lord. He comes bearing a message from Lady Night Shadow Star."

"Bring him forward." Morning Star had now fixed his hard, black eyes on Seven Skull Shield.

The fleeting thought ran through Seven Skull Shield's souls that he could charge, smash Five Fists off his feet, pivot, and sprint like a terrified fox for the gate and stairway. Maybe leap onto the mound's slope, hope he could slide down on the thick wet snow and not kill himself when he hit the bottom.

But even as he did, two warriors were closing in from either side to act as an escort when Five Fists led the way forward. All eyes in the palace were fixed on him. He felt like an orphan fawn being led to slaughter before the solstice feast—and the hungry diners were watching his every move in anticipation.

Five Fists stopped before the great fire, stepped to the side, and, when Seven Skull Shield hesitated, the warriors behind propelled him forward.

Had he ever felt so alone, vulnerable, almost naked and defenseless?

"Prostrate yourself, fool," Five Fists hissed before giving Seven Skull Shield a shove. Burning with embarrassment, Seven Skull Shield dropped and touched his forehead to the matting.

"Rise. What message do you bear?" Morning Star asked, leaning forward on his litter. The living god propped an elbow on his knee, painted face with its forked-eye design done in black and white. The shell masks in the form of human heads gleamed where they covered his ears.

Seven Skull Shield, figuring he was dead already, stood, shrugged. "L-Lady Night Shadow Star w-would like you to know that she has decided to deal with the problem in her own way. She said to tell you that she'd handle it. One way or another. That you'd know what she was talking about."

The fire snapped and shot sparks into the air, the only sound in the room.

Morning Star studied Seven Skull Shield, something cunning behind his eyes. "What are your thoughts, thief? Do you think she means it?"

Means what?

Think!

Seven Skull Shield pulled up all the courage he could muster. "Whatever this is all about, Lord, my impression was that she's determined. There wasn't any give in her."

Both Spotted Wrist and Rising Flame had clambered to their feet and were fixed on him the way a hawk fixed on a fat rabbit.

"When did she leave?" Morning Star asked.

"About midday."

"And you just came to tell me?"

"I would have come immediately, Lord. I was in the process when a bunch of warriors showed up figuring they were going to grab her. They tore her palace up looking for her. Someone had to make sure those warriors didn't steal the lady blind. Green Stick would have let them have—"

"Stop. Go back. What do you mean she's gone?" Rising Flame demanded.

"She, uh, left."

"Headed where?" Spotted Wrist stepped forward, a fist clasped before him. "And who are you? What are you doing with Makes Three's staff of office? You're not Bear Clan, and no noble I know."

"He's Blue Heron's thief," Rising Flame said. "The one she keeps around for entertainment. One of her spies. A clanless bit of human flotsam." She smiled, eyes hard. "And not the sort that Night Shadow Star would leave to keep an eye on her things while reputable warriors were around."

Seven Skull Shield shrugged, a cold sweat breaking out as people around the room began whispering back and forth.

Spotted Wrist reached out. "Give me Makes Three's staff, thief."

"Not mine to give." Seven Skull Shield hoped his voice wasn't the quavering warble he feared it was. "Lady Night Shadow Star said to tell anyone who objected that I was acting as her agent. You got a problem with that, you'll have to take it up with her when she gets back."

Spotted Wrist took another step, only to have Five Fists impose himself, breastbone to breastbone, and locked eye to eye.

"Stand down, Clan Keeper," Morning Star said softly. "This man is a messenger in the service of Night Shadow Star. You do not seize a messenger's staff, no matter to whom it once belonged."

Spotted Wrist turned to Morning Star, hands out, imploring. "Lord, we're to believe that Night Shadow Star, of all people, would leave a known thief unsupervised in her palace? Seriously?"

Seven Skull Shield finally managed to get a swallow down his too-tight throat.

"War Leader Five Fists," Morning Star spoke reasonably, "you have had dealings with the thief in the past. Have you any doubts about his service to Night Shadow Star?"

This is it. I'm dead.

Five Fists had never been anything close to sympathetic when it came to Seven Skull Shield—not that he'd started with a good impression that day when Blue Heron first found him in the shell carvers' workshop. Calling him "tow rope" was ample reminder of that.

Which meant Seven Skull Shield was going to have to make a break for it. Maybe get his hands on one of the warriors' war clubs before they knew what was happening. Do his best to take as many with him as he could before . . .

To Seven Skull Shield's total surprise, Five Fists said, "Night Shadow Star sent Blue Heron to find the thief when Walking Smoke was murdering Four Winds Clan nobles right and left, Lord. He played an important role in bringing that to a conclusion. He has served Morning Star House since."

"Preposterous!" Rising Flame hissed loudly enough that half the room heard it.

Somehow Seven Skull Shield managed to keep from wincing.

The living god, who had been staring thoughtfully at Seven Skull Shield, shot an irritated look at Rising Flame. "Do you wish to contradict the war leader, Clan Matron? Perhaps explain how Five Fists might be in error?"

"No, Lord. My apologies."

"I don't understand," Spotted Wrist groused. "Lord, granted, the Cofitachequi expedition is delayed, but it is still under the command of Lady Night Shadow Star. She most assuredly isn't shedding her responsibility for the expedition. I need to know her whereabouts."

"Why?" Seven Skull Shield blurted. "So you can send Blood Talon and twenty warriors to kidnap her like some petty chief's daughter? What's wrong? Can't find a woman who wants you?"

Snickers ran through the crowd. Spotted Wrist turned a shade of red.

Five Fists was glaring his own reprimand.

"Sorry," Seven Skull Shield muttered. "Shouldn't have noted the obvious."

"I'll give you one chance, fool," Spotted Wrist said through gritted teeth, a promise of death in his eyes. "Where is she?"

"Gone," Seven Skull Shield said warily. He glanced at Morning Star, the god taking in every nuance of the interplay. "My suspicion, Lord? This thing that has to be dealt with in Cofitachequi? After watching the expedition assemble? She's hired a canoe and gone to deal with it in her own way. Fast. Simple. And effective."

Morning Star's lips quivered in a knowing smile. "I suspect so. Thank you for delivering the lady's message. You may go on about your duties for her."

Seven Skull Shield dropped to his knees, touched his head to the matting, and rose. Spotted Wrist's glare was as dark and cutting as obsidian. Rising Flame's jaw was locked, her eyes drawn down to angry slits. Ooh, no love there.

As Five Fists led Seven Skull Shield to the rear, under his breath he said, "You're either an idiot, or you have a death wish. Spotted Wrist's never going to forget this night."

"Why'd you back me?"

"I don't like you. Don't approve of you. But you have your uses, thief."

"I'll remember you said that."

They were at the door, Five Fists throwing it open enough that Seven Skull Shield could slip out into the snow. As Seven Skull Shield hurried out, the old warrior added, "I'm tempted to say remember this night. But a memory is something you get to keep over time. And after tonight, time is something I don't think you've got a lot of."

The door closed, leaving Seven Skull Shield shaken down to his bones in a way he'd never been. Out in the darkness. And falling snow.

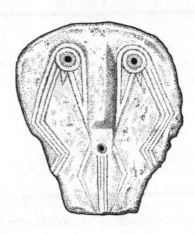

The Awakening of Sleep

The grassy rise, backed by pine, hemlock, bald cypress, and sweet gum, overlooks water. I sit, my attention on the swamp and backwater where it lurks just this side of the river. I come here to marvel. This land is different. Even from the swampy lower reaches of the Father Water where I traveled after my first exile from Cahokia. It has a different feel, a different Power.

My butt is perched on a fallen and rotting log surrounded by palmetto and supplejack vines; I am aware of the insects that swarm around me. My skin is rubbed to a deep-red sheen with puccoon root and sassafras extract to keep the mosquitoes and biting flies away. Diaphanous wings glitter in the sunlight as dragonflies dart and weave in search of prey.

At my feet, past the bulrushes and swamp grass, the water stretches—green with patches of duckweed, dotted here and there by yellow lotus. It is still, and dark, and murky. Frogs are singing, fish dimple the smooth surface. Towering bald cypress, tupelo, overcup oak, and swamp laurel cast shadows pierced by shafts of sunlight.

I close my eyes, take a deep breath, and inhale not only the perfume of vegetation, water, and damp earth, but the Spirit that pulses here. The swamp, I learned long ago, bursts with life devouring itself like no other place. Think of the Tie Snake that has swallowed its tail and continues to consume itself. Even as it digests itself, it grows longer.

In all the lands that I have ever traveled, this is the richest.

I can't tell you how I got to Cofitachequi. One minute I was in the depths of the Father Water, cold, water gurgling around my ears as I raged, clamped my fingers around my sister's throat, and sought to choke the life out of her.

The next I was here. Surrounded by fire, heat, and cracking bolts of lightning.

As to choking my sister to death?

That is the true measure of love.

One can't destroy what one does not truly love.

And I love my sister more than any woman alive.

My need to strangle her that day was as great as my need to thrust my bursting shaft into her warm sheath. Were I able, I would have driven it all the way through her, right into her heart. The explosion of my seed would have burst like golden light through her entire body. It would have shone from her eyes, nose, mouth, and ears. It would have glowed, lantern-like, from her fingers and toes and twinkled in the feathery tips of her ears.

You see, she ruined it all. And I was so close! I had the doorway to the Underworld creaking on its hinges. A flick of the blade, a few body parts to complete the vulva that would have opened Mother Earth's sheath, and Piasa would have been born into our world.

Would have found me. Waiting. My body the perfect host for his primeval Spirit.

But Night Shadow Star tricked me, lured me away from that last stroke of the knife that would have severed Sun Wing's throat.

Lured me all the way to the river with the promise of her body and the rapture it would have provided.

And somehow I woke up here. Different. Changed. With half of my face scarred from a terrible burn. I don't remember how it got burned, or the pain, or the time it would have taken to heal and scar. I just appeared in that burning charnel house wearing the shell mask to hide my hideous face.

From the depths of the Father Water and my hands locked on my sister's throat to here. In what seemed a single moment.

As I stare at the swamp I try to understand. I was choking Night Shadow Star in spring. I appeared in Cofitachequi in fall.

What happened to the time in between?

Why do I remember none of it, but I can recall every moment of my youth? I know I am Red Warrior Mankiller's second son. That my older brother, Chunkey Boy, became home to Morning Star's Spirit. That I am Thrown Away Boy, the Wild One, a force of chaos.

I remember using a beautifully flaked long chert knife to cut my sleeping father's throat. To sacrifice my sister, Lace, and to cut the fetus from her womb.

Looking down at my hands, I remember the hot blood shooting across them. That red was so much more Powerful than the color of the puccoon root now staining them.

In the distance, I hear the first rumbling of thunder. Through the trees I can just see the high billowing white towers of thunderhead.

It will build, carried by the prevailing winds, to unleash its fury over Cofitachequi where the town stands on its river's north bank.

The barest of movement in the duckweed catches my attention. I see the eyes, the slit pupils, and an arm's length in front of them, the two rounded nostrils. He's a clever fellow, hidden like he is. Alligator is a prized feast among the Muskogee hereabouts. I've come to savor it myself. Something about an ultimate predator's flesh being another ultimate predator's finest meal.

And I am the ultimate predator.

It is my birthright.

The first gust of wind comes rolling out from under the thunderhead. It rushes through the leaves overhead, shishing through the branches.

Lightning streaks out in multiple contorted and bent fingers, the white light jumping through the swamp.

I hear a name in the wind-blown leaves, it seems to be exhaled: "Joara."

I cock my head. I hear the voices periodically. Disembodied. Speaking out of the air around me. When I look, there is no one there.

"She is coming, isn't she?"

"Yes," the storm wind answers, using the trees to give itself voice.

"Then I shall go to Joara to await her arrival."

I look down again, flex my fingers, and remember their feel as I clamped them around my sister's throat.

Seventeen

What, by Piasa's hanging balls, is wrong with you?" Spotted Wrist thundered as he stomped before the fire in his palace great room. Warriors, various household staff, and a couple of messengers from Matron Red Temple of the Fish Clan tried to look in every direction except toward Blood Talon.

For his part, the squadron first stood at attention, chin up and out, fuming and burning on the inside.

"Well?" Spotted Wrist demanded, stopping to glare into Blood Talon's eyes.

"We followed orders, Keeper. From the canoe landing, we marched straight to Night Shadow Star's palace. We searched the place from top to bottom, figuring the lady had to be hiding there. When it was apparent she wasn't in the building, I extended the search, sending warriors to Blue Heron's, the Four Winds Clan House, the *tonka'tzi*'s, the Council House, and even to the Earth Clans healer's looking for her."

"But not the canoe landing?" Spotted Wrist's lips were quivering. Always a bad sign.

"We had just *come* from the canoe landing! Why would we have gone back? Surely if Night Shadow Star had magically appeared at the canoe landing, one of our officers would have immediately sent a runner, don't you think?"

"I think fine." Spotted Wrist looked as if he were having trouble breathing. "You, apparently, do not. I have to go to the Morning Star's palace and be humiliated in front of half of Cahokia. By a common thief, no less. A thief who not only knows that I've been made a fool of by Night Shadow Star, but that she's taken a canoe and headed for Cofitachequi."

Blood Talon blinked, tried to swallow. "She *what?*"

"You heard me. She sent a messenger, some clanless bit of human trash, to inform the Morning Star that she's gone to Cofitachequi to deal with some problem of the Morning Star's. The rumor is that it's Walking Smoke."

"That's crazy!" Blood Talon protested. "She's a noble. One of the highest-ranking women in the Morning Star House of the Four Winds Clan. She wouldn't just leave in a canoe. Not by herself. Not without an escort befitting her rank and status. She's the head of the entire expedition. She has responsibilities."

Spotted Wrist kept clasping his hands into angry fists. "You didn't know her as a girl. Didn't witness the kind of wild things she and her brothers did. Insane, undisciplined, and in many cases unconscionable. Had she and her brothers been anyone's brat offspring but Red Warrior's? If we hadn't had the power to cover for the crimes, the rapes those boys committed, the disrespect with which they acted? The situations they dragged their sister into?"

"Excuse me?"

"We *covered* for them." Spotted Wrist frowned. "Running away like this? It's exactly the sort of thing she'd do. I thought she'd changed. Seemed like it, anyway. She wasn't the same reckless girl, but a deeper, almost haunted woman. And she's got the Morning Star wrapped around her finger. Doesn't matter that she claims to serve Underworld Power. She can get away with anything again. *And I won't have it!*"

"Yes, Keeper."

Blood Talon waited until the Keeper turned away. Only then did he allow himself to take a deep breath and try to cool his suddenly hot body. Pus and blood, but he wished they were back in the north. Cold, miserable, and barbaric as it might have been, at least there was an enemy he could deal with up in those trackless forests. Villages he could burn. People he could kill.

Here? Trying to deal with this recalcitrant woman? It didn't matter how hard he tried, it kept turning to sand under his feet, making him look like a hopeless fool.

He managed to pull in a deep breath. If Night Shadow Star had—for some unearthly reason—taken a canoe and headed off downriver on her own, it meant she was no longer in Cahokia. No longer his problem.

Blood Talon could relax and go on about his usual business of keeping his warriors in line, training, drilling, preparing for whatever war-related duty arose next.

Surely, with Night Shadow Star gone, there would be no need for a large military escort for the expedition. That could be managed by whatever noble they'd now put in charge. No one remaining was of the profile, status, or rank that would demand an entire squadron of . . .

"You will take your twenty best warriors," Spotted Wrist's declaration broke Blood Talon's concentration. "You will find the fastest canoe you can, and you will pursue her. Find her. And bring her back."

Blood Talon's heart missed a beat, then began to hammer against his breastbone. "Er, Keeper? Excuse me? Go find her?"

"You do understand speech, don't you, Squadron First? At least you did. Once upon a time. Before you lost your wits and became the addle-brained fool I now find before me. Remember that man you used to be? Competent? Trustworthy? No task too difficult to tackle and persevere at? Whatever happened to that man?"

He came to Cahokia where he was asked to play silly games hunting a supposed wife who is smarter than you, War Leader.

But Blood Talon kept his mouth shut. Finally suggesting, "There are other men who might be better suited to chasing down a fugitive woman on the river, Keeper. My experience, as you just noted, is better applied to maintaining the squadron and the preparations that may be—"

Spotted Wrist whirled on his heel, pointing a hard finger. "You go get her, Blood Talon. Whatever it takes, you bring her back to me alive and unharmed or don't bother to come back. Get on about it. I don't care if you have to follow her all the way to Cofitachequi. Bring her back or be sure you die in the process. Fail me, and you will wish you'd cut your own throat."

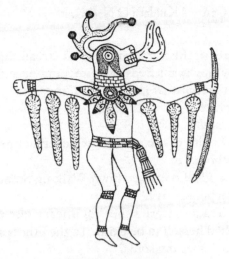

Eighteen

The river was mesmerizing. Constantly moving, churning, alive as it swirled, curled, and twisted. Forever changing its patterns while remaining the same. It felt eternal, yet forever fresh.

Night Shadow Star could stare at it, entranced, as finger after finger of time passed. Given the overcast and the few falling flakes, the surface looked opaque, leaden, with a galena-like metallic sheen. At least until she craned her neck to stare straight into the depths. When she got the angle right she could see down into the murky transparency.

Red Reed, true to White Mat's brag, slipped through the water like an arrow, steady as the Traders plied their paddles to keep them racing ahead of the main current. They proceeded past the tree-lined banks with a reassuring speed.

"Too bad the Father Water doesn't run all the way to Cofitachequi," Fire Cat noted from the seat beside her.

To her surprise, he'd picked up a paddle first thing and hadn't let up. Working just as hard as the others. As if he were one of them and not a passenger like she was.

She shot a glance over her shoulder, looking back upriver.

Piasa whispered, *"Say farewell to everything you ever knew."*

"Farewell," she whispered, glancing over the side again to see if there was a blue glow in the water beneath them. The river was Piasa's world. Down in those depths she'd come face-to-face with him the day she'd tried to kill Walking Smoke.

Right down there, in this same murky and streaming water.

For all she knew the Spirit Beast was keeping pace, racing along the bottom, his clawed feet disturbing the mud, moss, fish, and clams as he lurked under their keel.

"Yes, you understand."

She took a deep breath of the cold air, watched her exhalation fog and vanish into the chill breeze.

"Kill me, Lord, and who brings down Walking Smoke? You need me to make it to Cofitachequi alive."

The rest of the Traders were shooting uneasy glances her way. She closed her eyes, willed herself to be calm. To the others she said, "You've heard that Piasa possesses my souls?"

"Something," White Mat said tersely.

"The beast devoured them when I sent them to the Underworld in search of my dead husband." And then she lied. "You need to know that on this trip, you are doing Piasa's bidding. You have his protection. Sometimes I lose this world. My souls drift. It is unsettling, I know, but after the first few times, you'll become accustomed to it."

"Whatever you say," Half Root muttered uneasily from her seat behind Night Shadow Star.

Though she'd tried to say it nonchalantly, the woman might just as well have screamed her fear out loud.

"How will you win their trust?" Piasa wondered, his voice seeming to float in the air beside her.

She glanced again over her shoulder, looking upriver toward Cahokia. Everything she knew was back there. She had never traveled beyond The Chains, a day's travel to the south. Hardly traveled more than a couple of days' journey in any direction from the city, for that matter.

And here she was, headed at a rapid clip into the unknown. Into a world about which she had no clue. For the first time in her life, she was no longer Lady Night Shadow Star of the Morning Star House, of the Four Winds Clan, of the Sky Moiety. She had no House, no servants, no prestige or authority. On the river she was just a woman, nameless, helpless. Vulnerable.

That reality sent a sliver of fear into her. Yes, she had a couple of packs and a box of Trade, a couple of changes of clothes, one dress outfit, and a sack of her jewelry and paints. But beyond that?

"Who am I?" she asked plaintively, her half-panicked gaze on the roiling water they rode into the unknown.

"You have to ask that?" Fire Cat shot her a curious look.

"I mean, out here, on the river. Away from Cahokia." To the Traders, she asked, "Who am I to you?"

"Lady?" White Mat shot a wary glance over his shoulder. "You're, um . . . well, a Cahokian lady. Rich. High born. Makes us a little nervous. When Fire Cat came to us, we didn't really know who you were. I mean, we'd heard of you, but never figured a lady like you would be offering Trade to travel with us."

"Figured you were some Earth Clans noble, maybe a lesser family, you know?" Half Root added from behind.

"And then Crazy Frog tells us who you really are." Shedding Bird almost shivered. "It's like a sort of dream, huh? Kind of as if you're not a real woman, just a magical legend. But here you are, and you're real, and you keep talking to the Underwater Panther."

"Still not real," Made Man said from where he stroked his paddle next to Half Root. "And I'm right here behind you, seeing you in the flesh. Real. And unreal."

Shedding Bird spread his arms. "Since we're talking, why'd you need to pick us, Lady? We heard you were supposed to be in charge of that big flotilla of canoes and warriors. So, instead, one of the most important women in Cahokia hires us? Granted, it's for more than we've ever been offered in Trade to carry anyone, but what's the real reason you want us to take you up the Tenasee to the Shallows?"

"Anything special we need to know? Like who this Walking Smoke is who wants to kill you?" White Mat added.

"I want to go without anyone knowing who I am," Night Shadow Star told them.

"*Yes!*" Piasa hissed in her ear.

"Well, sitting there like a regal matron, dressed like you are," Half Root told her, "anyone with eyes in their head is going to know you're not one of us. Not with a hawk-feather cloak and a garish piece of polished copper with its Spirit Bundle box pinned to your hair bun."

"What would a normal woman do?"

Fire Cat had an amused look on his face.

"She'd be dressed in a Trader's tunic," White Mat said.

"Her hair would be in a braid like Half Root's," Made Man chimed in. "And she'd look like she had a job. Not like a passenger."

Reaching up, Night Shadow Star pulled the long copper pins from her headpiece, removed it, and carefully laid it in her bag. Then she pulled her hair loose. With nimble fingers, she began braiding it.

"Night Shadow Star should be left back at Cahokia," she declared. "I think it's time I become someone else for a while."

"Lady?" Fire Cat asked uneasily. "I mean, what's Piasa think of that?"

"Unsettling as it might be, I think he's purring."

With that she removed her feather cloak, shuffled her packs, and located the spare paddle she'd seen in the canoe's bottom. Lifting it, she inspected the long blade that ended in a pointed tip for poling. Word was that such a paddle wasn't an unhandy tool in a fight, either.

"Uh, you ever used a paddle before, Lady?" Half Root asked.

"I spent some time in canoes as a girl," she told them, then took a grip and joined their rhythm, letting the blade take a deep bite, water curling around the edges.

"You sure you want to do this?" Fire Cat asked.

"If we're going to make time on the river, I can't be Night Shadow Star. It will be a distraction at every colony we stop at. They'll want to feast, celebrate my presence, try and use me and my position for any gain. Think it through. Fire Cat, you and I have to vanish. The best way to do that is to become Traders. And even Crazy Frog says we have some of the best people on the river to teach us how."

On their seat up in the bow, White Mat and Shedding Bird were staring uneasily at each other. Now Shedding Bird looked back. "It's hard work, Lady."

"Fire Cat and I know the chances we're taking. Maybe, doing it this way, our chances get a little better."

"It's your Trade," Half Root told her. "We work for you on this trip. However you want to run it."

"I want to make time," Night Shadow Star told her, her arms warming to the effort of paddling. "Get us to your town on the Tenasee ahead of time, I'll throw in a piece of copper plate."

"Done," White Mat agreed. "But you better know in advance, it's going to be harder than you imagined. You just let us know what you want. One way or the other, and we'll see to it."

Every fiber of her being ached to order *Red Reed* to turn about, to paddle her back to Cahokia. Back to her safe palace and her familiar haunts. Down deep, she was afraid like she'd rarely been. Bad enough to be rushing headlong into the unknown. Now she couldn't even do that as herself.

But being Night Shadow Star, traveling without escort, vulnerable, would make her a target for every chief on the rivers. Many hated the Morning Star House. Others would see her as the perfect hostage for ransom. Still others would want to use her as a lever for their own political advantage, not to mention that as a single woman of incredible status, every chief in the country would be pressing for a marriage.

"I need to learn to act like a Trader." She glanced again at the banks as they rushed by. The dense gray mat of winter-bare trees gave way to sandstone bluffs on the east, their tops thickly forested with skeletal branches that almost vanished into the gray sky.

"Of course."

But she could tell White Mat didn't believe it.

Nineteen

Blue Heron wondered when she'd been as tired, cold, or numb. As her porters laid her litter on the ground before her palace veranda, she watched one of the shivering young men lift her blanket away. The covering of snow dropped from the wet cloth in chunks.

Still, it took her three tries to get her legs to hold her as helping hands pulled her up.

"Sorry," she muttered. "Not as spry as I used to be. Pus and rot, I'm worn."

"We could carry you in," one of the young men, a Hawk Clan youth, offered.

"I'd crawl first. Allow me some dignity."

The youth smiled, nodded, and blew into his hands to warm them.

Hardly willing to trust her wobbly legs, she nevertheless hobbled her way into the warm great room, calling, "All of you, come in and warm up. Smooth Pebble will give you something hot to put at least a little fire back in your bellies."

"Thank you, Lady," they all chimed, trooping in behind her.

"I'll get them fed, Lady," Soft Moon offered, hurrying toward the fire.

Smooth Pebble stepped forward, taking Blue Heron's hand, noting, "You're half frozen. Let me help you into your room, then I'll bring you a hot stew. Your porters aren't the only ones who need a little fire in the belly."

"Thank you."

Blue Heron allowed Smooth Pebble to help her back through the door and to her bed. The woman then left on her errands.

Blue Heron sighed, blinked. She perched on the bed frame and levered her wet and filthy moccasins off. She hadn't managed to remove her soaked cape before Smooth Pebble was back, a lamp in one hand, a steaming cup of stew in the other.

"Need help with anything?" Smooth Pebble asked.

"No, that's all. I'm going to eat and collapse."

"How did things work out?"

"Expedition's leaving tomorrow by midday. Though there was some sort of ruckus at the camp that may or may not affect that. I got them provisioned. Didn't want to wait around to get tied up in whatever new disaster was unfolding."

"Sleep well."

"You, too. Just don't wake me until it's midsummer, all right?"

Smooth Pebble left with a knowing smile on her lips.

Blue Heron sighed, slipped out of her cold and soaked dress, wrapped a warm blanket around her shoulders, and was halfway through the gut-warming rabbit and duck stew before she caught the glimpse of something moving in the dark corner of her room.

Heart skipping, she lifted her lamp. "Who's there?"

"Just me, Keeper."

"Blood and spit, thief! Have you ever considered just walking in the door and announcing yourself? Smooth Pebble let you in here?"

"I didn't think she'd want the bother of telling me no."

"Well, go away. I don't care what kind of trouble you're in. Get out. Vanish. Solve it yourself. I'm tired of fixing things. It messes with my time to sleep. And that's just what I'm going to do as soon as I have you pitched out into the snow and I finish this stew."

"Figured you'd want to know first thing: Night Shadow Star and the Red Wing left this afternoon. Apparently took a canoe and headed off downriver on their own. Piasa was whispering in her ear. Nothing else would explain why she left me in charge of her palace. Had me deliver a message to the Morning Star. Now, I've always considered myself a brave sort, but that put the trembles and shakes in my souls, let me tell you."

"She what? She's supposed to be escorted by that disorganized mess of an expedition."

"Maybe she didn't want to hang around that long and let Spotted Wrist's warriors grab her for an impromptu marriage. She wasn't gone a finger's worth of time before Blood Talon and his warriors searched her palace. I'm not sure but that they didn't make off with the occasional bit of Trade, either."

"Start at the beginning, thief."

He did. She listened straight through, sipping stew, trying to keep her muzzy brain working.

"So, you, of all people, are in charge of her palace? You? She and the Red Wing are gone to Cofitachequi, and you flung the whole mess in Spotted Wrist's face? He'll kill you for that, you know . . . and now you want my advice?"

"That's about it."

She placed the empty cup on one of her storage boxes, pulled her covers back, and slipped into her bed. As she closed her eyes, she said, "I'd say you would be best served if you hurried down to the canoe landing, stole a canoe, and headed downriver after them."

He said nothing, so she added, "Used Makes Three's staff? For some that would be a killing offense. Be glad the Morning Star backed you up on that."

This was all trouble. Night Shadow Star left on her own? What kind of insanity was that? She was wondering why the living god would have bothered, but never finished the thought, her exhausted body drifting into sleep.

Twenty

Blood Talon might have been in a fouler mood at some time in his life, but he really didn't remember when.

He sat perched in the bow of a sleek and high-prowed war canoe that he'd "requisitioned" from a group of Fish Clan warriors who'd camped on the mucky sands of the canoe landing. The craft was seven paces in length, could seat three abreast, had a shallow draft, high bow, and squared stern. Six poles, three per side, could be fitted to support a fabric tonneau for protection from the sun or storm.

No one had questioned his authority when he marched up to the freshly delivered baskets of corn, squash, and beans—meant to outfit the expedition—and commandeered what he thought he needed.

The same with blankets, water jars, fish net, rope, and cordage. Then, before it could really settle in between his souls, he ordered his warriors to stash their weapons in the trim vessel, and without further consideration had the war canoe pushed out into the current.

"Shouldn't be too hard," he muttered as he stared out at the roiling river. "There's twenty of us. Won't be but a day or more before we catch up with a bunch of lazy Traders."

"Not all of the men are happy, my friend," Nutcracker whispered as he perched in the bow beside Blood Talon. "They thought they were traveling with the expedition. Hot cooked food, nice large camps, just linger about and make sure that no silly downriver chief messed with the high and mighty. Dress up on occasion in order to impress some backwoods colony and its chief. Now they're paddling, headed off on some chase."

Blood Talon looked back at the warriors. They were lined out in ranks of ten on each gunwale. "Here's how it is: Yes, we're on our own. Our orders are to make do with what we have, and it won't be pleasant. But all we need to do is catch up with Lady Night Shadow Star, grab her, and kill the Red Wing. Should have done that last bit back in Red Wing Town and saved everyone a lot of trouble."

He got laughter for that.

"Once we have her, we paddle our way back to Cahokia, deliver her to the Keeper, and we're done. We relax. Take a half moon off to enjoy the city again. So, when you think about it, we're home in less than a moon and all those poor friends of ours are gone for more than a year, maybe two, before they see Cahokia again."

"Thought Night Shadow Star was doing something for the living god. Us going to get her? That's not going to have us in trouble with Morning Star?"

"That's the Keeper's problem. We're just following orders."

But the notion seemed to stick sideways down in his souls. Grabbing Night Shadow Star to be married before the expedition left? Simple. That wasn't interfering in anyone's business but Lady Night Shadow Star's. And it was done with the Four Winds Clan blessing, since Rising Flame herself had ordered the marriage. Dragging her back? That was something else. An event for which he was going to have to plan ahead.

"What are you thinking?" Nutcracker asked, reading his expression from long association.

"I'm wondering what happened to Spotted Wrist." Blood Talon kept his voice low. "Ever since we returned from the north, it's like he's a whole different person."

"He's always been ambitious. Of all the Houses, Serpent Woman has traditionally been the weakest. Suddenly he's the Hero of the North. They make him the Four Winds Clan Keeper. Used to be he'd be invited to Morning Star's palace before or after a campaign to either plan or celebrate a victory. Now he almost lives there."

"As I said, he's different. I wonder if I even know him anymore."

Nutcracker kept his gaze on the river ahead, adding, "It's like he's left the rest of us behind. But remember, he's the most gifted war leader since Black Tail destroyed Petaga. The man is a master of planning, tactics, and field movements. We've always won because he had a better plan for defeating the enemy. For now, he's fighting on a different battlefield, that's all."

"Of course."

"That doesn't sound like you really believe it."

Blood Talon took a deep breath, lowered his voice even further. "Think back over these last couple of weeks. We've been following our old friend Spotted Wrist's orders. Hopping, obeying, hardly getting time to catch our breath. We used to help him plan; we were the ones he tested his ideas against, used us to find the flaws. Now it's Rising Flame he depends on. We're not even consulted anymore, and what's happened?"

"We're on the river."

"And nothing's changed, Nutcracker. Every order he gave was for naught, right down to the burning of the warehouse. Old Blue Heron had the food replaced in a day. The only difference is that instead of us escorting Night Shadow Star and living in plush camps, we're still chasing her. And probably doing it in defiance of the living god's wishes. This isn't like working with the Spotted Wrist we once knew."

"So?"

"We're going to follow orders. Bring her back. And then, I'm finished. Back to Snapping Turtle Clan. Offer my services to High Chief Kills Four and Matron Wide Swallow."

"I see."

"Yes, you should. This is my last mission for Spotted Wrist." Blood Talon smiled warily. "Assuming it goes as easily as the war leader thinks it will."

"Why shouldn't it?" Nutcracker slapped him on the shoulder. "It's not so tough. Like you yourself said, all we have to do is run down a bunch of Traders, kill the Red Wing, and take a woman back to Cahokia. What could go wrong?"

Twenty-one

Here she was again. Back at the pus-sucking canoe landing. Blue Heron took a deep breath, blew it out, and watched it rise in the cold air. She was huddled on her litter, this time wrapped warmly in a hair-on buffalo robe. Her porters were standing, the weight of her conveyance spread between them as she watched from her vantage point high on the slope above the canoe landing.

Around her stretched the mass of humanity, perhaps a thousand people or more, all crowding down around the beached canoes, milling among the ramadas, calling among themselves, staring out for one last glance at loved ones, or gawking up at where Morning Star sat on his high litter, looking godlike in the midst of his perfectly dressed warriors. His eyes, too, were fixed on the departure.

In the river, like a school of slivers, the canoes were lined out on the lead-gray surface. The mighty expedition was finally, and hopefully permanently, on its way.

Blue Heron would have liked to have uttered a sigh of relief, gone back to her palace, and spent the coming days relaxing by her fire, sipping tea, and gossiping with Wind. Problem was, each time she fixed one problem, the doing of it created another couple of problems. Each ever more pressing in its own particular way.

She need only look past the far bank at Evening Star Town atop the bluff overlooking the river. Across the distance, Blue Heron couldn't be sure, but one of those little figures at the corner of Matron Columella's tall palace mound was no doubt Columella herself, having positioned herself on the high point of vantage to watch the departure of the grand expedition.

And to wonder if, by agreeing to supply it, she had become a participant in her own downfall, perhaps murder, but undoubted replacement as ruler of Evening Star House.

Unless that food could be replaced and her warehouses restocked.

Blue Heron turned her glance off to the right, seeing Wind. The *tonka'tzi* sat atop her own litter, her copper-clad staff of office held before her. Dull sunlight barely penetrated the cloud cover and reflected with a bloody tint off her headpiece. A bright red cape hung from her shoulders; her litter bearers were dressed in finery, each being a young noble from one of the Four Winds Houses. To serve as such was considered an honor.

Wind, too, had her concentration fixed on the flotilla of canoes as they slowly headed downriver.

Hope you're thinking how to pry that corn, beans, and squash out of these Houses and clans.

Beyond her, Morning Star's squadron beat their clubs against their shields, turned as one to face the rear, and began trotting back through the buildings that lay between them and the Avenue of the Sun. The moment the living god departed, people began to follow, pressing, ebbing and flowing up the slope.

"Shall we go, Lady?" her lead porter asked.

"Stay a moment. No need to get caught up in the press. Let the worst of it filter through River Mounds, otherwise we'll contribute to the mess."

As she waited, she watched the last of the canoes vanish to the south and idly wondered what could have possessed Night Shadow Star to undertake such a journey with only the Red Wing at her side. Not that anyone but a fool underestimated the man. Blue Heron had. Once. But once was all it had taken.

And, of course, her niece served Underworld Power. The Underwater Panther had to be playing his own game when it came to Walking Smoke.

"Lady?" A voice interrupted her thoughts.

She glanced down to see a messenger dressed in River House's characteristic smock. The young man bowed low, touching his forehead. When he straightened, he said, "High Chief War Duck and Matron Round Pot send their greetings. They would like to offer you a fine meal, lodging for the night, and seek the pleasure of your company. They stressed that this is their most earnest invitation. If you can spare them the time, they will be most grateful."

The young man's eyes were pleading, as if, should she turn it down, he would suffer the consequences.

"A meal and a bed?" She let the options run through her head. Disaster had struck River House last year when someone—and yes, she knew exactly who—had knocked over a boiling pot that drowned the sacred fire. Taken as an affront to Power, and a token of terrible bad luck, War Duck and Round Pot had been hanging on to their authority by their very fingernails. Three Fingers had been gaining in influence and was turning out to be pretty good at intrigue.

Seemed to be a lot of that going around.

In no way, shape, or form had the rulers of River House ever been allies of Blue Heron's. From her spies, she knew they'd been on the verge of letting loose mayhem last fall until their fire was put out. That they needed her now? Given that she was no longer Keeper? Was either a measure of their desperation, or they had something they wanted to barter for a favor. Probably wanted to use Blue Heron as an intermediary to get to Wind.

She was hungry.

The weather was blustery.

It would save her from arriving back at her palace after dark.

"I am happy to accept the High Chief and House Matron's fine offer of hospitality. Lead forth."

The young man led the way through a warren of warehouses, the passages clogged by people working through the buildings that packed the levy.

Breaking out into the elongated River Mounds plaza, they passed the Four Winds Clan House, the Men's House, several Earth Clans Council Houses, and the famed chunkey courts where the finest of the river Traders and professional players battled for wealth. Today, with its bone-numbing damp, the courts were forgotten.

At the northeastern extent, War Duck and Round Pot's palace stood atop a platform mound; *Hunga Ahuito*, the two-headed eagle that dwelled at the top of Sky, stared down from atop its guardian post, as did Falcon.

At the foot of the stairs, her porters laid her litter on the ground. She winced, mentally cursed her aches and pains, and rose stiffly to her feet. She made the climb up the wooden steps, touched her forehead reverently as she passed the guardian posts and the high World Tree pole in the cramped courtyard before the palace.

The steeply pitched roof looked shabby, covered as it was with gray thatch. Atop it, the ridgepole was adorned with weather-faded carvings of Snapping Turtle, Falcon, and Ivory-billed Woodpecker: all totems of war.

Blue Heron followed the young man through the carved double doors and into the delightful warmth of the great room. Maybe it was because of the disaster last fall or to make a statement, but the fire was roaring, flames shooting high, sparks winking out as they rose.

When it came to opulence, the lords of River Mounds House spared nothing in the decoration of their palace. They were, after all, perched above the canoe landing. That gave them first access to whatever Trade landed on their shores. Nor did War Duck shy away from nefarious dealings with unscrupulous Traders, let alone the city's morally questionable habitués like Crazy Frog, Black Swallow, and their ilk. War Duck wasn't too keen on bringing such miscreants to heel as long as he got a percentage.

As a result, the palace walls were hung with exotic artifacts, stunning textiles, weapons, copper embossing, shell, and statuary. Each of the sleeping benches was made of poles carved to resemble snakes, the uprights topped in renderings of deer, cougar, and bear heads, and leaping fish. The woven mat on the floor was stunning—a marvel of the weaver's art second only to the Morning Star's.

Behind the fire, seated atop the dais, War Duck's litter was perched beside Round Pot's. Most of the household servants were lined out along the walls, all seated in order, their hands resting on their knees in a posture of obedient readiness. The air was heavy with the odors of boiling hominy, venison, fish, and turkey. Through it all, Blue Heron could smell baking acorn, smilax, and goosefoot bread.

She followed her young guide up beside the fire, feeling the heat of it begin to roast the right side of her face. Felt good for at least a couple of heartbeats.

"Welcome, Blue Heron, of the Morning Star House, of the Four Winds Clan, of the Sky Moiety," War Duck called in greeting. Then he began the traditional recitation of ritual. A pipe was brought, lit, and shared, the bowl and stem being carried back and forth between them by the houseboy. If Blue Heron remembered correctly, the lad's name was Clicking Boy.

Finally, black drink was offered in ceramic cups, drunk in copious amounts, and the final prayers offered. This was no casual visit. Every bit of ritual was being attended to as if Blue Heron were a visiting chief from a foreign nation. By that time the right side of her face felt scalded, and she'd eased her way a couple of paces to the left to lessen the effect.

Ritual complete, War Duck and Round Pot rose, walked around the fire, and offered Blue Heron a seat on the matting back from the fire. In an unusual display of equality, they seated themselves to either side before clapping their hands.

As food was brought, Blue Heron gestured toward the fire and plates being set before her. "A bit dramatic, all this. It's not like I'm some foreign lord."

War Duck's good left eye fixed on her. "After last fall? In all of Cahokia, you will find no more pious, observant, or humble practitioners of ritual than River House."

"Why don't I believe that?" she noted dryly.

"It's not about what you believe," Round Pot confided, dipping bean mash from a bowl with a bit of goosefoot bread. "It's about everyone else."

"I begin to see."

War Duck gestured with a horn spoon full of hominy. "Right up front, we admit that we have not always been on the same side. But despite that, recent events dictate that perhaps you, the matron, and I might find some common ground. Our history is replete with stories about adversaries who once believed themselves locked in a battle to the death but, through better judgment, were able to find common cause, establish peace, and work toward some shared goal."

"Why me? Spotted Wrist is the Keeper now. I'm just a discarded old woman."

"A wealthy old woman with her own spy network and whose sister is the *tonka'tzi*. Not to mention that you have access to the living god any time you wish, or that your word can persuade some of the mightiest matrons to do your bidding."

"A couple of those spies you refer to tell me that your brother, Broken Stone, has been in touch with Rising Flame. They are putting together a coalition of cousins led by Three Fingers and backed by his brother Waving Reed. Word is that they're strengthening ties to Horned Serpent House and North Star House in preparation for the day when the two of you are politely asked to step down."

Round Pot's eyes were slitted as she absently fingered her long braid. "We hear these things, too. The fools are playing Horned Serpent House one way, North Star House another. Broken Stone has always been the affable host, the bluff and hearty teller of tales, exactly the sort to have around at a banquet. He's never had a head for, let us say, the intricacies of deal making."

"That's where Three Fingers comes in. Problem is, gullible as Broken Stone is, I don't think he realizes that Three Fingers isn't planning for an instant to leave your brother on the high chair."

War Duck ran a finger down the scar in his face. "I would hope not. Should Broken Stone become high chief, Wolverine, Slender Fox, and Green Chunkey will carve River House into pieces and devour them. Give it a year and one of them will have him assassinated. Then they will go to war over control of what's left."

"Which leads us to wonder, what's Rising Flame's interest in this? How does she gain if River House is destroyed?" War Duck arched his good left eyebrow.

Round Pot asked, "And most important of all, where does Morning Star stand in all of this? You, Wind, and Five Fists are close to him. You have his ear. That, in the end, might save Cahokia from a calamity."

Blue Heron noted dryly, "Like the one River House would have precipitated if Morning Star had died last fall? You had your squadrons ready to march before the others could have called an assembly. So don't play the righteous card."

War Duck shared a hard glance with his sister.

Blue Heron continued, "Yes, Five Fists, Wind, and I have access to Morning Star. That has all the value of spit in the snow. Morning Star plays his own game, for his own reasons. Half the time we don't have a clue what he's about, or why. Decisions he makes, orders he gives seem completely illogical at the time. Like with that Chickosi wife he took last fall. Five Fists says Morning Star knew she was going to poison him. That he knew full well that he was going to die. Still, he did it without any kind of guarantee that Night Shadow Star and the Red Wing would travel into the Underworld to bring him back."

War Duck continued to finger his scar, a sign of his worry. "Morning Star was responsible for Rising Flame being named high matron. Maybe he wants River House destroyed. But why? We send our share of wealth his way."

Blue Heron scooped a bite-size chunk of boiled meat from the bowl in front of her and swallowed it before pointing a finger for emphasis. "I spent most of my life as Keeper. In those early years I made a lot of mistakes, played the game for my House instead of the city. Wasn't until about ten years ago that I began to see that a balance had to be maintained. In the years since, when one House started to gain ascendancy, I'd work to chop it off, cut it down to size."

"Except for Morning Star House." Round Pot almost spat the words.

"Use your head," Blue Heron shot back. "Morning Star lives in the middle of it. Whichever territory the living god calls home will ultimately dominate the other Houses. That's just the way of it. Took me a while to learn, but the job of Clan Keeper is to keep the clans in balance. So I dedicated myself to making sure that Horned Serpent, River, and Evening Star Houses all had about the same authority and influence."

"Even if it meant assassination?"

"Even then," Blue Heron responded. "Now, knowing where I'm coming from, let's get down to business. You want my help to save your skins, keep River House from being destroyed, and ensure that Morning Star comes down on your side."

"What do you want in return?" War Duck asked.

"Beginning tomorrow morning, start shipping food stores to Evening Star Town to replenish Columella's warehouses."

"That camp bitch has spent years trying to cut our throats," Round Pot hissed.

"And you've spent years trying to cut hers. Sometimes she's come out ahead, sometimes you have. You want me to fight for your survival? Fine. You need her, she needs you."

Round Pot mused, "We might get a better deal from some of those cousins of hers who want to ascend to the high chair."

"And she might get a better deal from Three Fingers than she'd get from you. It's an obsidian flake that cuts both ways."

"Stripping our warehouses could be the action that brings us down. Broken Stone, egged on by Three Fingers, will be the first to protest. He'll be calling for our blood."

"It's your call. But if you want my help, Wind's, and Five Fists', that's our price."

The following morning, as Blue Heron's litter was carried out of River Mounds City's plaza and onto the Avenue of the Sun, the first canoe-loads of corn, beans, and squash were being paddled across the river headed for Evening Star Town's empty warehouses.

On the way out, she'd seen Broken Stone, backed by five of the River House Earth Clans chiefs, headed for the palace. None of them looked happy.

So, I wonder if I just witnessed the end of River House, and with it, the beginnings of the end of Cahokia?

Twenty-two

Two hard days on the river. Night Shadow Star had stepped out of one existence and into an entirely different one. She might have shed lives the way she did a change of clothing. But this new woman she sought to become was totally alien. Uncomfortable. She might have changed identities and at the same time become a stranger.

The transition from Lady Night Shadow Star of Cahokia into a common Trader had proved more than unsettling. It wasn't just the way she now dressed and the hard labor with the paddle. It felt like part of her was fading away that she would never get back again.

Piasa's ridiculing laughter, echoing from the air around her, only added to her discomfort and the deep-seated fear of some terrible thing hovering just over the horizon.

The only constant had been the rivers: alive, filled with the Power of the Creation and the Beginning Times. She could believe they were the Spirits of the magical Serpents of the Beginning Times, turned into water to forever flow from the highlands down to the sea.

Under her breath, she recited the myth to herself as she paddled. "Just after the Creation, Crawfish scooped mud from beneath the primordial waters and brought it to the surface to create the land. Vulture spread the land, contoured it with each beat of his mighty wings, lifting and dropping to shape mountains and valleys. From the heights, the Spirit Serpents crawled down through the lowest places, their bodies becoming the living waters, the rivers and streams."

The very waters *Red Reed* skimmed across with such apparent ease, its bow and stern leaving V-shaped wakes to vanish in the wind-borne waves and swelling and eddying surface.

Despite living on the Father Water as she did, she'd never really understood the vibrant Power that flowed through the river's soul. As *Red Reed* had proceeded, she had watched in wonder as the currents swirled and spun, how the little whirlpools had formed, and upwelling spread across the rippling surface, disrupting the waves.

Of course the river lived, filled as it was with Serpent Power that flexed beneath the canoe's keel.

Bedazzled, she watched as the south wind stroked waves from the water's surface, experienced the miracle of the waves marching against the current to create the illusion of the river running backward at the same time it bore them ever south. Were she to free her imagination, she might believe she was going in two directions at once.

"This is my world," Piasa said from just behind her ear.

She whirled, expecting to see him crouched there on the canoe's gunwale, only to find a startled Half Root who asked, "What's wrong?"

"Just Piasa. He's here. Pacing us."

None of which had reassured the Traders.

"You get used to it," Fire Cat had told the others reasonably.

The Traders' wary glances back and forth, not to mention over the sides—as if they were looking for the Underwater Panther—hinted that they did not believe him for a moment.

The river: realm of the Tie Snakes, stalking ground of Piasa, of Snapping Turtle, and Horned Serpent. Her souls had walked in the Underworld, wrapped in the arms of Sister Datura. Now her body floated on that thin veneer of surface. Such a fragile boundary between worlds. One she could whisk her fingers through. Only *Red Reed*'s slim hull kept her separate from the Power that surged, eddied, and flowed beneath her.

That night she walked out from the little village called Fish-on-the-Bank. A couple of families of Illini had built it on the north bank of the Mother Water just above its confluence with the Father Water. Normally some distance from the river, the flooded lowlands now allowed *Red Reed* to beach where the water was lapping within a body length of the lowest pole-topped structure in the tiny hamlet.

White Mat had bargained off a small clam-shell bracelet in return for a night under a roof in one of the bent-pole houses. The place wasn't much. A hovel. But after last night's cold camp on the beach below The Chains on the Father Water, just having four walls and a roof felt like a luxury.

Supper had consisted of boiled catfish and the earliest spring greens. Not a feast fit for high chiefs, but filling.

Night Shadow Star rubbed her sore arms and shoulders, wincing in the night. Something deep within her souls—a realization that she had just begun to recognize—was pleased that she'd picked up a paddle and joined in the work.

She'd always had a firm grasp of teamwork after her years on the stickball court, but this tight-knit bond she was developing with the Traders was something new.

Why am I out here wandering in the night? I should be in an exhausted sleep.

Earlier, Piasa's whispered voice had awakened Night Shadow Star from a sound sleep. Her thoughts wouldn't leave her alone. Rising, she had walked out into the quiet village, her presence only noticed by the village dogs who'd approached, tails wagging, looking for some kind of treat.

Pulling her blanket tight, she took the trail down to the water's edge beside the tied-off *Red Reed* and stared up at the night sky. The moon was almost dark, the heavens a mass of stars that reminded her of frost swirled across the blackness.

They had made good time. To her surprise, White Mat and Shedding Bird had acquiesced when she ordered them to travel late into the night and rise early before dawn to make additional use of the daylight hours.

"Happy to," Made Man had told her. "Headed downstream? That's the easy part. Find the river's thread—or fastest current—and hold it, keep steerage, and we literally shoot downstream like an arrow."

"Hard part," Half Root rejoined from where she stroked her paddle in the stern, "comes when we reach the Mother Water and head east. That's upstream, against the current. Then we have to read the river, stay as far from the thread as we can and paddle harder in the backwater and shallows, slip across the current as it twists back and forth. Then every bit of progress we make is paid for by muscle and sweat."

"Fire Cat and I will do our share," she'd told the woman.

"Don't push yourself too hard. We don't expect you to give up being a Cahokian lady the first day," White Mat had remarked skeptically.

"And since when can't a Cahokian lady do a full day's work?"

They'd laughed, and truth be told, she hadn't come close to contributing a full day's work. Night Shadow Star had thought herself fit, hardened by her dedication to stickball and running. Paddling, however, exercised muscles in her arms and shoulders she hadn't used in years.

"It's all right," Half Root had told her after a couple of fingers of time. "You're used up. Take a break. You're causing us more work missing strokes and dragging your blade than you help."

"Ease into it," White Mat had insisted. "It will take a couple of days to harden your body and hands. Bleeding blisters aren't worth it in the end, not when you can take the time and grow the calluses slowly."

The Trader had been right. Every muscle in Night Shadow Star's shoulders, arms, and back ached and burned. She massaged them as she strode along the bank. The night, so close to equinox, seemed particularly thick. The feeling was of eyes watching her from out in the flooded forest.

The Mother Water's black water pooled around the spring-heavy trees in the floodplain. The smell of mud and damp vegetation hung like a pungent perfume in the night. The water lapping at the bank mixed with the sounds of frogs and the first beetles. A fish splashed out in the dark water, and a night bird called.

She thought she caught a flicker of movement out in the flooded trees as Piasa slipped through the shadows. She could feel the beast, watching, biding his time, knowing how she chafed at his ever-present interference with her life.

Worse, she had to sit through the day, her body brushing Fire Cat's, aware of his presence, catching whiffs of his musky perspiration. Sharing his company, seeing his smile, watching his hands move on the paddle, added to the agony come night when she had to bed down across from him. To listen to his soft breathing, and know that she'd destroy them both if she slipped over to his bed and crawled under his blanket.

"We have a chance at the end of this journey," she told the night, knowing that Piasa was listening.

And, though it tortured her to avoid his touch, at least she could revel in his humor, his strength and honor. Having half of the man she loved was better than having none of him at all.

"You all right?" Fire Cat asked from the darkness behind her. Figured he'd have noticed her absence.

"Piasa was whispering into my ear. Words I could barely hear. Besides, I needed to walk. My legs are cramped. Sitting all day, every day. How do they do it?"

"Traders get used to it. You can stop, you know. Rest. They work for us, after all. We don't have to push this hard."

"*Yes, you do,*" Piasa whispered in her ear.

"I'll pay that price."

"Why?"

"Piasa says we have to."

She turned, seeing Fire Cat's night-shadowed form in the trees. "We're in the middle. Caught between two traps."

"I don't understand."

"Something coming from behind. Something awaiting us ahead. Both of them terrifying, both bringing pain and trouble."

"All right, we know that Walking Smoke is awaiting us in Cofitachequi, but what's behind us?"

"Who do you think?"

"The expedition? That mass of people, canoes, and supplies couldn't possibly make the kind of time we are. They have to unload, set up camp, build fires, cook food enough for an army."

"Spotted Wrist."

"You're sure? Piasa tells you this?"

"He does. But more, I can feel it."

"What does he want? Pay you back for outsmarting him?"

"He's not used to losing. At anything. I embarrassed him. Made him look weak. How can he be the Keeper, ferreting out threats to the Four Winds Clan, when he can't even compel me to marry him after the clan matron herself ordered it? That can't be allowed to stand."

"He can't leave Cahokia."

"It will be a party of his warriors. He won't rest until I'm in his bed."

"Won't that be a slap to the Morning Star's face? Chunkey Boy wants you to kill Walking Smoke. Probably hasn't forgotten how close Walking Smoke's assassin came to cutting his throat. Keeping you from taking out his rival in Cofitachequi? It's not healthy to enrage your brother. He holds a grudge."

"Spotted Wrist will have a plan, some way to soften the blow. Probably something with Rising Flame's blessing. After all, she appointed him. His failure makes her look bad as well."

"But you said that rushing ahead is just as threatening."

"Walking Smoke knows we're coming."

"*Yes,*" Piasa whispered from somewhere behind her ear.

"Ominous, indeed." Fire Cat bent his head back to stare up at the cloud-thick sky.

"And the jaws will be ready to snap shut around us the moment we are within reach." She tried to imagine what sort of trap her brother would set. Something intricate to pay her back for her part in ruining his murderous spree in Cahokia.

Chunkey Boy wasn't the only brother she had who carried a grudge. Even before the Morning Star's Spirit had devoured Chunkey Boy's souls, it had been Walking Smoke who was the most devious, and ultimately, entirely evil.

Twenty-three

In Trade pidgin, Blood Talon called, "We're looking for a Trader's canoe. We think with seven people. They're headed upriver with two Cahokians. At least one woman, young. She's a Cahokian noble, dressed well. Four spirals are tattooed on her cheeks. A warrior travels with her. A scarred man accompanied by armor, weapons, and chunkey gear."

Blood Talon perched on the high prow of the sleek war canoe as it was paddled along the edge of the flooded trees; his attention was fixed on the two dugouts proceeding in tandem across the muddy water. Lines attached to a submerged net were being towed by the two craft. Each held three fishermen, all bent to their paddles as they dragged their net through the shallows at the edge of the half-drowned trees.

"We might," one of the fishermen called back through an atrocious accent. "Such a party stayed at our village last night. They Traded for house for a lady and her warrior. They head for Tenasee. The canoe is *Red Reed*. They leave us at dawn."

"Was the lady called Night Shadow Star?"

"How do I know? They only talk to her in Cahokian. But she got those tattoos."

"Thank you. The Morning Star's blessing upon you!"

The man waved, bending back to his paddle, far more interested in loading his net than talking to passing warriors.

"Think it's her?" Nutcracker asked as Blood Talon lowered himself to a seat.

"Has to be her. How many Cahokian ladies do you know of headed for the Tenasee? If I were her? And I'd just embarrassed the war leader? I'd figure that Spotted Wrist would send someone to drag me back. One thing about Night Shadow Star, she hasn't proved to be stupid. Not even once."

"I never thought it would take us this long to catch her. It's almost like she knows we're chasing her."

"She knows."

"Do you really think she's that smart? Or are the tales true?"

"What tales?"

"That she's protected by Underworld Power. The stories are that she sends her souls there, you know. That she walks the Underworld with Piasa at her side. That the Spirit Beast whispers in her ear, and that she sees him."

"That's piss in a pot if you ask me." Blood Talon said it more for the men's benefit. No sense in spooking them or feeding any of their night fears.

On those occasions when he'd seen her, he thought her Spirit-possessed. That eerie look she got? The vacancy in her eyes? Well, it made the stories about her soul possession pretty easy to believe.

Once they caught her, maybe he'd take special precautions. Maybe cover her head with a sack so that she couldn't cast some sort of spell on his warriors. Keep her trussed up like a cocoon lest she invoke malevolence with her fingers.

Have to catch her first, though.

Blood Talon glanced over his shoulders at the warriors resting on their paddles. "She's a half day ahead of us. She doesn't know we're closing on her. I know you're tired. I know I've pushed you hard. But just a little longer. That's all I ask. We have to make up a half a day. When we have her, we can rest, feast for a day or two, and once we're refreshed, we can take our time getting her back to Cahokia."

The men answered with weary cheers, bending their backs to the paddles. The war canoe cleanly cut the waves. Broad-beamed as it was, it proved a fast vessel, built for moving men three abreast, and he had the toughest and strongest of his hand-chosen warriors to make up the difference.

Blood Talon smiled. These were his warriors, trained, battle-hardened, and proud of it. If anyone could catch Night Shadow Star, it would be them.

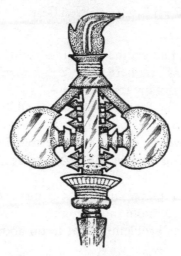

Twenty-four

The fact that a couple of warriors were watching Night Shadow Star's palace really annoyed Seven Skull Shield. And what did they think? That he was some three-fingered fool who'd just go tripping down the stairs and into their arms?

By Piasa's hanging balls, no way. He and Farts had waited until after midnight, slipped out the dark doorway, skirted around to the back of the palace, and eased down the mound's steep slope. In addition to being bundled in a mottled gray, completely unremarkable but very warm blanket, he carried a hemp-cord sack that dangled from a thin rope that secured its top. The contents he had carefully chosen from among the boxes of Night Shadow Star's wealth as he helped replace the carelessly tossed items left by Blood Talon's warriors.

For the time being, the problem of Willow Blossom was taken care of. She'd been awestruck at the notion that she could live in Night Shadow Star's palace, safe from retribution from her husband, surrounded by wealth.

This hadn't been approved of by the rest of the household staff, but they'd heard Night Shadow Star's order.

"Look, it's a simple fix to your problem," Seven Skull Shield had told Green Stick. "You take care of Willow Blossom, keep her fed, happy, and safe, and I'll stay gone and out of your hair."

"Are you insane? We don't know who this woman is. Only that her husband is hunting her. Why should we allow a stranger to just live in our lady's palace?"

Seven Skull Shield had grinned. "You're right. She might get lonely. Maybe I should leave Farts here, too. You know, company for Willow Blossom while I go about my business of—"

"No! You're right! She'll be no problem at all."

Just thinking back on it had Seven Skull Shield grinning. As he trotted down the cold Avenue of the Sun, he told Farts, "See, that's the thing about people. There's always a lever, a way to manipulate them to your purpose."

The big dog glanced up, darkness obscuring his blue-and-brown eyes, the tail lashing like a phantom in the night.

But that still left the problem: What to do about Spotted Wrist and Rising Flame.

"Sometimes I wish I could go back and sew my mouth shut," Seven Skull Shield muttered into the night, his breath clouding around his head. "Pus and blood, who does that arrogant overfed excuse of a Keeper think he is? Sending warriors to kidnap Night Shadow Star? Then trash her palace? Flip through her things, paw around her bed?"

He made a face, admitting to the dog at his side, "Old Five Fists was right. I'm going to remember embarrassing that weasel-shafted Spotted Wrist for a long time. And there won't be a person in that room who forgets it either."

And that was a problem. It was one thing to embarrass an influential man like Spotted Wrist. More worrisome that he'd also showed up Rising Flame. And even more vexing and dangerous, everyone who'd been in that room had seen him do it. All nobles, Lords of Cahokia. Four Winds and Earth Clans chiefs.

Depending upon who demanded what, most of Cahokia would be hunting him within the next couple of days.

As always, he turned his steps toward Crazy Frog's, finding himself in the gambler's front yard as Mother Otter stepped out with a pot. The woman gave him a disgusted look as she emptied the contents of the brownware pot into the latrine behind the ramada.

"I could name a thousand disagreeable ways to begin a morning, like having the cramps or a bloody flux, or maybe a toothache, but no, there's even worse afoot, and here it stands in my doorway."

"Good morning, Mother! Assuming that you've come to your senses and want to leave that rather sketchy husband of yours, I'm ready at this very moment to steal away with you. Show you the way to true love."

"The only thing I'd truly love is to see your burned, sliced, and twisted corpse in a square, thief. Stop where you are. And if that misbegotten beast you call a dog sets so much as a paw in my yard, I'm using a club to brain him. Then I'm feeding him to the crows, his meat being unfit for human consumption."

Seven Skull Shield looked down at Farts. "You might want to linger out here by the road. Stay."

As he took a step toward the house, Farts cheerfully leaped past, raised his leg, and peed on one of the ramada poles, wetting a roll of nearby blankets in the process.

"Foul four-legged beast!" Mother Otter cried in dismay. In her passion, she threw her pot at the dog, missed. It hit one of the hearthstones on the big central firepit. With a loud *pock* it shattered into a hundred shards.

Farts, having ducked as the pot sailed past his head, paused only long enough to lift his leg on a second post, and then ran as Mother Otter charged his way, her hands clawing at the air in an attempt to grab him.

Like a shot arrow, the big-boned dog was gone, stretched out with each leap, his floppy ears flapping like wings.

"Well, don't blame me," Seven Skull Shield told her thoughtfully. "I did tell him to stay."

The woman, panting with either rage, exertion, or both, just glared, her fingers working. "If I could have just one wish, it would be your polished skull tied above the doorframe. I would look up, smile, wave at it on occasion. A simple reminder of how much nicer the world was without you in it."

"I know you just say these things. It's a way to convince yourself that staying with Crazy Frog is in the children's best interest." He gave her a wink. "It will be our secret."

The look of wild rage slowly faded in her eyes. Then she shook her head. "You never cease to amaze me. Every time I think I have finally observed the most incomprehensible of human behaviors, you have the ability to prove me wrong."

"I just need to see Crazy Frog. I have something to give him . . . unless, of course, you'd like to run off with me."

"And you'd give it all up? For an older married woman who's getting thick in the hips? I've just got to hear how even you could delude yourself into desiring me."

Seven Skull Shield cocked his head. "If you could take all the things that make a woman and roll them into one individual, it would be you: strong, maternal, provocative, self-possessed, and competent. Makes you the end-all to womanhood."

She shook her head, sighed as she stared at the shattered angular bits of her pot. "They should have hanged you in a square years ago. Go on. Around back. I'll send him your way as soon as he has finished breakfast and had his fill of playing with the children. Meanwhile, I don't want you standing around out here. Gives the place a bad name."

"I meant it. I'd run away for you."

"Go. Before I change my mind." A pause. "And if I see that dog, I *will* beat his brains out of that oversized skull."

Never one to squander an opportunity, Seven Skull Shield beat a hasty retreat across the yard, past the firepit, along the wall, and into the narrow passage created by Crazy Frog's house and the warehouse next door. The space was a small triangular yard culminating at the thick-walled storehouse where Crazy Frog kept his wealth.

A burly Fish Clan man stood back in the shadows, his body wrapped in bear hide. A battered and well-used war club hung from one scarred hand. The look in the man's cold eyes suggested that he'd never been burdened by a sense of humor.

"Mother Otter sent me back. Said she'd send Crazy Frog out as soon as he finished breakfast."

"I know you. The thief, right? Heard that rope maker was looking for you. Says you warmed your shaft where you shouldn't have been keeping it warm."

"I am so misunderstood."

"Said he'd give a coil of good basswood rope to whoever turned you over to him."

"Your boss might not approve." Why was someone *always* looking for him? Robin Feather, Spotted Wrist, Rising Flame? The list went on and on.

"Seven Skull Shield," a voice called from the storehouse door. "It's all right, Six Claw, let him pass."

The Fish Clan man, Six Claw, gestured with his club. "Go on. Just be glad I serve Crazy Frog first and my own wants second."

"Got to say, you're everything I could never be." Seven Skull Shield gave the man a touch of the chin in salute as he passed. Not only was humor beyond Six Claw, apparently so was irony.

Seven Skull Shield almost missed the shadowed form in the doorway. He was looking man-height. The dwarf had hands propped on his hips, then he turned and led the way in past the hanging and into the storehouse proper. Here another guard sat with his butt on an oversized carved box, war club ready to hand while the man cradled a cup of steaming hot tea. A mound of coals glowed red in a ceramic bowl set on the bit of dirt floor that wasn't covered with large wooden boxes, ornate storage baskets, large seed jars, sacks of shell, a stack of copper sheets, and carefully folded textiles. Remarkable wooden carvings and beautifully tanned hides of deer, elk, panther, and bear were belittled by an imposing pile of hair-on buffalo hides in the rear.

Best of all, the place was warm. Seven Skull Shield sighed, bending down to extend his hands to the heat rising from the coals.

The dwarf clambered up onto one of the boxes where the rising warmth bathed his feet.

"Word is that you created quite the scene up in the Morning Star's palace," the dwarf noted, his keen eyes gleaming in the firelight.

"Good to see you, too, Flat Stone Pipe. How's the matron doing?"

"She's made the biggest gamble of her life. Despite River House's efforts, either Blue Heron replaces all the food within a half moon—which solidifies Columella's position—or she'll be lucky to get away with her life. Me, had I been there when Blue Heron made her plea, I would have advised that Columella respectfully turn it down."

"I heard that Wind and Five Fists backed it."

"And against them are Spotted Wrist, Rising Flame, and North Star and Horned Serpent Houses, all of whom would like to see a change in the leadership at Evening Star House. They want someone not so cozy with those overentitled and arrogant rulers of Morning Star House. By backing Evening Star, Round Pot and War Duck could be thrown out of their palace any day now."

"That would be bad. Old War Duck is about as crooked as a sassafras root, but at least we know his game."

"To say that their canoe-loads of food came as a surprise is an understatement. My lady was stunned. This sudden thawing of relations is uncomfortable, to say the least." As if it itched, Flat Stone Pipe rubbed his nose. "But what is this rumor that Night Shadow Star fled in the night?"

"In the light of day, actually. She wished to avoid an unwelcome marriage to the Hero of the North, and, I don't doubt, having to be in charge of that traveling festival of an expedition. I caught the merest of whispers that somehow Walking Smoke is at the bottom of it."

"Thought he was dead."

Seven Skull Shield gave a shrug of the shoulders. "Maybe. If she's off to kill him, I pray that Power bless her. I still have nightmares after what I saw in that burning palace. I wouldn't mind gouging the man's eyeballs out myself. And I'd make sure my thumbs were dirty when I did it."

"I'd Trade a copper plate just to watch," Flat Stone Pipe mused, eyes half-lidded. "Odd, but he put us on this path. Set events in motion that brought us to this." A pause. "You know that Spotted Wrist and Rising Smoke are both after your hide? And then there's the matter of Robin Feather. I do hope that you have that delightful creature he was married to hidden away somewhere safe."

"I might."

"Thief, you need to get a message to Blue Heron for me. Tell her that if she, Wind, and Five Fists can't get those granaries refilled, it will all come tumbling down. First, they will destroy Columella, then War Duck and Round Pot. After them comes Blue Heron, whose position is already tenuous, and then Wind."

"I know."

At that moment, Crazy Frog slipped past the hanging. The gambler wore only a hunter's shirt. He had a hair-on elk hide wrapped around his narrow shoulders. The man prided himself on looking nondescript and valued the ability to disappear in a crowd more than most nobles valued copper, spoonbill feathers, and seashells.

"Mother Otter said you were infesting my property like hornworms in a tobacco crop. What brings you this way? Or do I take it that I need to help sneak you out of Cahokia before either Robin Feather or Spotted Wrist can catch you?"

"Tempting," Seven Skull Shield told him, "but I came to give you this." He handed over the sack. "It's not what we initially agreed upon but should be fair compensation."

Crazy Frog loosened the rope tie, reached inside, and removed a huge shell cup made from a conch shell as long as his arm. "Where did you get this?"

"I have a source."

"And the original items?"

"You have to trust me on this, they are in a much better place for the time being. That cup, however, should be fair compensation."

"You'd better be right about this."

"Oh, I think you'll be mildly entertained by the use I put the original items to."

Flat Stone Pipe was watching from his box, his gaze fixed thoughtfully on the impressively large cup. "Thief, whatever stakes you are playing for, I hope they're worth your life."

Seven Skull Shield gave him a ribald wink. "You and your lady aren't the only ones playing a deep and dangerous game. Besides, I've got a bet with Meander. A big basket of shell is at stake. But either way, I win."

"How's that?" Crazy Frog studied Seven Skull Shield with suspicious eyes.

"If I win, he hands over a small fortune in shell. If I lose, I don't have to worry about paying up."

"Oh? Figure to just bilk him out of his winnings?"

"I'd never bilk anyone I liked. It's just that it is very hard to get a basket of shell out of a dead man."

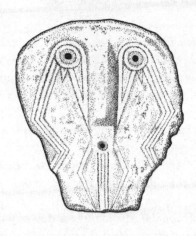

A Battering of Shell

*T*hese local Muskogee—despite having been occupied by Moon Blade's warriors for all these years—are still mostly forest hunters and plant collectors despite their corn, bean, and squash fields.

At the time of my arrival in Cofitachequi, only two small mounds had been built in the town. First was the palace where Moon Blade's eldest son, Streaming Stone, was orata, or town chief. The second had been the low platform mound where I magically appeared in the ruins of the burning charnel house.

Streaming Stone had been just as awed as the rest, and fortunately, along with most of his warriors, spoke Cahokian. He had agreed to anything I asked, including the addition of another layer of dirt to expand my mound before I had my temple built upon it.

Within weeks most of the locals had abandoned their houses within an arrow shot of my temple. The reasons they gave for leaving were some of the most facile and trite of excuses. Fact was, no one wanted to be that close to me.

How can I blame them? Being in the presence of Power unnerves people.

Not that it ever stops them if they need something. I cured Streaming Stone's son by his first wife, Blanket, of snakebite. Drove the evil Spirits of infection from old Bobcat Ear's swollen jaw and relieved the blockage of Turtle Woman's sheath so she could finally pass her infant daughter.

But people are people. When Throat Caller gave me a slave girl in return for cursing his lifelong enemy, Scoot, I conjured a spell that left Scoot choking to death on his own blood. Scoot's brother was found dead a couple of mornings later after a terrible storm. He'd been trying to sneak into my temple with *a war club, only be struck dead by lightning in the middle of the night. The burn along the left side of his body, his popped-out eyes, and the thick white foam bubbling from his mouth were full proof of the manner of his death. Not to mention that deafening crack of lightning that had brought everyone bolt upright out of bed.*

That the lightning killed him on my doorstep without marking my temple made an impression.

In addition, people who called me a witch, accused me of evil acts, and demanded my removal from the community kept winding up dead of unknown causes.

Oh, and there was Diamond Moccasin. He actually made it into my temple a couple of days after his little daughter mysteriously disappeared. He, too, had figured to brain me in my sleep, but the voices warned me that he was coming. From deep in the shadows I drove a spear into his side as he lifted his club high to strike my rumpled and stuffed bedding.

I flayed the hide off his body and draped it on a framework that I posted outside my front door.

Another couple of houses moved away after that. Odd of them, don't you think? It's not like I had anything against them.

I digress. When one is given a message by Power, as I was that day in the swamp, one shouldn't ignore it. The Thunder Beings had told me about Joara. And I could feel Night Shadow Star. Sense her purpose—even across the distance that separated us.

Therefore, I made my preparations. I had packed my Power items, including the cup I'd made from Diamond Moccasin's little daughter's skull. By the way, that's tougher to do than you might think. A child's skull isn't grown together as completely as an adult's. Lot of work to glue those bones together in a way that will let them hold water. But using a little girl's skull to drink out of carries a lot more weight than just any old adult's.

And besides, when I used the child's blood to fill a well pot, I was able to see visions of Cahokia, particularly Night Shadow Star's departure from the canoe landing. Who'd have thought she'd leave in a single canoe instead of at the head of a large war party?

One doesn't carelessly throw away body parts from a child who can grant that kind of vision, so I ate her heart, liver, and tiny little ovaries. I've been trying to craft a flute from her leg bone, but the sound just isn't right. That project might have to be abandoned in the end.

So, with my box packed full of the more delicate of my possessions, and having folded my clothing and placed it in a large basket, I make my way across the plaza to Streaming Stone's palace.

As a plaza, it's not much. The obligatory World Tree pole stands in the center, though its bald cypress trunk hasn't been carved. The stickball ground is relatively flat and groomed, but the poor excuse for the chunkey courts is laughable. Word is that Moon Blade was buried with his chunkey stone, so Streaming Stone uses one crafted out of wood. Nor does the local game have the religious majesty that it has at home. Here it is more of a recreation and excuse to gamble.

I lose sight of the fact that at home the dirt farmers are religious converts, and here the Muskogeans are effectively conquered. This is a colony, maintained by Streaming Stone's warriors, his alliances through marriage, and the fact that most of the old mikkos, oratas, *and their families were murdered in the aftermath of the conquest.*

Stretching back into the surroundings are the local houses, mostly bent-pole construction, bark-sided and similarly roofed, although the occasional split-cane or thatch roof can be seen. In addition, a "summer house" or ramada is attached. Like I'm familiar with in Cahokia, each has a small garden, and the dwellings here are grouped by lineage. An elevated corn crib is shared by every ten or fifteen families. The cornfields lie just beyond the houses, a mosaic of different-sized and -shaped plots that surrender to the forest. All told, perhaps a thousand people live in town, and another couple of thousand in the surrounding villages.

The day is marvelous, and I can look down the rise to the canoe landing where sunlight sparkles on the breeze-stirred water. On the far bank, the trees are dark green where they dominate the floodplain and stretch off into the haze-filled distance. Off to the west, thunderheads are rising into the pale blue sky.

I don't make the foot of Streaming Stone's low mound before the chief emerges and stands between the two pathetic Hunga Ahuito *guardian posts at either side of the top of the stairs. He is in his late thirties, muscular, with keen eyes. He wears a cloak, Cahokian style, with the traditional apron that drops to a point between his knees. He has his hair done up in a bun secured by an arrow-split cloud headpiece. I can tell he rushed to pin it in place because it sits crooked.*

"Greetings, Elder!" he calls in a much too jovial voice. "How may I be of service today?"

That he calls me Elder, seeing as how I'm at least ten years younger than he is, is a mark of the fear he has for me and my Powers.

"Great Mikko," I tell him, "I gave you word of my need of transportation to Joara. I have made my arrangements and am ready to leave. Could you have a litter brought? My packs are waiting beside my door. Just a box and a basket."

The conflict behind his eyes would be amusing if I were not in a hurry.

"Elder, with my deepest apologies. I've made the announcement—ordered it, in fact—but the people appointed seem to have vanished overnight. Gone."

While not entirely unexpected, this infuriates me. "I thought you had this under control, Mikko. Call your squadron first. Have him assemble warriors to scour the town for able-bodied men. And if he can't find any, I shall choose my own porters from among their ranks. If any hesitate, I shall initiate the growth of brown rot in their testicles and infect their shafts with pus. Those who carry me to Joara quickly and efficiently, I shall gift with the ability to win when gambling at hand game."

I have to tell you, being considered dangerous and Powerful, for the most part, delights me.

There are other times when it is as bothersome as lice in pubic hair.

Twenty-five

The turgid floodwaters were dropping, leaving shallows and muddy lakes on the narrow floodplain that lined the Tenasee River's winding banks. Fire Cat bent to his paddle, peering back into the trees.

This was all new. Everything he was seeing was like legend coming true. He'd heard about the Mother Water, the Tenasee, and the endless lands the rivers served. The effect was that his world was growing by the day, expanding into a larger universe with each bend in the river.

And the people? So many of them. *Red Reed* had passed the cluster of settlements that dominated the heights above the confluence of the Tenasee with the Mother Water. Along the banks, people had built farmsteads atop every levee. Passing dugouts—most of them crude hollowed-out logs—carried fishermen and local waterfowl hunters as well as the occasional family.

The smell of the Tenasee had a subtle tang that differed from both the Father and Mother Water rivers. And the Tenasee moved with a different character, as though it had a more serene soul.

The low, tree-lined knolls in the distance indicated bluffs beyond the thickly forested floodplain. The first greening of spring was coming to the forest, a land ready to burst into life. They'd cheered at the sight of the first great blue herons as they winged north, their twittering and flute-hollow cries carrying across the land.

Even as a boy Fire Cat had understood that rivers were the lifelines of his world; then he'd seen the swarms of vessels, people, and Trade that

clogged the canoe landing below River Mounds City. Traffic on the Tenasee wasn't as heavy as it had been since leaving Cahokia, but as the
broad channel began to narrow, they passed closer to the oncoming canoes, calling greetings.

Another of the giant Vs of migratory birds passed overhead, their
calls echoing over the land. Said fowl, along with fish, freshwater clams,
and mussels, were offered for Trade at any stop the *Red Reed* made—not
to mention bartered from one passing canoe to another, often for the
simplest of Trade such as a small hank of wooden Cahokian Trade
beads.

They also Traded such fare upon reaching shore in the evening,
exchanging the raw fish or plucked birds for whatever was in the village
stewpot where they landed.

Despite plenty to eat, even White Mat was looking weary. The one
who bore the brunt most, however, was Night Shadow Star. As fit as she
might have been as a runner and stickball player, paddling was a different proposition.

They had put in for the night at a small settlement that consisted of a
cluster of huts back from a canoe landing. The five bent-pole structures
were grandiosely called Great White Wolf village. The people—local
fishermen, hunters, and part-time river Traders—consisted of a small
displaced Michigamea band who'd come down from the north a generation ago to escape the constant raiding and warring in the northern
forests.

While their language was incomprehensible to Night Shadow Star and
Fire Cat when the Michigamea were talking among themselves, they
were fluent in Trade pidgin.

As morning broke, Fire Cat forced himself awake. Wincing, he
stretched, thankful that his own sore muscles were beginning to harden.

He sat up in his blankets, stared around at the bent-pole hut. The
construction was simple: Dig an oval-shaped series of post holes that
enclosed a space about four paces long and two across. Set the butts of
green-cut saplings in the post holes, then bend their still-pliable tops over
and tie them to their opposite across the oval. Doing so created a series
of bows. Lace them all together with vines or smaller saplings to make a
framework, and then cover the whole with peeled sections of overlapping
bark.

Fire Cat rose, walked out among the trees beyond the village to the
small glade that served as the local latrine, and watched his urine steam
in the chill air. Overhead, the branches showed the faintest trace of frost.
A couple of the buds had opened, the first flowers peeking out.

Next, he walked down to the river, stooped, and washed his face in the cold water. Fingers of mist were rising from the swirling, sucking, and swelling surface of the Tenasee; the graying dawn gave the water a dull silver gleam that reminded him of galena.

Ducks, geese, and morning birds were calling across the restless river, the morning oddly peaceful. He enjoyed the moment, knowing he should have been headed back to wake Night Shadow Star and the rest. Weary enough to simply enjoy the peace and solitude, he let it soothe the deep-seated fatigue that came from hard days of travel.

Night Shadow Star's words from a couple of days past returned to his memory: "You feel it, don't you? The Power of the river? It's alive, watching us, wondering."

"Wondering what?" he'd asked.

"Wondering which faction it will finally side with. Walking Smoke's or ours."

As he looked out at the endlessly moving water, he could feel the river's energy—something momentarily restrained, but impatiently awaiting that inevitable moment when it would unleash its physical and spiritual might.

He had grown up on the upper Father Water, had known its unique Power and moods. Had marveled at how it changed personality from the clear green waters of his home in the north to the murky expanse it exhibited at Cahokia.

The Tenasee had a completely different feel, as if it carried a long memory of pain and struggle. The sensations it stirred in his souls were anything but reassuring.

"Who are you?" Fire Cat asked. "Whose side are you on?"

He would have thought Piasa's, since rivers were the province of the fearsome Underworld beast and the lair of Tie Snakes, Snapping Turtle, and the depths.

The roiling lead-gray surface sent him no answers.

That's when he heard the distant voices. But for the morning's stillness and the way sound carried over water, he would have missed them. Even then, he was about to discount the faint chatter. There was no shortage of human beings crowding the Tenasee's populated shores. The words, however, were Cahokian in a land where most people spoke their own tongues or Trade pidgin.

"The squadron first says it's time to get your lazy carcasses out of your blankets. Today we catch them!"

Faint and incomprehensible complaints barely carried across from the far bank to where Fire Cat hunched.

The Tenasee curved here, a long loop that curled back on itself. With the next flood, the current would finally chew through the narrow neck of land across from him, effectively cutting off the ox-bow loop and eventually leaving it as an isolated lake.

The voices came from the other side of the narrow neck of land.

The camp might have been no more than ten, maybe twenty bow-shots away to the north on the opposite side of the loop, but perhaps a couple of hands' time to travel by following the river's channel.

Fire Cat was on his feet, pounding up the trail to the Michigamea village. He stopped only long enough to kick White Mat and Shedding Bird awake, then he ducked into Night Shadow Star's hut.

Dropping, he shook her. "Lady? We have to get up. Now. I think they're right behind us."

"Who?"

"Someone called 'squadron first.' That name conjure any memories for you? And it was uttered in good Cahokian. The sort of wake-up a war party would get."

"Where?"

"Remember that loop we rounded last night? Just across that neck of land."

She threw her blankets back. Combed long black strands of hair out of her face, then pulled her cloak on, saying, "Get these things rolled up and get them in the *Red Reed*. By the time you do, I'll be ready."

After rolling up her bedding, he stepped out, finding the Traders blinking, still sleep-bleary.

"You're sure you heard this war chief you've been talking about?" Half Root asked, her face wrinkled where she'd slept with it pillowed by a wad of cloth.

"Pretty sure. Nothing would make me happier than to get us out on the river, race *Red Reed* south, and discover later that it was all a mistake, a curious echo across the water." Fire Cat chuckled dryly. "But that's not the kind of break I get in my life. On your feet, people, we're leaving."

"You really think this is worth an extra piece of copper?" Mixed Shell asked White Mat. "I'm thinking maybe I'll sleep for another couple of hands of time and stay a poor man—but well rested—for the rest of my life."

The Michigamea were rising from their own blankets, curious about the visitors' rush to get on the river. Talking warily among themselves, they watched suspiciously. Fire Cat Traded the last of the ducks they'd bartered for on the river for all the lotus and cattail-root bread the Michigamea had.

Night Shadow Star was as good as her word. Fire Cat was securing the last of their belongings down inside *Red Reed*'s hull when she emerged from the forest trail leading back to the latrine area. She looked oddly fresh, almost nervous.

"You all right?"

A smile died on her lips. "Piasa tells me I'm a fool. That I'd sleep through my own abduction."

"How far behind us would you say they are?" White Mat asked.

"Maybe two, three hands. Other side of that narrow neck of land and screened from seeing us by that growth of willows. Oh, and keep your voices down. If I could hear them, they could hear us."

Together they pushed the *Red Reed* out into the silt-laden water, dipped paddles, brought the slim vessel around and into the current.

"You ask me," Mixed Shell grumbled softly, "the warrior here has an active imagination."

"Better awakened to a hard day and endless paddling than having to face down a war party." Fire Cat shot the man a knowing wink. "We'd lose."

"We've made outstanding time," White Mat muttered over his shoulder, digging deep with his paddle to send them forward. "Catching up with us? This must be some bunch of warriors."

"They'd be the best of Spotted Wrist's people—and his squadron is the best in Cahokia. You know what that means?"

"Not really," Shedding Bird shot back over his shoulder. He paused only long enough to stuff a piece of root bread in his mouth.

"It means the best in the world," Night Shadow Star told him.

"Assuming Fire Cat didn't hear something echo, maybe a turkey call he mistook for a voice. Sound does funny things on the river."

"If I mistook what I—"

"Hey!" The call carried from behind.

Fire Cat craned his neck, searched, saw a man break out from the willows. Across the distance he could still recognize a Cahokian warrior by the distinctive cut of the man's war shirt. The fellow carried a bow and arrows, looked more like he was hunting than anything else.

"Stop!" the man shouted, stumbling out onto the bank. "It's them! Night Shadow Star! Hurry. This way, all of you!"

As Fire Cat watched, five more warriors came crashing through the willows, all stopping at the edge of the water to watch *Red Reed* as the narrow canoe sliced along the bank opposite from them.

"Bring us Night Shadow Star. We only want to talk!" the lead warrior called. "Come back here!"

Shedding Bird was putting his back into the paddle. "So, that's the enemy, huh?"

"That's them," Night Shadow Star said wearily. "Piasa? Where were you? Why didn't you warn me?"

Fire Cat saw the absent look in her eyes as the Spirit Beast told her something she apparently wasn't keen to hear.

"Stop, or we'll shoot!" one of the warriors shouted from the far bank.

"Good luck with that," Fire Cat growled to himself, driving the paddle deep, matching his stroke with the rest.

Red Reed leapt forward, water splitting at her bow.

"They're shooting," White Mat said, taking a glance in the warriors' direction.

"The river here's a long shot across. We're at the limits of range," Fire Cat told him. "And as fast as we're moving? It would be a miracle if any of them even came close."

An arrow made a *thook* sound as it speared the water a stone's throw to their left, its passage marked by a trail of bubbles.

A flight of arrows hit the water in a staccato of *thook thook*s.

"Stop shooting, you fools!" an angry order carried across the water. "You'll hit Night Shadow Star!"

Across the distance Fire Cat could make out another warrior as he bulled his way through the thick screen of willows and charged out on the narrow beach. He drew up, fist knotted, berating his warriors.

"What will they do next?" Night Shadow Star asked.

"Depends," White Mat replied. "My suspicion is that they'll pile back in their canoe and put out, figuring they can eventually catch us."

"That or they'll unload it." Half Root was driving her paddle into the water with grim purpose. "Portage the hull over the neck, toss everything back in, and foam water trying to catch us."

Mixed Shell shrugged between strokes. "Lot of downed timber and brush in there to wrestle a war canoe through."

"Wait," Fire Cat noted. "Look, they're coming on at a trot. Following along the far bank. What's that all about?"

In the bow, White Mat glanced back. Considered. "I think I understand. For the moment the thread is on their side, which means the strongest current is running against their shore. But just up ahead, the river turns back on itself. They're figuring that we'll have to cross the current to keep headway. That or wear ourselves out tackling the river's full force head-on in an attempt to stay out of their range."

Fire Cat rose slightly, staring ahead. Indeed, the next curve was a tight one where the river looped back on itself. Maybe, fresh as they were, they could power *Red Reed* against the full strength of the current. That, or perhaps walk the boat along the shoreline if the bank didn't drop off?

"Got any ideas?" Fire Cat asked. "Or should we stop so I can don my armor and try a valiant rearguard action?"

"These are warriors," Shedding Bird told him, seemingly unconcerned. "We're Traders. They might be unleashed terror on the battlefield. But we're on the river."

"You'll notice," Made Man said from where he stroked behind Fire Cat, "that they're still a bit behind us on the outside of the curve, climbing over brush, slogging through the mud. Probably figuring that they'll catch us at the next loop."

"Shouldn't bet against a Trader," Half Root added. "Not on the river, anyway."

Fire Cat could see the ripple where the current cut across the river ahead of them, the water moving faster, not sucking and swelling like in the slower eddies next to the bank.

It wouldn't be long now, just another canoe length, and they'd be in the main force where it ran close to the curving bank.

White Mat and the rest took a couple of vigorous bites with their paddles, driving them into the bank.

"Let's move, people," White Mat ordered, bailing over the side and holding *Red Reed* against the river's pull.

Shedding Bird, Mixed Shell, and Made Man splashed over the side, Made Man retrieving a coil of basswood rope from under his seat and calling, "Fire Cat? You and the lady are with us."

"What are we doing?" Fire Cat asked as he and Night Shadow Star clambered over the gunwale. Across the river shouts of victory sang out from the pursuers. The Cahokians must have thought they'd won if *Red Reed* was no longer moving. In Fire Cat's mind, the smart thing would be to send four or five warriors ahead to swim the river, bottle up both sides, and hunt them down in a pincer movement.

"Half Root steers," White Mat said, lining out the rope that Mixed Shell was tying around his waist. "Mixed Shell uses his paddle to keep *Red Reed* off the bank, and the rest of us pull the canoe around the bend against the current."

"We're towing the canoe?" Night Shadow Star asked as she took a grip on the rope.

"And we're not taking our time about it either," Half Root said tersely, as she glanced across at the closing warriors.

"Let's go," White Mat called, getting a good grip and slinging the rope over his shoulder. Then the man bulled his way up the incline and started along the high bank, the rope lining out behind him.

"What do you think, Lady?" Fire Cat asked as he threw his own muscle into the task and tramped forward in White Mat's tracks. The whole weight of *Red Reed*, the current, and cargo made the rope strain. "Enjoying the coddled life of a noble these days?"

Struggling along behind him, Night Shadow Star laughed. "Can you imagine Rising Flame in this situation?"

Across the river, shouts of anger accompanied the Cahokians' realization of what their prey was doing.

Tossing a glance past the taut rope over his shoulder, Fire Cat watched in amazement as foam curled around *Red Reed*'s bow. Half Root had her paddle wedged against the hull, water angrily curling as she steered the canoe outward. Mixed Shell was using his paddle as a pole, forcing the craft away from the bank.

Now all the rest of them had to do was clamber across the roots, through the brush, over the logs and crumbling bank, and keep moving as the tow rope dragged *Red Reed* forward.

Within moments, Fire Cat began to pant, his hands biting into the rope. He, Made Man, and Night Shadow Star took the load as White Mat and Shedding Bird clambered over a deadfall and then took the rope while Night Shadow Star, he, and Made Man followed.

Sweat began to build despite the cool morning. The tow rope chewed painfully into his shoulder, the weight of the canoe, its load, people, and current's pull trying to topple him backward.

Crossing a shallow stream, Night Shadow Star slipped, fell face-first into the muck, clambered back onto her feet, and took her place again.

Past that, the bank was open along the river, thick with last year's grass. The pace picked up, coupled with their heaving and panting as they struggled forward.

And as White Mat had said, across the river, the pursuers were having their own problems where they splashed through the shallows.

All bends have to end, and as the current's pull faded, White Mat—panting and grinning—slowed, began coiling the rope. "We're there. Everyone back in the canoe. Now, let's make time."

Mud-spattered, scratched from branches, gasping for breath, Night Shadow Star shot one last wary glance back across the river. There, the warriors were even farther behind, bellowing threats, some stomping as they slogged through swampy low ground. One bent his bow back, aimed high, and sent a futile arrow to spear the water a half bowshot behind them.

Night Shadow Star seated herself, asking, "Do you think they'll keep up the pursuit on foot?"

"Not from here," Made Man told her, pointing upriver. "Gets pretty swampy on their side. No, they'll have to go back to get their canoe. We've just extended our lead."

As Fire Cat clambered into the canoe, he said, "We won this one. But they've had a taste. They've seen their prey. That sort of thing? It really motivates a warrior."

"They'll keep coming," Night Shadow Star said, pulling a thorn from her hand.

"Then we'd better be smarter as well as faster," White Mat told her.

Fire Cat hoped the Trader wasn't making an empty boast.

Twenty-six

Enraged, Blood Talon charged along the shore as one by one his muddy, frustrated warriors slowed and vented their anger at the disappearing canoe. When the excitement began, he'd been down at the river, filling a brownware pot with water to add to the corn gruel that bubbled on the fire.

A couple of the men, Three Bow and Whistle Hand, had taken their bows and slipped into the driftwood-and-willow tangle that had protected their camp from the chilly south wind. Their hopes had been to bag something for the pot, be it waterfowl, a raccoon, or best of all, a deer or turkey.

As the rest of his warriors rolled up their bedding, attended to their morning needs, and washed at the water's edge, Blood Talon had poured his water into the stew, only to hear "Stop!" and "It's them! Night Shadow Star! Hurry. This way, all of you!"

Chaos broke out. Nutcracker had charged headlong into the tangle of willows, old wood, and vines.

Additional shouts could be heard along with the ululating call of the hunt.

Blood Talon had grabbed for his weapons, among the last to claw his way into the screen of vegetation, battle his way through the mess of old driftwood, and stumble out of the willows onto the narrow beach.

In the heartbeat it took him to orient himself, it was to see a slender Trade canoe lancing its way parallel to the far bank, maybe a couple of bow shots away. Seven people, all bending their backs to the paddles, were driving the craft upstream at a quick clip.

His warriors were charging up the beach, some shooting, others howling with the thrill of the chase.

"You miserable fools!" Blood Talon roared. "You'll never catch them this way."

"They'll have to cross at the next bend," Wild Owl called back. "We'll trap them against the current."

Then the warrior was off and running, slogging through the muddy water, ducking around broken branches and deadfall that stuck out from the bank.

Blood Talon shook his head at the notion; surely the fugitives—if that really was Night Shadow Star and the Red Wing—wouldn't just paddle into the arms of their pursuers.

But it might slow them down.

Was there a way?

He and his men were charging along the outside of the curve, splashing through shallows, clambering up the places where the fast current had undercut the bank. Tough going, but his warriors were in good shape. If they could make it that far, the river's next loop would let them cut across the inside, maybe get far enough ahead . . . No, the quarry couldn't be that stupid.

Even if they could get ahead, maybe enough to allow several of their warriors to swim across, cut off escape on the other bank . . .

But then, what was to keep the quarry from simply doubling back, fleeing downriver and leaving him and his men upstream? Not to mention far from their now-vulnerable canoe. Which was unguarded and sitting right there on the beach where Night Shadow Star and her people could push it out onto the water, put a couple of paddlers in it, and race it downriver on the current.

"Halt!" Blood Talon bellowed. "Now! All of you! Get back to the canoe. That's an order!"

His party of warriors was strung out too far. Those closest to him slowed, looked back, and stopped. Fingering their bows, they shot uncertain glances at the distant canoe. It had beached on the opposite side, the occupants unloading.

To do what?

As soon as the rope was played out and the people on shore began towing the canoe against the current, Blood Talon cursed, kicked the water, and threw his hands up.

"Get back here. Pass it along. That's a direct order!"

He could just see the last of his warriors disappear around the bend, gesturing, giving voice to their rage, shooting the occasional and totally fruitless arrow as the Traders' towed canoe vanished around the far curve of the river.

"Back to camp! Now! And anyone who isn't present after a finger's time better not come back!"

Was that even Night Shadow Star and the Red Wing? Across the distance he thought he recognized the woman and her slave warrior. But he couldn't be sure. They'd been wearing slip-over shirts, some kind of cloaks. Not the sort of dress a Cahokian lady from the Morning Star House of the Four Winds Clan would wear.

The woman who might have been Night Shadow Star had bent to the paddle as furiously as the rest of them. A woman of her status would never have allowed herself to participate in such a menial task. Even more, the woman he'd seen knew what she was doing. Plied that paddle like a seasoned river traveler.

He angrily kicked a stick of driftwood out of his way, sloshed back through the shallows, and worked himself into a rage as he finally made it back to the willow screen and forced his way through the tangle to his beach camp.

Just the sight of the canoe brought a swell of relief, and the corn gruel had cooked down in the meantime. It needed another pot of water. As he bent to get it, watched the water flowing into the brownware pot, he realized that he was right back where he started.

Only now—if that really had been them—they knew they were being hunted.

"Of all the stupid stunts to pull," he growled.

"Thought we had them." Nutcracker bit off the words the way he did when he was mad and frustrated. "They should have had to cross at the next bend of the river."

In ones, twos, and threes, the rest of his warriors emerged from the tangle, all looking sheepish, mud-spattered, their skin scratched; and more to the point, the number of arrows in their quivers was considerably depleted.

They were all there now, trying to look busy with other things, avoiding his eyes as he filled the breakfast pot and set the brownware pot to the side.

"Someone tell me. Are you the same smart, canny, veteran warriors I knew up north? The ones who took Red Wing Town without a single loss? The ones who pacified the barbarian chiefs? Remember those warriors? Smart. Disciplined. Did any good sense you used to have up north vanish when you got back to Cahokia? Or just when you turned the bow of your canoe up the Tenasee? Is there something in the water that turned you all stupider than a rock?"

"We thought we had them." Old Scar pulled at his earlobe, eyes on the distant horizon.

"Are you even sure that was Night Shadow Star? Huh? Did any of you really get a good look across the water? Did you recognize the Red Wing? I've stared the man in the face. Fought him. I wasn't sure that any of those people were who you all think they are."

"They ran," Three Bow said in defense. "We called for them to stop, and they threw themselves into the paddles. If it wasn't them, why would they run?"

"You don't think that a party of men with strung bows who are pulling arrows out of their quivers might have that effect on a party of Traders? Who knows what the story is here? Maybe a couple of villages are at war."

"The canoe was like the one that's been described." Nutcracker squatted before the gruel pot, used a ceramic cup to scoop up some of the contents. "Same number of people. Just like all the informants have said."

Blood Talon laced all the sarcasm he could into his voice. "Ah! Good! So, there's only one canoe on this entire length of river that has seven people in it and is headed upriver. That just made my life so much easier. From here on, when we encounter a canoe, we just need to count. When we have seven, that's them. Grab them, take them back to Spotted Wrist, and be heroes."

Nutcracker chugged down the hot gruel, ordering the rest, "Come on. Fill your bellies. Then get the canoe packed. If that was them, they know we're behind them. It's just going to make the hunt that much harder, longer, and more difficult."

"Do as the second commands." Blood Talon stood. "From here on out, I don't want to hear a word of complaint. No matter how long it takes, just think back to this morning and how you had a chance to nab them without a fight."

Assuming it really was them.

But even as he considered the question, Blood Talon just had that feeling. Like a tickle along the spine. True, he hadn't been close enough to get a good look at that warrior—and just how did he know he was a warrior?—or the woman. No, they weren't dressed as Cahokians, let alone nobles. And yes, the woman was paddling as hard as the rest, but both of the women in that canoe had had their hair in braids. A Cahokian noble would wear her hair up. The women he'd seen wore common garments.

But this was Night Shadow Star.

Blood Talon had helped to capture the Red Wing with the understanding that Night Shadow Star could torture him to death, and instead she'd taken him into her bed. She'd been born to a Sky clan, and now served Piasa. Rising Flame had ordered her to marry Spotted Wrist, and she'd ignored it. She was supposed to be in charge of the Cofitachequi expedition, and she'd run off with Traders.

Given all that, why was he surprised she was acting like a common-born Trader? Since when had she ever done anything the way she was supposed to?

"Let's move, people. Something tells me this just got a whole lot more difficult."

Twenty-seven

The first time Matron Slender Fox had made love with her brother, Sliding Ice, had been when they were children. She had been nine, and Sliding Ice was just turned eleven. It had started because they'd hidden under one of the beds as part of a game, only to hear two of the household slaves, Slip Fish and Fern Flower, sneak into the room. The two adults had frantically stripped off their clothing, leaped onto the bed, and Slip Fish had driven himself into Fern Flower with a vigor that strained the leather strapping and had the bed's pole frame creaking. The event ended in a chorus of delighted yips and barely stifled squeals.

After the slaves had left, Sliding Ice had turned to her, saying, "I wonder what that's like. She sounded like I've never heard a woman sound."

"And he kept whispering, 'Yes, yes,' over and over."

"Must be wonderful. I can't wait to try it."

"We could, you know. Try it. Just to see. We're going to have to learn how sometime. You heard War Leader Black Stick. How he made fun of Tied Root. Said he couldn't pleasure a woman if he had a thousand years to learn. Well, you wouldn't want that, would you?"

"You could tell me what made you feel good." Sliding Ice had frowned. "And it's not like we're lowly Earth Clan or dirt farmers. We're Four Winds Clan. Nobles. I don't want people to make fun of me just because I don't know how to pleasure a woman."

"A woman needs skill, too, you know. Someday I'm going to be high matron. I should know what's good and what isn't."

Besides, Slender Fox had always found a certain excitement in the forbidden. And somehow, over the years, on rare occasions when she was feeling particularly frustrated, stressed, or just felt the physical need, she would arrange to have the palace empty. What she and Sliding Ice did on those nights wasn't love, but a physical release that still carried the added excitement of being forbidden.

Sliding Ice had indeed become expert at coaxing pleasure out of a woman's body, and she suspected that he kept a little extra in reserve just because it was her. In the end, he knew her needs in ways no other man ever had or would.

That night he had taken her from orgasm to orgasm. The warm and tingling glow was fading from her pelvis, thighs, and lower back as he slumped onto her body, breath shuddering in and out of his lungs. "How's that?"

"Never better, brother. No wonder White Phlox doesn't want you taking a second wife. She's probably afraid the word would get out, and you'd have a line at the door to your personal quarters."

Craning her head, she thought she heard a dog lapping water. Then wind in the thatch overhead drowned the noise. Couldn't have been. She'd personally secured the great room door and latched it with a thong. Anyone trying to enter the palace would have given her and Sliding Ice plenty of warning.

"All these years, I've wondered why this was forbidden." She wrapped a lock of his hair around her finger. "Coupling as brother and sister is supposed to result in evil Spirit-infested children with deformities. That man Jenis, the Ilini, remember him? He planted that child in his own daughter, and when the baby was born she looked normal enough."

"She was only three when Jenis was found out and they burned the girl alive. Maybe the evil hadn't had time to manifest itself. And don't forget Tharon. You know the stories about all those monsters he sired. And that's why we don't ever want to get found out. If anyone so much as suspected—"

"Too late," a voice announced in the darkness.

Before Sliding Ice could scramble off her, a heavy weight landed atop them, driving the breath from her lungs. Sliding Ice bucked, grunted, crying out, only to receive a hard cuff to the head. The impact of it banged Sliding Ice's skull against hers. Hard enough that lights flashed behind her eyes.

By the time she could fill her lungs, a couple of loops of thick rope had been wound around their bodies, locking them together, binding them to the bed frame.

"Who are you?" Sliding Ice cried, half panicked as he thrashed against the bindings. All he succeeded in doing was to hurt her.

"Stop it!" she ordered. "Hold still."

Looking up past her brother's head, Slender Fox could only make out the dark shadow of a man. He loomed above them, staring down. When Sliding Ice tried to slither forward, the intruder made a tsking sound with his lips.

"I wouldn't do that. No, you stay right there. Seriously, there are a great many worse places to be than naked against a beautiful woman's body. And your sister? There's not a man in Cahokia wouldn't mind being bound up tight with her. Especially after a session like you two just had."

"What do you want?" Slender Fox asked in her hardest voice. The paralyzing flood of fear was being replaced by the first fingers of panic.

"Who, me? I want all kinds of things. It took a good friend of mine to finally figure it out. She says I can't live without having a challenge. That I need the excitement. Like tonight. Sneaking in here like this. See, it's kind of a gamble."

"You know who we are?" Sliding Ice demanded indignantly.

"Sure. You're Lord Sliding Ice, who's punching his shaft into Matron Slender Fox's ever-voracious sheath. Daring of you, given the penalty for such doings with one's own sister."

"You know what's going to happen when we catch you?" Slender Fox asked in her most calculating tone. Who was this man? Why couldn't she place his voice?

"That's the gamble part. Suppose someone comes back? Wanders in the door. I'm betting I can get out of here, disappear, before they can get you untied and you can call out the guards to run me down. But then, that leaves you with the problem of having to explain why you're both naked, tied up in Slender Fox's bed the way you are, and smelling the way you do. Wonder what clever explanation you'll try and concoct."

The panic was now steady and enveloping as it rushed through Slender Fox's body. "I asked you what you wanted. Why are you here? Why are you doing this? Surely we can come to some sort of agreement."

The man's long silence just added to her terror. If she were discovered thus, it would be all over. There had to be something she could do to—

"You've got corn, right? Storehouses with dried squash? Baskets full of goosefoot seeds? Those big sacks of dried beans?"

"You want a storehouse full of food?" Sliding Ice muttered incredulously. "For yourself?"

"Well, no, not for myself."

At that juncture, the sound of the door opening into the front room sent ice into Slender Fox's veins. Someone was coming. Out in the great room she heard one of the cooking pots rattle as it was knocked against its neighbor. Then came the sound of slurping again. Most definitely a dog.

"You got 'em?" a voice asked in the dark.

"Sort of bound them up like fish in a net. Say, that's an idea. We could wrap them in a net, drop them just like this on the Grand Staircase on Morning Star's mound. Be a little cold, but they could huddle together for warmth. Should have seen how they were staying warm when I got here. Very athletic. But with lots of gasping, moaning, and frantic breathing."

"No, thanks. I never was much into watching."

That voice, old, female, slightly slurred from missing teeth. Something about it . . .

Then the old woman's dark form was leaning over the bed. "What do you say, Matron? Do we opt for the net? Or just wait until Wolverine, maybe the household staff, comes back? Your choice."

"I will burn you alive for this!" She let the rage loose, using threat and bluster as a tonic for desperation.

"You have a choice. Order your storehouses emptied and sent to Evening Star Town to compensate them for what they donated to supply the expedition, or within the next hand of time, you and Sliding Ice are going to find yourselves the center of most unwelcome attention."

"I'll kill you!" Sliding Ice bellowed in his impotence.

Slender Fox clamped her eyes closed. Pus-rotted gods! It had been her hope that Columella would be deposed over the donation of those stores. Now she found herself caught against her brother's trembling body, still wet with their combined fluids.

"How do I know that . . . that . . ."

"That I won't betray your secret?"

Slender Fox waited, the sensation like that of knowing a terrible weight was about to come hurtling down from the heights to crush her.

"I guess you'll just have to find out. Day by day. Forever worrying."

"I'll order it first thing."

"You'll order it now." The old woman raised her voice. "Runner?"

Slender Fox heard someone enter the great room, trot across the matting.

"Far enough," the woman ordered before the newcomer reached her personal quarters. "You know the matron's voice?"

"I do, Lady."

"Go ahead," the old woman told Slender Fox in a most agreeable voice. "Give the order."

Slender Fox, on the verge of tears, filled her lungs and called, "I want our granaries emptied. All of it. Every last kernel of corn, every rind of squash. The same for the local Earth Clans. We're . . . we're sending it all to Evening Star Town." The words tasted bitter in her mouth. "A gesture of gratitude toward our good friend Matron Columella."

"Yes, Lady," the eager voice called from the front room. "I'll have our people on it by first light."

Slender Fox felt Sliding Ice's body go limp against hers, felt his lungs pulsing, as if in silent tears.

"Is that sufficient?"

Silence.

"Have I bought your silence?"

She twisted her head past Sliding Ice's, stared up at the darkness, and saw no looming forms. Her room was empty.

Whoever had tied them had done so with expert knots. It seemed to take forever for Sliding Ice to wiggle free, help her out of the blankets. She pulled on her clothes and staggered out into the great room. Sliding Ice followed close behind her.

Someone had tossed a couple of logs on the fire. The flames now leaped to illuminate her empty great room. Everything seemed in order except for the ceramic vessels around the fire. The stewpot lay canted, empty. The loaves of bread were gone, only crumbs left. A wet stain gleamed in the firelight where it looked like a dog had urinated on the dais that supported her litter.

"I will find whoever did this," she swore, fist knotted. "And when I do, I will hang them in a square and gut them slowly."

"I think I know that voice." Sliding Ice looked sick in the firelight. "I think it was the Keeper."

"Are you crazy? If Spotted Wrist trapped us like that, he'd have hauled us up before the Morning Star and destroyed us. Besides, he's the last person who'd want Columella's storehouses restocked."

"No, I mean the old Keeper. Blue Heron."

Slender Fox pursed her lips. Thought it through. Yes, that's why she'd thought the voice familiar. "That, brother, is a different thing entirely."

Twenty-eight

The storm had rolled in at midday. A dark wall of clouds that had come sailing in from the northwest. It brought with it gusting winds, dropping temperatures, and unleashed sheets of cold rain that hissed as they slashed down on the river, the valiant *Red Reed*, and its exhausted crew. The camp that night was cold, miserable, and wet; a mixture of sleet and rain fell from low clouds.

Despite the welcoming villages they passed, Night Shadow Star couldn't forget the sight of those Cahokian warriors running along the shore, shooting, cursing. These were Spotted Wrist's men. Warriors who didn't stop just because the weather turned a little foul.

In the last glow of twilight, White Mat had passed a substantial village set atop a low bluff, and a finger of time later, steered *Red Reed* into a sluggish brush-choked stream that entered the Tenasee from the west. Night Shadow Star wouldn't even have noticed it, given that the mouth was partially obscured by willows and overhanging branches of water oak.

Through the entire day, she'd felt Piasa's Spirit lurking. Several times, she thought she'd seen his glowing presence in the depths, only to realize it was a trick of the storm light on the water.

The Tenasee itself had changed character; the currents and eddies began taking a hand in slowing their progress, and once a log, bobbing just under the surface, had almost capsized the *Red Reed*.

Usually White Mat spotted the danger by a careful reading of the water. Snags and obstacles beneath the surface, he'd shown her, could be detected by subtle upwellings and turbulence that betrayed their presence. For some reason this submerged log had waited until *Red Reed* was right over it to rise and knock the canoe sideways.

Only the veteran hands at the paddles had saved them.

Maybe it had been Piasa's work, flipping the log up with one of his taloned feet in a jest to ensure they were paying attention. A reminder that the river could kill them as surely as the pursuing warriors.

Throughout that long day, as the clouds moved in and the temperature dropped, she wasn't the only one throwing anxious glances over her shoulder. They were all expecting to see a Cahokian war canoe appear around the last bend they'd passed.

She shivered, cold to the core, as rain pattered down through the trees and onto her cloak. Her arms were going numb as they used the points of the paddles like poles to push *Red Reed* up the shallow channel.

Not more than a bowshot up from the confluence was a gravel bar, and it was onto this that White Mat ordered them to set up camp.

The cold rain had slowed, turned to a drizzle, but water dripped from the dark and shadowed branches that interlaced above them.

Night Shadow Star, for once, was happy to huddle and shiver in misery and let the rest attend to the making of camp as they tugged brush out of the way and secured the canoe.

I could quit. Surrender myself to Blood Talon. I wouldn't have to paddle. Wouldn't have to ache. All I'd have to do is share Spotted Wrist's bed, and in return I could be warm, fed, and pampered again.

"Not like being in a village," Made Man told them wistfully as he built a lean-to, then went about procuring dry kindling from a pack. Using a bow drill, he managed to conjure a flicker of flame, feeding it more kindling.

Meanwhile, Shedding Bird used a hafted stone celt to split some of the branches lying about, exposing the dry wood inside.

The fire smoked, but managed to shoot out feeble light as they set to making camp.

Night Shadow Star rubbed her aching shoulders. Another bout of shivering racked her body. This day she had blisters, but each time her protesting body had wavered on the edge of collapse, she'd forced herself to paddle harder.

A hank of wooden beads had been bartered off to a passing fisherman for a catfish as long as her arm in addition to a sack of freshwater clams. Not much in the way of variety, but it would be filling. And hot. Mostly she wanted hot. Something to rekindle even the tiniest sensation of warmth in her belly.

Mixed Shell, in the light of the fire, used a freshly struck gray-chert flake and began cutting strips from the catfish. The clams they placed at the edge of the fire to roast as the flames began to overwhelm the wet wood.

"We need a plan," White Mat said as he fixed his rain hat at an angle so the water dripped off the back. The man's breath rose like a white fog in the cold air.

"Can we outrace them upriver?" Night Shadow Star asked through chattering teeth.

Fire Cat had draped a hard-smoked hide over his head and shoulders. Firelight gleamed in his dark eyes as he studied the fire. "*Red Reed* is smaller and faster in a short sprint compared to their war canoe. But I counted close to twenty of them. Working in relays, they can eventually catch us over the long run across open water. All they have to do is get close enough to shoot a couple of us down, and we're out of the race."

"If they can find us," Half Root said as she used a stick to turn the clams. She had hunkered down, tending the clams as an excuse to huddle over the flames.

The first aroma of the cooking shellfish tickled Night Shadow Star's nose, making her mouth water. She tensed her muscles, jaws clamped tight to stop her teeth from chattering. If she just demanded that they let her, she could take the fire for her own. She was Lady Night Shadow Star. A Cahokian noble.

In the forest darkness behind her she could hear Piasa's laughter. Her jaws were too cold to chance a comment. It would embarrass her too much if the others heard her teeth clacking like a sack full of rocks.

"It's hard to think they can catch us," Shedding Bird replied as he propped sticks to support a length of catfish over the fire. "*Red Reed*'s one of the fastest canoes afloat."

"It's not the canoe," Fire Cat told him, "it's the manpower. We can distance them with that initial burst of speed, but they have endurance on their side. They can pull a third of their warriors out, let them rest, and rotate refreshed warriors onto the benches. Once we're spent, it's only a matter of time before they overtake us."

"Then how do we deal with them?" Half Root flipped one of the clams, water spattering on her rain hat from the trees above.

"We have to not be found." Fire Cat extended his hands to the fire. Night Shadow Star could see the blisters. She wasn't the only one who'd pushed as hard as she could.

How did he do it? Every muscle in his body had to be screaming like hers were, he had to be just as chilled to the bone, and yet he sat poised like a statue.

"The problem with that," Made Man said, "is that there's only this one river, and they know we're headed up it."

"They even know where we're going," Night Shadow Star said between shivers as she watched the catfish begin to sizzle. "The only thing we can do is beat them to Cofitachequi. Get there before they do."

"Won't work," Fire Cat told her. "We made good time from Cahokia, and they had to have left at least a day behind us. They already caught us once, they'll do it again. They're faster. Just accept that."

"So, what do we do? Head back downriver?" White Mat asked. "It's that or get caught, right?"

"We could go back," Shedding Bird said thoughtfully. "At the confluence with the Mother Water, turn upstream to the mouth of the Southern Shawnee River, take it up to its headwaters. You'd have to travel overland to the headwaters of the Tenasee. It would be longer, more complicated. Especially across the uplands."

"And maybe even more dangerous," Made Man said. "Those people up there don't take kindly to strangers. Let alone traveling Cahokians."

"Think tactics," Fire Cat told him. "We're going to have to play fox and rabbit with them. The only thing we have going for us is that they don't know where we are. So put yourself in Blood Talon's position. He knows we're close, and he will have pushed hard today, hoping to make up that couple of hands' time he was behind us. I'd guess he's pulled in at that last village we passed just before dusk."

"We're going to spend a really cold and miserable night because there's a chance that he's there. Blood and spit, I could sure enjoy being in a nice dry house this night," Half Root groused. "But what about come morning?"

"Come morning, we're going to let them pass," Fire Cat told them. "They'll be on the river at first light." He gestured around. "We're out of sight, and they'll be expecting us to have traveled ahead, to have made shore at the next village. Not to be back in the forest like this."

"I don't understand," Night Shadow Star said through her shivers. "Eventually Blood Talon will figure out that he's ahead of us. He'll lay a trap. Catch us on his own ground."

"That's the tricky part," Fire Cat agreed, looking around at the others. "But he's a Cahokian warrior. Our advantage is that we have White Mat, Shedding Bird, Mixed Shell, Made Man, and Half Root. Not to mention *Red Reed*."

"Traders," Night Shadow Star filled in. "People who know the river."

"Blood Talon doesn't have a chance." White Mat had a smug smile on his lips as he blew frosty breath into the firelight.

Everyone noticed when Night Shadow Star's shivering shook her whole body. This time she couldn't silence the chattering of her teeth.

"Come on," Made Man told her, offering the first of the catfish. "You first. Eat up. To have come this far, given who you are, and to have done it without so much as a single complaint, you can crew on my boat anytime."

"Seconded," Shedding Bird added solemnly.

The food did help. And she knew they all let her eat the lion's share.

It was later, when the blankets were rolled out and she stared down at the sodden protection they were going to afford her for the night, that the cold and exhaustion finally caught up with her. Blood Talon was out there. She was as cold as she'd ever been. Feeling defeated. Tears finally came.

"You all right?" Fire Cat asked, appearing in the night beside her.

"I don't think I've ever been this cold and miserable."

"Yes, you were. Once."

"When?"

"When I pulled you out of the river after you tried to kill Walking Smoke."

"How did I survive?" But she remembered. His body, atop hers, his warmth driving the cold from her naked flesh.

"Fire Cat . . ." She couldn't finish—not when she'd been possessed by that image, where it led to in her fantasies. How it would feel if she ever had his body against hers again.

"You're safe," he told her as he pulled her into his arms. "Cold as it is tonight? We need to sleep together, share the warmth. Trust me, those thoughts will be the farthest from our minds."

Which was a lie, she knew.

She reached down, took her blanket, and doubled it with his. When he laid himself down, she curled around his back, snuggled close to his warmth as he pulled the doubled blanket around them.

"*Beware,*" Piasa whispered out of the night.

"Oh, go drown a fish," she told the shadowy beast where it paced just beyond the fire's light.

But as she lay there with her body pressed against Fire Cat's, her heart beat hard, a tingle began to warm her loins. Every fiber of her being was throbbing. What if she asked? Would Fire Cat be willing? Was he as acutely aware of her as she of him? Was he, too, lying there with his heart in his throat?

And if he was, he'd never allow it to show. Yet again she cursed his incomprehensible sense of honor.

It would be so easy if he'd just roll over, drag her close, and slip his hand between her thighs. That was all it would take.

But he wouldn't.

So she spent that entire night too uncomfortable to sleep. The rough gravel poked up into her hips, shoulders, and thighs, which left her awake, frustrated, and longing to make love. If there was any consolation, it was that she was marvelously warm the entire time.

Twenty-nine

For the most part Fire Cat could cope with his physical desires. He'd been raised to be a war chief. Uncle had taught him to endure privation of every sort, be it cold, heat, pain, or the ragged edge of physical exhaustion.

He had fallen in love with Night Shadow Star understanding the bitter reality of his situation. He had pledged her his service on his honor and the honor of his ancestors. He was Red Wing—and when one's sacred word was given, that oath bound him until either it was rescinded by the person it was given to, or death.

As it was, he understood that Piasa had forbidden Night Shadow Star and him from ever sharing their bodies, though neither he nor she understood the why of it all. Power had decreed that they live chastely, and somehow that single abstention apparently had saved the city of Cahokia. And supposedly later, it had allowed them to free her brother's soul in the Underworld. Leave it to gods, Spirits, and Power to figure out how that balanced the scales of Cosmic Trade, but apparently it did.

Several times Fire Cat and Night Shadow Star had teetered on the edge, hearts pounding, blood racing, as they held each other and stared into the other's eyes. He'd seen her desire in the parting of her lips, the rising of her breath, the desperation with which she clung to him. Not that she could miss his own protruding arousal where she pressed herself against it. To tear himself away from her had been brutal.

Nevertheless, he lived with the knowledge that at least he got to share his life with her. Was able to watch her, enjoy her smile, and find ample satisfaction in his ability to make her already difficult life easier. Especially in view of her soul possession and the terrible strain it placed on her. That Power had chosen him to serve such a woman he considered a rare honor. That she understood and appreciated his sacrifice? That made any privation worth it.

He had come so close to failing himself and her last night. Had she given him the slightest encouragement, he would have ignored the voice of warning in his head. It had been torture enough to watch her suffering from exhaustion and cold; he'd have given anything to have pulled her close and hugged her to him at the fire. But that would have embarrassed her in front of the Traders. He'd taken risk enough to suggest they share bedding.

And I would have willingly condemned us to who knows what sort of disaster and tragedy. Sacrificed her future, perhaps even her life for a single night of sharing her body.

Fire Cat kept running that thought through his head as he crouched in the brush just back from the bank and kept watch on the river.

Beyond the gray screen of forest on the eastern bank, dawn was a dull gray glow in the east. The morning birds had begun to call, and fish jumped to leave rings out in the river.

Fire Cat fought the urge to shiver; the morning chill seemed worse than last night's, more penetrating, or else it was so deep in his bones it would take days to warm up.

Slipping out of his and Night Shadow Star's bed had been one of the hardest things he'd ever done. He could have spent eternity just being close to her.

The memory brought a smile to his lips.

What a fool a man could be when it came to a woman.

His duty was here, watching. Their lives and success would depend on knowledge and cunning from here on out. The only way to avoid a run-in with Blood Talon was to know where the squadron first was. Understand that, and the key to avoiding him was suddenly feasible.

"He's going to be coming soon," Fire Cat promised himself, checking to see that the breeze was still coming in off the river, that there was no way the smell of their small fire would carry to the Cahokians.

Fire Cat tightened his grip on his war club, hearing a stealthy foot as it rasped in the sumac behind him. He turned his head to see Night Shadow Star as she eased along the creek-side trail. He made room, allowing her a seat on the grass beside him. The patch of wild cherry that screened him from the river was just on the verge of blooming, leaving enough openings that he could see without being seen.

"How are you this morning?" He kept his voice at a whisper. "Feeling better?"

"I'll live," she whispered back, tucking her blanket around her. "I wouldn't have. I had that deep bone-cold chill. By myself, in my wet blankets, I'd have died."

"That might be an overstatement."

"As it was, I was warm. Slept well."

That was a lie, but he smiled at her attempt to put the best face on it that she could.

Then she surprised him. "Actually, it was a hard night. But not from the cold or that unforgiving gravel." She drew a breath. "What are we going to do?"

"Go to Cofitachequi and kill Walking Smoke."

She shook her head sadly. "This is torturing me. I want you as a woman wants a man."

"What does Piasa say to that?"

"He's out there," she gestured aimlessly at the forest. "He knows how I ache to live with you as a normal woman does with the man she loves."

"We paid a price, more than once, you'll recall, to save Cahokia. Doesn't matter that we don't understand the why of it, that's the bargain we made. Power doesn't like it when you break your word."

She glanced sidelong at the forest. "What if I ordered you? Right now. Told you to take me, here, on this little patch of grass?"

He smothered a chuckle. "I swore to serve you, so I'd decline."

"You'd disobey a direct order? You swore that night—"

"I swore I'd serve you without reservation. Violating a promise you gave to Piasa isn't acting in your best interest."

"Wrong. You swore that you'd follow my orders, no matter what they were. I don't remember your memory being so clouded."

"Are we really having this discussion? I am only a servant. You do remember that, don't you? You're the lady, I'm the one who's bound to you."

A saucy glint filled her dark eyes. "I free you. Absolve you of your oath. Now what are you going to do?"

He blinked, lifted an eyebrow. A curious unease filled his chest. "You mean that?"

She nodded sadly, rubbing her shins with nervous hands. "I'm tired, Fire Cat. I hurt all over. I'm afraid of what's going to happen to us up-river, let alone in Cofitachequi if we ever get that far. For the first time in my life, I am no longer Night Shadow Star, only a lone woman without station or privilege. Blood Talon is out here somewhere ready to kill you and the others and take me back."

She took a breath. "I'm possessed by voices telling me terrible things. I see flickers of light. Bits of movement that aren't there when I look twice. I don't know who I am anymore. I'm . . . I'm scared."

He reached out, laid his arm around her shoulders, and pulled her close. "Then it's no time to be making the kind of decisions you can't take back."

"In Cahokia, everything was . . . how do I say this? Familiar? Comfortable? Established? I knew who I was, what I had to do, and who I had to be."

"Ah, I see."

"Do you?"

"I've been there, remember? War chief to bound servant in the space of a single turning of the moon. One minute I'm a noble war chief, a hero, the next my wives are enslaved and my children are dead, my world conquered, and I'm oath-bound to serve a people I hate. Unlike your journey now, I spent that journey bound, in the bottom of a canoe, weeping."

She smiled wearily, her eyes losing their focus as they did when Piasa was talking in her ear.

When her expression cleared, she said, "Are you always so wise and courageous?"

"No. Remember when we began our journey to the Underworld in the Spirit Cave? I was a shivering, frightened wreck. Too terrified to move. I would have died there, consumed by my fear. You were like a pillar of stone, unwavering and strong."

"You were just in a place where you didn't understand the rules. In the end, you saved us all."

"And now the roles are reversed, that's all. For once in your life, you're cast loose without roots. You're cold, physically exhausted, in a totally unknown place, on a strange river, and you've just discovered the hunters are hard on your trail."

"So, let's run."

"Everyone has doubts in their moments of trial, Lady. For the moment you don't think you know who you are, but you will find that solid core again, and be all the stronger for it. Meanwhile, take the moment, live as someone besides yourself for once. Trust me on this."

She nodded, and he thought he could feel the resolve building inside her again.

She glanced at him. "I meant it. You are free. I take back your oath of service."

He tried to exhale around the sudden tension in his chest. "Let us see where the future takes us, Lady. For absolving me of my oath, I deeply and sincerely thank you. But for now, let it be our secret."

"Why?"

"Because while it might not have consequences here, it would anywhere else. What would they say in Cahokia? He's free, yet he still lives in her palace, orders her household staff around, stomps around behind her like her personal servant in his armor. Or do you wish me to remove myself from your life?"

"Yes, I see. Very well, we . . ."

He gestured for silence, withdrew his arm, and leaned forward.

It was the sound that tipped him off: soft voices carrying over the water, then the hollow thunk of a paddle on a canoe gunwale. The morning had brightened to the point that the leaden reflection off the water had turned silver where the current eddied and flowed.

He caught the first movement, watched as the war canoe's shape formed behind the mat of cherry stems and branches. The warriors were bent to the paddles, all stroking in unison as the sleek war canoe cut water like some mythical predator. The craft slipped cleanly past as it sliced crisp Vs of wake. The hull's bright red color looked dull in the predawn light.

For a moment, Fire Cat considered pulling up his bow, standing, and taking a shot. Blood Talon was passing no more than twenty paces away. With a single arrow, he could kill the squadron first. Pull a second and kill Nutcracker as the man stumbled to his feet in surprise.

After that, the rest of the warriors would be in a panic. As Fire Cat's arrows took them one by one, they'd break, turn, paddle like the Spirit-possessed to get out of range.

More than enough time to gather the Traders and slip away into the forest.

As if she shared his thoughts, Night Shadow Star's hand reached out, settled on his arm.

She barely whispered, "Piasa says 'Don't do it.'"

"It would solve so many problems, Lady."

By then it was too late. The canoe had moved on.

Night Shadow Star exhaled wearily, staring empty-eyed off to the side. "You had better be right, Lord. I'm unhappy enough with this whole situation."

Fire Cat made a face, really uncomfortable with the tone in her voice as she said, "I give you this, you give me something in return."

She cocked her head, shot a questioning glance to one side, and said, "That woman isn't here. This woman is, and she will make new terms." A pause. "I will kill him."

"What just happened here?"

"Hush, I'm bargaining," she told him.

"About what?"

"I'll know that when I finally make the bargain."

"Great." A person could never tell when it came to Power.

Blood Talon should be so lucky.

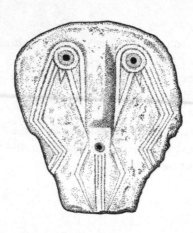

On the Trail

I love this country. I am carried along what's called The War Path between Cofitachequi and Joara. It's an old route, used by Traders, travelers, war parties, and peace embassies for generations. In places the path is worn into the ground, in others it winds around sections where the rut grew too deep. Here and there it now makes detours around the corpses of huge fallen trees.

I love this forest, given that it's filled with huge flocks of passenger pigeons that feed on the towering mulberry trees, the flocks of turkeys, the wary black bears, and the colorful tribes of parakeets. Topping a low ridge, we pass beneath the first great chestnut tree, its branches laden with flowers that—now at the end of their lives—drop a rain of petals upon us.

I can stare up by the hand of time as I am carried west through the vast immensity of forest. I never tire of the remarkable height. In some places, the lowest of the mighty branches are almost a bowshot above my head. The boles of the great black oak, hickory, ash, elms, and maples are so large a person could hollow them out to make a reasonable dwelling, provided he cared to invest the labor.

And then there are the vines, giant grapes, greenbrier, walking stick, honeysuckle, the list goes on. All of them, as ageless as the trees that support them. Huge, they twine up the bark, or hang free, like ropes for the gods dropped from high in the Sky World.

And up in those trees? A hundred hundred birds call, flit through the shadows, and dart from branch to branch. The squirrels mock us from above, barely visible as tiny darting shapes, so far are they above our heads.

The forest floor that we cross is knotted in places by great roots that trace lightning patterns across the ground. The leaf mat is thick, as deep as my arm where I tried to dig down through the black, molding compost. It gives the air a curious pungency that mixes with the scent of verdure and aerial flowers that floats down from above.

I don't think I've ever known such forest. Even in the southern nations that surround the lower Father Water.

Here I am surrounded by a massive pulsing of life, as if the forest transpires an eternal Spirit that echoes the Beginning Times.

While I am carried away in poetic rapture, my porters are as skittish as barefoot Dancers in a storage cist full of water moccasins.

Last night an owl hooted. If I hadn't already been on my feet and close to their fire, the whole lot of them might have bolted into the night before I could stop them.

My bellowed "Don't you dare run!" barely held them in place. I had to stalk into the light of their fire and pin them, one by one, with my glare and threaten to maim their souls if they ever showed such cowardice again.

You see, I took something from each of them: a lock of hair, a bit of cloth, a personal token. Took it with the admonition that if they didn't get me to Joara, I would wreak my revenge on their souls through that item. That they couldn't run, couldn't hide, and certainly couldn't protect themselves as long as I held that Spiritual link to them.

Needless to say, we make excellent time on the trail. Not a single one of them cares to linger even a moment longer than need be to get me to Joara.

And I must get to Joara.

Night Shadow Star is coming. The lightning has told me.

Thirty

If Seven Skull Shield had a weakness, it was Farts. Cahokia was lousy with dogs. Big dogs, little dogs, pack dogs, hairy dogs, dogs of all colors, they were everywhere. Some, like the big pack dogs, were prized bearers of burdens. Others, like the little dogs, were kept by families for their company. Some were bred specifically for the stewpot, and others were handy to have around as trash disposal to keep the garbage, old bones, and discarded food from piling up and drawing flies.

Had anyone asked Seven Skull Shield to explain his relationship with Farts, he'd have been hard-pressed. He told people, truthfully, that Farts was a Spirit Dog. A gift from Power. And in the past, Farts had kept him company during some of his most memorable adventures.

But above and beyond that, Farts had saved Seven Skull Shield's life. On numerous occasions. A man didn't forget a thing like that. Well, some men did, men not being the brightest of creatures, after all. But not Seven Skull Shield.

All of which made Farts something of a problem for the moment. For most of his life, Seven Skull Shield had made a habit of not being noticed. That was one of the prerequisites of being a thief. Thieves who got noticed got killed. A really simple relationship when one got right down to it.

In the matter of a moon's time, Seven Skull Shield had become what he always loathed: noticed. It hadn't been so bad when he was skulking along in the Keeper's shadow. After all, he could always just slip away, vanish into Cahokia's hidden nooks and crannies. Live off what he could stick in his belt pouch when no one was looking, perhaps beguile a warm bed from some young woman whose husband was off hunting or Trading. Then he'd move on. Catch a ride across the river to Evening Star Town, or perhaps down to Horned Serpent Town where he could renew old acquaintances, Trade for a warm spot by the fire in one workshop or another.

All that had been before Night Shadow Star had sent him up to deliver her message to the Morning Star. Before he'd made a mockery of Spotted Wrist, and more or less thrown it all in Rising Flame's face in front of half the nobles in Cahokia.

The only reason he was still alive was that he'd been painted up, dressed like a lord, and looked nothing like he usually looked. For that reason, like today, he could pack a bundle of sticks over his shoulder and pass for a dirt farmer carrying a load of firewood. Like this, he could march right past Spotted Wrist's warriors, as he'd just done, without a sideways glance.

Robin Feather, however, posed another problem. He was looking for that same old Seven Skull Shield everyone knew. The one dressed in a hemp-fiber hunting shirt who wandered around among the common folk with a big, thick-boned brindle dog. Worse, a special dog with floppy ears, a bearlike snout, and odd brown and blue eyes.

A dog that looked just like the one pacing at Seven Skull Shield's side, its tongue lolling out, nose working as it sniffed at every cook fire in every farmstead they passed.

"So, what do I do with you?" Seven Skull Shield asked. "That wooden-brained Robin Feather has now raised his offer to two coils of basswood rope. He has half of River Mounds looking for us."

Seven Skull Shield averted his face as a group of Panther Clan warriors with the traditional four-pointed star emblem of North Star House came clattering past, their shields over their shoulders. They barely spared him a look, their attention on the story the one who waved his arms about was telling.

"And that's another problem. You heard what that thatch Trader said at the plaza? Slender Fox has been in a rage. See, that's the thing. Now, you and me? We get caught in compromising positions all the time. Granted, not while we're sticking the old plug in our sisters, but you get my point here. We've got the ability to laugh it off. That woman I saw huddled down under the blanket with her brother? She's not the kind to just let it go. These Four Winds nobles are a bit finicky about things like that."

Farts glanced up, his tail slashing back and forth in time to his pace.

"I heard that first thing, when the household staff arrived the following morning, they found all the cooking pots smashed on the ground in front of the palace. Had to go find replacements. Which made breakfast late. Word is that enraged the matron even more. And when Wolverine heard about the food being shipped to Evening Star Town, he left the *tonka'tzi*'s at a run. That when he got to Serpent Woman Town, he and Slender Fox got into a downright brawl over it."

Seven Skull Shield turned off the Avenue of the Sun, fixed the widest and stupidest smile on his face that he could, and slightly crossed his eyes as he bobbed a nod in the direction of Spotted Wrist's supposedly unobtrusive warriors. The two men were still standing at the corner of the Morning Star's mound where they could keep an eye on Night Shadow Star's palace on the off chance that the notorious Seven Skull Shield might appear on the steps and announce himself.

They ignored him.

Seven Skull Shield sighed, plodded on down to where one of the warriors Fire Claw had assigned to guard Blue Heron's mound now stood. Seven Skull Shield wasn't familiar with this one. A completely new face.

"Got firewood for the Keeper. Um, ex-Keeper. Uh, you know, the Lady Blue Heron."

"Go. But not past the veranda. And show a little respect. You dirt farmers need to mind your place. And keep that dog away from the guardian posts. He pees on them, it'll be the last thing he does."

Of course, Farts had peed on them so many times already that Blue Heron had thrown her hands up in despair, calling on Sky Eagle and Falcon to wreak their revenge on the beast as they would.

To Seven Skull Shield's amusement, the Sky gods must not have cared. Farts remained hale, hearty, and unconcerned that he might be struck down at any moment by an enraged Sky Spirit. A fact that continued to irritate Blue Heron to no end. Where were the Spirits when you really needed them?

Seven Skull Shield looked back as they topped the stairs. The guard had turned his attention to the avenue; he completely missed seeing Farts pee on the base of Sky Eagle's post.

At the veranda, Seven Skull Shield dropped his load of sticks and sauntered into the palace great room. Smooth Pebble fussed over a pot of hominy that steamed by the fire. She glanced up, eyes narrowing. "If that foul creature takes so much as a sniff of this, I'm beating him with a cudgel!"

"Farts, maybe you better sit and stay." Seven Skull Shield pointed to a blanket beside the door. Then, as a way of making amends, he reached out a crusted half loaf of goosefoot bread and tossed it to the dog. Farts caught it in midair, the mighty jaws shearing the dried bread into gulpable hunks.

"Keeper?" Smooth Pebble called. "The thief's here. Miracle of miracles, he came in the front door in the middle of the day for once."

Blue Heron appeared in the doorway to her personal quarters. Her eyes had a puffy look, her hair mussed on one side. She wore a simple white skirt embroidered with the Four Winds spirals. A cape made of twisted strips of rabbit hide hung from her shoulders.

"What news, thief?" she asked as she stepped to her litter where it rested atop the dais behind the fire.

Seven Skull Shield snagged a cup, barely missed his stride as he scooped it full of hominy from Smooth Pebble's pot, and seated himself at the foot of Blue Heron's dais. "Just got back from the canoe landing. There's a whole string of hulls being paddled down from the north. Slender Fox didn't cancel the order. She's delivering. As to how much or for how long? That remains to be seen."

Blue Heron, looking tired, took a deep breath. "Well, at least there's that. How did you know? About Slender Fox and Sliding Ice, I mean?"

"I think her name was See Through-Leaf. She was a Snapping Turtle Clan woman. Married to that Go Throw. She was—"

"Down in Horned Serpent Town. Go Throw. I remember him. He's a cousin to Green Chunkey. Banished him for making trouble about six, seven years back. But what does See-Through-Leaf have to do with . . . Oh, don't tell me. You didn't. Not a woman married to a Four Winds Clansman."

"She was lonely. Go Throw was carried away with some sort of nonsense involving a couple of the Earth Clans chiefs who served his House. Figured they were going to get rid of Green Chunkey. Man really shouldn't leave a ripe young woman like that alone for such a long—"

"Would you get to the point?"

"One of the slaves started to get suspicious, went to Go Throw, so, of course, I got as far away as I could."

"Which meant Serpent Woman Town."

"My real interest was the Men's House. They had this wooden box they were keeping scalps in. Would have been worth a fortune at the canoe landing. A Pacaha Trader would have—"

"The point?"

"It was the middle of the night. I'm keeping watch, waiting for the right opportunity, and I see this girl come sneaking out of the palace. You know, Many Bows was still high chief up there then. And it's not but a hundred heartbeats later, this boy comes sneaking out with a blanket. They slip over to the shadows behind Old-Woman-Who-Never-Dies' temple, shuck off their clothes, and he's between her legs faster than spit.

"I sneak close and listen in, hearing, 'Try this. No, move like this.' And, 'That's really good, brother.'

"This goes on for maybe a hand of time, and he says, 'We've got to get back. If Father finds our beds empty, we're dead.' And they dress, and one by one, sneak back to the palace."

"And you've been sitting on this for all these years?"

"Me? Sitting? It's common knowledge among the house slaves and the, um, lower sorts that frequent Serpent Woman Town."

He made a tsking sound with his lips. "And you, with all your fancy spies, have to learn this from me?"

"Guess I don't know everything."

"Not nearly as much as the people who empty the chamber pots, that's for sure. But, getting back to it, I heard that Wolverine was bringing the entire household to Cahokia. Thought we might get lucky. We did."

"Let's hope they don't figure out who it was caught them in the act. They do? It'll mean blood. Me, I've got to be up at the Council House. The last bird to fall is Horned Serpent Town. Robin Wing is supposed to be there. If I can shame her into it, belittle her in front of the others, I think she'll cave and make the order."

"And if she doesn't?"

"Columella could still lose everything."

Thirty-one

*R*ed Reed may not have made its best time ever up the Tenasee that day, but the pace was definitely easier on the paddlers. Instead of a race, their progress was now a matter of stealth.

Each sinuous curve of the river had to be scouted out to ensure that Blood Talon's war canoe wasn't lying in wait just out of sight around the bend.

They queried each passing canoe, asking the locals if they'd seen the Cahokian warriors. In the beginning, most everyone had. As the day wore on, fewer people reported a sighting, and those who did claimed it had been several hands of time since the big canoe had raced south, headed upstream.

Not that such reports could be taken for granted. Before approaching each village, they had to ascertain if the war canoe lurked at the landing. If, perhaps, Blood Talon had somehow determined his quarry was now behind him and was lying in ambush.

If he had, at least he and his warriors could rest in the process. They'd be fresh when they sprang their trap, capable of running *Red Reed*'s tired paddlers to ground.

Fire Cat felt his own fatigue, could see it in the eyes and posture of his companions. They looked haggard, their eyes swollen, backs sagging. Solid folk, these Yuchi. They'd been pushed as hard as the toughest warriors, and never muttered a complaint. Part of that, he suspected, was because of Night Shadow Star. If a highborn noble like her could take it, day in and day out, they must have figured that they, seasoned river Traders, had to prove themselves even tougher.

Looking at Night Shadow Star, he could see her exhaustion; it lay in the flat-eyed and hollow stare, her slumped shoulders, and the clumsy strokes she now made with the paddle. How long before she just plain collapsed? And worse, she'd spent half the day mumbling, answering the voices she heard in her head. She'd start, glancing uneasily, obviously seeing things the rest of them didn't.

The Yuchi were on the verge of bolting. Fire Cat himself was getting antsy.

"You really think this is necessary?" Half Root asked as they paused in a backwater and peered through a screen of arrowwood and haw before attempting to pass a small village set back from the river.

"No," Fire Cat told her, "but we can only be wrong once. Want to take that chance?"

She'd given him a quizzical smile, arched an eyebrow. When they determined no war canoe was beached among the local dugouts, they broke cover to resume their progress. Took them right by the village as they skirted the current's pull.

No one was complaining about the slow pace. Maybe they were all close to folding.

"How long do you think it's going to take Blood Talon to figure out that we're behind him?" Night Shadow Star asked as they slipped across the shallows inside a loop of the current.

The river here was straighter, its banks restricted by elevated bluffs that had closed in and entrenched the Tenasee's channel. The thick forest that covered the highlands displayed the first fuzz of light green while the darker cones of cedar and the occasional pine could be seen scattered among the oaks, maples, elms, and hickory trees.

"Couple of days would be my guess," Fire Cat decided. "He knows his warriors can make better time upriver. And he's going to be asking every canoe he passes if they've seen us. He might even spend the time to send someone ashore at the likely villages where we might stop. Check to see if we'd been there. But eventually it's going to be clear to him that we've slipped behind him or taken off overland."

"And then what?" White Mat asked from the bow. He'd been carefully plotting their course along the shallows.

"He has several possible choices. He can stop, wait, and lay a trap for us. Probably at one of the narrows where the bluffs close in to create a choke point. The chances of that working will depend on how well we play the game. Our advantage is that you know the river, know the likely places he would lay an ambush. If we're clever, we'll discover it and figure out a way to get past him. Maybe in the middle of the night. Maybe a portage around the choke point."

"Here, on the lower Tenasee, there are only a couple of places. If he's waiting in ambush for any length of time, it will be the talk of the river among the locals. We should have lots of warning." White Mat slapped at a persistent fly that was enjoying the warm day.

"The real choke point," Shedding Bird added, "is up at the Mussel Shallows, but that's still days ahead of us around the Great Bend. That's a tough passage, depending on the water. In flood it's possible to tow the canoe up without much difficulty. If the river's low, running fast over the rocks and rapids, we can help you hire local Yuchi to portage the Trade and canoe. You'll have to walk around. Or you can make camp in our town and wait in hopes the river rises."

"Worry about that when we get there," Made Man muttered. "If we get there."

Fire Cat kept a wary eye on the river ahead as he paddled. "Another option is that Blood Talon will turn around, head back downriver in the hopes that he'll catch us out in the open before we spot him and can hide *Red Reed*. If he can just get eyes on us, it will all be over. But his decision to charge back downriver comes with its own risk: We might have decided the smart move is to camp up some tributary, wait him out."

"In which case he'll shoot right past our hiding place and travel who knows how far back downriver before he figures out that he's lost us for good," Made Man said.

"Finding a place to hide? I'm not sure that's a bad idea," Night Shadow Star told him. "The longer he goes without word of us, the more uncertain he's going to be. If it's a quarter moon or more, what's he going to think? If we're lucky, he'll decide that we turned around and fled back downriver to avoid capture."

Fire Cat took another stroke with his paddle, eyes still on the water ahead, afraid that the war canoe was going to pop into sight at any moment.

"You're right. The longer we're missing, the more he's going to fret and start second-guessing himself. The more his warriors are going to grouse as they give up ground they worked hard to paddle up. And he's still going to be asking about us as he heads back downstream. Someone's going to tell him they've seen us. The river's just too busy, too many villages, all these people drifting around fishing, diving for clams, checking fish traps and weirs."

"So, do you think we should go to ground?" Shedding Bird asked from his position up front beside his brother.

"Do you know of someplace where we could just disappear?" Fire Cat asked. "Some camp up one of the rivers? Maybe a small village where we could hide *Red Reed*? Stay out of sight for a while?"

"I do, but not right along this section. We're entering Casquinampo lands. They're still irritated and thorny over Cahokia establishing Canebrake Town at the mouth of the Sand River. That Cahokia has placed a colony on the northern boundaries of their territory, and another down south at Red Bluff Town, festers and is a source of resentment."

Night Shadow Star paddled thoughtfully. "It would be in their best interest to just accept it and get on with their lives."

"It's having to accept it that really chafes in their gullets, Lady. They know they could call up their squadrons and drive the Cahokians out any time they wished, but if they did, the massed might of Cahokia would come crashing down on their heads like a hail of boulders."

"Maybe we could be lucky enough that the Casquinampo will take their frustration out on Blood Talon." Fire Cat kept the rhythm as White Mat steered them just out from a screen of waterlogged brush.

"River's rising," the Trader said as he indicated a clutter of driftwood that broke loose from the haw and willows. "That works in our benefit. Easier to duck out of sight in the brush. Low water means we're exposed on the bank with nowhere to go unless there's a creek mouth handy."

"So, you're telling me that Blood Talon only has two options?" Half Root asked. "He can either stop and wait for us to catch up, or come looking."

"He also knows where we're going," Fire Cat told her. "That's his third choice. If he assumes he's lost us on the Tenasee, his only hope is to try and relocate us either on the way to Cofitachequi—maybe at these Mussel Shallows you talk about—or, as a last resort, try to intercept us in Cofitachequi. He knows we're after Walking Smoke."

"Long way to go just to catch the lady." Shedding Bird shook his head as he paddled. "Think he'd travel all that way?"

"He would," Night Shadow Star replied.

"That's crazy. Chase a woman halfway across the world? Especially when he's got no proof she's really going to go that far." Mixed Shell shook his head in disbelief.

"I am going that far, because I gave my word," Night Shadow Star told him. "And Blood Talon will because Spotted Wrist ordered him to."

"Duty, honor, strength," Fire Cat repeated. "Those are the tenets of Cahokia's Four Winds squadrons. They could add obedience to the list. Once they've been given an order they don't back off." He smiled wryly. "That's a weakness they have if you know how to exploit it."

Night Shadow Star gave him a sidelong knowing glance. She, of course, knew that he'd used it against Makes Three when he thought he was attacking massed warriors outside the walls of Red Wing Town. In reality Fire Cat had hidden his squadrons in the cornfields on either side of the broad trail leading out of the forest. His first objective when he sprang the jaws of his trap had been to take out the leadership. With Makes Three mortally wounded and the squadron leaders cut down, the Cahokians had stood and fought, caught in a crossfire of arrows. Then Red Wing warriors hit them from both sides until the crushed remnants had fled in disarray, running like rabbits all the way back to Cahokia.

"That tenacity, Red Wing," she reminded, "is why Cahokia will eventually conquer the whole world."

"Not to mention having the living god on their side," Made Man said with soft reverence. "How can anyone stand against the Power of the Sky World brought to earth?"

Fire Cat took a breath, studied the forest-covered bluffs that rose beyond the narrow band of floodplain. Spring green was in evidence in the grass, the first buds, and canebrakes. Figured he'd be better off not mentioning his belief that the whole "Morning-Star-the-living-god" thing was just an elaborate hoax that even the Four Winds Clan had talked themselves into believing.

"The strength of their military is only half of the genius that makes Cahokia great," White Mat said from up front. "Wherever they put up a colony, they build a temple, bring in priests, build chunkey grounds. Then they start preaching to the local farmers and hunters. My grandfather at Mussel Shallows remembers the first Cahokians who settled at Good Clay Town. They looked like they'd just dropped from the Sky World to earth with their feathered cloaks, masks, and finely dyed clothes. I was a boy when we buried grandfather in the clan mound. He'd been given a wooden Morning Star pendant by the priests when they finished building the first temple. He'd worn the paint off it, rubbed it with his thumb and fingers until the grain stood out. We placed it on his chest when we laid him in his grave so it would help carry his soul to the Sky World."

"Things have been good since the Cahokians came," Half Root agreed. "We still hear about the days before the priests came with stories of the resurrected god. What the Tenasee was like before the Cahokians."

"What do they say?" Night Shadow Star blinked, yawned, as if struggling to stay awake.

"Mostly good," Half Root told her. "Cahokia brought peace to the river, established the Power of Trade in a way that was only talked about in legend. The elders tell of the constant wars, endless raiding. In those days, they say, every town on the Tenasee was fortified with a palisade, the farms were all close by the town walls. Half the young men were relegated to the forest as scouts to raise the alarm before a raiding party could strike. They needed to buy enough time so the people could grab their weapons and defend themselves."

"Since the coming of the Cahokians," Mixed Shell said, "people have extended their farms, can travel farther afield hunting and collecting. They get a lot more use from their territory if everyone is carrying a bag during the nut harvest instead of a shield and war club."

"We're all richer," Shedding Bird agreed. "It's remarkable how much a people can flourish when they're able to farm, to hunt, and have children instead of bury them. Not being killed by one's neighbors has a lot to be said for it."

"We wouldn't be able to be Traders like we are now," Half Root added. "And even if we were, we'd never have been able to go to all the places we've been, let alone gone in safety."

"And they said Black Tail was crazy," Night Shadow Star whispered under her breath.

Fire Cat rocked his jaw, thinking back to the way he'd grown up. Life had had a very different feel when it was Red Wing Town that stood out as the target of Cahokia's wrath.

All those people, my family, my children. All dead now. Butchered and discarded.

Was that the price that had to be paid for the rest of the world to have peace? Even if it was at the point of a Cahokian lance?

As with everything else in Fire Cat's life, it always came back to that cosmic equation. For one people to have good things, another must be crushed and destroyed.

The white Power and the red, always teetering in the balance.

He glanced again at Night Shadow Star, remembering the ache in his loins as she'd pressed herself against his back under their shared blankets.

Yes. I would give the entire world in return for her.

Not to mention that she'd freed him from his obligation to serve her. That fact had been stuck sideways down between his souls. A sense of exultation on one hand, a curious unease on the other. He was free. He could go where he would, do as he pleased. Find a new life. But to what point? Anything he attempted would be as hollow as a rotted log without Night Shadow Star.

Somewhere along the line, he had bound himself unequivocally to her. Fallen in love with her despite her possession by Piasa and her scary reliance on the Underworld. That she so often sacrificed herself for her people had left him humbled and amazed. That she could be a stone-hard pillar of strength at the same time she was ultimately fragile and wounded left him in awe.

She was a woman worthy of any man's heart and faith. That she chose him filled him with pride. That she had freed him—no doubt to Piasa's displeasure? For that he would remain indebted to her for the rest of his life.

"Notice the water?" White Mat asked, using his paddle to point out the clearer water running closer to the shore.

"I do," Fire Cat said, his reverie broken.

"Sand River," White Mat told him. "It just occurred to me. We could take it, travel a short distance up its channel. There's a Casquinampo town, old fields that were abandoned when the Cahokians built Canebrake Town just above the Sand River's mouth. Assuming that no one from Canebrake Town observes our passage or finds it remarkable, that might be a place we could stay out of sight for a couple of days."

Fire Cat glanced at Night Shadow Star. "What do you think?"

She nodded, a vacancy behind her eyes as Piasa whispered something for her hearing alone. That or she was just so tired she didn't care.

"Let's do it." She smiled absently. "We're all exhausted, Red Wing. We've been pushing ourselves for days. If nothing else, Blood Talon can capture us rested and refreshed."

It would mean that for the time being, like Blood Talon, he was gambling. That he could guess when the squadron first would reach the limits of his patience. Unlike Fire Cat and Night Shadow Star's situation, time wasn't on Blood Talon's side.

We're in the same quandary he is: guessing.

But who knew, maybe for once on this trip, Piasa would finally decide to give Night Shadow Star some clue as to when and how to move.

Which was just as frightening as the alternative.

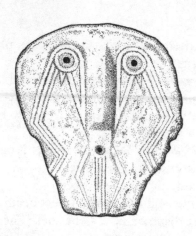

Joara

The town sits on the banks of Joara Creek—a small stream that runs down from the high mountain pass that leads across the Blue Mountains. It's a major Trading trail, a route that leads to one of the major tributaries of the Tenasee River.

The surrounding terrain is mixed, low ridges rise above fertile alluvial valleys, an area just east of the mountains where several creeks flow into the headwaters of the Cofitachequi River. It's rich country, forested with mature chestnut, mulberry, hickory, walnut, several varieties of acorn, hazelnut, pawpaw, chinquapin, grapes, berries of all kinds, maygrass, little barley, and soil that will grow just about anything a family might want to plant.

It was here that Moon Blade established his headquarters when he first invaded Cofitachequi. Strategically located, the site itself has ample agricultural land, doesn't flood like the lower areas, but still allows control of the Trade route leading to the divide and across to the Wide Fast River.

The day I arrive is sunny and hot—that sapping muggy summer heat that slicks the skin with sweat, and where, if a person makes a fist, he almost squeezes water from the very air. Even the birds had gone quiet for the most part, and the squirrels had retreated to the high shadows to pant in misery. Only the idiot insects seemed to be thriving, chirring, buzzing, and flitting about in the heavy and baking air.

My sweating, staggering porters flounder their way across the Joara ford, labor their way up the bank, past a line of crude dugout canoes, past the wilted-

looking ramadas where people fan themselves in the shade and barely wave a greeting.

The town itself stretches east-west along the terrace on the south side of the creek. A low mound has been raised on the eastern end atop which Moon Blade built the peak-pitched palace overlooking the feeble excuse of a plaza. The palace is now occupied by his second son, Sharp Path, who was born of a Muskogee woman called Mica. The small plaza, with chunkey courts, World Tree pole of red cedar, and remarkably confined stickball ground, was surrounded by a Men's House, Women's House, a couple of Clan Houses, and on the other end, a temple dedicated to Old-Woman-Who-Never-Dies.

Behind them I can see a haphazard collection of both bent-pole and trench-wall houses, mud-daubed, their peaked roofs either grass-thatched, cattail-thatched, or made from split cane.

Given the heat, people are outside, living in the attached ramadas, or what they call summer houses. Granaries in Joara are the southern type, elevated high off the ground on four tall poles, the floors and sides made of interlaced branches that allow air to circulate and roofed with thatch or bark to shed rain.

In the background, beyond the forest, I can see the high, flat-topped mountain, and know that beyond that rises the bulk of the Blue Mountains. Not that they really are blue, mind you; the thick forests that cover them are all shades of green, but when seen from any kind of distance they appear shrouded in blue misty air.

I am carried summarily to the flat in front of the Mikko's palace and carefully lowered to the ground. My porters step back as if a water moccasin is riding on the litter with me. Now they watch me, wide-eyed, as I stand, stretch, and take my bearings.

"Master," one asks. "If it wouldn't be taken wrong. Might we have our talismans?"

I consider, narrow an eye, which, if anything, makes the poor fool sweat even more. After just enough hesitation to rattle him to the bones, I toss him the sack in which I'd kept their personal items.

He snatches it out of the air, opens the drawstring with shaking fingers, and peers inside. "It's here."

They don't even take the time to divvy up their bits and pieces, but leave at a run. I watch them pelt past the ramadas. Don't even look back as they splash across the ford and disappear into the forest.

I would have thought they'd at least have found a meal, perhaps rested for a day or two. But then, who knows? Maybe there is something about the food in Joara?

"Who comes?" a voice asks behind me in rudely accented Muskogee.

I turn, see a young man dressed as a Cahokian lord. I place him as being *close to thirty, and he moves with that athletic grace of a stickball player—complete with the scars to prove it marking his tanned and sweat-gleaming skin. He has that arrogant look to go along with his Four Winds Clan tattoos.*

Something about that square face, the set of the jaw . . . Oh yes, now I recognize him: my cousin Fire Light. Out of Slick Rock's lineage. Takes Blood and Eel Woman's oldest son. As boys we used to practice chunkey and stickball.

I should wonder why he is here in Joara, but I'm sure I know the story. He was always a bitter young man, chafed at the fact that he wasn't part of the privileged side of the family. As if, being a parallel cousin, he wasn't one of the most important young men in the city. My bet? He made a play for the tonka'tzi's chair, or involved himself in some other disruptive political shenanigans, and got himself exiled.

I study him thoughtfully.

Of course, he doesn't recognize me. Not with the left side of my face ruined and scarred. His gaze is locked first on the damage, and then he takes in my light cloak, more of a net fabric woven from hanging moss, and the wrap of airy fabric at my waist.

Beyond lies the litter, my box and basket. He glances around, as if in search of the porters, and then, puzzled, back at my twisted smile.

I can see it as he places who I am. The frost of recognition cools behind his eyes, but I give him credit. He doesn't slowly back up the low stairway to the safety of the palace mound.

"*Greetings, Lord,*" *I tell him in Cahokian.* "*Have you a place where I can stay? I'd suggest the Clan House, such as it is. Don't worry about moving the others out. For reasons that elude me, people seem to shun my presence. Not sure why, I wash with great regularity.*"

"*Lightning Shell. What are you doing here, witch?*"

"*I have business. Power is afoot in the land. Trouble comes this way.*"

"*Do I know you? Something about . . . ?*"

"*Does anyone really know anyone else? Well, except for when you can slip your soul into another person's body. Listen to their deepest, most secret thoughts?*"

This time he does take a step back, heel striking the bottom stair. I can see the worry growing behind his eyes.

"*Oh, relax, Fire Light. I'm not here for you. I'm laying my trap for another. And there's plenty of time. Even for you. I can help you, you know.*"

"*Help? Me? How?*"

"*I can give you what you want more than anything else.*"

"*What's that?*"

"*A way out of this desolate end of the world. A way back to Cahokia, back to the warm embrace of the Four Winds Clan.*"

"*How did you know I was Fire Light?*"

"*I know a great many things. Especially the hidden and secret ways of the heart. For instance, you've known for a moon now that your sister, Rising Flame, is the Four Winds Clan matron. And why are you here, in Joara? Because you've been waiting for a messenger who has never come. Irritated, tortured, you twist in your blankets at night, wondering why she hasn't lifted your ban, sent for you to come paddling back to Cahokia as fast as the rivers can carry you.*"

Center strike! I can see the truth of my words in the familiar tightening of his eyes, that pinching at the corner of his mouth.

Oh yes, I know you, cousin.

"*You, a witch, can get me home?*"

"*What is the control of Power good for if you can't use it?*" *I give him a lopsided grin, which is all I'm allowed given the scar tissue around my mouth. Then I add,* "*What would you give to go home? Take your place at the side of Morning Star's high chair?*"

I'll say this for Fire Light. He's a lot more careful than he was in his youth. Maybe the exile has been good for him, taught him to think things through.

"*Anything!*"

On the other hand, maybe it hasn't.

"*I need someone to carry these things to the Clan House. After that, I need food, some sassafras tea, water to wash with.*"

"*I will have to get the* orata's *approval. He is currently—*"

"*Sharp Path is a smart man. He will have no objection. And if he does . . . Well, that's silly. Like I said, he's a smart man.*"

With that, I turn on my heel, take two steps toward the Clan House where it sits diagonally across the plaza. Then I turn back.

Fire Light hasn't moved.

I tell him, "*Come tonight. After dark. There are some things I will need. If you can procure them, I would be most grateful.*"

"*Things? Like what?*"

"*A little girl. Two would be better.*"

I see the color drain from his face.

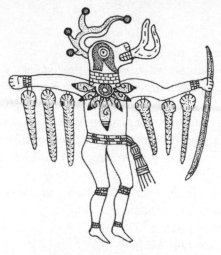

Thirty-two

I'm getting too old for this. The notion kept rolling around in Blue Heron's head as she climbed the stairs to the Council House Gate. The wind whipped at her cloak. Tried to topple her off the squared-log steps set into the ramp. Above her, Morning Star's great mound, topped with its steep-roofed palace, soared against the sky.

She stopped at the top. Nodded to the guards who monitored the Council House Gate, then turned her attention to the Great Plaza where men were practicing on the chunkey courts, flinging lances after the rolling stones. A pickup game of stickball was being played on the other side of the tall World Tree pole in the plaza's center. Around it, vendors had set up stalls, booths, or spread blankets to hawk their wares. At this time of year there weren't as many of them. Gaps could be seen between the various potters, weavers, meat vendors, and Traders.

She sighed, rubbed her hip, and entered the gate. A scattering of people stood around in knots before the Council House door: lesser nobility, personal servants, and the like. Partially sheltered from the wind by the palisade wall and the bulk of the Council House, they were trying to reap whatever benefit could be had of the post-equinox sun where it peeked through the clouds.

Blue Heron made her way to the doorway, nodded at the warrior who stood guard there, and entered.

Immediately the warmth bathed her cold face, made her grin with relief. People nodded, called greetings, and stepped aside as she crossed the matting, passed the fire, and made her way to the rear of the room where Wind, seated on her litter, was talking to one of the recorders. Matron Robin Wing stood behind her. Arms crossed, face stiff and flinty, as if in distaste.

The recorder, a man in his early forties, had a long string of variously sized, colored, and shaped beads. These he was running through his fingers, reading off, ". . . seven hundred and fifty-seven standard baskets of corn, one hundred and ninety-five standard baskets of goosefoot seed, one hundred and fifty-three standard baskets of dried lotus root, two hundred and ten standard baskets of dried acorns, three hundred and twelve standard baskets of hickory nuts . . ." on and on until he reached the last of the beads.

"Quite a haul," Wind remarked, turning her piercing gaze Robin Wing's way.

The Matron's long face reflected nothing. She'd always been able to adopt the gambler's expression: impassive, her dark eyes inscrutable. Now she ran a long-boned hand over her graying hair, pulled her thin frame to full height. "That was the fall inventory. We've just passed the spring equinox celebration. All that feasting and dancing, our stores are depleted."

"So are the stores for Morning Star House, River Mounds, and North Star House." Wind arched a suggestive eyebrow as she resettled herself to glance Blue Heron's way.

"Then you might ask North Star House to open their storehouses as well."

"We have," Wind told her, then glanced again at Blue Heron, the question hanging there between them.

"The first canoe-loads have already landed. Slender Fox and Wolverine began shipment yesterday." Blue Heron kept her expression neutral, as if she was having a conversation about the strength of a cup of tea. "And it's not like we're asking you to strip your warehouse down to nothing, though Slender Fox ordered exactly that. We only need to replace what Columella offered and some additional as reward for her loan."

"Why a reward? What's that all about?" Matron Robin Wing crossed her thin arms.

"Because she came through at a desperate moment," Wind snapped. "Because she took a gamble that the rest of us would do what she was willing to do. Replace those burned food stocks."

"I still don't think that warehouse catching fire was an accident." Robin Wing narrowed an eye.

"No one does," Blue Heron replied. Then added, "Well, but for Spotted

Wrist and Rising Flame. Probably because they have their reasons for believing as they do."

"What a surprise, eh?" A sour smile bent Robin Wing's lips. "Slender Fox and Wolverine really opened their storehouses?"

"They did," Blue Heron said.

Robin Wing closed her eyes, took a deep breath. For a time she held it, no doubt considering her options and trying to calculate the ramifications of refusing. Hard to do when Horned Serpent House would be the only one to hold out.

"The Earth Clans are contributing?" Robin Wing asked hopefully.

"Everyone is," Wind told her. "We all share the pain. If bellies end up ganted by the time the first greens are imported, it will be all the way around. And it is spring. The migrations are starting. It won't completely fill the gap, but a lot of people are going to be spending a lot more time hunting ducks, geese, herons, swans, cranes, and pigeons. I think we can organize a mass netting in the river. Get enough canoes together, tie enough nets together, and trawl it upstream and we should be able to make a substantial catch. Working together we can manage."

"Slender Fox really agreed to this?" Robin Wing's desperation was almost palpable.

"She did," Blue Heron said mildly. "And with remarkable alacrity. She barely hesitated . . . considering that her attention was on her brother. She's such a sharing woman and so open to family needs."

Robin Wing lifted a skeptical eyebrow.

"You could always say no, but we could really use your help," Wind added. "Might stir a little resentment, being the only House to refuse to help out."

"We shouldn't be in this mess to start with."

"No. Too bad, really. Makes you wonder what kind of man could possibly have so much trouble snaring himself a wife." Blue Heron shrugged. "But then he and Rising Flame have made such a difference. Things run so much more smoothly now. Like getting all the Houses but one to pitch in and fix the problem created by the burning of the expedition supplies."

Robin Wing grunted under her breath. "Green Chunkey will be livid."

"He will," Wind agreed. "But I suspect he will be more livid when North Star House comes out looking selfless, interested in the good of all, and Horned Serpent House looks like stingy misers interested only in their own bellies."

Blue Heron gave a sagacious nod. "I can just hear Wolverine and Slender Fox in the next full Council meeting: 'And where was Horned

Serpent House when bellies were empty? Were they sharing? Did they place the good of Cahokia before their own?'"

Robin Wing bit off a curse, jaw muscles bunched. "You know we *hate* those people."

True, not that many moons past they'd been fit to open combat against each other, and Piasa take the hindmost—even if it meant the destruction of both their Houses and Cahokia as well. Slender Fox had called Green Chunkey a walking piece of shit to his face.

Wind said, "I think that come the Green Corn Ceremony, we shall have a feast for the Houses who pitched in. In fact, as *tonka'tzi* I hereby order it. I wonder who will be left out, most noticeable by their absence? People will talk."

"All right! I will send the order." Robin Wing shook her head. "My brother will scream."

"His voice will be drowned by the cries of thanks," Wind said amiably. She turned. "Messenger."

One of the young men along the back wall sprang forward, his staff of office in hand.

Robin Wing made a face. Seemed to flinch, then said, "Tell my stewards that the storehouses are to be opened, and all but a third part of what's left is to be sent to replace Evening Star House's stores." She glanced at the recorder, who stood still holding his string of beads and looking uncomfortable. "Will that be enough?"

"Yes, Lady. Just about perfect."

With that, Robin Wing growled something unpleasant under her breath. Then she stalked off, crossing the room and calling, "Have my litter made ready. I need to return, now!"

Wind chuckled. "That went well, unless, of course, it turns out that North Star House really didn't send their share."

"Given what I've got hanging over Slender Fox? Believe me, she'll deliver."

Which was when Blue Heron turned. There, leaning against the back wall, his muscular arms crossed and knotted, Sliding Ice watched. The man's eyes were slitted, angry, promising mayhem and violence.

Does he know it was me?

Somehow, that seemed a safe bet, and it sent a shiver down her spine.

Thirty-three

The way his warriors avoided his eyes, Blood Talon's men understood the extent of his foul mood. He hung on the ragged edge of an explosion. He dared not. He was a squadron first, and his warriors took their cues from him. They relied on his sense, intelligence, and composure. Stomping around, kicking things, cursing, and waving his fists wasn't the kind of behavior that would allow him to keep his command, let alone their respect.

So he bottled his anxiety and fuming frustration as his warriors paddled for the canoe landing at the Cahokian colony at Red Bluff Town.

To get to the colony they had turned up the River of Ducks, a tributary that entered from the eastern highlands. Red Bluff Town stood a short distance back from the confluence, atop the heights, on the tributary's south side. At that place the limestone bluff extended like a finger above the floodplain, providing a point of vantage above both the Tenasee to the west and the River of Ducks.

A generation ago, an expedition under Red Tooth—one of Black Tail's famed squadron firsts—had brought colonists here to hack out a settlement on the heights. For the first two years they'd battled with a tribe of forest farmers called the Tasi. At the same time, they ringed the old-growth trees, built their town, and hung on by their fingertips. Reinforced twice with additional warriors and colonists, Red Tooth finally prevailed. The Tasi had been overcome, enslaved, and the survivors had been absorbed by the Cahokians.

From there, additional settlements had been established ever farther up the River of Ducks until the entire valley had been brought under Cahokian control—or at least pacified and converted. Since then, the fertile valley had become a breadbasket exporting canoe-loads of corn, beans, squash, tobacco, and dogbane fiber as tribute to the Morning Star.

For the colonists' purposes, the town's location proved ideal. Not only was the location defensible, and with a good view of any approaching body of warriors, but it was well above the occasional flood, cooled by breezes that kept the bugs down, and on well-drained soil.

For Blood Talon, however, it meant he had to leave the main course of the Tenasee, and while the big river might be observed from the Red Bluff heights, it was so far away that his passing quarry would only be visible as a dot on the water. And only if they were passing on the far side where the view of the near shore wasn't screened by trees.

His solution had been to leave Three Bow and Split Limb at the confluence to keep watch from the bank. If Night Shadow Star happened along, there wasn't much the two warriors could do but wave as she went by. But at least Blood Talon would know if his quarry had passed, and how long ago they'd done so.

For a whole day, he would have to take the risk. He needed both supplies and help. Not to mention that his warriors were worn out. He could see it in their movements, in their haggard expressions, and more so, in their ever more surly behavior. They might be his most elite, but even the best had their breaking point.

For his arrival at Red Bluff Town, he'd had them dress in their armor, paint their faces, and don their finery. Not only did it serve to remind them who they were—Cahokia's best—but he wanted to make the right impression on the local chief.

With a final burst of effort, his warriors sent the war canoe flying toward the landing, the bow cutting a groove in the sand as it literally speared the beach.

Then they were out, dragging the craft up on the landing where a line of crude dugouts of various sizes had already been beached. Several small camps of locals, dressed in crudely woven textiles, tanned buckskin, and wearing hair-on capes crafted from raccoon, beaver, bear, and wolf hides, watched from around smoking fires.

Blood Talon stretched his legs, took in the shoreline and the trail that led up to the town. The fact that Red Bluff Town was surrounded by a palisade wasn't lost on him.

"Form up," he told his warriors. "Wild Owl, Old Scar, keep an eye on the canoe. Not that I think the locals would cause us any trouble, but there's no sense in tempting them."

"Yes, Squadron First!"

Shouldering his quiver, taking up his shield, Blood Talon led the way, his legs finding the climb something of a challenge after days in the canoe.

The trail zigzagged up the grassy slope, around rotting stumps and crumbling limestone outcrops. He was cognizant that a small crowd had gathered above, that the entire climb was subject to observation and a potential rain of arrows from the heights.

At the crest, a small delegation approached at a trot. In the forefront, a young man, early twenties, wearing a blue tunic woven from fine dogbane fiber, carried himself erect, his step almost pompous. His hair had been wound up in a bun, a small copper headpiece topping it. A quick application of white had been dabbed on his cheeks, indicative of peace and welcome. In his hands he held a Four Winds Clan staff of office. The four men and single woman who followed appeared to be household staff, given their dress and manner.

Red Bluff Town centered around the palisade and the buildings within it, but most of the settlement lay outside the walls. Locally designed pole-frame dwellings were intermixed with Cahokian-style trench-wall houses. Each was surrounded by small garden plots. A spacious chunkey court was built just behind the towering World Tree pole. Drying racks, ramadas, what looked like sweat lodges, Council Houses, and a couple of temples gave the place a cluttered yet prosperous appearance. A stickball field lay beyond the houses where it butted up against the distant forest. People were coming from all directions, obviously curious about the newcomers.

"Greetings, warriors," the young man called. "I am Whistle, of Horned Serpent House, of the Four Winds Clan, and nephew to High Chief Tanned Wolf, who bids you welcome to Red Bluff Town. Had we known of your imminent arrival we would have made the appropriate arrangements to receive you, but you catch us by surprise."

Blood Talon bowed low, touching his forehead; his men mimicked the gesture. Then he straightened, stating, "I am Blood Talon, squadron first for War Leader and Four Winds Clan Keeper Spotted Wrist. My warriors and I appreciate the kind welcome to Red Bluff Town. We are in need of resupply and a short rest, along with some assistance if it can be had. These things I would discuss with High Chief Tanned Wolf at his soonest convenience."

"You serve Spotted Wrist? The Hero of the North?"

"The very same."

Whistle inclined his head, gesturing toward the palisade gate. "If you and your valiant warriors would accompany me, we will make you comfortable. Black drink is being prepared, and I've ordered food to be readied. My uncle, unfortunately, is upriver. Every spring he makes a tour of the towns and people under his supervision. In his stead, I will be happy to extend whatever hospitality and courtesy I can."

With his practiced eye, Blood Talon took in the palisade and its condition. "Looks like you need to replace your fortifications. You've got rot eating through the posts."

"Actually, we're going to take it down this fall after the harvest comes in. We haven't had the threat of an attack for years. But I can tell you, in the early days, things around here were different. The name Red Bluff Town? You'll notice the soil is pale here. From the limestone. It was named for the blood that soaked into this ground during the fight to take this land."

"Must have been difficult."

"Let's just say that no one slept well back then."

"Looks like most of the activity is outside the fortifications."

"It is. We keep the central area imposing for ritual purposes. Ceremonies for the visiting chiefs, the needs of state. It serves as a reminder of Cahokia's grandeur and authority, not to mention the miracle of the living god."

Inside the palisade Blood Talon saw raised granaries atop greased poles, closely packed trench-wall houses, and a palace at the far end of a small courtyard. A temple with a high roof had been erected on a low earthen platform immediately inside the gate. Everything here looked tidy, the thatched roofs in good repair. A World Tree pole—not as large as the one outside—dominated the center of the plaza.

People hustled about, mostly locals. The men and women wore their hair in styles Blood Talon wasn't familiar with. Their facial tattoos came in patterns and designs he'd never seen before.

Whistle led them into the small plaza, indicating the building standing on the east side. "We offer you the Men's House for your stay. Make yourselves at home. I have ordered food prepared. When you are ready, I will receive you at the palace."

Blood Talon looked to his men. "Go, get some rest. When I need you, Nutcracker will sound the horn. Don't wander too far, not more than a half-finger's time to assembly."

To Whistle, he said, "The sooner we talk, the better."

The young man inclined his head. "Then come with me. If you don't mind that black drink isn't prepared, that the food is a half a hand of time away, and that the palace is in disarray, I will hear what you have to say."

The interior of the palace might not have been outstanding in Cahokian terms, but for the wilds of the lower Tenasee, it was probably more than fine. The walls were decorated with carvings of the Morning Star, with skulls from vanquished foes, the occasional war trophy, and colorful fabrics. The central fire burned, as it would in any Cahokian palace. A rendering of *Hunga Ahuito*—the two-headed eagle who lived at the top of the Sky World—dominated the wall behind the raised dais where High Chief Tanned Wolf would sit during official state functions. The floor mat, made of woven rushes, though serviceable, wasn't anything like the ornate examples in Cahokia.

"Have a seat," Whistle offered, and spoke to a young woman in some local language. She immediately retrieved a long-necked jar and cups. These she filled and offered to Blood Talon and Nutcracker.

"Mint tea," Whistle told them. He seated himself on the dais behind the fire as if he were high chief. "Now, what can I do for you?"

Blood Talon studied the young man, wondered if he had the authority he claimed. "I am on a mission for the Four Winds Clan, authorized by the clan matron herself, as well as on the orders of the Keeper. I am in pursuit of a criminal. A woman who has betrayed her clan, her people, and her honor. Perhaps betrayed the Morning Star himself. She is a desperate fugitive. I have been tasked to find her and take her back to Cahokia."

"And what do you need from me?"

"You have people who know the river, the places she can go to ground. You have spies who can send word. I want help finding her, capturing her, and taking her back to Cahokia. Whatever it takes, I will do. Even if it means turning this entire river upside down."

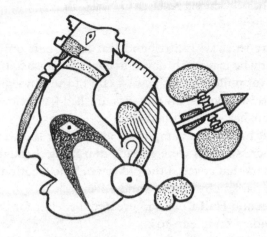

Thirty-four

The Casquinampo had called it Maygrass Town before they abandoned the location. It once stood on a raised terrace above the Sand River and a tributary called Creek-Where-Raccoons-Play that ran down from the uplands in the west. An old Trader's trail could still be seen headed up the valley that—according to White Mat—ran across the limestone uplands, across the divide, and joined the headwaters of a creek that flowed west into the Father Water a ten-day journey away.

When the Cahokians had established their colony at the mouth of the Sand River, the Casquinampo had abandoned Maygrass Town, unsure of the Cahokians' ultimate goals. They had been unwilling to have their people corrupted by the Cahokian priests with their stories of gods come to earth in human bodies, not to mention their insidious game of chunkey. All things that might subvert impressionable Casquinampo youths.

That had been almost a generation ago. The fields had gone back to wild, but still sported stands of the maygrass for which the town had been named. Remains of a rotted-out palisade—most of its posts hauled off over the years—forty or so house depressions, the structures long since collapsed, and a low, square mound that had once supported the chief's palace, remained. A bowshot to the north stood a conical burial mound—grassed over now, and with saplings furring its slopes. Several prayer sticks—offerings to the dead—were weathering away.

Behind the old town limits, new-growth forest dominated, covering the gentle slopes back from the terrace. The trails that wound through the trees were thick with litter and leaf mat, their only use apparently from the deer who cautiously dared to pass this close to Canebrake Town.

Red Reed was pulled up at the west end of the canoe landing along the Creek-Where-Raccoons-Play and was masked from view by once-tended chokeberry bushes gone wild.

White Mat had set up camp back away from the water, and close to the forest where saplings were already marching through the thick grass and wildflowers that covered the old town. The location was out of sight from anyone passing by on the Sand River.

Made Man and Half Root had erected a shelter for themselves, while the other Traders built lean-tos.

Fire Cat and Night Shadow Star had put their efforts to building a bedding of grass, topped by blankets, and then draped tanned hides over a framework of branches to keep them dry.

Mixed Shell turned his attention to the stew, starting water to boil over the fire, while Shedding Bird sorted through their food stocks.

As soon as they were laid out, Night Shadow Star had crawled into her blankets; she was now sound asleep.

Fire Cat, for his part, strung his bow, collected his quiver, and took the old Traders' trail that paralleled the creek bottom headed west.

As the day waned, the sum total of his hunt came to three large fox squirrels who'd forgotten just how accurately an arrow could be dispatched.

It was a measure of their exhaustion that the rest of the camp was asleep by dusk.

I should be as exhausted as the rest.

Instead he pasted his exposed skin with insect repellent made from something red called blood root and spruce sap mixed with sassafras extract. Then he walked down to the bank and looked out over the smooth waters of the Sand River. On the opposite shore willows, water oak, and cottonwood surrounded older bald cypress in the swampy low ground. Real bald cypress. He'd marveled at the trees, having never seen them alive and growing before. White Mat had assured him that as they traveled farther south, he'd see some giants. To a man raised in the northern forests, they were magical.

The first frogs were croaking; the night came alive with the sounds of insects. A fish splashed out on the river, its rings quickly devoured by the swelling and sucking water.

He watched as a bat flitted about in search of insects, its shape outlined against the dying light in the sky.

The sound of her steps as she made her way through the grass brought him back to the moment. Night Shadow Star seated herself beside him.

"Thought you'd still be asleep."

She pulled her hair back, tilting her face to the evening sky. "I would be . . . but it was get up and find a place to relieve myself or spend the night in soaked blankets." She glanced at him. "What are you doing out here?"

"Worried about Blood Talon. About getting past him. And once we do, there's still Walking Smoke waiting for us at the end of the journey."

She reached out, took his hand, her touch sending a tremor though him. "Wishing we could just run away?"

"Always."

"The voices get louder when I'm tired. They're telling me terrible things. Piasa has been flashing at the edges of my vision. I hear him speaking to me, but I can't quite make out what he's saying. It's not good. It's like he's furious. That he needs to punish me for failing him."

"How?"

"I don't know."

"I need you to tell me something."

"What?" She shot him a quizzical look.

"Is Piasa mad about you freeing me? If he is, tell him I serve you and only you. When it comes to you and me, nothing has changed. Bound or free, I remain yours. Whatever it takes, no matter the sacrifice. Make sure he understands."

She stared at him, her eyes like dark holes in her face. "You should go. Make a life for yourself. Any people, any chief, any woman would be honored to have a man like you."

"I have a life, an allegiance, a ruler, and a woman all rolled into one. She is outstanding, courageous, and all that I will ever need."

She sighed, looked self-consciously away. "If I could change things . . ."

When she couldn't finish, he gave her hand a reassuring pat. "We've had this conversation."

"When we reach Cofitachequi . . ." She tightened her grip. "Fire Cat, I don't know what happens beyond that. Piasa gives me glimpses in my dreams. Something terrible happens there. I can't quite see it. I just know I am alone and terrified when it happens."

He took a breath, used his free hand to swipe at the humming mosquitoes that had collected in a wavering column above his head. "If I am not at your side, I am dead. Nothing else would explain why you would be alone. Ever."

"Do you really care so little for your future? You could live to an old and honored age. Have children . . ." Her voice faded.

"What? Why did you pause?"

"Piasa is laughing." She glanced off into the gloom. "Yes, you miserable beast, I know he's dedicated his life to me. I'm trying to get him to see reason."

"I had children," he told her. "Two charming wives. I was a famous war chief and considered a great man. Beloved by my people. It was all taken away from me. The price I paid to come into your service. If I'm to die keeping you alive—even if it be but for a matter of time—I need nothing more."

Again, she was giving him that intent stare. "Do you really love me that much?"

"And more."

She let go of his hand, lowered her face into her palms, her hair spilling around her like a mantle. He could hear her taking deep breaths, could see the slight shake of her head. "You are a fool."

"People have told me that before. Didn't believe it then, don't now."

"That, or you have a death wish."

"Not particularly."

"I'm sorry for the pain I've caused you. For my part in bringing you to this."

"Do you know the most terrible day of my life?"

"When Red Wing Town fell."

"No."

She raised her head, looking at him with that intensity he could feel more than see in the darkness.

"It was the day you married that Itza lord. Nothing—not the death of my children, the loss of Red Wing Town, or even the fear I felt in the darkness in that cave when the terrors of the Underworld hovered around me—was so terrible. But for the thief . . ." He shook his head, laughed in a vain attempt to make light of it.

"It was my duty to my clan."

"I know."

"We beat him, though, didn't we?"

"We did."

"Together," she said thoughtfully.

"Together."

"You know how much I would give to leave all of this behind?"

"I do."

"I was cursed. It began the moment I was born. It's because of who I have to be. Maybe, if we can kill my brother, it will be enough of a balance, a sacrifice to Power, that you and I can make a new life."

"Maybe."

She placed a reassuring hand on his shoulder, yawned, and climbed to her feet. Looking out into the darkness off to one side, she said, "Yes,

Lord. I *am* thinking about it. Wondering what price I would have to pay, and if it would hurt more than living this way."

"What is the beast saying?"

"Just meddling," she told him as she walked off into the night. "Like he usually does."

Meddling in what? But he knew from her tone of voice she'd never tell him.

It didn't usually help matters when he tried to understand what went on between his lady and the Spirit monster who owned her.

Tossing a stick out into the dark water, he stood, clawed at the mosquitoes so they'd be as out of sorts as he was, and turned his steps toward camp. There, he knew he'd spend the night aching to hold her. Satisfied to know that she slept but an arm's length away, and that he would be there if she needed him.

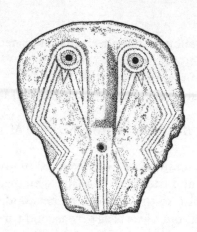

A Tedious Predictability

One would think that warriors, of all people, would have an oaklike grain of fortitude within their flinty hides. After all, they march out, blood in their hearts, death in their eyes, as they form up behind their shields to face the arrows and war clubs of the enemy. These are the wielders of pain and death. Not the sort to give in to night terrors or show the slightest squeamish side of their natures.

The Joara Clan House, hardly to my surprise, was vacated within moments of my arrival. Seriously, I just entered the place, picked a sleeping bench in the back, and had Fire Light's runners place my box and basket. The other five occupants whispered, "Lightning Shell!" back and forth a few times as they hastily threw their things together and rushed for the door. One—apparently bunked next to me—didn't even bother to pick up his blankets. He just hurried out. Made warding signs with his fingers the entire time. Must have had a guilty conscience.

I spent that first night pleasantly alone, listening to the warriors singing over at the Men's House a couple of structures to the east. They were involved in some kind of ritual. Along with the drumming and flute music one had a particularly fine baritone voice.

I found it irritating, therefore, that the following night, the Men's House was dark. That it remained that way thereafter. I asked Fire Light about it, and he told me that though there was no threat in the country thereabout, the war leader had taken his squadron for a "patrol of the mountains," whatever that meant.

Which brings me back to Fire Light.

He only shows up after dark. On this, the fifth night, he comes in the company of a large-boned and rather scurrilous-looking fellow with a sack of something over his shoulder. At the door, he calls a cautious, "Soul Flier? Hello?"

Indeed. Soul Flier? At first, I'm puzzled and amused, but when I think about it, does he really want to stand at the door and call, "Hello? Witch? Are you there?"

Not that I think of myself as a witch. I've always considered witches to be those narrow self-serving individuals who are bent on creating havoc, seeking to fulfill only their personal lust for aggrandizement, authority, and personal gain.

I don't need aggrandizement. I already know I am born to a higher calling: that of remaking the world.

For the sake of the moment, I slip my shell mask over my face. The mask is made from a large half of a whelk shell. Triangular in shape, it has eye holes, an incised nose, and a round hole for a mouth. It hangs on my head by means of a thong over the top and another around the sides. Wearing it gives my face a ghostly, pale look, and I have carved the zigzag symbols of lightning under the eyes and down the cheeks. It almost resembles the scar patterns.

I toss another couple of branches onto the fire and take a position behind it. Only when I have my cloak hanging just so with the flames casting dancing light over my body do I say, "Enter!"

Fire Light comes first, and behind him, nervous to the bones, comes the burly fellow. Maybe a Trader, but certainly not a warrior. He has the kind of crude face that could be fashioned out of a stump. The forehead sort of slopes into the cheeks—a broad face, with almost no setback for the eyes. His nose is a flat and wide thing like a rolled-on triangle, nostrils are two round holes. Jaw and chin made to match.

His eyes flick back and forth, going everywhere but in my direction. He stoops and lays a large thick-weave burlap sack on the floor. As soon as he does, he touches the top of his forehead and he's gone. Big feet thumping on the matting as he rushes out the door and into the night.

On the floor, the bag is shifting and squirming, muffled whimpers and cries coming from within.

"Two," Fire Light announces. "As you asked."

He pauses, looks slightly sick. "It wouldn't do to have them talking. I mean, you know, shouting for help. Calling for their parents. That sort of thing."

I can tell that my mask, my silence, is really eating into him. Like when he was a boy, Fire Light can be read the way a recorder can read a string of beads.

In a detached voice, I say, "I don't think that will be a problem."

"Good." He claps his hands together. "Now, I've taken your word that you

can get me back to Cahokia. If it turned out . . . Well, you know. It wouldn't make me happy. Especially after going to such lengths. Taking the kind of risks involved in . . . Well, you know." He gestures toward the squirming sack on the floor.

What sounds like weeping can be heard through the coarsely woven cloth.

I ignore his words, stepping over for my little-girl's-skull cup. Retrieving it, I bend down by the fire and dip it into the pot that contains steaming sassafras tea. This I offer to Fire Light. "Drink?"

He is staring wide-eyed at the cup, cut halfway through the eye sockets as it is. The dull ivory color of the bone looks almost ruddy in the firelight.

"No, thank you, Soul Flier."

"I am not a soul flier. That's for the likes of those who can send their souls into the Underworld, or up into the Sky World in search of the Spirits. Me, I have only ridden the lightning."

I reach up and touch the zigzagging lines on the cheek of my mask. "It left me marked, you see. Imbued with its Power. It speaks to me. Tells me things from around the world.

"For example—and the reason behind why I needed your help procuring the little darlings in that sack—someone is coming to Cofitachequi. Someone Powerful, filled with Underworld Spirit. She is coming for me. Thinks she's going to destroy me, pull my corpse down into the Underworld where Piasa can rip me limb from limb, tear my stomach open and devour my intestines like a robin sucks a worm from damp soil."

Fire Light swallows hard. "I see."

"No, you don't. I hope to keep her from making it this far."

"Her?"

"What makes you think that only males are gifted with Power?"

"I, uh . . ."

"When you take your report back to Sharp Path, tell the orata *that I am in the process of doing everything in my Power to keep this woman from arriving here. I have no desire to fight this out in Joara, especially if I can destroy her on the way."*

This is all a lie, of course. I would love nothing better than to get Night Shadow Star here, alone, and defenseless. She and I have unfinished business from those last moments in the canoe. I feel my penis harden at the mere thought of her.

"How can you do that, Soul . . . er, Lord?"

I gesture to the sack that is bunching, shifting, and twisting on the floor. "There are ways of striking across distance, just as there are ways of seeing. Power, however, needs to be fed. Life is filled with Spirit, and that energy can be harnessed to a purpose. I can't conjure something from nothing."

I pause, knowing full well how to torment my dear cousin. "Understand. If

I lose this, you have a long and happy life to look forward to right here in Cofitachequi. It's not that bad of a place. I've traveled most of it. In the event I fail, you should consider it not an exile, but a remarkable opportunity that . . ."

I tilt my head curiously. "What? I see that expression on your face."

He struggles, futilely, to hide his horror. "Let's just see that you win then, Lord."

"Help me, and I will accompany you back to Cahokia. Personally take you with me. You will walk at my side as we ascend the Grand Staircase to the Morning Star's palace."

He is about as keen to share my company as he would be to clutch a full-grown water moccasin to his breast. But he hides it well, even plastering a cheery smile onto his face. It doesn't go all the way to his eyes.

"Anything I can do to help, please call on me."

I incline my head. "We sit right on the Trade route from the sea to the head of the Wide Fast, the Tenasee, and the whole of the world."

"Yes."

"If you should happen to stumble across some Traders? You know, the kind who really don't spend their nights agonizing over the Power of Trade? You might send them to me. I would be willing to make them rich, drowning-in-copper-shell-and-property rich. But they have to be the right kind of men. Um, not the sort you would invite into your palace, but the kind who still know the river. Maybe the sort who are traveling to this part of the world because they can't stay back in theirs. You see what I mean?"

Fire Light chews on his lips for a moment, a churning behind his eyes. "I think I do, Lord."

"Last offer of a drink." I extend the cup his way again.

"No, thank you, Lord. Um, I should be going. Thank you again."

And with that he turns, doing his best to pretend he isn't hurrying for the door.

After he leaves, I lift my shell mask, take a drink of sassafras tea and let the taste, sweetened with honeysuckle nectar, run over my tongue. What a remarkably refreshing drink. And it always puts me into a good mood.

Then, lowering my mask again, I step over, drag the bag back past the fire, and untie the knot.

The fabric falls away from two little girls, maybe four and five, their hair mussed. They look like sisters. Their eyes are huge, dark pupils overwhelming the brown irises. Both are gagged with knots of cloth, and the cords eat deeply into their round cheeks.

At the sight of me, they try to scream into their gags. It sounds like rabbits being crushed under a too-large boulder.

I pull the older of the two up onto her feet, bound as they are at the ankles. The knot that holds her skirt up surrenders to my first tug and the slip of home-woven fabric falls away to leave her naked and terrified. Her squealing into the gag is almost comical.

"Well, dear one. You need not fear. I have yet to meet a people who don't believe that everyone who has a name also has a soul. And everyone knows the soul continues after death. So, whatever happens tonight, it's not like you will cease to be."

With that said, I reach for my knife.

The muffled squealing gets louder and louder.

Thirty-five

Time to go now." Piasa's voice came as a whisper. Night Shadow Star could feel the Spirit Beast's breath against her ear as she jerked her eyes awake to the night.

It took her a moment to realize where she was: the Traders' camp. An abandoned village called Maygrass Town.

A cool breeze blew the last of the clouds from the moon's face as she sat up, peered out from under the cover of the hides draped on the pole frame overhead.

She took a deep breath, hearing the crickets and insects on the warm night. The perfume of spring flowers carried on the somnolent breeze, mixed as it was with the scents of water, mud, and freshly leafed-out vegetation.

She glanced at where Fire Cat lay sound asleep in his blankets, fought the impulse to reach out and reassure herself by touching him.

The fire popped in the hearth, the faintest red glow around the bottom of the boiling pot that rested at the edge of the coals to stay warm.

"You must leave now!"

Piasa flickered at the edge of her vision, but when she turned her head, he'd already vanished into the shadows.

"Got to go now," an ethereal voice insisted from air around her. *"They are coming."*

She reached out with a foot and shoved Fire Cat. "We have to go."

In an instant he was awake, reaching for his weapons. "Trouble?"

"A warning from the Spirits. Piasa is most insistent."

"Thought you and he weren't on the best of terms these days."

"We're not."

But she didn't dare tell him the thoughts that had possessed her as they'd traveled farther and farther from Cahokia and all that its environs had meant to her. She'd keep the torture of her temptation to herself. No sense in adding to the burdens he'd already assumed on her account.

The Spirit Beast knew that she balanced on the fine edge of betrayal. Even as she thought it, she could hear her Spirit master's hiss of displeasure.

"What do you know of sacrifice, Lord?" she muttered to the dark as she stood and began rolling her blanket.

"What are we doing?" Fire Cat asked, crawling out of his bedding.

"We're leaving. Wake the others."

"It's not even midnight," Fire Cat protested as he glanced up at the position of the stars in the moonlit sky. "You want to take your chances on the river? In the dark? You know the dangers, floats of driftwood, half-sunken logs."

"Piasa will warn us if there's trouble," she lied, hoping the malicious beast would accede to her wish since she was giving in to his.

"The Traders are not going to like it."

"It's been five days, Fire Cat. We're rested, you've killed two deer, we've caught fish, Half Root's been diving for freshwater clams, it is time we got back to our duty."

"Right." He promptly began rolling his bedding and taking down their shelter.

The others complained, even after Fire Cat threatened them. With grumbles, much stumbling about in the darkness, and no little confusion as things were remembered at the last moment, *Red Reed* was ultimately shoved into the current. Taking paddles, they got under way. White Mat was in his usual position in the bow, paddling shoulder to shoulder with Shedding Bird.

"It's too dark. Hard to see the thread of the current," Half Root groused.

"If Piasa woke Night Shadow Star out of a sound sleep," Fire Cat told them, "it was for a reason."

"You put a lot of faith in the lady's visions," Made Man muttered.

"When you've lived in the shadow of Power for as long as I have, seen the things I have seen, you'll understand," he answered.

"I think we do," Half Root said from the stern. "Downright spooky the way she gets when she hears the voices. Sees all those flashes of light and flickers of movement that we don't."

"Half the time we're in awe," Mixed Shell said softly. "The rest of the time we're more than a little scared. Like when she gets that vacant look, sways, her hands in her lap and all filled with visions."

"We mean no offense, Lady," Half Root added quickly.

As Night Shadow Star paddled, she said, "It's no blessing to be half in the Spirit World. I would Trade my Power to live your lives in an instant. You could have it all, the palaces, the wealth, the prestige and servants, the knowledge that you have been chosen because of your birth to be the tool of Underworld Power. In return I could simply be myself, unmolested by voices, free of everyone else's expectations. No one would be hunting me to make me marry a man I didn't want. I wouldn't have to cross half the known world to kill a brother who's as twisted and evil as any man alive."

"Thanks, Lady," Half Root replied. "I think we'll just stay happy being ourselves."

"That's the smart bargain," Fire Cat told them. "Get us to your town at the Mussel Shallows, and you'll be the stuff of legends for the rest of your lives. Think of the stories you'll be able to tell of the time you took Lady Night Shadow Star of Cahokia on the epic journey to her confrontation with Walking Smoke."

"Assuming we don't get capsized by a sunken log first because we can't see the slick it makes on the surface," White Mat replied.

Night Shadow Star chuckled softly. "I don't think Piasa will let that happen." Not yet anyway. "He wants me in Cofitachequi. He's not going to let anything interfere with that. Until I'm face to face with my brother, you can be assured that this journey has Power on its side."

"Hope you're right, Lady," Mixed Shell told her.

They had progressed down the channel of the Sand River, could see the open water of the Tenasee at the confluence. And there, on the sliver of beach exposed by the falling water, lay five canoes. Three fires had burned low. The dark forms of men sleeping in blankets could be discerned on the pale sand.

"*Quiet*," Piasa whispered from behind Night Shadow Star's right ear.

"Not a sound," she whispered. "Don't so much as knock a paddle to the hull."

Letting the current carry them, they drifted past the sleeping camp. Paddling wide, they cut across, hugging the Tenasee's far bank as they turned upriver.

"Who were those people? Why were they camped there, of all places?"

"Blocking the river," Night Shadow Star said with certainty. "Making sure that no one passed them in the night. Perhaps their guard is asleep? Piasa's reason for waking me when he did?"

"Wonder if they were going to search up the Sand in the morning?" Fire Cat was stroking vigorously with his paddle. "If they're looking for us, it means that Blood Talon has allies. I wonder who?"

"Tanned Wolf," Night Shadow Star guessed. "Blood Talon made a fourth choice, Red Wing. Something we should have anticipated. He stopped at Red Bluff Town and talked the High Chief there into using his people to search for us."

"Blood Talon figured out that he was ahead of us," Fire Cat mused. "So, of course he would have badgered the local colonists into helping. He would have placed scouts to watch the river, made sure we didn't pass. Then he would have gathered his men, sent them all searching downriver, having them check camp spots, search villages and inlets, anyplace we might have holed up."

"Like Maygrass Town," Shedding Bird said through an exhale. He bent his head around, staring at Night Shadow Star in the moon-bathed light. "And they'd have found us tomorrow morning. Lady, I'll never doubt you again."

In the night, Piasa hissed his delight.

So, we've escaped the net this time. Now all we have to do is get far enough upriver to be beyond the search.

But how were they going to manage that? Every man, woman, and child between the River of Ducks and the Sand River would be on the lookout for *Red Reed*, and dawn would come long before they could make that passage.

Thirty-six

The day had been sunny, hot, the first real hint of summer. It had come so quickly that, with its fire, the interior of Blue Heron's palace felt like an oven. To escape, Blue Heron had retreated outside to the southwest corner of her palace, her back to the wall, a bowl of coals by her side, her stone pipe in her hand.

This was how Seven Skull Shield found her: sitting braced, puffing a cloud of blue smoke, eyes on the Four Winds Plaza where a group of young nobles were locked in a game of chunkey. Like so much of Cahokia, they were preparing for the lunar maximum moonrise that lay just days away.

"Keeper, so here you are."

She glanced up at him. Shot a distasteful look at Farts. "Didn't think I'd see you. Not given the number of people looking for you. And what on earth are you dressed as? You've got mud all over you."

"Crawfish trapper," he told her, flopping down next to her and giving Farts the "down" signal. "No one would suspect a crawfish trapper of being Seven Skull Shield."

"That's dirty work. Wading around in the mud to set out and pick up crawfish traps. Didn't figure you for the kind who'd stoop to that kind of labor."

"I'm not. I stole the catch from a dirt farmer over south of the lake outside Serpent Woman Town." At her irritated glare, he admitted, "All right, I 'Traded' for it. But I have standards. I stole the blanket I Traded for the crawfish from a Deer Clan chief over at that mound group east of Serpent Woman Town."

"So, there's really crawfish?"

"There's really crawfish. A whole basketful. I left my 'catch' inside with Smooth Pebble. She'll cook them up for us to share."

"Share? As in you think you're eating supper here?"

"Speaking of which, you going to strangle that pipe? I think you should hand it to me, rest your fingers a spell before they cramp up and ache."

She glared at him, only to have it fade into a weary smile as she handed her precious pipe over. "No other human being on earth would have the nerve or guts to ask me to share my smoke."

He puffed, enjoying the wonderful rush of fine tobacco. Not the mix of leaf, stems, berries, and other additives his less-exalted associates could afford down at the canoe landing. This was the real thing, straight, unadulterated. Traded up from the distant south along the Tenasee.

"You still got that woman hid out over at Night Shadow Star's?"

"I do."

"See her much?"

"Every couple of days or so."

"How's that go over with Green Stick and the rest?"

"They howled at first. Willow Blossom, she was bored in the beginning. But she was raised by good people. Wasn't long before she was cooking, helping to keep the matting clean. She's been going down to the plaza to Trade for food. Believe me, she really enjoys that. Thinks it's a challenge to Trade a trinket for all she can get. Winter Leaf goes with her. Says she's pure cutthroat when it comes to making the Trade. So, yes, she's fitting in."

"Half of Cahokia's looking for her, and you let her wander around the plaza? The most public place in the city?"

"Best place to hide her. Right out in plain sight. Besides, she paints her face like a lady, wears fancy stuff from out of those baskets Fire Cat won in the chunkey game with the Natchez. If I didn't know better, I'd never know it was Willow Blossom. She's taken to it like she was born a high chief's daughter."

"You sound like you're smitten."

"I'm with her every chance I get."

Blue Heron took her pipe back, puffed, held it, and exhaled streams of smoke through her nose. "What about Wooden Doll?"

"What about her?"

"There is a woman after my own heart. She knows exactly what she wants . . . and will do anything to get it."

"Well, she doesn't want me."

"And you think this new one does?"

"Willow Blossom. That's her name."

"Don't sound so thorny, thief. Willow Blossom. Came from over by the Moon Mound. Panther Clan girl. Oldest of five children. Her father sold her to that rope maker, Robin Feather. Essentially Traded her for a coil of rope. Did you know that she'd been married a couple of times before that?"

"What? No!"

"First time was to a Bear Clan boy just after her first woman's moon. She went with him and his family down to the Mother Water. They were supposed to help hack the Rising Moon site out of the forest. Apparently, wilderness living wasn't her preferred brew of tea. It was a bad breakup. Almost led to violence. Next, her people married her to a Raccoon Clan fellow from up on the bluff. She left him and went home to her people with a pack full of shell, tool stone, and other valuables. Never heard from the Raccoon Clan fellow again. Not more than a moon after being home, she's married off to Robin Feather. And, less than three moons later, she's living happily in Night Shadow Star's palace Trading for goodies with my niece's wealth."

"What are you saying?"

"Be careful."

Seven Skull Shield took her pipe, sucked the last of the smoke from the bowl, and handed it back. Counting to ten, he finally exhaled as she knocked the dottle out, repacked the bowl, and used a coal to bring it to life.

"She's not what you think, Keeper."

"What is she?"

"She's kind, and a bit fragile. The way she looks at me, I can see her souls, sort of swimming there in her eyes. She has wonderful eyes. Large, deep. And the way her face lights up when I walk into the room? It's not that she needs me, but . . ."

"Uh-huh. And you can't wait to snuggle up against that nice soft body? And when you're locked together, it's more than just coupling? She's giving you all of herself because she's finally discovered what being a woman in love's all about?"

"Well, I guess you could . . . I mean, how did you know?"

She sighed, shook her head. "Nothing I say would matter, would it?"

"You don't know her."

"Actually, I do, but we'll let that pass for the moment. Where's the Koroa copper?"

"How should I know?"

She gave him a crafty sidelong look. "Tell me you didn't leave it with Wooden Doll."

"No, I . . ."

"Well, that's one bit of good news. I like Wooden Doll. Wouldn't want her snapped up in the mess that's going to come when someone finally stumbles over it."

"What makes you think I've got it?"

"Thief, I was Keeper for three tens of years. I didn't survive for as long as I did by being a fool."

"That makes two of us."

"Maybe. Or you're just lucky. Although given your feelings for Willow Blossom, I could wonder. But here's the thing"—she gestured with the pipe—"for whatever reason, Morning Star has taken an unusual interest in that copper. Consider it hot poison."

"Why bring this all up now?"

"Because I keep track of all the pieces. That copper will come to light. And if you're holding it when it does, I'm Powerless to help you."

"Trust me, I'll be all right."

She shook her head, took another puff from her pipe before handing it over. "Spotted Wrist and Rising Flame want you dead. Robin Feather has half of Cahokia looking for you. Sliding Ice knows a man was with me the night we caught him sticking his shaft in his sister, which means he'll suspect you. Morning Star will have whoever stole that Koroa copper cut apart in the square, and all you can think about is making that calculating bit of fluff gasp and coo as you bounce her up and down on that oversized rod of yours."

"Hey, we saved Columella, didn't we?"

"That's the thing about victories, they always come at a price."

"What price? Columella's still sitting on the high chair over there."

Blue Heron narrowed a knowing eye, pointing at him with her pipe stem. "North Star and Horned Serpent Town were blackmailed into helping. River Mounds resents it because they were in a position of weakness that Three Fingers is going to exploit the moment the time is right. It's going to fester. Especially with the moon ceremonies looming. The lunar maximum only happens every eighteen years, it's big. And the traditional feasts are going to be small affairs, barely enough to fill bellies. The dirt farmers are going to be blaming the Earth Clans for the empty larders, and the Earth Clans are going to be blaming the Houses. That leaves a bitter taste to go along with all of those empty bellies. And you think there won't be a price?"

Seven Skull Shield winced. "So, who's going to pay it?"

"That, thief, is the question. And you'd better hope it's not you and me."

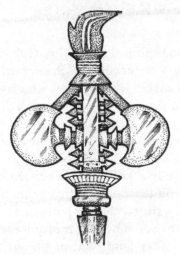

Thirty-seven

It took *Red Reed* a quarter moon to make the distance upriver that separated the Sand River from the River of Ducks. Most of the distance was made after dark, under the cover of night as White Mat and Shedding Bird, in the bow, felt their way upstream. Often it was done at a snail's pace, literally pulling the canoe along the shore by grasping overhanging branches and tugging themselves forward.

Other times they proceeded by wading through marshy shallows on the inside bends, one hand grasping the gunwales, the other casting about for balance as they sloshed, stumbled, and dunked themselves in hidden holes.

When the waxing moon was at the right angle, they paddled across the backwaters. More than once, disaster was averted by mere seconds when Piasa whispered some warning in Night Shadow Star's ear, urging her to order the canoe left or right, or to beach. Sometimes it was because of an approaching canoe, or a spinning log that came spiraling down on the current. A couple of times it was floating rafts of driftwood broken loose from some lodging upriver.

During the day, they hid wherever the opportunity presented. Several times, they slept uncomfortably in the canoe, propped on the packs, chewed on by biting flies, gnats, and, of course, by the plagues of mosquitoes that hummed about them at dusk and dawn.

But as the near-full moon shone from the night sky, they paddled past the mouth of the River of Ducks and, hopefully, any alert pursuit.

That night, on a sand spit just above Fire Oak village—the northern-most Yuchi settlement—Night Shadow Star crawled, aching, sore, and bug-bitten, into her blankets. To Fire Cat, who lay just across from her, she said, "I never knew that humans could work this hard. What kind of people are these Traders? It seems that anything we, or the river, throw at them, they just grit their teeth, put their heads down, and work their way through it."

"Seriously? You have to ask?" Fire Cat shifted in his blankets, where they were thrown out under the spreading branches of a sassafras tree. Exhausted as they were, they'd chopped into one of the roots to taste the sweetness, taken bark to boil down for mosquito repellent.

"I'm just trying to understand," she answered, hearing Piasa laughing in the shadows of an oak that stood to one side. She could feel the beast's disdainful humor.

"The answer lies inside you. Tell me. You're dog-weary, you're scratched, covered with welts, half devoured by mosquitoes and biting flies. You beat a cottonmouth to death with a paddle today, and you're absolutely filthy and sun-browned. But you've outsmarted a renowned war chief, worked your way up a hostile river undetected, and are in the middle of an epic journey. So, given all that, how do you feel about yourself?"

"Proud. A kind of pride I've never felt before. It's a particularly reward-ing feeling. Not like winning a stickball championship, or some race, or a noted clan coup, but deeper. A fierce sense that I have accomplished something miraculous."

"Now, put yourself in the Traders' moccasins. They're escorting the Cahokian Lady Night Shadow Star on an epic quest. They're doing something mythic. As if they've been chosen out of all the Traders in the world because they are the best. If they can do this thing, it will be the greatest accomplishment of their lives, and they'll push themselves past the limits of endurance."

"Their limits exceed mine. They keep going when I'm too exhausted to lift the paddle for another stroke."

"That's one of the reasons they do it, you know. Because they've watched you give everything you've got, then pull up more from some deep part of yourself. Because you might be one of the most highborn women in the world, but you work in the mud and the cold side by side with them."

He paused. "Though, I have to admit, having Piasa whispering in your ear, watching you lose yourself to the visions, that hasn't hurt, either."

"I don't understand why that would be. I'm scared, right down to the bottom of my souls. And the visions . . ." She clamped her eyes shut, as if to forever blot them out.

"It adds to the sense of Power that you radiate like a white-hot stone. Remember when I said mythic? Knowing that Piasa talks to you makes you even more special."

"I don't feel special. I don't know who I am anymore. This new me is nameless, clanless, and all of my existence is focused on the river, on reaching Cofitachequi. On finding out who the woman will be who finally gets this body. She frightens me. And most of all, I worry that Piasa isn't going to like her."

"Why is that?"

"Because I no longer know if I can trust this new woman to serve him as he wishes to be served. I'm just not sure if I care what the consequences would be."

"*There is always a price,*" Piasa's voice whispered from the night air.

"Yes," she told the beast. "I'm just tired of paying it."

"What's he saying?" Fire Cat asked.

To change the subject, she asked, "We can't forget that Blood Talon is behind us. He's not to be underestimated."

"By now he's frantic, wondering if he made the right decision. If I were him, I'd be terrified that we turned and paddled flat-out down the Tenasee to the Mother River, maybe cut east to the mouth of the Southern Shawnee. I hear it's only a hard day's paddle to the confluence. We might have headed upstream for the Southern Shawnee's source. From there we could take the trails cross-country to the divide with the upper Tenasee."

"That, or he knows we've managed to get ahead of him again."

"In which case, he will be coming. Maybe sending scouts in search of us. It all depends on what he could force or cajole the high chief at Red Bluff Town to do."

"Remember, a whole string of Cahokian colonies lie farther up the Tenasee as far as the Mussel Shallows," she reminded, fixing the image of the map she'd seen in the Recorders' Society House as she was preparing to leave. "And many of the local towns, especially the Yuchi ones, are friendly to Cahokia's colonies. They'd be willing to turn us over in hopes of currying favor."

"Only if they knew who you were."

She stared thoughtfully across the gap between their beds. "I don't even know who I am."

"You just said you were no longer Night Shadow Star. You most assuredly don't look like her. Well, but for the Four Winds Clan tattoos on your cheeks. You could cover them with paint. Maybe a red circle?"

"And be who?"

"A Trader. You look like one wearing your hair like that, with your arms and shoulders packed with smooth muscle and your skin tanned the color of old leather. You've perfected your pronunciation of Trade pidgin. As long as you kept track of your tongue, said nothing in Cahokian that would betray your accent, who'd know?"

Again, Piasa was laughing from the shadows.

I could do this.

But doing so would be letting loose of yet another piece of who she had once been. Cast her further adrift in the gray haze of oblivion. The notion both frightened and excited her.

She lay there for the next few fingers of time, head pillowed on her hands, staring thoughtfully across the narrow space where Fire Cat's deep breathing indicated he'd fallen into sleep.

"It was Night Shadow Star who promised that she would not share her body with the Red Wing. If I were someone else, a simple Trader . . ."

Piasa hissed a subtle warning from the darkness behind the sassafras tree.

If only I dared.

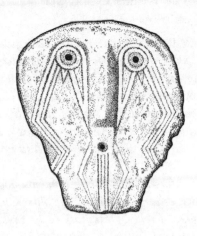

The Casqui

*T*here are three of them. A Casqui, who is the leader, a Yuchi, and a mixed-breed fellow who's half Hiawasee and part Muskogee and a bit Shawnee.

I have to hand it to Fire Light. He still has no clue about who I am. I scare the man down to his bones, but through my goodwill, he really thinks he's going to go home. That once he's there, back in the graces of his clan—his sister being Four Winds Clan matron—he will finally rise to his proper place in the hierarchy that governs Cahokia.

He has brought me the Casqui and his two companions. I've enjoyed their arrival. The three of them came trooping in, looking dangerous. Or trying to. I've seen the kind so many times. They think they're bad. The sort who aren't frightened by any comeuppance short of the square. Especially when it's anything Spiritual.

They don't know who they really are. Not the deep cracks and crevasses between their souls. Down in those dark shadows is where the stories they were told—and believed as children—still live. Sometimes it just takes the right lever to pry them free.

I find that lever when I let them see me staring into the well pot I've made out of one of the little girls' skulls. The blood is dried and blackened, of course, and the surface is no longer smooth and reflective as it had been.

"There is a woman coming," I tell them. "She comes with a single man, transported by canoe up the Tenasee. She is a Cahokian noble. A woman by the name of Night Shadow Star, though she will be traveling under another name. Passing herself off as just an ordinary traveler. You will know her by the tattoos *on her cheeks. The Four Winds, two spirals on each side of her mouth. She is young, early twenties. She will come bearing Trade packs.*

"You know the Tenasee, the points through which all must pass. Go, watch. And when you find her, bring her to me. Unharmed. Unmolested. That latter will be a difficult challenge for you, I'm sure. If you deliver her here, your semen dripping from her sheath, I will give you each a single shell and send you on your way. Within a moon, your shafts will burn and begin to rot from the inside out.

"Bring her to me fit, unused, and I shall give you Joara."

"What about the orata *that lives here?" the older Casqui asks.*

"He is no longer here," I reply. "He has, as he says, 'relocated' to Cofitachequi to build a new palace and, as he says, 'wants to help his brother better govern' the nation. But even if he were, he would accede to my request. Declare you each an orata, *and the town would be yours to rule and govern as you saw fit. Placed as it is, on the route to the sea and the crossroads of major Trading trails, you could live quite comfortably for the rest of your lives."*

"What makes you think we'd want that?" the second asks.

I lift my ruined eyebrow—well, as much as it would lift given the scar tissue. Doing so does absolutely wonderful things to my expression. Makes it almost monstrous instead of simply hideous. "What do you want? Why are you slipping up and down the rivers? I think it's because you have nowhere to go. Here I can make you oratas, *and you will never have to suffer privation again."*

"We just take your word for that?"

"Just bring me the woman, in the condition I ask. I'll give you Joara as well as all the Trade she carries. You will be both rich and landed."

"That's all there is to it? Take her away from one man? Bring her here with her sheath unused?"

"Must be a pretty important woman," the mixed breed finally chimes in, his hard black eyes on mine. Of them all, he seems the least intimidated.

"I'll warn you now. She reeks of Power. In fact, you might want to carry her with a sack over her head. And when she talks to the Underworld, you really don't want to be listening in."

Thirty-eight

The Yuchi settlement called Rainbow Town consisted of a palisaded central plaza that served the people's two moieties. The Chief Moiety was in charge of the northern half of the town, the Warrior Moiety of the southern. Their Council Houses stood on opposite sides of the plaza from each other. An open-roofed temple perched atop a platform of earth on the plaza's west, and the high chief's residence on the east. The rest of the space was occupied by various society houses and granaries.

Each moiety conducted its own affairs, moderated by the clans. Children were born into one of four clans, the Wolf, Bear, Panther, or Deer Clan that their mother belonged to, but also into the same moiety as their father.

In their own language the Yuchi called themselves the *Tsoyaha*, or the Children of the Sun, believing they were sprung from drops of Mother Sun's menstrual blood that had fallen to earth as she crossed the heavens in the Beginning Times.

In their cosmology, the sky had the three great lights, the sun, moon, and stars, each of which they depicted as circling the heavens. From them, the rainbow served as a bridge to the earth. In the Beginning Times, a mysterious stranger had descended from the rainbow. Called the *Kala Hi'ki*, the mysterious stranger had taught the Yuchi all the ways in which to deport themselves as brave, honorable, wise, and respectful people.

Rainbow Town was their westernmost settlement just below the Great

Bend of the Tenasee. Surrounded by Muskogean peoples to the north, west, and south, the Yuchi had been in a state of constant war until the coming of the Cahokians. As the first colonial expeditions pushed down-river, the Yuchi had quickly allied themselves, accepting priests, Traders, and even allowing a colony on their southern boundary. They had rightly figured that it was smart to have a Cahokian colony situated between them and the bellicose Sky Hand Muskogeans who had recently conquered the Albaamaha and Koasati nations on the southern side of the divide.

It was toward this western Yuchi city that *Red Reed* now traveled. This was familiar country for the Traders. And they put their backs into the paddling, for this was a holy day that marked the lunar maximum.

"It's like a homecoming," White Mat called over his shoulder as *Red Reed* was driven up the Tenasee's eastern shore toward Rainbow Town. He and the others cried out greetings in their native Yuchi tongue to locals who were on the river checking their weirs, fish traps, and crawfish pots.

Night Shadow Star enjoyed the rising sense of anticipation as they passed the first Yuchi villages. Most were either empty or vacating as people left for the lunar celebration in Rainbow Town. *Red Reed* joined a growing flotilla of dugouts paralleling the bank as they paddled their way upstream.

"It's the moon ceremony," Half Root told Night Shadow Star. "To-night, the moon will set at the northernmost point in its cycle."

Of course. Cahokia, too, would be awash in celebration. Not with as grand and sacred a pageant as the southern lunar maximum, but still a major marking of the eighteen-and-a-half-year lunar cycle.

Have we been on the river that long?

A canoe landing lay on the river's west bank, below a wide and shallow slope created by a long-ago slumping of the high bluff that over-looked the Tenasee. The lowland was bordered by a stream that ran down from the uplands; and a moderate incline allowed easy access to the high bluff.

The landing itself was packed with canoes, many of them pulled up and crammed together so tightly a person could barely squeeze his way between them. On the slope above, campsites had been established with slapped-together ramadas, tents, and simple collections of packs and bedrolls. Late arrivals were climbing the trail that led up to the town.

A festive mood filled the air; drums, flutes, and rhythm sticks *zizz*ing could be heard in the late afternoon. A thousand fires had to be burning atop the bluff, given the pall of smoke that rose and trailed off to the east like a plume. The roar of the crowd rose and fell as something monumental occurred beyond view on the bluff.

"Auspicious, don't you think?" White Mat called as they drove in for the shore. "Coming here on this of all days."

"It is indeed, brother," Shedding Bird agreed. "We have kin here. Chief Moiety, Wolf Clan. I wonder if they'll have room for another bed in their house?"

Half Root called, "If not, Made Man has a brother here. You can come camp with him."

"Hey, woman, that's my brother's house you're giving away," Made Man chided his wife.

"He'll be happy to see us. More so when he hears what we're about on this trip. Who we carry."

"No!" Fire Cat said sharply. "Think, my friends. They may be family, people you trust. They may only tell people they trust, who will tell people they trust. But do you want the news that you carry a lady from Cahokia passing from lip to lip? Somewhere along the line of 'trusted people' telling each other, the word will spread like wildfire through the entire celebration. Everyone will come to look, to see the lady. And then the word will be carried to Blood Talon. He will know not only where we are, but who you all are, and when we were here."

White Mat sighed as he shipped his paddle and stepped from the canoe, looked at the rest, read their disappointment. "You all know he's right, don't you?"

One by one, they nodded, slightly crestfallen looks on their faces.

"All it would take is one slip," Mixed Shell said. "We could lose everything we've worked so hard to accomplish."

"As for me," Shedding Bird added as he stepped out of *Red Reed*, "when the story is told, I don't want to be remembered as the one who acted foolishly, bragging, and brought disaster down on everyone's heads."

"Me, either," Made Man agreed.

Together they all pulled *Red Reed* as high as they could on the swampy land just above the creek mouth—the only unoccupied area remaining. White Mat tied the canoe off to a bald cypress sapling, lest the water rise and float the *Red Reed* away.

Up to her ankles in mud, Night Shadow Star dabbed some of her red paint onto her cheeks and asked, "How do I look?"

"Like a red-cheeked Trader," Fire Cat told her with a smile before smearing white onto his own cheeks to cover the Red Wing tattoos. Then he shouldered a small pack filled with just enough Trade to see them fed and perhaps housed for the night.

"What about the Trade and our things? Should someone stay to watch *Red Reed*?"

"It will be safe, Lady. This isn't Cahokia. These are Yuchi, on a most revered holiday. Not only would no one so much as think of stealing, they'd be horrified about the repercussions from the Spirit World if anyone did so on such a sacred day."

Given the crowding, they had to wade through muck for a half a bow-shot to reach solid ground.

The climb up to the bluff actually felt good, having been too long since they'd used their legs.

Atop the high bluff, camps had been set up in every direction and against the palisade that surrounded Rainbow Town. The palisade itself served as a reminder that while the Cahokian Peace might be on people's lips, the *Tsoyaha* didn't take it for granted.

Situated as it was on the edge of the bluff, the town overlooked the Tenasee, with a good view of the river and the thickly forested rolling country off to the east.

People and dogs were everywhere; the breeze blowing in from the west carried the odors of cooking fish, roasting duck, geese, cranes, venison, turkey, and turtle along with the smells of boiling crawfish, hominy, greens, corn stew, baking smilax, and countie root. The odors of fresh cattail and yellow-lotus-root bread made the mouth water.

It sounded like chaos: drumming, flutes, laughter, shouts, clapping hands, the roar of the crowd surrounding the stickball field. Children raced by, half of them laughing, the others blowing on willow-stem whistles. Dogs were barking, running around in packs that people alternately chided, chased off with thrown sticks, or called to.

Everyone was dressed in colorful clothing, and in places Wolf, Deer, Bear, and Panther Clan standards marked hastily contrived clan grounds. Outside the palisade gates, Traders had set up pavilions, stands, or just bowed to expediency and spread a blanket on the ground to display their wares.

"Should we join them?" Fire Cat asked. "Consider it part of our disguise?"

"If you'd like," White Mat told him. "Me, I'm off to see kin. Everyone, meet at the canoe tomorrow, midday. Tonight, feast, dance, sing, and find someone to share your blanket with."

With that, he whooped, slapped his brother on the back, and the two of them marched off toward the stickball field and chunkey court along the town's western wall.

"Find someone to share a blanket with?" Night Shadow Star asked.

"It's a lunar celebration." Half Root arched a suggestive eyebrow and gave Made Man an intimate glance. "Fertility. Making the world new. Think red Power: creative, chaotic, and lusty. You follow my path here?"

To emphasize her words, she squeezed Made Man's hand and grinned. "But no coupling until after moonrise. Those are the Yuchi rules."

"What about people who aren't married?"

"Oh, there will be plenty of partners," Mixed Shell told her.

With that, he, too, gave them a ribald wink and set off for the stick-ball grounds.

"See you at the canoe. Midday tomorrow," Half Root reminded. Taking Made Man in tow, she headed off for the town gates.

Another frantic cry rose from the crowd around the stickball field. Night Shadow Star stared longingly at it. Back in Cahokia, she'd be playing. Probably at this very moment. There, she'd be leading the Morning Star House women's team against the other Houses and the Earth Clans as well.

"Want to go see?" Fire Cat asked amiably. "Just to get an idea of what the competition is like?"

She couldn't stop the grin. Together they walked over to join the crowd. That no one realized who she was came as a shock. In Cahokia, she was a renowned stickball player; people recognized her even when she was present only as a spectator. Here, no one gave her so much as a second look. The feeling was . . . peculiar.

And then liberating.

She found it almost impossible, however, to just let herself go. To simply be herself. Not to worry about what people were thinking, seeing.

This was a grudge match, Bear Clan against Panther Clan, each side fielding more than a hundred players. Amid the screaming and yelling of the thousand or so spectators she could hear the grunting of the players, the clacking as they banged their racquets together and shouted encouragement to each other.

Down the court, she could see the scoring sticks: sixteen for Bear Clan, fourteen for Panther. If this was like the Cahokian game, the first side to reach twenty would win.

As the game progressed, she lost her self-conscious feeling, whistling and clapping as the play intensified. Both teams collided down by the Panther goal, tens of bodies slamming together in a melee of confusion as both sides fought over possession of the deer-hide ball. Someone screamed in pain.

The press of men surged back and forth, seeking by sheer mass to force the others away from the ball.

And miraculously a young man appeared out of the chaos of straining bodies and charged for the Bear goal on the opposite end of the field. Shouts rose, the whole pack of sweating and gasping men pounding after him.

Fleet as the young man was, others were closing, and at the last instant, he reached back, used his racquet to catapult the ball toward his teammates. The forward players for Bear Clan knew their game, four blocking the Panther Clan guards while the fifth neatly caught the ball with his racquet, spun, and raced wide around the defenders. With a series of brilliant passes, Bear Clan managed to close with the goal. A forward caught the ball, feinted, ducked around a Panther Clan guard, and used his racquet to whip the ball between the goalposts.

Bear Clan erupted, shouting, leaping, clapping, and whooping.

"Did you see that passing? They practiced that," Night Shadow Star told Fire Cat.

He gave her a grin, reading her delight. "Wish you were playing?"

"Of course. I wonder if any of the women's teams need a volunteer."

"As good as you are? They'd want to know who the new phenomenon was who made all those goals, which would lead to uncomfortable questions about who you are and where you came from."

For the next few fingers of time, she lost herself in the game, joining the crowd as she enthusiastically rooted for the Bear Clan. In the end they won by two, Panther Clan never managing to close the gap.

Huge amounts of goods had been wagered on the outcome, including blankets, pots, lances, bags of food, articles of clothing, ritual dress, slaves, and even canoes. Half the wealth of the western Yuchi changed hands, the losers dismayed, the winners delighted.

"Looks like they bet the town," Fire Cat told her.

She shot him a smile. "Nothing like what you won when you beat that Natchez war chief." She paused, heart swelling. "I never told you everything about him. About what he was going to do to me when Thirteen Sacred Jaguar was away. So many things would have been different if you hadn't won that game."

"Swirling Cloud was a vile human being in a lot of ways."

"I should have freed you from your oath right then and there. I wanted to. But for Piasa . . . Pus and rot, I'm tired of being his plaything."

He laid a reassuring hand on her shoulder, telling her, "You are who you are, and Power has made you its instrument. My life is dedicated to yours, Lady. Wherever it takes us, I'm yours."

She closed her eyes, let herself settle against him, reveled in the sense of safety and security imparted by his muscular body against hers. His arm was around her shoulders, holding her close.

"Why does it always have to be so difficult?" she whispered.

"Because you and I can stand it," he told her reasonably. "Anyone else? Power would have broken them long ago, and they'd be corpses." A pause. "Now, let's go find food. I'm starved."

They traded a string of Cahokian shell beads for a feast of roast goose, acorn bread filled with sunflower seeds, and boiled crawfish all washed down by strong black drink that sent shivers of energy through her body.

As the sun set, teams of men carried whole logs into the middle of the stickball field just west of the sacred red cedar. They stacked the logs in a tall cone shape and lit it on fire. The flames slowly ate their way up the structure until a roaring fire not only illuminated the grounds and town, but its roar sent sparks whirling into the sky.

Night fell, the priests called out the prayers. Then drummers, singers, and flute players were assembled beneath the palisade walls. Accompanied by the clapping of hands, lines formed in circles around the enormous bonfire. Men took positions across from women. As the music carried in the night, the men began their dance, stepping, clapping their hands, turning and stomping.

"Want to try?" Fire Cat asked, taking Night Shadow Star's hand.

Her body almost vibrating from the strong black drink, she took position opposite him, watching the women around her, copying their steps, the swing of the hips, the timing as they clapped their hands together. The movements were intoxicating, as if she were one with the people, all moving together, a swelling sea of shared consciousness.

How long had it been since she'd danced like this? Allowed herself to be free, to just express her joy at being alive?

Not since she was a girl. It seemed an eternity gone, from some other life. Here, this night, for this moment, she was just herself with no one to judge, no one to expect anything from her.

I feel free!

Letting the music, the movements of her body buoy her spirits, she let herself go. Each step, each thrust of her hips, the sensual movements of her arms were magic. Her toned legs might have had a mind of their own. Her entire body became the music, swaying and undulating with the song.

She turned her gaze on Fire Cat. Firelight cast gold on his skin, alternating with shadows as he stepped, swayed, and clapped his hands. It accented the contours of his muscular body, slipped along the scars he'd received in her service.

The man moved with a fluid motion, his body in perfect time with the rising and falling music. Strong, supple, he turned, stepped, and clapped, the muscles in his broad shoulders knotting and swelling. Just watching him ignited some understanding in her core, aroused her in a way she'd never felt. Every move he made was born of innate masculinity.

It spoke to her soul, stirred a liquid warmth at the root of her spine that spread through her hips, up through her heart and chest.

She matched her swaying body to his, stepped closer, until they moved as one. Each motion of her arms, her matching steps, her clapping hands in perfect sync with his. Locking her eyes on Fire Cat's, she matched his smile, wondered if even her heart was beating in time with his.

Everything faded, the night, the people around them, all lost in the dance, in the rhythm and perfect harmony of their bodies. A unity of soul and motion.

We are one.

The clear sound of a conch horn carried on the night, the dance grounds going suddenly still, music and movement stopped in an instant.

All eyes turned to the northwestern horizon where the first sliver of the moon topped the distant rolling forest on the far side of the Tenasee.

The lilting voice of a priest could be heard in the silence. While the Yuchi words were incomprehensible, the deep emotion, the reverence the voice communicated, couldn't be missed: Here was a moment of bliss, the northernmost movement of the moon across the Sky World. A special time, a moment of renewal when the world was changed. One cycle was ended. Another began.

All around them, people began to sing, the Yuchi voices rising and falling, seductive and plaintive at the same time.

Men moved next to women, laid their arms over their shoulders, and began swaying, hip to hip, bodies in motion.

Night Shadow Star curled herself against Fire Cat's side, both of them copying the Yuchi step-slide-step, adding a playful shove as she matched her movements to his.

Couples were leaving, arms around each other, heading off into the darkness.

Still keeping step, she slipped around, face to face, her body pressed against his. Her heart was pounding, her breath short, as she clung to him.

"No!" Piasa almost spat from the darkness.

She closed her mind. Forced the beast out of her head. Let the ache in her heart, the liquid tingle in her loins drown any doubt.

I am no longer Night Shadow Star. She's back in Cahokia.

She reached down, slipped her hand past Fire Cat's breechcloth and grasped his hardening shaft. Every muscle in his body knotted when she tightened her grip. His gasp filled her with excitement.

"Lady?" he whispered.

"Come."

"You know what the—"

"I know what I owe Power. There is also what I owe myself, and what I owe the man I love."

"Not that I don't want this more than life itself, but what Piasa might do . . ."

She placed fingers to his lips, saying, "My love, this *is* Power. This whole night is sacred. The moon has reached its maximum in the north. All around us, people are coupling, building the Power, celebrating. Now come, let us find some dark place. I want you."

He didn't resist as she took his hand and led him into the darkness.

She thought she heard Piasa scream from a great distance away.

There would be a price. But for this night, it would be worth it.

Thirty-nine

For four days Cahokia had prepared for the lunar maximum moonrise. Each night, crowds gathered at the observatory to watch the Sky priests take their measurements. Despite the fact that clouds obscured the sky for three of the four nights, the excitement grew.

The whole city seemed to be holding its breath, waiting, expectant. The lunar maximum was a rebirth. The second-most-important ceremony in the Cahokian world, it was eclipsed only by the lunar minimum ceremony when the moon rose at its northernmost point on the southeastern horizon.

The lunar maximum only came once every eighteen-and-a-half years. On that special night, the entire nation was transfixed. While the biggest celebration—overseen by the reincarnated Morning Star—was held on the Great Plaza, every family, every farmstead, had their special temple or shrine. Everything, even elongated fire hearths, was oriented to the northwestern horizon.

Out at the Moon Mound and temple a day's travel east on the Avenue of the Sun, the moon priests would be offering sacrifices, many of them human beings. Some were slaves, taken in war or bought for the purpose, but often a family would offer one of their own. A child. A brother. A young woman. Most went joyfully, fully convinced that after they'd been strangled, their souls would enter the Land of the Ancestors as honored dead.

Some of the sacrificial dead would be cremated on elevated racks oriented to the moonrise—their souls borne up to the Sky World. Others would be interred with their corpses oriented to the northwest if they were from the Earth Clans. For them it was but a short moment and their souls would be welcomed into the Underworld by Old-Woman-Who-Never-Dies, with the arms of their ancestors ready to embrace them. Wherever the souls of the dead ended up, they carried with them the prayers and pleas of the living, whether it was for luck, prosperity, a good harvest, or forgiveness for some transgression or crime.

For those less in need of such important Spiritual intercession, the sacrifice of an animal, a bag of corn, or perhaps some precious personal possession would do. A prized bow might be burned, an expensive pot might be smashed, or a treasured stone effigy broken into pieces. In some cases, buildings would be incinerated—even great palaces if the chiefs were desperate enough to curry divine favor from the Powers of the Sky.

For four days prior to the event, Cahokia fasted, prayed, cleansed, and purified itself. Priests, warriors, and volunteers stalked through the avenues, peered into yards, and kept an eye on their neighbors to ensure the sanctity of the preparations.

For Seven Skull Shield—who thought that most religious rituals were nonsense—the four days passed in an agony of boredom. His friend Black Swallow was being watched by some of Robin Feather's agents. So, too, was Crazy Frog. Additional warriors had been stationed around Night Shadow Star's mound by Spotted Wrist. With the preparations and purification rituals, traffic on the Avenue of the Sun was but a trickle of what it normally was.

The one dark and cloudy night he and Farts could sneak up the back side of Night Shadow Star's mound and inside, Willow Blossom had flatly denied his attempt to slip under the covers with her.

"It's two days to the lunar maximum! Do you want to condemn us? Bring down all the disaster and grief? That's *forbidden!*"

His sharp ears had caught the muffled mirth as Green Stick and Clay String snickered from their beds across the room.

In Cahokia the sacred fast, asceticism, and sexual abstinence lasted until the first glimpse of the rising moon as it crested the high bluff that rose above the floodplain to the east.

Not that Seven Skull Shield or Farts went hungry that day. He'd managed to steal a couple of loaves of walnut bread from a lazy Hawk Clan vendor who'd come in early to get one of the better places along the western margin of the Great Plaza.

And come the throngs did: an endless stream of humanity arriving from all directions to pack the Great Plaza. There they stood, anxiously awaiting both the rising moon and the appearance of the living god. At moonrise Morning Star would take his place at the Council Gate to signal the beginning of the celebration.

It was easy pickings for a thief of Seven Skull Shield's ability, people with open packs hanging from their backs, distracted parents trying to keep track of their children lest they get lost in the crowd. But, as a gesture to the sanctity of the day, for the most part he restrained himself from temptation.

Well, all but for one particularly gorgeous redstone effigy pipe. The pipe had been carved by a master to represent Sky Eagle, and the bowl rested in the bird's back between the folded wings. Its owner, one of the recorders, was bragging to his companion about how he'd stand on the corner of the society house atop the recorders' mound, smash the pipe with a stone, and offer his prayer that he be made the next Master Recorder when old Lotus Leaf died, as the old recorder was sure to do in the coming moons.

Something about the man's wheedling voice just set Seven Skull Shield on edge. And the pipe was a beautiful thing, much too nice to be broken into bits for one man's vainglorious ambition.

The recorder had absently dropped the pipe back into his belt pouch, his hands waving busily as they added emphasis to his tirade on why he would be a better Master Recorder than someone named Flicker Beak. People never thought things through. Gaping open like the man's pouch was? All it took was a deft sleight of hand, and Seven Skull Shield disappeared into the crowd with his new pipe bowl. He'd have to carve a stem for it, but the thing was well worth the effort. And, if it didn't draw well, it would bring him a fortune in Trade down at the canoe landing.

Assuming he could ever ply his old Trade at the canoe landing again.

He glanced down at Farts who was pacing along at his side. "You know, I'm getting tired of always being hunted."

Since evening was falling, he picked his way through the crowd. To his immense relief, the usual warriors were missing from their station at the foot of Morning Star's great mound. No one was watching Night Shadow Star's mound that he could see. It was, after all, one of the most important holidays in Cahokia. Everything stopped for worship, reflection, purification, and prayer. Even, apparently, vendettas.

Seven Skull Shield skipped his way up the steps, kept Farts from peeing on Piasa's guardian post, and found Willow Blossom sitting on the veranda with Green Stick, Clay String, and Winter Leaf. They were in the process of shelling corn, rubbing two dried cobs against each other to break the kernels loose. As they did, a rain of yellow kernels dropped into the large basket they huddled around.

"A glorious day to you. Salutations."

"So, you're back. Noticed that Spotted Wrist has called off his warriors for the day, did you?" Green Stick looked up.

Willow Blossom dropped the cobs she'd just shelled into a sack, leapt to her feet, and ran to greet him.

Her expression was alight with joy, her eyes dancing as she took his gnarled hand in hers. "You're here! I'm so glad! What are we going to do tonight?"

"See the sights. The lunar maximum in Cahokia? It only comes around once every eighteen years or so. We're going to walk in the crowd. Watch Morning Star call the Blessing, see the Dancers, eat what we can—even if it's scarce—and join the celebration as the Sky World renews itself."

He paused, smiling down at her, feeling his heart lift. After being constantly on the run for the last moon or so, the joy at having this wonderful woman staring up at him with delight sent his spirit flying. "Now, go find something fine to wear. Something not too gaudy, but rich."

He watched her whirl and run for the palace.

"We've got a roof leak," Green Stick remarked as he shelled corn.

"Well, get it fixed."

The servant shot him a reproving look. "That's *your* job. The lady left you in charge. Seems to me all you do is slip around and do your best to keep one bunch or another from hanging you in a square or bashing your brains out."

"What do I know about fixing roofs?"

"You're the great Seven Skull Shield. You're supposed to know all the common folk, the Traders and artisans. Surely you've run across some thatch Traders somewhere who would know someone who could fix the roof."

Winter Leaf and Clay String were now giving him the eye.

"I can probably find someone. That's, well, like a special sort of builder." He could figure this out. What was the point of knowing all the people he did if he couldn't tackle as mundane a chore as getting a roof fixed?

Willow Blossom emerged wearing a striking white skirt that was belted around her narrow waist and accented the enticing swell of her hips. A fine dogbane cloak hung at her slender shoulders. Shell necklaces fell to the tops of her perfect round breasts. She'd pinned her hair with a feather splay that appeared to radiate from behind her head.

In her arms she carried a red war shirt that she tossed to him, saying, "Put that on. I don't want to go with you looking like some dirt farmer from up on the bluff. You can disguise yourself just as well by looking like a noble."

Seven Skull Shield grinned, glanced down at Farts. "So, dog, what are we going to disguise you as?"

"Most people already mistake him for a bear," Green Stick muttered sourly.

As the sun set, fires began to spring up, casting their light into the gloom. The sky in the west had gone from orange to indigo while the eastern sky darkened from bruised purple to charcoal and the first stars poked out.

As Seven Skull Shield and Willow Blossom, arm in arm, wended their way through the pack of humanity surrounding the Great Plaza, she asked, "What happens if Night Shadow Star never comes back?"

"She will. What makes you ask that?"

"How long will people wait, like the *tonka'tzi*, before she declares Night Shadow Star dead and missing for good?"

"Cofitachequi is a long way away. Even if Night Shadow Star and the Red Wing are making good time, it's still a couple of moons before they could get there."

"What if she never makes it? Rivers are supposed to be dangerous places. People drown. There are barbaric tribes out there. Accidents happen. Illness. A lot could go wrong."

"Why are you worrying about this?"

"Well . . . what if she never makes it?"

"Someone will eventually bring word back. Probably from that big expedition that left after she did. They're headed to the same place. They'll be asking about her. She's not the kind of woman people don't remember."

"So, if word comes back that something happened to her?"

Seven Skull Shield shrugged, stepping wide around a group of dirt farmers who'd plunked themselves down in the middle of the way. The men were seated cross-legged, the women with their knees together to the side. All were clapping their hands, singing in some incomprehensible language in time to a drum and flute. Their eyes were fixed on Morning Star's Great Mound, as if they expected him to appear in a blaze of light at any moment.

"I suppose if word came back that she was dead, maybe Morning Star or the *tonka'tzi* would order her palace burned. Maybe a new layer of earth laid atop it, and another palace built. Or maybe not, since she didn't die there. I don't know."

"But what would happen to Green Stick and the others? They'd have to go live somewhere else, right?"

"Like I said, I don't know. They're her slaves. If she died here in Cahokia, they might be sacrificed to follow her to the Underworld. If she dies someplace far away and there is no soul to attach them to? Maybe they'd be freed. Maybe given to someone else, I don't know. That's noble stuff."

She had tightened her hold on his arm, her brow deeply lined as if vexed. "What about that old lady, Blue Heron?"

"She's not exactly old. Just, well, older."

"Would she take in Night Shadow Star's people? I had a cousin who took all of one of his cousin's slaves once. And she's Night Shadow Star's aunt, after all."

"Why are you so worried about this?"

"Oh, it's not me," she insisted. "The others are worried."

"Don't worry about Night Shadow Star. Whatever she's about, she has Piasa's protection. If a person has to have an ally, there are worse to have on your side."

But Willow Blossom continued to frown. "Have you ever thought about moving in with Blue Heron?"

"Where did that come from?"

"Well, I was thinking you serve her, and I could serve you. Sort of keep it all in one palace."

Seven Skull Shield thought back to Blue Heron's apparent dislike of Willow Blossom. Surely this eager-eyed young woman would be an asset in Blue Heron's household. She could run errands for Smooth Pebble, help with—

Pus and blood, what was he thinking? A soft and tender thing like Willow Blossom in Blue Heron's household? With Smooth Pebble, Dancing Sky, White Rain, and Soft Moon? They'd eat her alive.

"Hey, don't you worry. Not that I believe anything will happen to Night Shadow Star, but if it did, you'd always have a place with me."

She squeezed his arm, looked up at him. Her smile wavered the slightest bit, her eyes didn't have the dazzling warmth, but that was probably because he couldn't see them in the dark.

And later, after the moon rose, the Dancing began. When feasting had filled people's bellies, Seven Skull Shield led her back to Night Shadow Star's palace.

Willow Blossom must have been tired, maybe a bit under the weather. Or maybe she'd just eaten too much. As they made love that night, she only seemed to be going through the motions. Her movements seemed lethargic, something forced about her little gasps and moans.

But it's probably just me. Too many worries. Too long living on the run.

Forty

Fire Cat and Night Shadow Star spent that night of the lunar maximum rolled in a blanket somewhere in a freshly planted cornfield outside the Yuchi's Rainbow Town. It would be the most memorable and wondrous night of his life.

Maybe it was the black drink that pounded in their veins, or the Power of the full moon beaming down from the northern sky, or maybe it was just that he had come to love her with all of his being. Whatever the reason, they consummated their relationship in every way. Nor did they finally succumb to sleep until the first rays of the sun were turning the forest behind them golden.

The sound of a stone ax striking wood brought Fire Cat awake when the sun was nearly two hands high. He and Night Shadow Star lay naked, her supple body teasing one memory after another from down between his souls. This morning he saw her as he'd never seen her before, knew her as he'd never known her.

Together they had broken Piasa's deal, and who knew what that might entail? He tried to convince himself that it was all right, that they'd done it in the midst of a new-moon ceremony that celebrated the glory of the act.

He wondered if he was deluding himself.

Rising, he slipped into the forest to relieve himself, then walked back. Took a long moment to fix the sight of her perfect body in his memory. If he died this day, he wanted to take this image with him to the Underworld, or wherever his souls ended up.

Finally, he knelt, took her hand. "Lady, wake up. It's full day. We need to get dressed, find some food, and be ready to meet the Traders at the canoe."

She blinked, came awake, and fixed on him. A smile bent her lips. "When did waking stop and the dreams begin?"

"I don't understand."

"I was dreaming it just now. You and me, shaft and sheath. Still locked together. I don't ever want to stop. Let's just fade back into the forest, go find a meadow, and we'll stay that way. Your shaft locked inside me from now on. Maybe I'll draw you in. Shaft first, then your balls and legs, hips, your chest and arms, and finally your head." She tapped over her heart. "I'll keep you here where you can never be taken away."

"I can think of worse fates."

He took her hand, pulled her to her feet, and together they dressed, grabbed up their pack, and went in search of breakfast.

After they'd Traded an oyster-shell bead for a thick goosefoot-seed stew, they watched a makeup stickball match. Checked out the Trade before the gates, and finally wandered back down to the canoe landing, knowing they were about half a hand of time early.

Wading across the muck to *Red Reed*, they were able to drag the canoe over and beach it on the landing where enough vessels had left the celebration to make room. They washed the sticky mud off their feet as best they could and sat on the gunwale, toes in the water, watching the people coming and going.

The place was like a hive. Just about everyone looked tired, but happy. Well, all but the family of seven. Three of the little boys had done something so terrible their parents were absolutely enraged as they loaded kids and camp into the canoe and shoved out for home.

"You've been thoughtful," Fire Cat noted. "More than once I've seen your gaze go vacant. What's Piasa saying?"

"We're bargaining."

Fire Cat's stomach dropped. "Over what?"

"My services."

"And?"

She shot him a sidelong glance, a steely brightness in her dark eyes. "The world changed last night. It's not the same place it was. Every time I took you inside me. Every time you cried out as you shot your seed. Every time I gasped with the fire of delight running through my body, we changed the world. Drove it further and further from the way it was into something different."

"I'm not sure I understand."

"In return for my city and people I gave up any chance to share my life with you as a woman does with a man, and I did it again in exchange for Morning Star's soul in the Underworld. That was Piasa's price. Last night, you and I joined our bodies under the light of the reborn moon. That's Sky Power. Things are different. Unfamiliar voices are talking in my head."

Fire Cat looked out over the river; he counted fifteen canoes coming and going at the landing.

She said, "I have given him my word that I will deal with Walking Smoke. If I do that, Piasa and I start from somewhere different. Go from there."

"He won't just leave?"

She tapped the side of her head. "He's in here, Fire Cat. He devoured my souls in the Underworld. He made me part of him, and he will be part of me for the rest of my life. It's just how it is."

"I'm still worried about this bargain."

"My decision to lock hips with you last night was made with the understanding that Piasa might very well kill me. I offered him my life in exchange for what we did. But what good does it do the Lord of the Underworld if he kills me? Alive, I still serve him. So, I'll go kill Walking Smoke, and by doing so, he'll keep you alive."

"Let him kill me." Fire Cat gave her a brave smile. "For last night? It was worth it."

She took his hand, gave it a squeeze. "That's a negotiating point. If you are dead, I have no reason to live." A pause as her gaze went unfocused again. "Funny, isn't it?"

"What's that?"

"I would have never found this courage or freedom if we'd stayed in Cahokia. I would have been Night Shadow Star forever. Here, on the river, I can finally see and understand. It's as if my world has been covered with a thick black smoke that obscured so many simple truths. If having you in my bed means I have to pay with death, I am ready to die."

"Lady, don't speak flippantly, not where Power can hear."

She shook her head sadly. "Without you, I have nothing."

"You have me. In your bed or not. I'd already made my peace."

"That's one of the reasons I made the decision I did. How can I live with any man after living with you? It's you and me. Or nothing."

"Let's just hope that Piasa knows how far we'll go to keep his . . . Wait, what's this?"

Fire Cat fixed on the big war canoe that appeared from behind the mat of vegetation downstream from the canoe landing. It cut the water, gliding gracefully across the murky surface of the river. Lines of paddlers were driving it for the landing with rhythmic strokes. Two men, dressed in war regalia, were perched in the high bow.

Fire Cat's heart sank, and he reached for his sacked weapons where they lay in the bottom of the canoe.

"Wait," Night Shadow Star told him, placing her hand on his arm. "We're not undone yet. Sit here, like we are. Our faces are painted, we're Traders."

"As long as Blood Talon doesn't walk right up and look me in the eyes." Fire Cat took a calming breath, his heart beginning to pound. "If he does, Lady, I'm going to kill him first thing." And with that, he slid his copper-bitted war club from its sack.

The Cahokian war canoe was coming fast, water roiling at its bow. Blood Talon—Nutcracker behind him—stood in the high prow and looked as if he were master of the river.

Forty-one

Night Shadow Star watched the Cahokian war canoe slide up on the beach not twenty paces down from where she and Fire Cat sat on *Red Reed*'s gunwale, their feet dangling in the water.

Fire Cat was as tense as a bent sapling, his hand resting just above his war club where it lay hidden by the hull.

Since waking that morning, she had been living a confusion of thoughts and hearing strange disembodied voices—though she'd struggled mightily to pass herself off as unconcerned about her nightlong need to fill herself with Fire Cat's body.

The voices had been howling, especially Piasa's, and she kept seeing flickers of movements, flashes of light at the corner of her vision. Her thoughts had been scattered, her memory replaying one particular copulation: She'd leaped on Fire Cat with a shrill yip, bit him on the shoulder. The coupling had been wild as she hammered her body against his. Then burst into a climax like she'd never known. Over and over the memory repeated, as if her souls couldn't recall the other times, but had fixed on that one explosive event.

Each time it replayed down in her souls, she could feel Piasa's rage. Hear his sibilant hiss as it mixed with the sound of people and the clamor of the celebration.

What have I done? Who have I become?

Her thoughts were reeling, confused. One part of her reveled in her mating with Fire Cat. She had relieved a suffocating weight that threatened to crush her. Another part of her experienced a sense of fulfillment as a woman—that she had finally been able to express the love she felt, that even if they died within the next moments, Fire Cat had shared her heart and soul. Then, an instant later, she was consumed by a sucking sense of guilt. That she'd somehow betrayed herself and Fire Cat, that her selfish actions would destroy them both.

That, in turn, led to panic.

How could a person be so torn inside?

"Because now there is no way out for you," Piasa hissed from the air above her head.

She kept thinking: *I've doomed myself . . . and him.*

And all the while, she'd been bargaining with Piasa, whispering, "I know what I promised. But I'm not sorry. I will bring Walking Smoke down. If you must punish, take it out on me. Not Fire Cat."

"And if I do?"

She glanced at the flicker of light at the edge of her vision, whispering, "Then I will never serve you again."

"I could devour your souls."

"Without Fire Cat, I have no use for them."

With all her might, she concentrated, imagining ways she could kill herself. Insisting that her threat was no bluff.

She needed only to stare into Fire Cat's eyes, send him that shy and intimate smile, and watch the light of love fill his eyes. When she did, she knew she had the courage to defy her lord.

Life without this man was simply not worth living.

"You try me."

"Then pick a more compliant woman next time, Lord," she growled under her breath as the Cahokian warriors leaped over the sides of their canoe and pulled it up onto the ash-stained sand of the canoe landing.

"Easy," she told Fire Cat as his fingers strayed toward the war club. "We're just harmless Traders. Remember?"

"You would have made a good war chief," he told her, sticking to Trade pidgin.

"How's my face paint?"

"A little smudged, but the tattoos are still illegible. And you have grass in your hair."

She laughed at that. "You look like you spent all night copulating with a bobcat yourself. But then, that's half the town."

Blood Talon and Nutcracker were issuing orders, the squadron leader surveying the landing, hands on his hips. With barely a flicker, his gaze traveled over *Red Reed* where Fire Cat and Night Shadow Star remained seated. They were just a couple among the fifty or so people thronging the hundreds of other canoes. Some were loading packs and pushing out. Others just came to retrieve something from the boats.

"Bring the packs and that Trade," Nutcracker called. "Take your weapons. Let's make a good show of it, but I want bows and quivers slung, war clubs on your belts."

"Old Scar, Whistle Hand, you stay and watch the canoe." Blood Talon pointed at two of the warriors.

"All right, Piasa," Night Shadow Star whispered under her breath, "let's see if we have a deal."

"What are you doing?" Fire Cat demanded.

She dragged a blanket out and draped it over his battle-scarred legs. That, if anything, would give him away upon close scrutiny. "Stay here. I have to find out something. Trust me."

She pushed off *Red Reed*'s side, reached for her small pack of Trade, and started for the warriors. She gave a slight, saucy swing to her hips, head back so that her long hair spilled down her back, her chin up.

"Hey, warriors," she called in Trade pidgin. "We've got Trade. Where you from?"

Blood Talon and Nutcracker stopped short, giving her appreciative glances.

"Now that's a nice sight," Nutcracker told his commander in Cahokian. "Too bad she isn't in my bed on these lonely nights. Hope that Trader over there knows what he's got."

Blood Talon shrugged. "Too much muscle for my taste. I like more cushion. Still, I'd Trade a shell gorget for a chance to slip my spear into this one."

"Hey," Night Shadow Star continued as she stepped up to them, fully aware the rest of the warriors were gathering around. She kept her smile in place, ignoring the comments they were making about how they'd do what and where in her body. "Where you from? What language is that?"

"Cahokian," Nutcracker told her in pidgin, cocking his head and smiling. "We're from Cahokia. Under direct orders from the Morning Star. We're looking for a woman."

"Apparently you're very good at your jobs. You've found one. Cahokian, huh? You know the living god?"

Nutcracker jerked a thumb at Blood Talon. "The squadron first here, he sits at the living god's right hand. We're his finest warriors."

"Then you'll have his finest Trade." She arched a challenging eyebrow. "I have spoonbill feathers, stingray spines, yaupon, even southeastern copper"—she pulled out a nugget—"which is worth ten times what that poor stuff from up north is worth."

"What about for you?" Nutcracker asked, lips breaking into a know-ing leer. "Say, you and me, for a hand of time? That brush over there would have some nice secluded spots."

She tossed her head toward where Fire Cat waited. "My man might take offense. Now, if you'd been here last night . . . Well, you know how it is when the moon rises on the night of the lunar maximum. We were both a little wild last night. Today? Sure, but I'd want your canoe in ex-change."

"Our canoe? Just to slip my shaft into your sheath?" Nutcracker laughed. "What do you want for that piece of copper? The Morning Star's palace?"

"Sure. You got a deal," she told him with a disarming smile.

"How about some information?" Blood Talon asked, clearly irritated to be delayed. "We're looking for a Cahokian woman, travels with a warrior. She's Four Winds Clan. You know who they are? She has spirals tattooed on her cheeks. They'd treat her specially, and her slave looks like a battle-hardened warrior. Tough man. Pretty scarred up. Traveling with five Traders, we think the Traders might be Yuchi."

"Lot of Yuchi Traders, look around," she rejoined. "You, war chief, you sure—"

"Squadron first," Blood Talon interrupted.

"—you don't want to Trade for this copper? Since you don't have the Morning Star's palace with you, you got art? Maybe a gorget? Some of those remarkable Cahokian fabrics?"

"This woman we're looking for," Blood Talon insisted. "She's called Night Shadow Star. Her slave is Fire Cat, he's a Red Wing. You tell me where I can find them, I might just be tempted to Trade you this canoe."

"You serious? You'd Trade that canoe for this woman?"

In Cahokian, Blood Talon told Nutcracker, "We can always get an-other canoe." In Trade pidgin, he told her. "Find me the woman, the canoe is yours."

She cocked her head, narrowed her eyes. "The living god must want them pretty bad if you'd Trade a big bald-cypress canoe like that. How long will you be here in Rainbow Town?"

"Overnight. We're headed upriver in the morning. Put the word out. I mean it. You find Night Shadow Star for me, I'll make you one of the richest women on the Tenasee. Now, nice talking with you, but we have to be on with our duties."

As he turned away, Blood Talon added in Cahokian, "As if you could find Night Shadow Star, you southern swamp slut."

The rest of the warriors laughed, winking, shooting her lascivious grins. Nutcracker was bold enough to reach out and cup his hand around her right buttock before giving it a squeeze. Her startled reaction brought more jeers from the rest of them as they filed past.

How dare a common warrior take such a . . .

Her reaction was instinctive. She barely stopped herself from ordering him back, telling Blood Talon exactly who she was, and demanding the second's death on the spot.

"*Careful,*" Piasa's voice whispered.

"Close. Too close." She had to bury the part of her that was still Night Shadow Star. She was a Trader. Only a Trader. She forced her heart to slow, made her expression blank. Got her breathing under control.

As the Cahokian warriors headed up the slope, Old Scar, one of the guards, walked up, saying slyly in pidgin, "I'd Trade. I've got a string of shell beads here, given to me by the Morning Star himself. Now, we'd have to be discreet, but you could have these for a couple of fingers of time over in those bushes."

He pulled a sweat-stained necklace from under his war shirt.

She gave him a bitter chuckle. "Those are freshwater clamshells. Not even cut round. The way I hear it? The Morning Star only wears necklaces made from perfectly cut shell Traded all the way up from the Gulf."

She turned, sauntered back in her saucy walk, aware that Old Scar and Whistle Hand were still watching.

"Well?" Fire Cat asked, his fingers playing just out of sight within reach of his war club.

"They're headed upriver in the morning. Offered that big canoe in Trade for you and me. That's a lot of incentive, provided it wasn't a trick."

"But they didn't know you?"

"Didn't have a clue." She frowned. "But I learned what I wanted to know. Piasa could have turned me over to them, but he didn't. That was the test. I think, Fire Cat, for the moment, you and I have dodged the arrow of fate."

"Let's just hope we keep dodging it."

Piasa laughed from so closely behind her left ear that she couldn't help but spin, expecting to see the Spirit Beast. She only found empty air.

Forty-two

Blood Talon studied the throngs of people. Many were packed around the plaza immediately west of the Rainbow Town palisade. Must have been quite the celebration. While many of the participants were drifting away, the town and its surroundings remained crowded. The grass had been trampled, the thick ash lens left in the wake of a bonfire smoked in the middle of the stickball field.

Despite that, a pickup stickball game was in progress, the teams avoiding the hot spot as if it were but another hazard in the play.

Surely, here, among all these people, he would find some kind of word about Night Shadow Star. The woman couldn't have just up and disappeared. *Red Reed*, and the Traders who accompanied her, had to be somewhere on the river.

Despite the number of searchers he had lured, threatened, and wheedled out of the chief at Red Bluff Town, no hint had come as to his quarry's location.

So, had Night Shadow Star given up? Headed back to Cahokia? Perhaps slipped over to the Southern Shawnee River? Or had she just gone to ground, hiding somewhere along some backwater where she hoped she wouldn't be spotted?

Given the manpower he'd turned loose on the sprawling waterway, he should have heard.

Beside him, Nutcracker chuckled.

"Something funny?"

"Just thinking of that sassy Tenasee Trader. I think I'll dream of her tonight. Nice one, that. You should have felt her rear. Solid, muscular. Just the thought of wiggling my shaft inside her makes me so hard a dog couldn't chew it."

"You could find out," Split Limb told him. "She said she'd warm your shaft in return for the war canoe. Suits the rest of us. We can always find another canoe to get our sorry hides back to Cahokia."

Blood Talon shot them an irritated glance. "No one is going anywhere unless it's after Night Shadow Star. We've been given a task to complete, we're going to finish it. Even if we have to go all the way to Cofitachequi to hunt her down."

"Long way," Nutcracker said as he watched three young Yuchi women pass. They were all giggling, sharing something either humorous or salacious, given the way they shot dark-eyed sidelong glances at Blood Talon and the rest of the warriors.

His men were back to uttering ribald comments, which, fortunately, the young women found as incomprehensible as he and his warriors found Yuchi.

"All right, let's get about it. The best source of information is going to be in the palisade. This place has to have a chief, and he has to have an interpreter. Time to see what we can pry out of these barbarians."

He turned, leading the way past a camp of Yuchi who were seated around a large stewpot. Apparently it was their last meal because they were ladling out the dregs of what had been a feast of hominy.

Even as he did, he couldn't help but remember the expression on that river Trader's face as Nutcracker grabbed her nicely rounded rear. That look of absolute shock and disbelief. Woman like her, as worldly as she'd sounded, she should have been used to being groped. So why the stunned expression?

He just couldn't get it out of his mind.

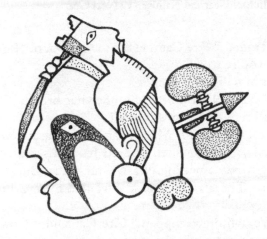

Forty-three

There was nothing like being face-to-face with one's enemy to spur an increase in pace. At Night Shadow Star's first telling of the encounter, the Traders had been incredulous. Needless to say, all it took to convince them was a casual head nod toward the two Cahokian warriors who guarded the big war canoe. It remained beached just down from *Red Reed* on Rainbow Town's busy landing.

White Mat and the rest wasted no time, tossing their belongings, a couple of packs of food, and some gear into the *Red Reed*'s waiting hull.

As Old Scar and Whistle Hand watched suspiciously from the war canoe, *Red Reed* had been shoved into the backwater, turned, and vigorously paddled around the confluence. Night Shadow Star had tossed one last look over her shoulder an instant before the steep bluff hid them from view.

"You went over and talked to them?" Shedding Bird asked incredulously. "What if they'd recognized you?"

"Then it would have been all over," Night Shadow Star told him. "But they didn't. They thought I was a Trader, and if I can fool them, I can fool anyone."

"What did they try and Trade?" Made Man called from where he paddled behind Fire Cat.

"Me. For a half hand of time in the bushes. I told them they had a deal, but it would cost them that war canoe. I think Nutcracker might have considered it."

"I'd have Traded," Fire Cat told her in Cahokian. "But after last night, I know what you're worth."

She shot him a flirtatious smile.

"Uh-huh," Half Root muttered under her breath. "I thought something was different between you two."

"Blame it on the moon." Made Man wore a lascivious grin.

"About time," Mixed Shell offered from his seat. "The rest of us weren't going to say anything. Wasn't our place. But watching you two up until today? There's times we just wanted to say, 'Just go do it! Stop the pain.'"

"The pain's definitely stopped," Fire Cat said. "Now we just have to figure out what it means in the grand scheme of things."

Piasa hissed his rage from just behind her head.

Night Shadow Star bit her lip, concentrating on her paddle as they passed beneath the sheer bluff, dominated by Rainbow Town where it perched on the heights above.

With nothing to do but paddle and listen to the voices in her head, she finally had time to face the fact that her future had changed. Her relationship with Fire Cat had been forever altered. Somehow, being in love with the man who had killed Makes Three had been one thing. Platonic love didn't reek of betrayal. Having taken Fire Cat into her bed, however, left her uneasy. She had loved her first husband, had centered her life around him, especially after having been taken by Morning Star after his reincarnation and then her subsequent rape by Walking Smoke.

Both events had traumatized her. That Morning Star had taken her to his bed the morning after his reincarnation was unsettling enough; she'd ultimately been able to convince herself that it wasn't her brother who drove himself into her. That she was the first woman the living god had wanted upon his rebirth in Chunkey Boy's body, uncomfortable as that had been.

But Walking Smoke? That he had beaten her, choked her, and savagely raped her had been so repellent she'd blocked the memory. Locked it away in some dark place between her souls. A place so deep it had taken Piasa and Horned Serpent to dig it out while she lay dying in the Underworld.

Looking back, perhaps that was why she'd placed so much dependency on Makes Three. He had been a kind, compassionate, and loving man. The kind of decent human being she'd clung to desperately as a reminder that not all men were sordid, vile, and heartless.

"Thinking something?" Fire Cat asked, his paddle stroking rhythmically in time with the others as they paralleled the bank.

"About my first husband. About you. About what it all means."

"We can always go back to the way—"

"No. Not only is it impossible, but I don't want to. Do you?"

"Not a chance. I just thought—"

"It's appreciated, but stop it. I loved Makes Three. We were young. Our lives were built on passion. You know first love? That initial hot burn in a person's life? A consuming ache for each other? That was what I felt. And I needed him. Clung to him. Made him the center of my life because I had no center of my own. Which was why, when he died, I sent my souls to the Underworld to find him. I wanted to die there so I never had to come back and face the world without him."

"If I could go back . . ."

"Don't be silly. When Piasa ordered me to cut you down from the square that night, I loathed you with all my soul, hoped you would spit out some vile curse in defiance. Free me to cut you apart piece by piece."

"I would have, if I'd known who you were."

They paddled for a time, her thoughts going back to that night, wondering how, in his pain and delirium, he could have mistaken her for First Woman.

Because he did, he bound himself to me. Was there to save my life, to save my city from the Itza, to rescue Morning Star, and ultimately to accompany me here.

"Now you begin to understand what you are throwing away," Piasa's voice sounded off to the side where water roiled and swirled.

"Lord, maybe you are more than just a vicious beast," she replied. Piasa's essence slipped along just beneath the river's surface. She could feel the Spirit creature, smoldering, uneasy, and not a little curious.

"The mysterious ways of Power, Lady," Fire Cat whispered. "It played us both. Not sure what it means now that we've shared the robes."

"Me, either. Nor is Piasa. Not that his demands ever made sense. I can understand throwing us together. We defeated Walking Smoke, defeated the Itza, saved the balance of Power, and retrieved Morning Star from the Underworld. But surely, by sending us on this journey, Piasa had to know that once we were out of Cahokia, it was only a matter of time. The beast lives within me, it knows the ache I have for you. Place a smoldering coal in a pile of leaves, Red Wing, and it's only a matter of time before it burns free."

He pursed his lips, frowned, the muscles in his arms tensing and flowing as he helped drive *Red Reed* across the green-tinted water.

Finally, he said, "I think you're right. Piasa knew it would happen. Knows what we mean to each other. As dedicated as I was to you before, my life and yours are now inseparable. Consuming. What does that gain the beast in our current endeavor?"

Piasa laughed inside her head.

"Clever man. He is indeed worthy."

"Oh, go drown a crawfish," she told it.

"What's the creature say?"

"Nothing reassuring."

Which turned her stomach. She glanced sidelong at Fire Cat; her heart and chest burned with her love for him. How many ways could Power use that? Manipulate her? Drive her to act, even against her own interests?

Too many.

Forty-four

Four major cataracts impeded the Tenasee River's flow along its central section. The first was located in the lower half of the river's Great Bend where the channel changed to a northerly route and headed for its confluence with the Mother Water. A Cahokian colony called Reed Bottom Town had displaced—or rather conquered and enslaved—a village of Koasati who had once lived there. The location was strategically located astride the great war path and Trading trail. The route—used for generations—ran from the lower Father Water, northeast to the ford at the Tenasee at the lower cataract. From there the trail continued northeast to the crossing of the Southern Shawnee River, and hence to the headwaters of the Mother River in the Algonquian lands. Anyone now traveling that route found it squarely blocked by the Cahokian presence at Reed Bottom Town on the Tenasee, and the newly established White Swan Town on the Southern Shawnee.

In addition, Reed Bottom Town controlled the river. When the water ran low, the cataract prevented all upstream travel. At those times the rushing water had to be portaged around, or men had to be hired to physically tow canoes up the fast water—a feat filled with danger and potential disaster for the canoe and to whomever was trying to steer the vessel and keep it from capsizing.

On Fire Cat's advice, they passed Reed Bottom Town at night. Not only did it buy them time—for the squadron first was sure to stop there—but if no one saw them pass, no one could report the same to

Blood Talon when he demanded information from the Fox Clan chief in charge of the colony.

Red Reed, by luck, arrived at the first cataract after a heavy rain, and with the river up, they were able to tow the slim canoe through the areas where the current ran swiftly. As a result, they made the passage in a single long day.

Advancing up the river they came to the Koasati Shallows, where again they were able to both pole and tow *Red Reed* through the fast water. From there the river ran east to the Mussel Shallows cataract and the settlement established at its lower reaches: Big Cane Town.

This final stretch had the Yuchi Traders in a rare good mood. This was their home river, the section of the Tenasee where they'd grown up.

"If it wasn't for that bunch of unruly warriors following us, Lady," White Mat told her, "we'd stay every night in a warm and snug house. Be fed the finest of boiled mussels, fresh venison, and roast turtle."

"But he's still back there," Fire Cat reminded them. Then he gestured to a passing dugout filled with waving locals. It was headed downstream bearing a family on some business. "Too many people know we're on the river. Sure, we're not the only red canoe on the Tenasee carrying five men and two women, but Blood Talon is going to get enough reports to suspect we're ahead of him. In his position, he can't allow any rumor to go uninvestigated."

"We can only hope the river has dropped by the time he hits the lower cataracts," Shedding Bird said as he shot a look back downriver. "It would make his passage that much more difficult. Hold him up. Or, better yet, maybe he'd be so desperate he'll try the rapids and capsize."

"He could also command the chief at Reed Bottom Town to portage his boat and equipment around the cataract," Night Shadow Star said. "With the whole town at his disposal to help portage the canoe, it might not take him any longer than it would take his warriors to walk the distance."

"And that means he could be even closer behind us than we think," Half Root added. "Wish we knew where they were."

"They're wishing the same thing."

Big Cane Town lay on the south bank of the Tenasee, just above a long island that split the river, and below constricting bluffs that forced the channel through a narrow canyon.

The cataract—called Mussel Shallows for the shellfish that thrived in its rapid waters—created a barrier to further progress. Here the river's course was broken, interrupted by more than sixty flood-scoured islands and outcrops of hard chert that jutted up like craggy teeth during low water. The river itself dropped in a series of low falls and rapids that tumbled over ledges of resistant rock. Nor did the steep sandstone canyon walls above allow much purchase around the drops where whitewater thrashed and thundered.

All Trade and travel came to a temporary halt at Big Cane Town; from there trailheads had been established south to the various nations, or help had to be procured to portage around the wicked channels, shoals, rapids, and falls.

The big stands of cane for which the town had been named had long ago been cut, used for various constructions, and split in half—the over- and under-sides overlapping for roofing.

Forested bluffs rose behind Big Cane Town, and several small creeks led back into the hills. A well-defined trail paralleled the river's southern uplands. This was the portage route.

As *Red Reed* arrived at the landing below Big Cane Town, Night Shadow Star handed over the agreed Trade, adding the copper plate she'd promised for their extra hard work. Here was a goal reached. Literally half the distance covered to Cofitachequi. But thinking back to that woman who had left Cahokia in a snowstorm, both the woman and the world had changed into something different, almost unrecognizable.

Knowing the landing would be a flurry of questions, they made their farewells early. She was saying good-bye to close friends, companions she had come to value as equals, whose skill and courage she cherished. And whose acceptance and respect she was honored to have earned. The experience proved surprisingly painful. Hugs. Tears. Promises to get together again.

The feeling was bittersweet in a way she'd never known before.

I have lived my life in a cocoon. The sensation might be likened to stepping out from a cold cave into glorious hot sunshine.

The jubilant mood among the *Red Reed* Traders filled Night Shadow Star with both joy and worry. She need only look downriver, along that murky and roiling surface they'd just crossed to imagine Blood Talon's canoe as it sliced water, driven by strong warriors paddling in unison.

"How long do I have, Lord?"

"Soon now. They come. Everything will be different."

Forty-five

From the moment of *Red Reed*'s arrival, the greeting the Traders received had been anything but subdued. As the canoe grounded on the sandy, charcoal-stained landing, a young man carrying fish traps on his back had called out, "It's White Mat and Shedding Bird! The *Red Reed* is back!"

Up at the head of the landing, a man stepped out from a cane-roofed ramada and blew a long note on a conch-shell horn. As the hollow sound carried up through the trees, people appeared from all directions. They called out in Yuchi, swarming the landing, grabbing packs out of the canoe, slapping White Mat and the rest on the back, laughing, crying out greetings.

To Fire Cat and Night Shadow Star—who stood back and remained mostly ignored—the few people who found themselves face to face had been most polite, asking in Trade pidgin, "And who are you? How did you get to travel with *Red Reed*?"

"Just Traders," Fire Cat replied as he retrieved his and Night Shadow Star's belongings.

Satisfied, the Yuchi turned away.

White Mat and the rest were hoisted up on the shoulders of brawny young men, as were the Yuchi's packs of Trade from inside *Red Reed*'s hull. And once the canoe had been manhandled further up on the beach, the entire entourage started up the bluff trail.

From the canoe landing the way led up a steep slope to the palisaded town. Given Fire Cat's canoe-cramped extremities, the climb brought an unfamiliar ache to his once-formidable legs. Had he really been that long-ago war chief who'd run for days along the leaf-shadowed trails of the north?

On the other hand, his arms and shoulders, back and stomach had never had the strength they now possessed.

He carried his weapons, chunkey gear, and kit in a bag thrown across his right shoulder; a pack with his and Night Shadow Star's bedding hung over his left. She, in turn, carried a pack full of their remaining Trade, and another with extra clothing. Two youths had been enticed to carry the engraved wooden box.

This was, after all, as far as the Yuchi Traders had contracted to carry them. In distant Cahokia, Big Cane Town had seemed an admirable goal. A place halfway across the world. Surely, once there, they would find someone to take them the rest of the way to Cofitachequi.

"So much for a quiet parting of the ways," Night Shadow Star told him as she preceded him up the worn trail. "Good thing we said our farewells earlier."

"I don't think White Mat could have kept it quiet if he'd tried," Fire Cat told her. "They may be young, but they're celebrities here."

"Being picked up and carried like that?" She indicated the mob ahead of them. "In the southeast it's a sign of the highest respect. Usually it's reserved for chiefs, visiting ambassadors, and victorious war leaders. I've never heard of such an honor being given to mere Traders."

"I guess they're not just 'mere Traders.'"

They crested the summit, following the others out into a flat terrace covered with corn, bean, and squash fields, goosefoot stands, and rows of freshly sprouted tobacco. Field houses dotted the flat before giving way to thick forest. Huge trees obscured the actual lay of the land, but it appeared to rise, hilly and broken, to the south.

Looking northeast, across the Tenasee Valley, it was to see gnarled, high bluffs capped with thick timber. Along the sheer slopes dropping toward the river, exposed sandstone, limestone, and shale cliffs could be seen where the underlying rock refused to support vegetation.

Down on the river, the lower rapids were plainly visible. Whitewater boiled around outcrops of chert that tore at the current. Driftwood had snagged on some of the rocky islands, and between them the water ran fast, flexing like liquid muscle between the scoured bedrock shores.

Like all Yuchi settlements, Big Cane Town was divided in two between the Chief and Warrior moieties, each having its Council House, a conical burial mound, and sharing the central plaza between them.

The chief's palace stood on the eastern side, atop a head-high platform mound. It was toward the ramada immediately to the palace's south that the procession made its way.

There White Mat, Shedding Bird, and the rest were seated in the place of honor at the rear, their packs laid out before them.

People arranged themselves, obviously by rank and status, and began filing past, nodding, touching their foreheads or hearts respectfully, and then shaking the Traders' hands. And more people were coming, appearing from the hodgepodge cluster of bent-pole houses, from the fields, and the Council Houses. Every now and then the conch horn would blow, just in case anyone had missed it.

Fire Cat and Night Shadow Star took a position in the rear, watching, amused, and not a little worried as they shared uneasy glances.

"Not exactly like we'd hoped, is it?"

"Think we ought to just strike out on the trail around the Shallows? Maybe see if we can hire a canoe on the upstream side?"

"Maybe. One thing's sure. Everyone in Big Cane Town's going to remember we arrived on *Red Reed*. Even if Blood Talon was a two-thumbed idiot, he'd be able to figure out it was us."

"And he'd know we were on our own as of today."

From behind them, a voice, in perfect Cahokian, asked, "Who is Blood Talon? And why would you be on your own?"

Fire Cat whirled, found himself eye to eye with a broad and muscular man, perhaps in his early thirties. The fellow's square face reminded Fire Cat of a block; the nose had been broken so often it was now permanently mashed to the right. A scarred and jutting brow shadowed wide-set, clever eyes. What should have been tattoos on the man's cheeks looked more like smudges. Totally illegible.

In contrast to the rough appearance of the man, the clothes he wore were those of a noble. A stunning spoonbill-feather cape hung from those wide shoulders, his startlingly white apron—secured by a braided leather belt with beaded pouches—exhibited a beautifully embroidered image of *Hunga Ahuito*, the Cahokian two-headed eagle and supreme deity. Thick shell necklaces, hanging down over the man's deep chest, gave him a garish appearance.

The young woman who clung to the man's muscular right arm appeared to be in her twenties—a ravishing beauty with thick midnight-black hair and large dark eyes to match. Her full lips were pouty in defiance of her delicate jaw. She stood with her hips cocked, one bare brown leg forward, as if to accent the perfectly flat stomach, the shadow of her navel, and full breasts.

She, too, was decked out in wealth, wearing a skirt feathered with turkey breast feathers that glowed copper in the light. A finely tanned buffalo-calf cape hung over her slender shoulders, and a wealth of gleaming white beads wrapped tightly at her throat.

"We're just Traders," Fire Cat said, reverting to Trade pidgin. "Looking to work our way east to Cofitachequi."

"We don't get many Cahokian Traders," the man said, fixing on Fire Cat's tattoos. "And most definitely we don't get Red Wing Traders"—the man turned his attention to Night Shadow Star—"in the company of a woman from the Four Winds Clan. Something tells me I'd really like to hear the tale of how and why the two of you are traveling together."

Reflexively, Night Shadow Star had started to reach up, as if to cover her cheeks, and let her hand drop with a sigh. The stranger missed none of it, an amused smile on his lips.

Something about his attitude, the way he was looking at Night Shadow Star, triggered Fire Cat's sense of impending trouble.

The woman—still clinging to the man's arm asked something in Yuchi. Fire Cat had heard enough of White Mat and the others' conversation on the journey upriver to have picked up a smattering of the tongue. She asked, "Who are these people, husband?"

His response was unintelligible, but he turned his attention back to Night Shadow Star. "From the artistry of those tattoos, I'd say you were Morning Star House."

Fire Cat narrowed an eye. "Who are you?"

"In these parts I'm called the River Fox. A man without a nation, a Trader, who—"

"Winder." Night Shadow Star crossed her arms. "I would have thought you'd have gone back to the lower Father Water. Or did the Quiz Quiz make that country a little uncomfortable for you?"

Fire Cat tensed as Winder's eyes flickered, one instant curious, the next deadly. Cold. Snakelike. "You take chances, Four Winds."

So, this was the legendary Winder? Fire Cat was trying to figure out how to rip his war club free from the pack without scattering his chunkey gear and armor all over the ground. And if he killed the man, what were the surrounding Yuchi going to do?

"As do you." Night Shadow Star had a knowing smile on her lips. "But my understanding is that you never go back on your word. Tell me, how did you escape the square in Evening Star Town?"

Winder's eyes were steady, implacable. "It doesn't matter who you are back in the city. Here, you're on my ground."

Fire Cat figured he was just going to have to swing the whole pack, try to knock Winder off balance to gain the time to pull his war club free.

From the looks of the man, he'd spent his life as a knuckle-and-skull scrapper. Sort of had the same look that Seven Skull Shield had, and when it came to a no-holds-barred brawl, the thief was among the best.

But can I take him hand to hand when it comes right down to it?

Fire Cat shifted, only to have Night Shadow Star reach out and place a hand on his arm. "Stand down, Red Wing."

To Winder she said, "Crazy Frog said that if I were in need, I should look you up. White Mat and *Red Reed* have carried us this far, and as soon as we arrive, who should step up? I would think it was Power working to both of our benefits."

Winder relaxed the barest bit, the woman at his side still spouting questions in gobbling Yuchi as she shot uneasy glances at Fire Cat and Night Shadow Star.

"How would you know Crazy Frog?"

Fire Cat said, "It's a curious and mutually advantageous relationship: We do business together."

"And what is this sudden need of yours?" Winder asked.

"Our destination is Cofitachequi." Night Shadow Star unslung her pack. "We have Trade. But I can offer something more than just pieces of copper, shell work, and exotics. I can give you something that no one else in Cahokia can."

"What's that?"

"A couple of things. For one, the Morning Star's personal pardon for your part in the theft of the Surveyors' Bundle. Serve me with the same dedication as you did the Quiz Quiz, and Cahokia is yours again." She paused. "With the added benefit that while you are working for us, we won't stupidly compromise you the way the Quiz Quiz did."

Winder's eyes had narrowed, his thumb and forefinger stroking his wide, square jaw. "A high-ranking Four Winds lady accompanied by a scarred-up Red Wing warrior. Traveling as common Traders. Why do I suspect there's more to the story?"

Fire Cat thought Night Shadow Star lied admirably when she said, "I am White Willow, of Wild Cat's lineage. This is Two Coups, a warrior of the Red Wing Clan. In this day and age—as you have noted—a Four Winds woman and Red Wing man are not exactly welcome in Cahokia. None of which precludes our usefulness when it comes to the living god and his goals."

"That's where Blood Talon comes in," Fire Cat added. "Him and about twenty Cahokian warriors. They'd really like to see us not make it to Cofitachequi."

"And whose authority are they acting under?"

"Clan Matron Rising Flame's." Fire Cat gave the man a wicked grin.

"She declared Lady White Willow an exile. Something about White Willow's particularly low standards when it came to her association with a certain heretic man. You want to jab a stick in the eye of the high and mighty at the same time you get your banishment lifted? Help us get to Cofitachequi. It'd be giving the Four Winds Clan a bit of payback."

"Four Winds Clan makes a pretty formidable enemy."

"Morning Star trumps even Matron Rising Flame," Night Shadow Star replied.

"And what gives you the right to speak for the living god? If that's what he really is?"

Fire Cat gave the man a big smile. "I could get to like the way you think." *But I don't trust you any more than I would a water moccasin.*

Night Shadow Star shot him a sidelong glance of irritation. "Let's just say that Morning Star and I are in this together. His goals—and mine—transcend the petty preoccupations of the Four Winds Clan. As to proof that I'm his agent in this, you'll just have to take my word." She smiled. "And some pretty fantastic Trade."

Winder's hard gaze remained on Night Shadow Star.

Fire Cat could almost see the man's souls working to figure out what her presence in Big Cane Town meant, and how he could benefit from it.

Worse, something about the way Winder's continued appraisal of Night Shadow Star's body spoke of more than just a financial interest. A fact that the raven-haired beauty also picked up on. She had tightened her hold on the man's bicep, as if to physically claim him.

Fire Cat felt his hackles rising, the way they did when a possessive male perceived too much interest from another dominant.

"Cofitachequi," Winder mused, so lost in thought he didn't even react as the Yuchi in the ramada erupted in delight at something White Mat told them.

Night Shadow Star glanced up at the midday sky. "We have half a day. By taking the trail, can we arrive above the Mussel Shallows before dark? We really need to get there and hire, or Trade, for a good canoe."

"I haven't said I'm taking you anywhere. In fact, I think I'll—"

"I have one last item to Trade." She extended her hand, something tightly clasped in her fist. When Winder reached out, she dropped the little carving of the fox that Crazy Fox had handed her that day on the canoe landing.

Winder stared at it, disbelief in his eyes. Then he again turned his attention to Night Shadow Star's tattoo. He glanced again at Fire Cat's. "I think I can get us a canoe in the pond above the shallows."

"The pond?"

"That's what the locals call the still water between the Mussel Shallows and the upper cataract. That's known as the Suck and Rage. You'll learn why if you ever make it that far. A fast and light canoe? I know a family with such a boat. One that can be carried over the chert-hard rock if local porters are hired to carry the packs. The locals are easy, they can be bought off with a hank of beads, maybe a pouch of black drink tea. That's the way to make time from here to above the Suck and Rage."

"Suck and Rage?" Fire Cat mused. "Sounds ominous."

"A really violent patch of water where the Tenasee cuts through the mountains a hard week's journey east of here. Pass that, and paddling a canoe up past Hiawasee island, to the Wide Fast, a portage through the mountains to the Beautiful River, then crossing the divide to Joara Town can be made in a moon's cycle."

"You've done this?" Night Shadow Star asked.

"Five—no, that would be six times."

Fire Cat felt the first faint slivers of hope. Winder's slightly dismissive shrug added to the feeling that the man knew of what he spoke.

The Trader glanced down, studying the little carved fox, rolling it between his thumb and forefinger. Shifted his thoughtful gaze to her tattoos. What was his preoccupation? Everyone had tattoos.

At that instant something seemed to change in Winder's appraisal, as if he'd stumbled upon a revelation. The barest flicker of a smile died on the man's lips, his eyes suddenly veiled as he said, "I'll take you to Cofitachequi. I want your Trade, and your word on that pardon."

"Half of my Trade, and the pardon."

He began to shake his head, reconsidered, and said, "Done."

"I give you my word." Night Shadow Star touched her chin. "Now, we have a half day's light. Shall we be at it?"

"As soon as I wrap up some personal business here," Winder told them. He winked at the young woman now grasping his arm in a stranglehold as she shot a jealousy-filled glare at Night Shadow Star.

Fire Cat experienced a crawly feeling down in his stomach. As Winder stepped away, he said, "Why do I sense that this isn't going to work out well?"

Forty-six

In the weeks since the lunar maximum Seven Skull Shield had spent much of his time in Evening Star Town. Not only had he found a use for himself while helping Flat Stone Pipe with a recalcitrant relative, but for whatever reason—probably because he simply didn't know better—Spotted Wrist had only two of his warriors prowling around Evening Star Town in the quest to find Seven Skull Shield, the Koroa copper, or any other salient information that the new Keeper might find useful in his pursuits as Four Winds Clan Keeper.

So ham-handed had the warriors turned out to be that Seven Skull Shield had actually befriended them, offering items of food, telling them stories, and generally providing helpful tips in their quest for intelligence on the operations of Evening Star Town, its politics, and, of course, its ever potentially dissident matron.

Flat Stone Pipe, to the dwarf's absolute delight, got the greatest pleasure out of feeding the two warriors conflicting, imaginary, and particularly damaging information about the other Houses and their supposed machinations against Morning Star, the clan matron, and the new Keeper.

These bits of intelligence were dutifully transmitted back to Spotted Wrist by a runner who checked in with the spying warriors every two days.

On the down side, Seven Skull Shield ached to see Willow Blossom.

"Got it hard, huh?" Flat Stone Pipe had asked the day before. "You keep looking off to the east. What is it about this one?"

"She's just special. Maybe it's that she's so innocent, you know? When she smiles up at me, it makes my heart leap. There's something about her laugh. It just comes out. All bubbly and joyous. And you should see the way her eyes light up, sort of sparkle just for me."

"You sure?"

Seven Skull Shield had given the dwarf his most disapproving look. "Who do you think you're talking to? I know more about women than any ten men alive. Sometimes a man and woman just fit together." He demonstrated by interlacing his fingers so tightly they'd hold water. "That's Willow Blossom and me."

"And how is this perfect woman of yours taking these long absences? Must be hard on her, pining away for you while you're hiding from half of Cahokia."

"She's happily safe in Night Shadow Star's palace. She understands, little man. This isn't forever. It's just going to take some time to bring all the pieces together. Spotted Wrist isn't going to last. All you need to do is think of those two idiot warriors he's got 'keeping an eye on things' here in Evening Star Town."

"Must be one really remarkable woman." Flat Stone Pipe's expression was anything but reassuring.

That had been the final straw. Seven Skull Shield had mussed himself up, found an old basket that he filled with scraps of cloth, and bartered his way across the river. Farts trotting at his heels, he'd hurried his way up the Avenue of the Sun, looking for all the world like another of the dirt farmers engaged in some venture of his own.

Arriving at the Great Plaza, he'd been delighted to note that the warriors who spent their days watching Night Shadow Star's palace were gone. Where they'd usually stood, a boy—maybe in his early teens—now sat, butt just shy of the sloping side of Morning Star's great mound. The kid was playing in the dirt, drawing figures with his fingertip and glancing periodically up at the Piasa and Horned Serpent guardian posts where they frowned down on the avenue.

Never one to take things for granted, Seven Skull Shield studied all sides, found no one suspicious, and with relief, pounded up the steps.

He gave the perfunctory salute to Piasa and Horned Serpent and snapped a "No, you don't" as Farts started to hoist his leg on Horned Serpent's post.

He dropped his basket of rags on the veranda and strode in the door, calling, "The wandering thief has returned! Was I missed?"

"I had a boil on my neck once," Green Stick called from the back of the room where he used a thumbnail to peel the tough outer skin off a small wild onion, the first of which had started to show up in the plaza markets. "I missed you about as much as I missed that boil after Rides-the-Lightning lanced and drained it. I used to spend my nights saying, 'I sure wish I had that boil back.' And I did it in the same voice as I say, 'I sure wish that shiftless thief would come back.'"

"Do you know the difference between you and dog shit?" Seven Skull Shield asked. "No? It's the dog."

"I don't get it."

"Think it through, Green Stick. Where are the rest?"

"Winter Leaf and Clay Stick are gone for water and firewood. I was just—"

"Seven Skull Shield!" Willow Blossom cried as she appeared in the doorway leading back to Night Shadow Star's personal quarters. She tossed a folded blanket onto the Red Wing's bed and came at a run, throwing her arms around Seven Skull Shield, clamping her body tightly to his.

"That's what I call a welcome," he greeted, lifting her off her feet and whirling her around. "I have so missed you. Figured it was worth the risk." He cast an eye at the stewpot, adding, "Farts, get away from that."

The big dog dropped on his butt, scratching at a persistent flea, mournful eyes on Seven Skull Shield. It might have been the ultimate betrayal.

Seven Skull Shield set Willow Blossom down, taking the moment to savor the happiness in her eyes, and yes, it was back, that sparkling joy that said she was delighted to see him. The smile was on her full lips, a radiant excitement in her expression and in the way she held him.

"I can't stop thinking about you," he told her. "Through the day and filling my dreams at night, you are always there. I want you to come away with me."

"Away? From here?"

"It won't be much. Not at first. I've been talking with Flat Stone Pipe. There is a farmstead out west of Evening Star Town. It's got a good house on it, water in a creek just down the slope. Nice soil for a garden. Peaceful. I Traded a beautiful redstone eagle effigy pipe for the place. I tell you, it will be perfect. No one will think to look for me there, and in a couple of moons they will have forgotten all about me."

"A farmstead?" The dullness only flickered behind her eyes for a heartbeat, and then she broke out in laughter, the sparkle back. "Of course! Wouldn't that be wonderful!"

She broke free of his arms, turned, and told Green Stick, "You promised."

"Promised what?" Seven Skull Shield asked.

"He promised me that the next time you showed up, he, Winter Leaf, and Clay String would leave. Give us a couple of hands of time alone."

Green Stick tossed the last of the onions into the stewpot, scooped up the skins, and consigned them to the fire. "Of course, he'd show up at the most inconvenient moment. It's not like I didn't have ten tens of things to do today. Or like Winter Leaf and Clay String won't be back with their wood and water anytime soon."

"So, go watch a stickball game," Seven Skull Shield told the man with a wave of the hand. "Wasn't it you complaining that you never had the time to watch a game all the way through? That Duck Clan team from over east is playing a Snapping Turtle team from down at Horned Serpent Town this afternoon. I heard talk of it all the way from River Mounds. People are wagering a fortune."

Clapping his hands to free them of clinging onion, Green Stick gave a mighty sigh. "Very well. Guess we know what you two are doing while we're out and about. You going to be gone for that farmstead by the time we get back?"

"Might," Willow Blossom called gaily. "Can't wait to see it. But it depends on how distracted we get in the meantime. Might wait until morning to leave."

"Enthusiasm is nice, and the vigor of youth is wonderful, but don't break the bed strapping," Green Stick muttered as he grabbed up his cloak and headed for the door.

A feral excitement had filled Willow Blossom's eyes as she stared up at Seven Skull Shield. Her quick fingers slipped past his breechcloth, grabbing his shaft. He sucked a breath as she squeezed.

"Why don't you pull those ugly clothes off. Make the bed ready. Me, I'm going to check that he's really gone." She turned, almost skipping out the door to the top of the stairs between the guardian posts.

Seven Skull Shield watched her wave, make a sign with her hand. Must have been some curious good-bye to Green Stick.

He had slipped out of his cloak, shirt, and breechcloth by the time she had returned to set the door so that it blocked the view from outside.

Farts had flopped on his side by the fire, filled his lungs, and vented one of those canine sighs of resignation.

Willow Blossom slithered out of her skirt as she crossed the matting and pulled the pins to let her silky black hair cascade down her back. She struck a pose, let him enjoy the perfect symmetry of her body, and then leaped on top of him where he had reclined in her bed.

Maybe Green Stick was right to worry. Willow Blossom's exuberance did strain the bed straps, but they held. Though it had to be a close-run thing.

He'd barely caught his wind when she managed to tease his shaft to attention again. This time he slowed her, savored the sensations of her body against his. Yes, he could spend the rest of his life enjoying this woman. She had him . . .

The only warning was Farts' growl. Seven Skull Shield was barely aware when the dog stood as Willow Blossom tightened around him. Squealed with delight.

He glanced over as the door was thrust wide.

Warriors, in a stream, burst through the door, charging across the floor.

Seven Skull Shield tried to throw Willow Blossom to the side, but she clung to him, arms and legs wrapped desperately around his body.

A hollow-sounding blow was accompanied by a yelp, and Farts streaked for the door, three warriors hot after him, swinging war clubs the whole way.

Seven Skull Shield bellowed his rage, still trapped by Willow Blossom's clinging body. He couldn't, he just couldn't fling her off. Might hurt her. And the poor woman was just terrified.

Stuck as he was, Seven Skull Shield watched the ring of warriors close around the bed. Never, ever had he felt so trapped, helpless, or frustrated.

"All right," the big warrior with the stone-headed club said. "You can let loose of him now."

Willow Blossom scrambled away, slipping between the warriors to collect her skirt and cloak. "I've kept my part of the bargain. Now it's time for the Keeper to keep his." She tossed her head to throw her tousled hair back.

Seven Skull Shield gaped, staring at her where she stood behind the warriors. "You what?"

"Oh, come on. A farmstead? After everything I've done to get this far?"

At her words, he leaped. Might have had a chance, but the straps gave way under the strain. His legs and butt crashed down between the bed-frame and the wall.

They were on him like flies on fresh dung. He howled, flailing, but his struggles were cut short by a clipping blow to the head that left him stunned, his ears ringing, and his vision blurred with little stars of light dancing before them.

His last memory was of Willow Blossom saying, "Bet he'll never forget his last moments with me."

Forty-seven

Winder proved as good as his word, employing a Muskogean team of five brothers from Mussel Midden village. The small Muskogean band—mostly Albaamaha intermarried with some Koasati—had built their village on a terrace at the head of Mussel Shallows. In a remarkably light-hulled canoe loaded with Night Shadow Star and Fire Cat's possessions and Trade they made their way past the shallows at the mouth of the Elk River and on into the "pond."

The exiled Cahokian Trader hadn't lied when he talked about his expertise on the river. From Night Shadow Star's perspective—city-bound as her life had been—Winder came across as having been everywhere. At night, seated at the cook fire, he told wondrous stories of Yellow Star Mounds in the distant west, of the lower Father Water, and the nations who lived there. He claimed to have been on the Gulf, to have Traded down the peninsula, to have traveled the Mother Water to its headwaters and Traded with the Haudenosaunee.

While Night Shadow Star might not have been to those places, she was familiar with those distant locales. Not only had she been present as Traders and embassies described them in the Council House, but she was passingly familiar with the maps and records, the latter woven into shell-beaded mats. It all sounded just the way she'd always heard. Odd, but now that she'd been on the rivers, a part of her was jealous. She envied Winder the depth and breadth of his travels.

"Imagine going to all those places," she'd told Fire Cat that night after they made love. "Think of the sights, the people, the places."

"Changes the way you've always thought of the world, doesn't it?"

While her nights might have been filled with dreams of faraway peoples and nations, Night Shadow Star's days were consumed with paddling, her thoughts invaded by the soft whispers of voices in the air around her. Flickers of light, fleeting glimpses of movement at the corner of her eye, fragments of images tried to distract her from the river and the chore of driving the canoe upriver.

If there was any solace, it was that after a hasty supper cooked by the Albaamaha men, she could wrap herself around Fire Cat's warm body beneath their robes. Each time they joined it was with a gentle desperation, as if they understood that time was not on their side. That each mating of their bodies made up for the lost past and served as hope against a fragile and uncertain future.

The thought *This is too good to last* kept whispering in the silence between Night Shadow Star's souls.

They knew each other now. Had learned each other's secrets. Fire Cat proved to be a most remarkable lover, had discovered how to use his shaft just so, delay his emission until he could coax her loins into a series of tingling explosions.

"Are you a perfect man?" she asked, her arms wrapped around him as mosquitoes hummed above their bed. The little beasts were put off by a mixture of puccoon root, sassafras root extract, and well-smoked blanket.

"No. Just lucky," he told her.

After a pause, he asked, "What do you think of Winder?"

"He's a curiosity. A blend of competence, craftiness, and honor. I don't—for so much as a heartbeat—doubt that he's playing his own game. That somehow he knows more than he lets on. It's in the way he looks at me."

"I know how he looks at you. And then at me. The man is envious every time we retreat to the blankets. That Yuchi wife of his back in Big Cane Town? She was a beauty, but the moment he fixed on you . . . Let's just say my first impulse was to club him in the head."

"Like Seven Skull Shield?"

"He and Winder, they're two of the same kind."

"Winder and the thief grew up together. You can see it, the similarity, I mean. Makes you wonder, did Seven Skull Shield learn his peculiar code of honor from Winder, or was it the other way around?"

"You haven't mentioned that you know the thief."

"I don't know what Winder knows. Were I to say, 'Oh, by the way, I left Seven Skull Shield in charge of my palace during my absence,' Winder might get that startled look, and say, 'Ah, good to finally make your acquaintance, Lady Night Shadow Star.' "

"You think he suspects?"

"I don't know. Nor do the Spirits tell me anything. But something is coming, Fire Cat. It's in the air, in the feel of the river. Even the land seems to be holding its breath. We know that Blood Talon hasn't given up, and every day we travel we're closer to Walking Smoke. I can feel his growing menace. He knows we're coming."

"How?"

"He has his own allies in the Spirit World. It was the Thunderbirds, after all, who snatched him away from Piasa that day in the Father Water. Just as Piasa uses me for his purposes, the Thunderbirds are using my brother."

"But he's evil."

"It's not about good and evil. It's about balance. The white and the red. Order and chaos, wisdom and creativity, peace and war, harmony and confusion. He serves a purpose on the Sky World's side as I do for the Power of the Underworld."

Fire Cat remained silent, his arms warm around her. The night sounds of the river, humming mosquitoes, a thousand croaking frogs, water lapping at the shore below them, a whippoorwill, some night bird, and the wind in the leaves of the great chestnut beneath which they slept, all whispered their unease.

"What?" She could tell he was disturbed.

"Balance? If only you survive, Piasa comes out ahead, doesn't he? You kill Walking Smoke, that's an imbalance."

"So, you think we're both supposed to die?"

"I've been worried. Like you said, it's the symmetry of it all. Walking Smoke came to Cahokia, and almost to the instant, you sent your souls to the Underworld to be eaten by Piasa. Walking Smoke's threat immediately had a counterweight."

She snuggled her head under his chin, understanding the harsh logic of it. Terrified by the implications.

"If all I have is this time on the river, I want to live it with you. I will cherish each moment, each meeting of our eyes, every last smile and the warmth of your body."

"We're a long way from the end of the journey, my lady. And when we get to Cofitachequi, nothing is certain. Whatever it takes, I will be there to keep you safe. Perhaps to serve as your instrument. I will see that you prevail. I promise you that on my honor."

She smiled, a flutter of relief in her breast mixing with a hint of dread. What if he did manage to save her at the last instant? What if he gave his life in place of hers? Could she live with that knowledge?

Better to curl up and die.

She expected to hear Piasa's laughter come spiraling out of the insect-laden air. Instead, lightning flickered in the distant east. And then again, and again. Strobes of white light in the night. As the far-off clouds flashed and blinked, it was as if the Thunderbirds had taken their place at the gaming blanket and were casting dice on the outcome.

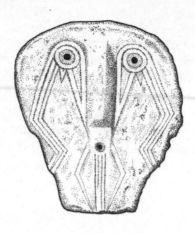

The Storm

As lightning flashes and bangs in the night, I sit naked before my fire. With a hickory baton, I beat on the small pot drum. Match the resonant thumping to the rhythm of my heart.

Another crash of thunder shakes the very walls, rattles the thatch overhead.

Lowering my drum, I walk to the door, throw it open, and stare out at the night, torn as it is with lightning that flickers and Dances among the high-packed clouds that obscure the sky.

The air hangs heavy, the scent of rain filling my nostrils.

An instant later a wicked flash of lightning contorts its way across the sky. Bent and twisted. As though in eternal agony. The quick double flicker burns itself into my eyes, sears a path across my brain, and snakes its way through my souls.

Stunned, I collapse onto the beaten ground before the Clan House veranda. Even as I sprawl there, nerveless and limp, the rain slashes down.

Blinded by the fierce black-on-white afterimage, I stare sightlessly up into the unleashed torrent. Feel the huge cold drops as they smash into my face.

In that moment, I see: Night Shadow Star is looking up into the night. I could be an owl, circling silently overhead as I stare down into her eyes. She is standing by the river; a canoe is grounded on the beach. A low fire burns, two men, cross-legged, sit on either side of it. They are talking as men do in companionship.

But it is Night Shadow Star who draws every bit of my attention. She remains as beautiful as ever. Her face unforgettable if I should live a thousand years. Only now her hair is down in a Trader's braid. A simple cloak hangs from her shoulders; an unadorned fabric skirt is tied at her hip.

I turn my head from the rain, letting it drain from where it has pooled in my eyes. Then I struggle to my feet, raise my arms. Again, lightning curls just over my head. White, hot, it burns through my eyes and lights my insides. Makes my bones shine white, glows through my guts. My liver turns that same shade of pale as a stone in the heart of a bonfire.

I am the lightning. Frozen for that one actinic moment, cast through the Sky World, discharged from the Thunder Being's taloned foot. I sear the world, stretch my burning essence through the heavens, displacing eagles. In that moment, the whole of the earth cowers beneath me.

"The storm. Call the storm."

The words thunder down around me as the glow fades from my flesh.

Fixing my entire soul on Night Shadow Star and the river, I pull my knife from my belt, extend my arms to the tempest, and slice down the insides of both my arms, crying, "Brother Lightning! Go! Find Night Shadow Star! Unleash your Power. Drown her! Wash her down into the river. And when her Lord Piasa rises to save her, blast them both!

"Strike her! Wound her! Hurt her where her heart lies! Take from her what she loves more than life! Show her your Power and sicken her souls. Blind her so that she doesn't see me. Deafen her so that she hears not my approach! Send her to me, stumbling and alone, without her protector!

"Set my world free!"

In answer to my plea, a bolt of lightning forks and strikes on either side of me. Pillars of a light so intense I am knocked from my feet even as the blast breaks my ears. For long moments I can't catch my breath.

Nothing.

I am only an empty husk, unable to breathe. To feel. Even to know.

The first sense that returns to my numb body?

Rain.

I gradually grow aware of the pounding, as if it will batter its way through my hollow skull. Beat my flesh into the very mud. Splinter my bones.

A series of thunderous booms, the flashing of lightning in the clouds, finally begins to register in my vision and hearing.

And still the rain falls, ceaselessly trying to hammer me senseless where the lightning has failed.

As the storm lessens, I begin to take heed of my surroundings.

I am sitting in the mud, water streaming down my body, blood washing down my arms in watery sheets.

Looking around, it is to see some of the people of Joara, standing like ghosts, staring anxiously at me. The measure of their disquiet can be seen in their postures, in the solemn way they gape. As if they have found something more unsettling than thunder and lightning.

And it is me.

Forty-eight

Lightning burned brilliant white, twisted. Bunched and throbbing like an old man's veins, it seared the purple-bruised heavens. Thunder boomed and crashed; rain slashed down out of the storm-torn sky. Bits of low-scudding cloud seemed to have been ripped loose from their brooding black brethren, and like errant feathers were cast to the angry winds.

The storm had come upon them like vengeance—as if the Powers of the Sky World had declared war upon the earth. It seemed to hurl itself down on the valley of the Tenasee with a special fury.

"It's just a little farther," Winder declared from the bow where he paddled into the relentless downfall. The water around them was lashed and pelted, tiny bits of hail mixing with sheets of angry rain.

"We should make for shore! This isn't going to let up," Fire Cat shouted over the hissing of rain on tormented water.

"Can't," Winder called back over his shoulder. "River's already high, and it's going to rise. Low as these floodplains are on either side, once it's over the banks we'll be underwater within a hand's time. The only choice is to head back downstream to that island or make the next bend where the channel cuts up next to a terrace where we can be above any flood."

"How far?" Night Shadow Star's voice carried that familiar note of desperation. She was paddling, hunched, a mist of water bouncing off the top of her head where the big raindrops and small hail battered her.

Like the rest of them, she'd been instantly soaked and made miserable when the heavens opened.

"Should have stayed in camp." Fire Cat winced as little balls of hail bounced off his bark rain hat. Cold streaks of water were running down the side of his face, along his neck, and into his shirt.

But had they, they wouldn't have made the couple of hands of progress up the Tenasee. And every measure of river traveled was that much closer to the goal. Besides, as Winder had just pointed out, the camp had been on a narrow sandbar, and behind it had been a low-lying swamp thick with bald cypress and water oak. Had the river risen just a couple of hands, their camp would have been inundated. Nothing to it but to forge ahead.

"You want to get out of this?" Winder bellowed over his shoulder as lightning illuminated his silhouette. "Paddle like you've never paddled before. The harder we work, the sooner we're off the river and safe."

How could the man read the thread of the current in such a downfall?

"Pus and blood," Night Shadow Star swore between chattering teeth, "I'm cold and totally miserable."

"Welcome to life on the river." Fire Cat gave her a smile as he fought his own shivers. "We get to that high ground, at least you and I have each other to wrap up together. And maybe there's going to be enough shelter that we'll be out of the worst of it."

"There's a village," Winder called back. "Black Clay Bank is what it's called. Bunch of fishermen and clam divers. Not my preferred place to put in. The brothers tell me they've had trouble with them before. But they probably won't mess with us since you're a warrior, and they know my reputation."

Winder paused. "But it's another hand of time to reach it beyond the first opportunity to land."

"We'll take it," Fire Cat growled, ignoring Night Shadow Star's look of incredulous dismay. From her expression she really wanted to get off the river and under some kind of shelter.

To Fire Cat's way of thinking, a roof and a fire would more than make up for the additional misery.

Through it all, the Albaamaha kept their heads down, paddling in unison, looking wet and dejected, breath fogging as they drove their slim craft across the rain-lashed backwater.

Fire Cat hadn't quite been sure what to make of them. Their language was incomprehensible to him, their religious observances oddly quaint and mystifying. In camp they kept to themselves, and while they built the cook fire and prepared the meals, they established a separate fire and sleeping area for themselves a stone's throw away.

Night Shadow Star they ignored completely. For all the notice they gave her, she might have been invisible.

Winder, they treated with particular regard and respect.

"Makes you really miss White Mat and the Yuchi, doesn't it?" Night Shadow Star had remarked the second night. "Odd how we became part of their group."

And miss them he did.

At the thought, Fire Cat shot a look over his shoulder. The patterns of rain on the river stood out, the surface savaged by bands of harder downpour. A white mist seemed to hover a couple of hands above the rain-pocked waves. A thousand rings and ripples interlocked, expanded, and died on the churning background.

Where the river lapped at the low and muddy banks, it gave way to thick forest, grape, smilax, and thorny walking-stick vines laced through the brush and into the low-hanging branches of bald cypress, tupelo, water oak, cottonwood, and shagbark. Streams of water poured off the leaves.

The river was rising. A twirling raft of driftwood set free by the rising water floated past. Fire Cat took a moment to glance back at it.

Lightning picked that instant to flash—burning and white—the after-effect searing Fire Cat's vision. A second later the blast almost deafened him, making the others jump.

But in that instant, he saw it. Blinked. Tried to clear the spots from his vision.

He was sure the lightning had illuminated a canoe. Back behind them. Maybe three or four bowshots back.

As he peered, all he could see was falling rain, the misty haze rising from the impact of countless cold drops hammering the surface. Nothing but curtains of falling water.

He turned forward again, putting his back into paddling.

Couldn't fight the impulse, kept throwing glances back over his shoulder.

Was that just his imagination? It wasn't like he didn't dwell on the fact that Blood Talon was back there, somewhere. Only in his wildest dreams did he delude himself into believing the squadron first might have given up and headed back to Cahokia. This was Spotted Wrist's man, after all. Not the sort to give up—even when the odds were against him.

Fire Cat turned, just as another bolt of lightning flashed. And, yes. He saw it. Like an apparition in the storm. A canoe. A big one. High prow, like a Cahokian war canoe.

The lightning had flashed on the paddles. Two rows of them, stroking in unison.

"Raft!" Winder's call intruded on Fire Cat's sudden sensation of sick inevitability.

He jerked his head around, saw the dim mat of swirling wood. Bigger this time. A huge and sprawling tangle of interlocked branches and entire trees. A mass of timber floated loose from whatever shoal it had been grounded on. Now it came spiraling down upon them. Given the size of it, it covered half the river.

Another look over his shoulder, and Fire Cat could make out the closing canoe. In the bow, defiant to rain and wind, stood a single figure. Wind whipped at the man's cloak. Gave him the appearance of flying.

What to do?

Drenched, cold as they were, the Albaamaha weren't up for a spirited flight. Put to shore? Trust themselves to the swampy floodplain? And have twenty desperate warriors tracking them through the swamp?

In an instant, Fire Cat saw it. How it would have to happen.

He glanced again at the floating raft of driftwood, the sleek wood gleaming in the eerie storm light.

"Winder! Blood Talon is behind us! Get Night Shadow Star to Cofitachequi. I'll catch up."

As he called, Night Shadow Star whirled, first to stare at him with wide and disbelieving eyes, and then to glance fearfully behind them.

"Paddle," Fire Cat ordered. "Paddle hard. I'm going to slow them down. I'll catch up. I promise. That, or meet you in Cofitachequi."

"What are you—"

"Can't take the time to explain. It's going to work. Now, paddle! I can't do this if you don't give them a hard chase. Do you promise?"

"I . . . Yes."

"Give me your word."

"I do."

He laid his paddle down, seeing that she'd ceased to stroke. "Hurry! Paddle. Now. You've got to outrun them!"

To Winder he called, "Don't let her come after me. I'll catch up."

Then he grabbed up his war bag from the sloshing water at his feet.

Night Shadow Star was staring at him, then glanced back over her shoulder at the now clearly visible canoe. A shout could be heard as the pursuers realized that it was only a matter of time.

"I love you! Make it to Cofitachequi. Do it for me. I'll meet you there!"

As the Albaamaha paddled just clear of the floating raft of timber, Fire Cat slipped over the side. Towing his heavy bag, he struck out for the floating tangle of wood.

To his surprise, the water felt warm. Night Shadow Star was screaming something at him from the canoe, but bobbing and ducking as he was, he couldn't make out the words.

His sack, loaded with his chunkey stone, copper-bitted war club, bow, quiver, and armor, kept trying to drag him down.

Everything depended on Winder now. Could he keep Night Shadow Star in the canoe? Could he stay far enough ahead of Blood Talon?

Would the Cahokians see the low-floating raft of wood in time, or would their attention be riveted to the fleeing canoe?

As the heavy bag pulled him down again, his fingers slipped off wet wood.

Fire Cat gave a last desperate kick, got an arm around a slippery log, and pulled his head above water.

All he could see was rain splashing down around him. He pulled himself up, higher, could just make out the war canoe, and—as if Piasa himself were helping—the raft was spinning its way toward it, bearing almost straight for the war canoe.

Please. Let this work.

Shooting a quick glance back at the fleeing Albaamaha canoe, he could see nothing as the rain hammered down harder, enveloping the river in a hissing roar of back-splashing water.

Lightning seared the sky, blasted the top of a towering oak just back from the shore. The cracking *bang* left Fire Cat's ears ringing.

In that instant, the raft of driftwood spun. The Cahokians, aware now, were staring at the interlocked tangle that bobbed in their direction. Fire Cat saw the confusion, could see the expressions on the warriors' faces as they lost the rhythm of their paddling. Some tried to back water with their paddles. One reached out to block a wicked-looking spear of wood.

Fire Cat hung the carry strap on his war bag to a broken snag of a branch, dove, and stroked.

A paddle slashed down beside his head.

Grasping it, he pulled, broke water. Jerking down with all his weight, he tore the paddle free from the surprised warrior's grip. Caught the gunwale with one hand and let the paddle go with the other.

He felt the big canoe shiver as it collided with floating wood.

Warriors were shouting, moving to Fire Cat's side, staring down at the impossibility of someone rising like magic from the river. The rest were prodding with their paddles to keep the driftwood raft at bay.

As the warriors crowded his way the canoe tipped. The gunwale to which Fire Cat clung dropped low. Enough so that he could grasp it, brace his feet on the hull, and throwing his weight back and out, capsize it into the water.

In an instant Fire Cat was surrounded by clawing, splashing warriors.

He dove, stroking down, caught a thigh, and jerked the man under. Then he was in the tangle of wood. Used a snag to pin his victim's cloak so the warrior couldn't resurface. The Cahokian was jerking, kicking violently. A burst of bubbles, like silver vomit, gushed from the warrior's mouth. For an instant the man's dark eyes fixed on Fire Cat's.

Fire Cat swam free, clawed his way up the wood, and broke the surface. Gasping for air, he searched around. Men were flailing in panic, trying to climb over each other, screaming and choking as they went under. A couple were clinging to bits of driftwood. The war canoe, swamped, spun in the current to one side.

Lightning strobed, coiled, and blasted the sky overhead, as if the Thunderbirds were unleashing all the rage in the universe.

One of the warriors splashed his way toward Fire Cat, only to have one of the trees in the raft ground and roll, then a falling branch trapped the man before it dragged him into the depths.

Another was thrashing about a pebble's toss away, screaming, coughing, his head going under. Within moments, the man's struggles ebbed. The last time his head broke the surface, he coughed out a great gout of water. He was trying to suck a desperate breath, his lungs expanding as he went under one last time. The man's body spasmed, slowed, and relaxed to spin away with the current.

As Fire Cat clung to the wood, he took note. Counted only three or four heads. The tangle of driftwood had begun to break up as the ripples and eddies of current slowly pulled it apart.

Fire Cat noticed his original log, now in a separate mat of wood, perhaps a stone's throw away.

Striking out, he dodged a spinning branch and swam for his tree. The thing seemed remarkably stable, and he realized when he got to it that his weapons bag had acted like a drag, impeding the dead tree's spin.

Clinging to his tree, he shot another look back toward the Cahokian canoe. He saw no heads now. Only the rain-battered hull where it had somehow become entangled with one of the bobbing rafts of driftwood.

How could he be the only one? It hit him like a thrown stone: Most of these were Cahokians. City people. Men raised on corn farms and in the uplands. Cahokians weren't raised on the river; they had others to do their swimming, fishing, clamming, and mussel diving.

They didn't know how to swim.

The storm gathered its fury, lightning savaging the sky, thunder booming down on the hills to either side.

As the rain picked up in intensity, Fire Cat came face-to-face with the realization that it was just him, a floating log, and the real chance that he was going to wind up just as dead as the Cahokians.

Forty-nine

Spotted Wrist's palace. Seven Skull Shield knew the place—every nook and cranny of it. He had been here before. What was new? The pole cage that the Keeper had had built. Spotted Wrist had ordered one of the beds taken out in the south wall and the cage built in its place. The thing was stout: a construction of hickory poles, the crosspieces lashed with wet rawhide that shrank into stone-hard bindings as they dried.

Being the Hero of the North, the Four Winds Clan Keeper, and a renowned war leader, apparently Spotted Wrist had no trouble finding people to do his bidding. Seven Skull Shield's cage had gone up in less than a couple of hands' time. Built even as he lay, bound like a fish in a net, on the man's mat floor.

Spotted Wrist had taken no chances. Once the still-naked Seven Skull Shield was placed in the cage, he was left with his hands bound behind him and confined by a short sinew rope that allowed him just enough movement to position himself over the small crudware pot they left in the corner for him to urinate in. Defecation was a more difficult proposition since he had to contort into the most uncomfortable posture.

If he missed, they unlatched the cage door and beat him. These were trained warriors. Men who'd spent their lives swinging war clubs. They had become very good at it. The beatings hurt. Painful enough to make him not want to be beaten again, not so damaging as to leave him crippled.

Spotted Wrist didn't want that.

"I want you kept as an amusement," Spotted Wrist had told him that first night when the Keeper had come home late from the Council House. "You'll die when the time is right. Probably on a square hanged along the Avenue of the Sun somewhere east of Morning Star's mound. By then you'll be begging for death. I'll let the people finish you off. Amazingly cruel, they are. Downright malicious, in fact."

"What did you offer Willow Blossom?"

"What she wanted all along: luxury. Wait, I see pain in your eyes. Oh, that's rich. You're Seven Skull Shield, renowned seducer of women, and you thought she cared about you?"

Spotted Wrist had cocked his head, staring past the bars at Seven Skull Shield, before saying, "You poor deluded fool. You fell all the way for her, didn't you? All the time you were pining for her, she was playing you for all you were worth. You got her out of that rope-maker's house, all the way to Night Shadow Star's palace. And then you got her that final step when she Traded you to me. You were the final price that earned her all she ever wanted."

Seven Skull Shield's heart sank. It couldn't be!

"What about my dog? You kill him?"

"No one's seen him. The beast turned out to be smarter than you are. He knew when to cut his losses. Must be tough to be you. You've been betrayed by the woman you love, abandoned by your dog, Blue Heron sure won't raise a finger on your behalf—assuming she'd even want to. And as I hear it, most of your friends on the waterfront could care less if you lived or died."

And then the man had turned on his heel, sat atop his dais, and had eaten dinner while he and his warriors shared jokes, sent taunts Seven Skull Shield's way, and watched him squirm uncomfortably on the short tether that bound his wrists behind him.

Food was offered twice a day, one of Spotted Wrist's slaves reaching past the bars with a horn spoon full of stew or extending bits of bread just far enough that Seven Skull Shield could grab them with his teeth.

Nights were agonizing. The tether allowed Seven Skull Shield just enough room so he could perch on his knees, back wedged in the corner of the cage.

During the day, the warriors, who were constantly passing through, did their best to humiliate him, spitting on him, poking at his exposed genitals with sharp or burning sticks, or dousing him with water. Spotted Wrist had precluded the tossing of anything that smelled bad or was too foul.

Willow Blossom arrived on the third night, escorted into the great room just after nightfall. She barely cast Seven Skull Shield a glance as she shared pleasantries with Spotted Wrist, enjoyed a wonderful supper, and let the Keeper lead her into his personal quarters.

Seven Skull Shield winced, could imagine with perfect clarity what the Hero of the North was enjoying.

How could I have been so blind?

His cramped posture hurt even more than usual. Unable to sleep, his scattered thoughts were interrupted by the occasional faint squeal of delight coming from Spotted Wrist's personal quarters. The warriors sleeping on the surrounding benches would chuckle softly, and then turn over.

He finally slept.

Seemed like Seven Skull Shield had barely closed his eyes when a loud clatter started him awake. He jumped, pulling his strained arms painfully behind him. His legs had gone to sleep and wouldn't hold him.

Blinking his bleary vision clear, he fixed on Willow Blossom as she ran a stick along the bars, the clattering loud in the room. She was staring down at him, that old familiar gleam of excitement in her eyes.

"Have a good night?" he rasped hoarsely.

"He's not the best I've ever had, but I can make do." She paused. "He has wonderful things."

"What did he give you?"

"For you? A nice house just a little to the east. Close to the Grand Plaza. It belonged to one of the Panther Clan nobles who backed Slender Fox and Wolverine when they were going to take Morning Star's mound with warriors last fall. Oh, and he gave me a couple of boxes of Night Shadow Star's things that I liked. Enough to see me through for a while."

"Those aren't his to give."

"And Lady Night Shadow Star isn't here to object." Willow Blossom studied her fingernails thoughtfully.

"Did you care nothing for me?" His heart skipped, waiting for her answer.

"You're a man. No different from any of the rest of them."

"Got news for you, Spotted Wrist's a man, too."

She smiled, her face shifting into the excited and animated glow he'd fallen in love with. Her lips bent into their familiar soft hint of anticipation. Her eyes seemed to expand, to sparkle just for him. "He is, isn't he?"

At her loving expression, he felt a leap of relief. "If you really care for me, I need you to do something for me. I just need you to—"

"You can rot, thief." And just as quickly the look of joy and anticipation vanished, replaced by a blank emptiness. "You humiliated him. He's not going to forget."

"But I love you. I'd do anything—"

"Men are so easy. Just give them a smile"—the loving, enchanted look was back, warm love reflected from her eyes—"and they're like potter's clay in my fingers."

The look of blank emptiness was back again. "Hope it's quick for you." She turned to leave.

"You're telling me I didn't mean anything to you? I was just a convenience?"

She shot a look over her shoulder. "Never had a man send sparks through my sheath the way you did. But a person can't make a life out of that." A pause. "After last night, I think I'll be back on occasion. Don't bother to act like we're old friends, all right?"

And then she was out the door.

Fifty

The island was a long ridge of stony ground, tree-covered where angular bedrock didn't protrude from the soil. It stuck up from the middle of the Tenasee like the elongated back of a snapping turtle. Roiling floodwaters, muddy brown in color, bearing floating yellow foam, sticks, and debris broke at the island's upstream point and rolled down the sides in rippling currents.

Fire Cat's log had grounded at the tip, twisted along the rocky bottom, and spun away along the river's southern channel. In that time, Fire Cat had grabbed his bag, picked his way through the accumulated driftwood that was still piling up on the rocks, and slogged his way ashore.

Cold and shivering, wet to the bone, he'd stared glumly around as rain hammered on his head, ran down his face, and streams of muddy water drained from his long shirt. Then he'd upended his war bag and poured the river out. No sense in trying to deal with his bow, arrows, armor, or chunkey lance.

The first thing was to find some kind of shelter.

A bolt of lightning cracked over his head, so close the *bang* almost made him jump out of his skin. But then he'd been terrified of the Thunderbirds ever since they'd blasted four lightning bolts around him that day up on the Father Water.

Old sun-bleached driftwood, laced and woven through the brush, gave him some idea of where high water had crested in the past. Taking his time, he studied the river, searching to see if any survivors from the war canoe were bobbing in the water. Perhaps headed his way. That was when his eye spotted the fish trap. The pointed end now stuck up from the water. He clambered over a mat of interwoven branches, twigs, and what looked like old roots to the trap. Woven from willow staves, tied to a float, it had washed loose in the flood and landed here. And, best of all, a good-sized catfish was desperately thrashing in the wide end as Fire Cat tried to pull it free from the tangle.

Ultimately, he had to break it apart, grab the fish, and sling it up onto the bank. Clambering his precarious way over the debris, he pulled out his war club, brained the fish, and strung it on his bow string—the sinew cord being much too wet to serve any other purpose for the moment.

His war club in hand lest he encounter any Cahokian survivors, Fire Cat found a trail leading to higher ground and followed it up the island's spine.

He remembered the island. They'd paddled along its length that very morning. What looked like a fisherman's hut had been perched on one of the high points on the downstream end. Toward that, he made his way. All the time wary, searching the rain-battered leaves, looking for any sign of Blood Talon's men. Not that he thought there was much chance that any had made it this far, but it just wouldn't do to stumble upon a couple of them who'd somehow managed to avoid drowning.

As the shivers racked his body, he wondered if he could even fight them, cold as he was, almost stumbling and brain fogged. Just walking took all his concentration. Thank the Spirits for Uncle, who'd trained him to take the cold. Had taught him to reach down inside and find that hidden reserve.

Two whitetail deer broke cover as he wound through a patch of brush and young oak and hickory. The deer crashed their way through the wet vegetation, stopped at the river, hooked back, and circled behind him. Good to know, if he ever dried out, got his bow string back in working condition.

The storm continued to rage, rain falling endlessly. Thunder boomed and roared. Teeth chattering so hard his vision blurred, shivering so hard he could barely walk, it was all he could do to keep from tripping over his own feet. Maybe he'd been colder, sometime, probably up in one of the northern winters. Thick as his thoughts were, he just couldn't remember. And that was back then. This was now.

In the end, Fire Cat located the hut, stumbled his way inside, and let his eyes adjust to the gloom. Water pattered from a leak in the roof, but it looked mostly sound. Barely two paces across, it wasn't roomy. He identified what appeared to be drying racks stacked against one wall. A brownware ceramic jar with a lid stood in the rear behind a firepit. To

Fire Cat's delight it contained a small fire bow, dowel, and starter stick as well as kindling.

With a distinct sensation of guilt, he broke the drying racks apart. Struggled to control his shivering muscles, and somehow managed to assemble the fire bow, fit the dowel into the starter stick, and began sawing back and forth. As the first tendrils of smoke rose, the shakes made it almost impossible to nudge the tinder into place. Took him five tries, but finally he was able to coax a flame.

Bit by bit, he added tinder, then a couple of twigs he found back in the corners. Discovered some old leaves that had blown in and wedged against the wall. Those he fed to the mix. And finally, a couple of the smaller lengths from the broken drying racks.

Sighing, he extended his hands to the crackling flames. Pulling his shirt over his head, he stepped outside to wring the water from it, decided it was raining so hard it wet the fabric as fast as he squeezed the water out. He compromised by crouching in the doorway and twisting the garment. Using three of the thickest lengths of the old racks, he made a tipi of the poles and draped his shirt over the fire to dry.

He lost any track of time, numb, shivering, feeding bits and pieces of the broken racks into the fire. As his brain began to work again, he used the sharp edge of his copper-bitted war club to cut the catfish apart, hung small pieces over the fire to cook, and wolfed them down as they browned.

Lightning continued to flash. Thunder rolled endlessly down the valley, and on occasion a bolt would hammer the sky just overhead with enough force to shake the hut.

He hoped that Night Shadow Star wasn't as miserable as he was. Winder should have found her some sort of shelter by now. Given the number of camps, villages, and towns they'd passed to this point, nothing had indicated that they were close to the end of habitation on the Tenasee River. Surely, they'd come to some place where they could get in out of the rain, Trade for a warm meal and a dry place to lay out their beds.

"Not that I trust that two-footed weasel, Winder," Fire Cat told the flames. "But Blood Talon and his little band of warriors won't be dogging Night Shadow Star's trail."

That had worked out a whole lot better than Fire Cat had anticipated. All he'd hoped to do was slow them down. Buy some time. The idea that he'd destroyed the lot of them was just beginning to filter through his cold-numbed head. He'd either had a hand in, or watched, the drowning of the entire party.

"Piasa? Were you down there in the depths, tugging them down, one by one?"

As if in response, the Thunderbirds unleashed a maelstrom of lightning that flashed white light through the hut door. Immediately it was followed by a fierce crackling and banging of thunder, as if the mighty Sky beasts were hammering at the very fabric of existence.

Fire Cat smiled in weary triumph.

Odd how the circle of events went around. He'd just killed warriors who had sacked Red Wing Town. Men who had murdered his children, uncle, so many of his kin. Among the men were those who had raped his wives, violated his little daughters. Some might have been among the ones who had carried him, bound and struggling, to be tossed in the canoe that had taken him, his mother, and sisters to captivity in Cahokia.

They had chased him to this far-off stretch of distant southern river, only to leave their corpses in Piasa's watery realm. The place to which they had consigned Fire Cat's children and relatives. Different river, same Underworld.

What kind of symmetry was that?

He plucked another piece of fish from where it roasted above the fire, let it cool to just bearable, and chewed the tasty meat. Hot food had an amazing ability to restore the body and souls.

"But I still have a problem," he told the leaping flames. "I've solved the problem of Blood Talon and his warriors, but Night Shadow Star is alone with that slippery Winder. Now they're headed upriver in a fast canoe, and I'm stuck on an island, in the middle of a flood, with a swamp on either side. Every day that passes while I'm stuck here, they're traveling farther upriver. Stretching the distance between us."

And that, he realized, was the terrible cost he'd paid to save her from Blood Talon.

Another bolt of lightning shot blinding light through the hut, the crack of thunder deafening, as if the Thunderbirds were laughing.

Fifty-one

Standing in water up to his thighs, rain pattering down from the forest overhead, Blood Talon stared into the snake's eyes. Of course he knew about water moccasins. He'd seen plenty in his day. Most had been brought to Cahokia in baskets, paraded around by Traders, especially down at the canoe landing where just about any kind of creature was exhibited, ranging from white foxes trapped in the distant icy north to a spotted jaguar hide from the far tropical south.

Because Blood Talon knew about the reptiles didn't mean he enjoyed being eyeball-to-eyeball with them. Worse, unlike the snakes he was familiar with, water moccasins were unpredictable. Strike at them with a stick, and the things were just as apt to viciously attack as to flee.

This one was dangling from a branch at head height. Its tongue kept flicking in and out of its mouth. The beady little eyes communicated malicious menace.

"I wish you no harm," Blood Talon told the snake, backing slowly away. He wished desperately for his war club. Instead he had only a broken hickory branch about the length of his arm for protection. Even then it made a poor club, being crooked, poorly balanced. It did end in a wicked point that he could use to spear things if they got close enough.

The snake, in this instance, appeared willing to let him go.

Blood Talon sloshed his way backward, then circled wide.

He *hated* this Spirit-cursed swamp. Floodplain, really. But the Tenasee was over its banks, leaving Blood Talon to flounder around in water up to his balls with only a hickory branch to fend off the drifting flotsam of old leaves, sticks, and forest litter clotted with yellow-brown foam.

And still the storm raged; torrents of rain hammered the forest canopy high overhead. The water then wended its way down to him falling in drops the size of small acorns, and in places actual streams. He'd never seen anything like it. Never *imagined* anything like it.

In every direction, all he could see was an endless expanse of thick tree boles—forest giants that rose into an impenetrable mass that blocked the light. Vines, many as thick as a man's leg, wound up their trunks to disappear into the canopy. Dead saplings—spidery in the dim storm-grayed light—added to the dreary effect.

How in the name of the Morning Star did I ever come to this?

The image, however, remained frozen in his mind. It played over and over in his head: the closing raft of driftwood, the rain-savaged surface of the river, slick wood gleaming, hazed by a mist of bursting raindrops . . . and a man's head emerging from the water. He'd appeared like a mythical river creature, water sluicing off his hair and face, mouth opening to gasp for air. The eyes had been closed, at least until a hand emerged from the depths to scrub his face clear. Then the eyes had opened, black, penetrating.

Blood Talon had frozen, disbelieving. Tried to understand what, or who, the man in the water might have been. Struggled with the impossibility of place. Then glanced at the closing raft of tangled driftwood.

As his warriors rushed to the side of the canoe to fend off the threat, the man in the water had ripped the paddle out of Split Limb's hands. Tossed it away. And as the canoe tipped, Blood Talon couldn't believe his eyes. The man had climbed up on the gunwale, leaned out, and rolled the canoe on its side.

In that last heartbeat, Blood Talon's gaze had fixed on the man's face, on the Red Wing tattoos on those wet cheeks. He'd glimpsed the burning triumph in those hot black eyes, seen victory, a sort of exultation.

Less than a heartbeat later, Blood Talon had been in the water, thrashing, clawing, and sinking. Water had rushed into his nose, bubbles gurgling around his ears, the cold shock hitting his entire body.

Despite the panic, he'd held his breath, fought his way to the surface. In the melee of screams and thrashing limbs, he'd been kicked free of the mass of entwined men. Got an arm around a floating piece of debris. The current had whipped it around, pulled it free of the mass of floating timber and trash. He'd been whisked to one side. Glanced back. Saw the sleek side of the war canoe tattooed by rain. Caught the image of the Red Wing thrusting one of Blood Talon's warriors deep down into the water.

Then there was nothing but the backsplash from rain on the water's surface. And the cold eating into his flesh. The feeling of absolute unreality that he had just seen the impossible.

One moment they had been closing on their prey, ready to bring the long hunt to its end. The next, he was alone, adrift and terrified, trying to get his souls around the shocking reality that he was going to die.

He didn't. His small raft of branches and litter might have been a leaf, tossed and played with as it was by the current. And in the end, as the cold sapped Blood Talon's fear-paralyzed body, the river had washed over its banks, carried him ashore. There, in a tangle of brush, he'd found footing.

Looking back at the river, it had been to see the head of the island they'd passed that morning; it split the water downstream like some fantasy vessel belonging to the Beginning Time Spirits. Rain, lightning, the crashing of thunder, and the angry river, swelling, rain-lashed, muddy, and full of floating debris.

The body that floated past was Nutcracker's. Facedown. Arms out. Slowly spinning in the current. Identifiable only because of the decorations on his war shirt.

The war canoe had been carried to the opposite side of the river and disappeared around the far channel.

Then the rain had increased.

If anyone was alive, Blood Talon figured he'd find them upstream. He'd tried slogging along the bank, but as the river rose, he'd been forced ever farther from its shore. Inland, into the inundating floodplain.

Now, here he was, up to his testicles in water, lost in the trees, and as miserable and broken as he'd ever been. The rain did not let up, nor the thunder cease. It just kept on, and on, and on.

Was the Red Wing a lunatic? He'd killed them all, and himself in the process.

Another snake slithered across the water, a copperhead this time, its body forming sinuous waves as it swam. The thing didn't even slow when it encountered floating wood; it just glided right over.

A chill shivered its way up Blood Talon's back, his skin crawling as a black-and-yellow spider as big around as a plum leaped from a floating leaf onto his war shirt.

Blood Talon batted the creature into the water and whacked it with his club. Looked, didn't see the body floating anywhere, was horrified that it might have splashed back onto him in the aftermath. He almost dislocated his neck in the frantic search of his person.

Spiders had never bothered him before. They were everywhere in Cahokia. Encouraged, as they helped to keep the endless plague of flies at bay. But here, in this floating morass of horrors? And especially a monster like that?

It's just being here. You're unnerved.

How right that was!

"Think." He looked around at the water and floating scum that ringed the flooded trees. "Use your smarts. There's got to be an end to this."

But which way? Here, under the thick forest canopy, he had no idea which direction was which. No stream flowing toward the river. All he could do was face a direction at random. Walk in a straight line for as far as he could see. Stop. Make sure he was still facing the same way. Walk in a straight line for as far as he could.

He did, slogging through the muck, feet slipping on the goop underneath, tripping over roots and submerged obstacles. With his hickory branch he fended off the worst of the floating debris.

Just as his confidence began to build, he encountered brush sticking up from the flood, oriented himself on the surrounding tree trunks, and sloshed his way into an opening between the brush.

He took a step, found no bottom, and sank up past his ears.

Panicked and thrashing, he fought his way back to good footing. Fighting for breath, he pulled at the sticks and flotsam that stuck in his hair. Realized that he'd lost his orientation, that the open space in the brush had been a creek of some sort.

But which way did it run?

And was he on the same side as when he stepped off, or had he crossed to the other side while he floundered about in the water? The club was floating out in the middle where he'd dropped it in his panic.

Pus and blood!

Not since he was a little boy had he ever wanted so much to simply sit down in the mud and bawl. Would have, but the water was too deep.

I am a warrior!

But that had been back in the world of men. Here, in this flooded forest, he was nothing.

Tears streaking down his face, he tried to catch his breath. Turned, followed just in from the brush that marked the creek. Water continued to cascade from the canopy, and the thunder boomed and banged.

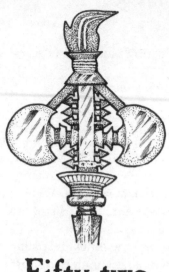

Fifty-two

For two days rain fell in sheets; lightning blasted the long and forested ridges on either side of the Tenasee River valley. Funnel clouds hovered over the land, dropping to tear through timber like it was kindling. The Powers of the Sky World unleashed their full fury.

One of the great black oak trees behind Black Clay Bank village was sundered in two, half of the forest giant falling to crush one of the huts, killing four men, five women, and seven children who huddled inside.

By day Night Shadow Star alternately watched the flood-swollen river and then the Trade trail that led down the northern bank and back toward the narrow channel where Fire Cat had disappeared in his attempt to deal with Blood Talon's pursuing canoe.

With the coming of full darkness, she would retreat to the house: a bent-pole frame structure, bark-sided, with a thick thatch roof. Mostly dry inside, it sheltered two families, and was warmed by a smoke-spewing fire that gnawed slowly through the wet wood it was fed.

When she rolled out in her mostly dried blankets it was to remember that look on Fire Cat's face as he slipped over the side and into the river. A calm confidence laced with desperation. Not for him, but for her. His insistence that she not follow him. That she trust him to complete this one last mission. That he would either catch up or meet her in Cofitachequi.

She'd watched him swim to the tangle of floating driftwood, latch onto the log. She had scrambled to her knees to peer back at the raft as the current whipped it toward the Cahokian war canoe.

After that the details blurred. She'd seen the Cahokians scramble toward one side, watched them fending off something hidden by the rain. Then she'd barely made out the melee as the canoe rolled onto its side.

Despite her pleas, the Albaamaha had doggedly continued to paddle upriver. Only Winder's hard hand clasping her upper arm had stayed her from leaping over the side and swimming in pursuit. She had ached to ride that current down, to discover for herself if Fire Cat lived.

"Don't do it, Lady." Winder had sounded so sure of himself. "He said he'd catch up. He will."

"You don't understand! That's Fire Cat! What if he—"

"You go after him, you'll undo everything he's done! You understand that?" He'd glared into her eyes. "Do you trust that man, or not?"

Numbly, she'd nodded, sank down to stare over the stern as the rain pounded them. The rest of that journey remained blurred in her memory. Just an endless jumble of shivering cold, pounding rain, and disbelief that Fire Cat was gone. She had kept her gaze on the river, the rain, and the distance. Shiver she might, but her imagination kept conjuring Fire Cat. That each bobble of the current, each bit of twirling flotsam or bobbing bit of wood, had to be Fire Cat, swimming strongly in pursuit.

They'd carried her up from the canoe, her flesh as senseless and inert as the clay for which the village had been named. She dully remembered sitting in the doorway, a warm fire at her back, watching the flooding river, knowing that Fire Cat would appear.

That had been two long days ago. Now she made her way back to the hut, wrung out her wet hair, and shook off her cape before entering the low doorway.

The smell of hominy boiling, roasting squirrel, and acorn bread sent pangs through her empty stomach.

"Lady," Winder greeted her where he sat in the visitors' place just inside the door; their Koasati hosts were seated in their places just behind the fire. "If he landed on the other side of the river, it will take him a time to catch up. And the lowlands will be flooded. Don't lose hope."

She ducked in, settled herself in her place opposite him by the door, and extended her hands to the fire. "He wouldn't have drowned. He's Red Wing. Raised on the river. He told me how he used to dive, how his uncle insisted he be able to swim across the river by the time he was seven. It would have taken more than Blood Talon to drown him."

Winder gave her that emotionless look she'd grown used to. The one he adopted when he wanted to remain completely neutral.

"Storm's going to break in the morning. I know you want to wait, to go in search of him, but I need you to think this through. Yes, your man Two Coups is back there. But so are any surviving warriors. And you can bet that this Blood Talon you talk about isn't going to give up. If you choose to wait here, I will not stand in their way when they take you prisoner. I'm not hired to do so."

She took a deep breath. "No, you're not."

"You heard your warrior. He said to continue, that he would catch up. There is no telling what he's going to have to do to avoid those selfsame surviving warriors. Maybe loop wide of the river. He may already be on his way to Cofitachequi, and you'll be here, waiting, while he travels on."

That was indeed a possibility.

Winder continued. "I don't know what your goal is once you reach Cofitachequi, but for you to have traveled this far, being the kind of Trader you are, it must be an important mission. Do you want to simply abandon it? Sit here in Black Clay Bank village, waiting? If so, for how long? A couple of moons? A year? What if Two Coups never comes? If the worst happened and Blood Talon's warriors killed him that day in the river, what then?"

She clenched her teeth, eyes going out to the growing darkness and the roiling flood beyond.

"*Cofitachequi,*" Piasa whispered.

"Is he alive?" she asked the air around her.

"*He lives for Cofitachequi.*"

"How do I know you're telling the truth?"

"*Our new bargain. Your brother for Fire Cat.*"

Night Shadow Star stiffened. Realized what the Underwater Panther had done. "He was in the river, your domain."

The Spirit Beast hissed his amusement. Two words formed in the air around her. "*The price.*"

For daring to consummate her love for Fire Cat?

She closed her eyes, heart pounding in her chest. Her master had just been biding his time, letting her fall ever deeper into her love, knowing that when the beast took him away from her, she'd be totally at Piasa's command.

"So," she mused, "the only way to get him back is to finish what I started?"

She could imagine Piasa's gleaming eyes, the feral smile, a half snarl that bent the beast's cougar-shaped muzzle.

"We go as soon as it's safe to travel the river," she told Winder. "And the faster we get to Cofitachequi, the better."

"And Two Coups?"

"He will find us there."

As if the Trader had heard Piasa himself, a contented smile, almost triumphant, seemed to animate the man's square face.

"In the morning, Lady," Winder told her. "Now, get a good night's sleep. We can make the downriver end of the Suck and Rage by tomorrow night if we're on the river by first light."

As she laid out her bedding, she pleaded, *Fire Cat, tell me I'm doing the right thing.*

Because if she got to Cofitachequi, killed Walking Smoke, and her Spirit master didn't produce Fire Cat? Well, should that be the case, her lord had better prepare for war.

Fifty-three

Make way! Make way!" Blue Heron's porters called as they steered her litter through the cramped back ways just off the Avenue of the Sun in River Mounds City. This was a warren of warehouses, workshops, and craft specialists, all packed together in the close confines that made up the area just back from the canoe landing and River House's elongated plaza.

All Blue Heron had to do was crane her neck, and she could see the River Mounds palace roof between the spaces as she was carried through the maze. That her people could find the way was a sort of miracle in itself.

She had worked for days to set up this meet. Sent stealthy runners off in the night to ensure that all the pieces were in place. And now she would discover if she still had the old touch.

The way led past an old weaver's; the woman was sitting out in the sun, squinting at her work as she ran weft through the stays of her loom. She glanced up, shot a sour smile Blue Heron's way that exposed pink gums long bereft of teeth.

And then Blue Heron's litter rounded the old woman's house and into a small yard bounded on one side by the weaver's, by a ramada on the second, and by a prosperous-looking house and ramada on the third. A young woman waited beside the door, a pretty thing, with long glossy hair, a triangular face, and large eyes. She rose, displaying a pregnant belly, as Blue Heron's litter was deposited in the yard.

Bones aching, Blue Heron climbed to her feet and grabbed up the sack she'd brought with her.

"Lady?" her head porter asked. "Can I be of assistance?"

"No. I don't think I'll be long. You and the rest, relax. Enjoy the shade in the ramada. I'm told that those jars contain water and there's a latrine around the back."

"Yes, Lady."

Blue Heron walked over to the young woman. "Whispering Dawn. You've changed since you first appeared before me with a leash around your ankle."

"Keeper?"

"Not anymore. I need to see Wooden Doll. She knows I'm coming."

"This way." Whispering Dawn opened the door, asking shyly, "How is Seven Skull Shield?"

"In trouble, if I was to guess. But then, what's new about that? He been here recently?"

"Haven't seen him."

"That makes two of us." She stepped into a well-furnished room, a stack of firewood by the door. Thick rugs and hair-on hides partially obscured an intricately woven floor mat. Wall benches were opulently furnished with blankets, robes, and fine furs.

A small fire, just enough to provide illumination, burned in the central hearth. Several corrugated pots steamed on stones at the side of the coals. The smells were delightful—mint, black drink, and something made from boiled flower petals.

In the rear an ample bed had been built into the wall and was thick with pillows, blankets, and soft furs.

Wooden Doll rose from the bed, a warm smile on her full lips as she strode across the floor. She took Blue Heron's hand in her own. Keeping her grip, she bowed low, touching her forehead respectfully, and said, "Lady. I bid you a most warm welcome. Please, have a seat. Dawn? Pour the Keeper a cup of that black drink."

To Blue Heron she added, "I've brewed it specially for you. If you're hungry, I can lay a feast for you in less than a finger's time. I have roast venison, stuffed duck, acorn bread seasoned with blueberries, or stewed buffalo tongue in onions and tender goosefoot leaves."

"I thought times were lean, given the near-empty storehouses in River Mounds."

"They are." She smiled, leading Blue Heron to one of the benches. "For those who can't afford it. Your preference?"

"Buffalo tongue?"

"Dawn? Please?"

"Yes, Matron." And the young woman was out the door, shutting it behind her to give them privacy.

"Thanks for seeing me."

Wooden Doll seated herself a respectful but intimate distance from Blue Heron, her keen brown eyes measuring. "What can I help you with?"

"I take it that I don't have to explain the political situation in River Mounds. You are aware that Three Fingers and Broken Stone are about to move on War Duck and Round Pot. Broken Stone's faction is using the opening of the storehouses to replenish Columella's stores as a rallying point to topple his brother and sister."

Wooden Doll's arched brow indicated the obvious. "I don't take sides."

"We both know better than that. I'm here to do business, and I think you're the key to River Mounds City and River House."

"Me? I'm just a woman who sells herself."

"And I'm just a has-been Clan Keeper." Blue Heron grinned. "Kind of nice being dismissed as irrelevant by the rest of the world, isn't it?"

Wooden Doll's almost deadly smile proved more eloquent than words. "What exactly do you need from me?"

"Three Fingers, using Broken Stone, wants to ascend to the high chair. I don't want to see him do it."

"Why should I care which side wins? War Duck, bless his sordid soul, takes a portion of what I make. Tribute, he calls it. Broken Stone might not take any, assuming he even knows who passes what to River House when it comes to wealth."

"What if I could put in a good word for you? You see, War Duck is in need of friends these days. He might be persuaded to forget any 'tribute' his few friends might owe. Given the right circumstances."

"Neither War Duck nor Round Pot have ever been friends of yours. I'd think, Keeper, that you'd want them gone, as many headaches as they've given you over the years."

"You know Three Fingers." She pointed. "He's been in that bed of yours a time or two."

"So has War Duck. What's your point?"

"My point is that you know that if Three Fingers ultimately takes over, he's going to go about shaking things up. What's the point of suddenly having all that authority and prestige you've longed for all your life if you can't flaunt it? And there are paybacks that will need to be made. People, lineages that have stood in his way in the past, need to be dispatched. Additional purges on top of the ones Rising Flame just made prior to sending that expedition off to the south. The old familiar structure is going to be turned on its head. A major disruption of business.

"Might even drive some of the Trade to other places. Perhaps Evening Star Town, or worse, Horned Serpent Town, despite the lack of a close canoe landing there.

"Not to mention that keeping War Duck and Round Pot in control lets me deal with the enemy I know. It would take time, effort, and distasteful means to educate either Broken Stone—if he's left alive—or Three Fingers as to where his best interests lie."

Wooden Doll laughed. "I thought Rising Flame knocked you off your pedestal as Clan Keeper."

"Oh, she did. Cut me right off at the ankles and left me impotent, as you can see. Poor me."

"Why do you care who controls River House? You could sit back, enjoy good food, sleep late, and be lazy. Watch from afar, saying, 'Told you so.' "

Blue Heron sighed. "The problem with Cahokia, from the very beginning, is that it has the fundamental impulse to tear itself apart. It did in the days of Tharon and Petaga, and it does now, despite the living god. I've worked all my life to keep the city together, and now we're building an empire. After all these years, all the sacrifice and blood, I don't want to see Spotted Wrist lose it because he doesn't know his job."

Wooden Doll considered. "I didn't know you were such a starry-headed idealist."

"I'm more of a self-centered pragmatist, actually."

"You know where my interests lie. I expect compensation."

"You'll have it. If I can pull this off. I'll do my best to get that 'tribute' taken care of."

"Done."

As Whispering Dawn brought in the food, Wooden Doll asked, "Where's Skull? He been with you?"

"Saw him a couple of weeks ago. Him and that disaster of a dog that goes everywhere with him." She made a face, inhaling the scent of roast buffalo tongue. "He's in love."

"That woman of Robin Feather's?"

"That's her."

"She's trouble. Just ask Robin Feather. He's still searching for her and Skull. Keeps a constant eye on my place. She's going to break Skull's heart."

"Can't tell him that. As he insists, he knows all there is to know about women."

"If he knew half of—"

A discreet knock came at the door, a young man sticking his head in. "Mistress," he said, looking out of breath, "you asked me to keep an eye on the thief? He's been taken. Took me a while to find out where. That war leader, Spotted Wrist. He's got him locked in a cage in his palace."

Blue Heron felt her gut drop, then shot a look at Wooden Doll, who'd turned a shade paler. "You were saying?"

Fifty-four

Nothing was working the way Fire Cat hoped it would. His days in the island hut had ended in misery as his search for any kind of dry and burnable wood grew ever more futile. Nor did he want to employ his copper-bitted war club as an ax to split open logs in an attempt to reach the dry interiors—not as wet as his club was with the wood and sinew bindings soaked. He might loosen the hafted blade to the point that he'd never be able to fix it solid again.

The storm hadn't abated for two days, and then he'd had to make a raft from the soaked driftwood that lodged on the bank as the river fell. After all his work to keep his bow stave from warping as it dried and the effort he'd put into maintaining his wood-and-leather armor, he didn't want to get it all soaked again. Hence the raft to keep it above water as he kicked his way across the north channel to the bank. That looked like the easiest crossing compared to the swifter water on the south.

After making shore, it had taken two days to slip, slog, wade, and occasionally swim his way through the swampy floodplain. Along the way, every mosquito ever born accompanied each step; the constant humming cloud wavered around him like a perverted shadow, moving as he did. Constantly biting, getting in his ears, nose, and mouth. He teetered on the verge of madness, periodically using his bow to whip the air in an attempt to disperse the beasts.

It worked. For a moment or two. Then the humming column would re-form around him. Maddening. Totally, completely maddening.

The night of the second day—a thick layer of mud daubing every bit of exposed flesh to protect him from the mosquitoes, ticks, and chiggers—he found better footing, the land rising.

He worked his way up the slight incline, the mud underfoot turning from slime to something sandier. He could tell it was a trail, and more to the point, he encountered a ragged stump where someone had used a stone ax to cut down a tree.

The trail wound its way through thick boles of oak, hickory, ash, and the huge smooth-barked trunks of mighty beech trees. Melodic birdsong and the buzzing of insects was broken by the occasional chatter of a fox squirrel.

The light was deepening, indicating that somewhere above the vast forest canopy, evening was descending on the land.

In the growing gloom, he could see more evidence of human presence: a broken pot, places where bark had been stripped from the trees. The forest litter had vanished, any fallen branches having been collected for firewood. And then he passed white bones left by a hunter: leg bones from a deer. Why pack the parts that couldn't be eaten?

As the first bats came winging down to ravage his cloud of mosquitoes, he reached the edge of the forest, a place where the trees had been ringed, left to die, and then burned to open a mixed field of corn, beans, goosefoot, squash, and tobacco.

Across the open space he could see the village. Not much to brag about, just a collection of bark-sided bent-pole huts. One in the rear was freshly crushed, a huge section of newly fallen oak lying across the flattened remains.

Firelight danced, voices carried, along with a clacking of rhythm sticks accompanied by the hollow tones of flute, and melodic singing in some language Fire Cat couldn't place. Might have been a Muskogean dialect.

His first impulse was to rush into the village, desperate in the hope that Night Shadow Star might be there waiting.

Caution, his old ally, however, reared its wise head, caused him to stop, to pull his war club from his bag, and use the last of the light to strap on his armor.

No telling who these people were. Nor did he possess any kind of Trade, not to mention that they might not understand Trade pidgin. Though that was unlikely, given that they lived on the banks of the Tenasee. He was a lone man, a stranger, appearing out of the night.

Creeping through the crops, Fire Cat kept the wind at his shoulder, letting it carry his scent down toward the river. Any village had dogs. Moving carefully, he circled downwind, edged his way around blackberry bushes, and found a point of vantage behind a small conical burial mound. From the soft dirt on the river side, more than one body had been recently interred. Maybe from the crushed hut?

Fire Cat wriggled up to the top, peered over. His view covered the small open space in the middle of the village. Maybe thirty people sat around the crackling fire. They sang, clapped hands, and played their instruments. An older man, white-haired, his body tattooed in geometric patterns, was wearing a cougar-hide cape. The man's face sported a painted mask of red and black, and in his hand he held a burning brand.

Just behind the man, two poles had been set in the ground to make an X. Tied within it, arms to the upper sections, legs below, a naked man struggled to keep his head up.

The white-haired and painted elder thrust his burning stick against the hanging man's side, causing his victim to jerk tight against the frame against which he was tied.

Something about the prisoner, about the way he wore his hair, the beaded forelock hanging down over his forehead . . .

Fire Cat slipped down the front of the burial mound, eased to the protection of the closest hut where it overlooked the canoe landing and the dark river. Carefully, he peered around the side of the bent-pole structure.

He could see the prisoner's tattoos now: Snapping Turtle Clan. Those eyes had stared into Fire Cat's, hard, desperate, ready to kill. Now Blood Talon's face was a sweaty mask of determination. He was a warrior, a squadron first, supposedly the bravest of the brave. Knowing him, as Fire Cat did, he suspected that every fiber of Blood Talon's being was focused on showing the forest barbarians just how a Cahokian warrior died.

Served him right.

Fire Cat considered, glanced back at the canoe landing. He could take one of the dugouts, slip it down the bank, and be gone into the night. The villagers were more than distracted, all attention on the suffering Blood Talon. Even the village dogs were watching, rapt, probably anticipating scraps of meat as the victim was burned, sliced, and dismembered.

I could just go.

Fire Cat hesitated, made a face. The memory remained as clear in his souls as spring water, every detail of his pain, his despair, so keenly felt in the days after this man had captured him and destroyed Red Wing Town. Each of the bragging taunts echoed in Fire Cat's ears.

He stopped short, staring at the canoes where they'd been pulled up beyond the river's edge. He should be going. His concern was Night Shadow Star. Blood Talon had once challenged him with the express purpose of murdering him. Had led one of the squadrons that had sacked Red Wing Town. Raped his wives, perhaps even thrust himself into one of Fire Cat's young daughters before he cut her throat and threw her corpse into the river.

Let him die.

With a sigh, Fire Cat closed his eyes, shook his head.

The man had chased them halfway across the world. Would have taken Night Shadow Star back to marry a man she despised.

"I am such a fool," Fire Cat whispered.

From his bag, he took his bow, strung it, and slung his quiver over his shoulder. He had fifteen arrows. Maybe thirty villagers surrounded the fire.

Walking out from behind the hut, he pulled a shaft, nocked it, and drew. At his release, the shaft drove into the old white-haired man's chest. The fellow started, eyes going wide in his painted face.

Fire Cat was already drawing, his second shot taking a muscular man who plucked at a bowstring and sang with gusto as he watched Blood Talon being tortured.

The third arrow stopped in the next man to rise, the fletching protruding just below his left nipple.

The fourth caught a young man in the hollow of the throat just above his breastbone. Probably severed his spine because he dropped as if head-clubbed.

By the time the villagers figured it out, Fire Cat was in their midst. Head back, he screamed his old war cry: *"Hoookaaaiiiiaaawww!"*

Then he pulled his war club from his belt, striking right and left as the villagers screamed, scrambled to their feet, and broke for the darkness. Their wails of terror, the sight of them running full out, filled him with exultation.

Only one of the dogs, a vicious-looking beast with matted fur, turned at bay, snarling, most of the teeth already broken out of its mouth.

Fire Cat leaped at it, swung his war club, and roared his rage.

The dog turned, apparently having had previous experience with armed humans. Tail between its legs, it sped for the dark haven of the forest, overtaking the last of the fleeing villagers.

Fire Cat stepped across one of the dying men as the fellow pulled feebly at the arrow sticking out of his chest. Frothy blood bubbled from his lips and nostrils.

With a swing, Fire Cat's copper-bitted blade severed the rope at Blood Talon's right wrist. Then the left.

"Can you walk?"

A weak smile bent Blood Talon's bruised lips. "If it means getting away from here? I can fly. Just watch me."

Chopping the last of the ropes away, Fire Cat turned, heading for the canoes. "Watch yourself. I'm done with this place. You can keep up or not. Your choice."

Wobbling and staggering, Blood Talon made it to the canoes. The level of his pain was evident in the half-strangled sounds he worked diligently to hide.

Most of the canoes were clumsy-looking dugouts, or much too large for two men, but one—a thin-hulled craft—might fit Fire Cat's need. He tossed his war bag and weapons inside. With Blood Talon's feeble help, they dragged it down to the water.

Feeling around inside, Fire Cat found three paddles, handed one to Blood Talon, and said, "Get in." Then he pushed the canoe out into the dark water.

"How long do you figure before they're after us?" Blood Talon asked, stifling a groan as he dipped his paddle into the dark water.

"Maybe a hand of time, depends on who's the new leader. How do I know? These are barbarians."

"Taking a real risk, out on the river in the darkness like this. Anything comes floating down, some log, maybe a raft of driftwood, and it could turn us over."

"You'd rather be back at that village?"

"I'll take the river."

"Thought you would." Fire Cat smiled warily into the night. "How'd you get hung up on that scaffold?"

"Accident on the river. Got lost in the swamps. I was on my last legs when I stumbled out, saw a party of fishermen. Called to them. I kept telling them I was Cahokian. Repeated the word over and over. Pointed out my clan tattoos. Told them I'd give them a great reward if they'd help me."

"Don't speak Trade pidgin?"

"Not well enough, I guess. One had a bow. Pulled a shaft and drew. What could I do? All I had for a weapon was a stick. Figured that they'd untie me when we got back to wherever they'd come from and I could explain myself. Instead they just strung me up to that scaffold."

"Not smart, calling yourself Cahokian on this part of the Tenasee. Gets even worse up past the Suck and Rage, I'm told."

"Haven't they heard? The Morning Star protects Trade. Cahokia won't stand for people taking and murdering Traders. It's the living god's law."

"Squadron First, you've got a lot to learn." Fire Cat shook his head in disbelief. But then, what should he expect? Blood Talon hadn't ever dealt with the world except as the leader of a war party. His entire life, everything the man knew, was oriented around Cahokia and the prestige of command. He'd never known any other perspective.

"How'd you know I was a squadron first? Who are you?"

"A bound man. A lowly servant."

"That's the worst lie I've ever heard. I couldn't believe it. You came walking out of the night like some monster, all covered in mud like you just emerged from the swamp. And wearing armor! No servant ever used a bow like that. Wasn't a heartbeat between the sound of arrows spitting those men. *Thwap. Thwap. Thwap.* And the way you lit into them with that war club? That copper shining in the firelight as it . . ."

Blood Talon stopped paddling. "I know that war club. But you're . . ."

"Paddle the canoe, Squadron First. I can still finish what those barbarians started."

"You? After what you did to me? To my warriors?"

"You want to go back into the river? Take your chances when those folk back behind us get themselves organized and come looking for whomever took their canoe?"

Blood Talon straightened, and resumed paddling despite his obvious agony.

Fire Cat had to hand it to the man. Burned and bruised as he was, he still forced himself to at least make the attempt at paddling.

By Piasa's balls, what am I going to do with him now?

Fifty-five

I have never been so alone. The words kept repeating down deep in Night Shadow Star's souls as she and Winder's crew paddled the Albaamaha canoe around a slight bend.

She was among strangers, in a strange land, a world that had been beyond her imagination. This river, these mountains, the smells and colors, even the people with whom she traveled, all were alien. For the first time in her life, she knew no one. The only things she was familiar with were the Trade items she had packed in her box back in far-off Cahokia and her clothes.

Even the country was alien. The green-forested ridges had been closing in on the river for days, narrowing, growing ever taller and steeper. Now, ahead of them across the roiling surface of the water, she could see the canyon at the mouth of the Suck and Rage. With a sense of desperation, she dug her paddle deep, as if the exertion would earn her some peace in her bruised souls.

Not even in the days after she'd learned of Makes Three's death had she felt so bereft. She'd been in her palace, after all, surrounded by her household staff, visited by her mother, father, and aunt. She needed only to step out her front door to see the sprawling Great Plaza, crowded with people, or look down on the Avenue of the Sun where the throngs of Traders, farmers, embassies, and travelers passed relentlessly below.

Totally alone.

The reality possessed her, left her aching inside and desperate for Fire

Cat's reassuring presence. Blood and piss, but she ached for him. Kept expecting to see him every time she looked around. His absence tore a hollow in her, one she longed desperately to fill.

She had known how much she loved him. What she hadn't fully understood was how much she depended upon him.

It's easy to be strong when Fire Cat's at your shoulder, his war club at the ready, that reassuring smile on his face.

Without him—not even knowing for sure that he was alive—she lived in new and unfamiliar terror.

At times in the past she had thought she was alone—but the realization now crept in that her circumstances in Cahokia had been entirely different than here on the Tenasee, accompanied by the affable, but untrustworthy, Winder and his five Albaamaha. The latter didn't speak a word of her language—and studiously ignored her to the point they pretended she wasn't even there.

"They remember when Moon Blade brought his army through here a generation ago," Winder told her. "In far-off Cahokia, the story is told of a valiant expedition that traveled across half the world to found the Cofitachequi colony. Here it is remembered as a horrible conquering army moving up the Tenasee, murdering, enslaving, and robbing. Entire villages of Albaamaha and Koasati were plundered and exterminated along the middle reaches of the Tenasee. As were the Hiawasee Muskogeans, and even the Mountain Chalakee. Then came the brutal conquest of Cofitachequi. And in the years after that followed even more expeditions as they founded the Cahokian colonies along the lower river. All those lands seized by force from the local peoples by means of blood and violence."

"The Yuchi like us."

"The Yuchi have used their alliance with Cahokia as a means of settling old scores. These days they can raid their enemies with impunity. If, for example, after a raid, the Koasati or Biloxi strike back, retaliation will come in the form of a combined Cahokian and Yuchi army. Remove that benefit, and what do the Yuchi have to gain?"

"Trade." Night Shadow Star gestured at the river. "Free Trade has enriched all people. Even you—as you no doubt are fully aware. And you're a Cahokian yourself."

He smiled as he paddled. "From here on, Lady, trust me. Once past the Suck and Rage, you are beyond the reach of the Cahokian colonies on the Tenasee. Oh sure, there are some small outposts, Traders and the like. But they tread lightly and go heavily armed on the upper river and its tributaries. In these parts people fear Cahokia. See it as a looming threat and wonder what the future portends should the Cahokians take an interest in their lands. They worry as Cahokian priests travel the back country, preaching the resurrection of the living god."

"The reincarnation of the Morning Star is a miracle."

"Is it?"

Some wariness kept Night Shadow Star from taking his bait. She was, after all, supposed to be White Willow, a minor cousin, generations removed from Black Tail's lineage.

She let the conversation drop.

Fought the urge to burst into tears.

Turned her thoughts to the beauty of the land instead. She would have never imagined that such country existed. As they'd traveled upriver from the Great Bend, the long valley of the Tenasee had turned to the northeast.

Even the smells had changed, filling her nose with a growing fragrance, a perfumed mix. Call it sweet pungency: the odor of forest, grass-rich fields, the damp soils, and smells of the river itself. All of it pulsed with a Spirit she'd never felt before. This land was possessed of a different Power than her native environs. Wilder, more vibrant.

The exact place where the transition lay between hill country and mountains eluded her. But on this section of river she was in mountain country. She could see it in the high, almost vertical inclines, in the nature of the stone that outcropped atop the soaring peaks, gray, rounded, and devoid of vegetation. That such thick forest could cling to such steep and dizzying slopes filled her with awe.

Though she'd been told stories all her life, nothing had prepared her for the vista as she stared up at the remarkably blue sky, the vivid greens, and the occasional fluffy white clouds. She'd once thought the Morning Star's mound to be the highest place on earth. Now, looking at mountains, she found the notion ludicrous.

The earth had always been a presence in her soul; it imparted an almost serene sense of nurture and permanence. But this land? It filled her with wonder as she gazed up at the heights.

"That's our goal for the day," Winder told her, using his paddle to point.

Ahead, on the river's southern bank, she could see a settlement located on a terrace. Smoke rose in thin fingers from the town's fires, though hickory and mulberry trees screened most of the structures from view. Behind it the ground sloped, rising in benches that surrendered to rounded heights on the far southern horizon.

From the town a trail descended to the canoe landing. Maybe fifteen or twenty craft had been pulled up on the shore. A smattering of ramadas and what looked like warehouses were set above the high-water line.

"The town is called *Haktimikko* in Muskogee. It means White Chief.

The legend is that a terrible chief once ruled here. He had his body tattooed entirely in black, and he stole all the Trade coming up or down the river. That in order to pass his lands, he demanded terrible sacrifices in payment for passage. One story tells of how he made a Trader sacrifice his only daughter, and that the terrible chief then cooked her body and fed it to the Trader at a feast in the man's honor.

"Then came a White Chief, who, through Powerful magic, destroyed the Black Chief by lifting him with a whirlwind and dropping him in the narrows. When the whirlwind hit the river, it pulled him down, creating the great whirlpool in the middle of the canyon called the Suck."

"Are the people here friendly to Cahokians?"

Winder shrugged. "Lady, everyone is tolerated here as long as they don't behave unreasonably. White Chief Town survives on Trade, prides itself on keeping with the old traditions of the Power of Trade. Anyone who enters its grounds is supposed to maintain the peace. As a result, even bitter enemies come here to negotiate the return of captives, solve grievances, and sometimes broker alliances."

"White Chief Town has a large military force to ensure the peace?"

"No, Lady. The various nations hereabouts, they just respect the tradition. Mostly I guess because it serves everyone's purposes. And anyone who broke the peace? They'd pay for it in the end. No one would deal with them. Not even Traders. It would cost them any allies they had."

Night Shadow Star studied the place as the canoe glided in and slid onto the beach.

Winder climbed out, laughing, slapping the Albaamaha paddlers on the back. Then he reached into one of his packs, handing each of the men a string of shell beads. Upon receiving their payment, the men bowed, grinning. Then, calling happily to each other, they muscled the canoe up on the sand, ignoring Night Shadow Star in the process. Without a backward glance they started up the trail, headed for the town.

"What just happened?" Night Shadow Star asked.

"They're looking to find a meal, spend the night, do a little Trading, find a woman to share the blankets with, and in the morning, they'll head back for home."

"But I thought they were going to take us all the way to Cofitachequi?"

Winder gave her a crooked grin, jerking his thumb in the direction of the canyon. "You and I are walking. We'll take the river trail. Hire porters to carry our packs and your box up past the Suck and Rage to *Ikansofke*, or Canyon Town, at the head of the narrows. From there we can hire another canoe to take us the rest of the way to the mouth of the Wide Fast River."

"I didn't know it would be so difficult."

"Most people don't."

Winder called out in some local tongue. A band of boys, in their early teens, swarmed down from one of the ramadas, picked up the box and remaining packs in the canoe and, laughing and chattering, started up the trail with them.

"Let's go find a bed, get some food," Winder told her, and spinning on his heel, the big man set out up the trail.

In the steeper spots, squared logs had been set as stairs in the trail, making the climb easier. Topping onto the flat it was to encounter a moderate-size town of perhaps two or three hundred people. The houses were mostly the traditional bent-pole construction, though to Night Shadow Star's surprise, here and there newer trench-wall houses of Cahokian design could be seen.

The layout followed the usual southern habit of building around a central square plaza that served as the stickball and Dance grounds, though this one had a large, round, earthen structure smack in its middle.

"That's called the *Tchkofa*, or Council House." Winder pointed. "And over there, that big square open-sided building? That's the summer house where most business is transacted and Trading takes place. You and I, we'll be trying to secure a bed in the Trade House. That's the log-sided building just the other side of the White Chief's palace atop that low mound."

"Why are these towns all so alike?"

"It's the *talwa*, means town. It's the way the Muskogeans tend to organize their politics. Goes back to the old days. Reflects the origin stories of the people. Each of the clans has their place on the square. A family can move clear down to the Gulf. Whatever *talwa* they arrive at, they know where their place is in that community."

"As long as they're Muskogee."

"That's right. Timucua are different."

"Are we going that far south? I thought they were down in the peninsula."

Winder studied her thoughtfully, that clever glint in his quick black eyes. "No. It's mostly Muskogeans we're going to be dealing with. And when we get to the eastern mountains, we'll find the Chalakee. They're a mountain people, high-country Traders."

She followed him as he wound through the houses, each with a garden. The granaries here were all elevated on tall posts. Ladders allowed access, and the cone-shaped roofs were thatched.

People, working at milling corn, pounding smilax root, and minding boiling pots, watched her pass with curious but hospitable glances. The occasional dog approached, tail wagging, but lost interest when it became apparent they had no food.

Ahead of them, the boys led the way, packs bobbing as they crossed the plaza to the Trade House.

At the door Winder reached into his belt pouch and produced a handful of small reed whistles. Each boy dropped his burden and received his, then joyously went running back the way they'd come; their progress was marked by the shrill hollow tones of tooting.

"I thought it was curious that you spent most of the night carving them."

Winder gave her a wink. "Pays to know what people want, Lady. Figure that out and you have the world in your hand."

She felt a sense of wariness, Piasa's uneasy hiss seeming to warble in the air around her. .

Winder, missing nothing, just chuckled and turned to an old man seated on a stump next to the door. In rapid-fire Muskogean, a bargain was struck. Winder produced a small packet of some organic substance and handed it across.

"And what was that?" Night Shadow Star asked as Winder led the way into the gable-roofed structure.

"Old man Seven Root, back there, has a weakness for a certain forest mushroom that, when mixed with tobacco, allows his souls to fly from his body."

"Your knowledge amazes me."

He gave her a knowing smile as he tossed one of their packs onto the lower of two bunk beds built into the back wall and separated from the other beds by a cane-wall divider. "I'll give you the bottom," he told her. "Trust me, it's a little more private."

From the packs, she took her and Fire Cat's blankets and laid them out. Hesitating as she did, she lifted his blanket, smelling, trying to find his scent in the woven buffalo wool.

How was he doing? Out there. Somewhere on the river. She knew he was alive, could feel it in her souls. But he had nothing but his weapons, not his blanket, not his fire starter, sewing kit, his knife, abrader, knapping tools, or cord.

Be well, my love. Come find me.

Piasa's laughter seemed to echo from the split-cane roof overhead.

"Don't worry about your packs," Winder told her. "No one will bother them here. That's another of the understood rules."

"Not even if it's a fortune in copper, shell, and carvings in an ornately carved Cahokian wooden box?"

"Not even then, Lady. Old Seven Root might like to send his souls flying, but not while he's on guard at the Trade House. Come, let me show you the town. And then I'll treat you to one of the finest roast cat-fish suppers you've ever eaten."

She gave him a suspicious sidelong glance. The man was just too smooth, too at ease, as if he possessed some special advantage she couldn't quite comprehend.

Nevertheless, as the sun sank behind the distant ridges and cast the most spectacular blue shadows over the valleys beneath, Night Shadow Star savored one of the most delicious meals she'd ever eaten. Given that she'd been raised in the *tonka'tzi*'s palace, that was saying a lot.

Winder explained, "Old Woman White Egret roasts the fish in a spe-cial pit. Uses salt she Trades up from the peninsula. She places sassafras root in the gut hollow, then wraps the fish in grape leaves interlaid with rose petals."

From where they sat on a log bench on the east end of the plaza, Night Shadow Star was able to watch a practice stickball match. She desperately missed the game.

Missed having Fire Cat at her side even more.

"What are you after?" she asked.

Winder took another bite of fish, chewed, and swallowed before wash-ing it down with a cup of mint tea. "After?"

"Fire Cat's not dead. He's following us."

Winder's gaze remained fixed on the sunset. "You sure?"

"Piasa would tell me."

"Now, that notion that the Underwater Panther—"

"Answer me. What are you after? Clever man like you, you're playing the perfect host. So genial. Everything seen to. Not a single misstep. Not a single hint of dishonesty. Always the smile in place, best side forward, and never a slip. Never an unmanaged moment when you're not playing the part."

The flicker of a smile teased the corners of his mouth, his eyes still guarded. "What if I told you I was just being myself? That this is who I really am. Just Winder, the River Fox, a successful Trader who is adept at his craft."

"And you lie so facilely and with such simple sincerity. I have to ad-mire how good you are in the practice. If I didn't know the depth of your involvement in the Surveyors' Bundle theft, in the way Blue Heron was treated by the Quiz Quiz, and the fact you almost got a lot of people killed, I might even believe you. Though how a clanless thief, orphan, and ne'er-do-well child like you could grow into such an accomplished pretender is a story worth hearing. You almost pull it off, you know. The genteel nobility act."

He shot her a hard look, no amusement now in his square and hard-used face. "I spent years learning. Studying the chiefs, from the Chitimacha down in their swamps by the Gulf, to the Tunica, Pasqui, the Quiz Quiz, Casquinampo, and Sky Hand. Learned how to posture my body, the movements of the hands, how they smiled, and how they scowled. Did the same with the House chiefs in Cahokia. Oh, not the Morning Star by any means. Not even I could weasel my way up into that sacred height. But Green Chunkey? War Duck? Those were chiefs who'd deal for my goods."

A pause. "Then there's the fine ladies. Bored with their noble husbands. Looking for something different, something a bit dangerous and forbidden. Looking to dally with a man who has made a study of the ways to coax every bit of delight from a woman's body."

"Why play the game with me? I don't have the slightest interest in being 'happy' with you. So, I repeat, what are you after?"

He stared off into the distance again, gaze fixed on the purpling sky and soft shadows of evening. Finally, he said, "I'm not the only one playing a game, Lady White Willow. Remarkable choice of a name, don't you think? Especially for a minor cousin several steps removed from the central authority vested in Morning Star House. But I must admit, you've surprised me. Actually, earned my respect. Never thought you'd be capable of work, and hard work at that. I begin to understand."

"Understand what?"

"Your Power, Lady. And why so many fear it."

She took another bite of fish. It really was marvelous. She wondered if she could explain how to make it well enough that Clay String could cook the like. Assuming, that is, that she ever got home.

"I have no Power."

"And I'm a simple river Trader," Winder asserted. "One good game deserves another."

She took a deep breath. "You are hired to take me to Cofitachequi. That is all you are expected to do. I don't need any special coddling. I'm far from bored with the man I already have, so you can cease wasting your time trying to seduce me. Beyond that, if I have secrets, they are my own. For my own purposes. Do we have an understanding?"

The mocking hint of a smile began to play at the corners of his mouth again. "I think, Lady, that you and I understand each other perfectly. Now, enjoy your fish. You won't taste the like until you come back this way again."

She caught a flicker of Piasa at the edge of her vision, as though her Spirit Master had been listening from the deepening shadows behind them.

Fifty-six

Screwing up all the courage Blood Talon could manage, he kept his expression stoic. Tried not to flinch. And prayed that tears would not come to his eyes as Fire Cat daubed a grease-based unguent onto the hideous burns that peeled and bled on Blood Talon's ribs, under his arms, and on the inside of his thighs.

The old man who'd been torturing him hadn't gotten to his penis and testicles, or to the point that they'd set his hair on fire. Nor, thankfully, had they pulled his eyeballs out of their sockets, cut out his tongue, or severed his fingers, one by one. Generally, the practice was to wait for that. Build up to the final indignity that left a sightless husk hanging from broken bones where the arms and legs had been smashed.

As to whether the barbarians would have chosen to either pluck his eyes from the sockets, or just burn them out on the end of a fiery stick would remain speculative, and a subject that would return to haunt Blood Talon's dreams for the rest of his life.

Not that Fire Cat's miraculous appearance out of the night wasn't without problems of its own. Blood Talon owed the man his life. This man. The one who had murdered his men and now daubed medicine he'd traded a catfish for at the last village they'd passed.

Looking back at their now-entwined histories, Blood Talon found himself more than a little troubled. In the beginning, Red Wing Town had incited its destruction by remaining a hive of heresy. Then, partly because of Fire Cat's military brilliance, the Red Wing Clan had destroyed several Cahokian armies, not the least of which was Makes Three's.

Blood Talon himself had led the raid on Fire Cat's palace, had helped to subdue the man and saw him safely shipped off for Cahokia aboard a canoe. Then he had helped himself to the spoils, including the degradation and abuse of Fire Cat's wives, relatives, and children. While he hadn't sexually violated the young ones, he hadn't forbidden it, had casually ordered their execution, and had their bodies disposed of in the river.

By the time he and his squadron had returned to Cahokia, the Red Wing—now Night Shadow Star's slave—had saved the city, not once, but twice, and supposedly had helped to bring the Morning Star's souls back from the Underworld.

And he could have killed me that day I challenged him on Night Shadow Star's mound.

But Fire Cat hadn't retaliated, even though he understood the stakes. The gentle feel of that blade against Blood Talon's neck remained as clear as yesterday.

But it hadn't stopped there. The man had precipitated the deaths of so many of Blood Talon's warriors when he capsized the war canoe: Nutcracker, Three Bow, Wild Owl, Old Scar, and Whistle Hand among them. Comrades from countless war trails. Men whose laughter, smiles, and privations Blood Talon had shared over the years. In a bond stronger than that shared by brothers, they'd trained, fought, shivered, and sweated. The notion that his erstwhile savior had murdered them? It left him confused and wanting to scream at the injustice of it.

"You killed my men."

"You destroyed my town and family. Sent me into slavery. Would have killed me and taken Night Shadow Star back to that foul master of yours."

"I was following orders," Blood Talon whispered past his gritted teeth as Fire Cat used a finger to smear more of the grease onto the underside of Blood Talon's right arm.

"Funny thing, your orders," Fire Cat answered. "Who were they to benefit? The Morning Star? The people of Cahokia? Certainly, they didn't benefit Night Shadow Star, or, I'm sure, the Four Winds Clan. I'm not sure they actually benefited Rising Flame, either. Not in the long view of things."

Blood Talon made a face, flinched at the bruises on his lips and cheekbones where they'd beat him. "I serve my war leader."

"Ah yes, the noble Spotted Wrist. In line for the chieftainship of North Star House. Now he's the Four Winds Clan Keeper, a rising star. And here you are, halfway across the world, your canoe gone, your warriors drowned, and the one man in life whom you could really call your enemy has plucked you from the hands of barbarians. Two-footed vermin who were going to torture you for as long as you held out." Fire Cat frowned. "What was that all about? Did you ever really get the gist of why they wanted to burn you alive?"

"Part of a burial ritual, I think. And something to do with being Cahokian. I think they wanted to send my soul to their afterlife to serve their dead. Some kind of funeral for a bunch of people killed by a falling tree."

"Poor choice on their part. You'd have made a pitiful and nasty servant. You don't have the qualities of soul required."

Blood Talon snorted a laugh, immediately regretted it as it pulled his bruised ribs and burned skin.

"I suppose you'll tell me all my failings now?"

"I suspect that you already know them, Squadron First."

"Where's the Lady Night Shadow Star?"

"Somewhere upriver, traveling with a Trader. Instead of spending every spare moment trying to catch up, I find myself tending my enemy's wounds and asking myself why."

Blood Talon tried to read the thoughts behind that implacable face. "You could go on. I'm all right on my own."

Fire Cat studied him for a moment. "We'll reach White Chief Town by midday tomorrow, sooner if you can find the strength to paddle. Word along the river is that it's a neutral town. Some sort of Power of Trade rules there. Everyone respects the peace. You'll be safe. Can take the time to heal, broker some sort of deal with a Trader to carry you back to a Cahokian colony. From there they can see to getting you back to your war leader."

"That's a problem."

"How's that?"

"The war leader told me not to come back unless I had the Lady Night Shadow Star in my company, safe and sound for marriage."

"Then I guess you're just running from one bit of bad luck to the next. I'm leaving you in White Chief Town, and, to be honest, if I find you on my backtrail again, I'll finish what those barbarians back there started."

Blood Talon nodded, stared out at the night-shadowed river. "Why didn't you kill me that day? You knew it was a trick, challenging you to train like that."

"I came close, Squadron First. So very close. But I didn't know who was playing which of us for what advantage. I assumed it was Spotted Wrist and Rising Flame who wove that little scheme together. And when it comes to Cahokian politics, you have to think several layers deeper than the obvious. So, whoever planned it, or permitted it, was fit to gain one way or the other. If you killed me, they figured Night Shadow Star would fold and marry that overbloated weasel. An error on their part, by the way. My lady isn't the same delicate flower she was when Makes Three died.

"The other way, if I killed you, would have also given them some advantage. Maybe it would have been some claim against Night Shadow Star? Maybe it would have been justification for your men to swarm me, murder me in their outrage and grief. What no one counted on was that both of us would come out of that alive. Least of all me, and with my honor intact."

"Do you always think so far ahead?"

"If I did, I'd have left you to those barbarians. Given that—wounded as you are—a ten-year-old girl could paddle with more vigor than you do, and realizing that you might still stab me in the back, I'm thinking I'm not nearly as smart as you seem to think I am."

Blood Talon fought his urge to laugh again. "I am many things, Red Wing. One thing I am not is ungrateful. If someone sticks a deer-bone stiletto into your back, it won't be me. And, for so long as I stand behind you drawing breath, no one else will either. Upon that, I give you my word as a Snapping Turtle Clan warrior and squadron leader."

"Accepted."

Fire Cat resealed the small pot of grease, handed it over to Blood Talon. "I suspect you'll need that a lot more than I will."

"How did you do that? Just Trade that catfish in the last village? Where did you learn that? I'd have thought you'd been Trading all your life."

"You might give it a try sometime, Squadron First. Trading rather than taking. You might learn a great deal about the world and the people in it."

And with that Fire Cat turned away to throw another stick of wood onto the fire before digging himself a hollow in the sand to sleep in.

Blood Talon stared thoughtfully at the man, tried to come to grips with his own situation. This man was his enemy. Still an unreconstructed heretic. Somewhere in the future—assuming they ever got home—he would be called on to kill Fire Cat.

And when that day comes . . . ?

Fifty-seven

Life in the cage had turned from dull misery to outright torture. Where the bindings restricted the blood flow, Seven Skull Shield's hands had swollen. Looked terrible. The ache in his back and legs just got worse. He couldn't sleep. At best he could take catnaps, at least until something went numb and he toppled forward, which jerked his arms painfully backward and strained his shoulders.

Unable to stand straight, every muscle in his back, shoulders, and neck pulsed with pain. His captors never gave him enough to drink, leaving him in a constant state of thirst; his hunger was barely cut by the few morsels they passed through the bars.

Worse, naked and restrained as he was, he had no ability to protect himself when the warriors "entertained" themselves. The constant baiting with pointed sticks, burning brands, and the occasional strike from a war club continued. His skin was scabbed, burns untended. So far, he'd been able to keep them from poking out one of his eyes by twisting his head away. But losing strength as he was, groggy as he was getting, the day would come when he didn't see the stick coming as it speared for his eye.

Worst of all—because of the way the cage was constructed—the warriors could swing a club through the bars. The blows to his head, shoulders, knees, and elbows were bad enough, but one clever warrior had figured out how to aim an uppercut from down low. If Seven Skull Shield didn't hunch and twist just right, the stone-headed club would hammer into his genitals. His unusual endowment was already a source of amusement and ribald jests; the warriors now made Seven Skull Shield's privates their favorite target of abuse. Each successful blow to his swollen and bruised penis and testicles brought tears to Seven Skull Shield's eyes.

Night had become his only limited refuge. During those few hours his tormentors were asleep. He could allow himself the sanctuary of Dreams. In them, he was a boy, slipping through the back ways with Winder, his empty stomach his only concern.

Or he would once again be sneaking carefully into some lesser noble's palace, tiptoeing past the sleeping chief to reach out and remove some precious statue, a well-crafted bowl, or a remarkably woven blanket from its place of honor. The sleepers still undisturbed, he would pick his way through the great room, past the household staff, careful to drop the occasional morsel of food to the household dogs. That was the thing about dogs. It took time and stealth, but with food they could always be turned into allies.

Then came the Trade down at the canoe landing. His stolen goods—worth a fortune in the south—would earn him the kind of wealth that kept him in food, drink, and enjoyment for days.

But most of all, he Dreamed of Wooden Doll. Not so much of the magic their bodies made when they were locked together, but of later when they lay with their limbs entangled, arms around each other, talking, laughing. In the Dream, her eyes expanded, became dark pools that sucked him in. Adrift in the depth, he sank into her, floated down into her soul to a place where he was warm, safe, and beloved.

Which was about the point at which he'd start to topple over, the short tether pulling his arms painfully behind him. Jerking awake, he'd pull his shoulders half out of their sockets, struggle to find his balance. By then his legs, cramped beneath him, would be numb from restricted circulation.

The fading memory of Wooden Doll's eyes would shift into Willow Blossom's. Her soft delight, that eager smile that he'd thought was just for him would hang in the back of his souls, mocking, taunting, torturing him.

I loved her.

In the end, the question was always left for him to ponder: How had she taken him in so completely?

"Was I really that much of a fool?"

But the dark palace beyond his cramped cage gave him no answer. At least, not until morning when the warriors would arise, begin cooking their breakfast, the odors of simmering stew teasing his growling, empty stomach. The knot of thirst tight and desperate in this throat.

He'd lost track of the days since his capture. Time had turned into an eternity of pain. The pain, now a constant, had numbed his soul, drained his senses, weakened him to the point that tears came unbidden and heedless of the moisture they wasted to the air.

"So, there he is." The contralto voice intruded on Seven Skull Shield's wheeling thoughts.

He blinked, looked up to see Clan Matron Rising Flame staring down at him. Beside her stood Spotted Wrist, resplendent in a bloodred cloak, his hair in a high bun pinned with a polished copper headpiece. The man's beaded forelock hung down over his forehead. The sharp eyes were mocking, disdainful.

"There he is. In his proper place at last."

"What could Night Shadow Star have been thinking? Asking this creature to act as her agent? I've had people check. She really did leave this bit of trash in charge of her palace."

"Matron, you've got to understand. That whole line of Black Tail's lineage is possessed and insane. If Chunkey Boy hadn't been consumed by the Morning Star's Spirit, he'd have become another Tharon. And we all know what kind of monster Walking Smoke turned out to be. Night Shadow Star, in her own way, is just as possessed and incomprehensible. Unlike her brothers, she may not have been evil, but she's always been disruptive. Never understood her place."

"She was a wild thing when she was a girl."

"Played chunkey, shot a bow, wrestled like she was just another boy. Failed to act responsibly like a proper female should. For a while her father feared she'd run off to be a warrior, as much as she favored her bow."

"Knowing all that, and you still want to marry her?"

"It's not like taking her to my bed would have been an act of undying love or done without full knowledge of the trouble she was capable of causing me. All I needed was her name and to have shot my seed into her sheath. After that, a wife's been made a wife. Doesn't matter what happens later. By keeping track of her woman's flux during those first months, I would have ensured I bedded her during her heat. Once a child is planted in her . . . Well, if she ever comes back, we'll see. Until then, she might have humiliated me, but she's also out of sight and out of mind for the majority of the dirt farmers and Earth Clans who'd care."

Rising Flame bent down, her curious gaze on Seven Skull Shield. "What? No witty comeback? Interesting, isn't it? You always wanted to be front and center in Four Winds politics. Now look, here you are, living in the Keeper's palace. Which, when I think about it, has always been your ultimate goal."

"Not mine," Seven Skull Shield rasped. "Piasa's. He sent Blue Heron after me way back when."

"Then let me guess." Rising Flame arched an eyebrow. "You just couldn't ever get away. Figured you were on a mission blessed by Power. You, a clanless orphan. Oh, I know all about you after that charade with the Quiz Quiz War Medicine last year. You might have bought your way out of a square, but I think your time has run out."

"Did you really think you could be one of us?" Spotted Wrist asked.

"What could have possibly possessed you?" Rising Flame asked.

Seven Skull Shield gave her a saucy grin through his bruised and swollen lips. "Don't think you'd understand. It's a bit beyond your experience. Something you've never known."

"What's that?"

"Friendship."

"I've had plenty of friends."

"Good as you are with that lie, you've been telling it to yourself for years."

"I'm not lying."

The quick way she said it made Seven Skull Shield's smile widen until it opened a crack in his lower lip. "Sure, Clan Matron. Out of respect, the war leader here and I will nod, wink at each other, and let you keep that mask front and center for the rest of the world to see."

"Impudent bit of maggot puke, isn't he?" Spotted Wrist noted, crossing his thick arms.

But Rising Flame was watching him, eyes thoughtful, her souls apparently considering something.

She said, "Where are your friends now, thief?"

"Doing just what I'd want them to."

"And that is?"

Seven Skull Shield chuckled. "Too bad you don't have a competent Clan Keeper. But then, I suspect he would just as soon forget about that stolen Koroa copper, wouldn't you, Keeper?"

"I don't know what you're talking about."

Seven Skull Shield shot another grin at the woman. "The day will come when you really need to remember he said that."

Rising Flame waved Spotted Wrist's protest down. "The Morning Star was embarrassed. Had to send additional copper to the Koroa embassy. Bigger pieces, of even greater value. What would a common thief like you know about it?"

Seven Skull Shield shrugged, ignoring Spotted Wrist's building anger. "Common thieves hear about uncommon thieves all the time. Famous people get noticed when they're skulking around."

"Are you insinuating that I had anything to do with the theft of that copper?" Spotted Wrist's face had turned an angry shade of red, his eyes almost popping from his face. "Guards! Beat this piece of walking vomit until he understands his place."

Seven Skull Shield caught that crafty glint as Rising Flame gave the war leader a new and calculating appraisal.

As the Keeper's warriors came trotting across the room, war clubs in hand, anticipation in their eyes, Seven Skull Shield chuckled to himself.

This was really going to hurt, but he'd just planted a weed in the new Keeper's garden.

I wonder if I'll live long enough to see it flower?

Fifty-eight

The River Trail, clinging as it did to the steep slopes, crossing creeks, winding over boulders, and around the boles of giant trees, ran from White Chief Town to Canyon Town. Making the passage took Night Shadow Star and Winder two hard days.

For Night Shadow Star, the trail came as a revelation. She'd never known such country. She'd thought the sight of whitewater back at the Mussel Shallows a remarkable vista, but it paled in comparison to the stunning canyon through which she now climbed, scrambled, and ascended. The smells of the forest, the roar of the river below, and the fantastic heights rising around her were magical, especially given her limited Cahokian upbringing.

Night Shadow Star was delighted that—scoundrel that he might be—Winder knew what he was doing. She'd thought the number of porters he'd Traded for had been excessive, perhaps hired out of pique for her stinging words during the catfish supper.

Turned out every man was needed on the rough trail that paralleled the Tenasee. Just below them the river thundered, roared, and crashed through the narrows, only to run smooth for a short distance before the next cataract turned it wild.

The Rage was aptly named: a section of tortuous whitewater that seemed impossible to equate with the same placid Tenasee she and Fire Cat had paddled up. And then the Suck, a swirling and awe-inspiring whirlpool where the river dropped between great stony outcrops and literally twisted around itself. She could believe that the Spirit of an evil chief was entombed there, and his anger remained manifest in the roiling depths.

They camped that night at sunset. Ate cold food for supper and breakfast and were on the trail again as the morning broke at false dawn.

She wondered if Winder wasn't punishing her, pushing to see just where her breaking point would be. As though trying to expose her as some sort of fraud.

Doggedly, though her legs ached and her feet hurt, she kept to the trail. When fatigue's painful fingers began to eat into her muscles, tendons, and bones, she forced herself to look up, to marvel at the steep-sided canyon. How, she wondered, did the oak, hickory, and maples cling to such places? Where the forest couldn't find root, the outcrops of exposed bedrock—the bones of the mountains—were weather-rounded, glistening, gray in the light.

She inhaled the rich scents of the forest, admired the thousands of wildflowers that lined the grass-thick sides of the trail. Let herself drift in a world she'd never have dreamed existed.

And longed for Fire Cat.

Time after time she would glance back along the trail, almost desperate to see his muscular form trotting effortlessly over the tricky footing. That smile would be on his face, the subtle humor in his eyes.

Piasa has promised. Walking Smoke for Fire Cat.

Fire Cat himself had promised: *"I will meet you in Cofitachequi."*

Instead the only people she saw were locals, or the occasional Trade party. Either Winder or the approaching Trader would—depending upon the trail circumstances—yield the way, allowing passage on the precarious sections. She'd never seen such amicable greetings called between strangers, as if they shared some common bond on the tenuous trail. But pass they did, each porter bent under the load of his pack, his or her bare brown feet seeking purchase in the dark soil or among the thick roots or rough stones that laced the way.

Her limbs heavy with exhaustion, her mind dull, she followed the others as they wound down through the trees to Canyon Town.

Like so many of the communities she'd grown used to, this one, too, was mostly composed of bark-sided bent-pole structures around a square. A couple of conical burial mounds were placed opposite each other across the central square with its *Tchkofa*. Along with a stickball field, she could see a crude chunkey court, indicating the game was played here. Below it, down on the river, lay the requisite canoe landing where the Tenasee rolled smoothly toward its alternate existence in the narrows.

On either side the mountains rose, taller, rounded, massive. She took in the towering peaks with their outcrops of high granite, the thickly timbered slopes, and wondered at the hazy vista.

"It gets better once we're up in the headwaters of the Wide Fast," Winder told her.

"What does?"

"The mountains. They're higher, wilder. Even more stunning than this." He smiled. "I remember the first time I saw them. I was, what, just in my twenties. Couldn't believe what the Traders had told me. One of the things you learn is that the world is a great deal more varied, Powerful, and interesting than you had been taught to believe back in Cahokia."

"It is that." She threw a glance back at the trail, still anxious to see Fire Cat step out from behind the screen of trees and brush.

Winder noticed, amused, and said, "They have a Trade House here. That one, with the split-cane roof. Same arrangement as at White Chief Town. I'll see if I can get us beds. Then we'll start asking around for a canoe to take us all the way to the Wide Fast."

He paused, studying her. "Might cost you a couple of pieces of copper. That or all of those carved shells you've been hoarding."

"And what's beyond that? The pass you said. And then we reach Joara?"

"Which is the gateway to Cofitachequi."

"So how much Trade do I need?"

"Keep that last copper plate, the embossed one of the Morning Star. Being a Cahokian colony, that will have the greatest value for whatever you need to acquire in Joara."

As at White Chief Town, a small bit of Trade was all that proved necessary to obtain one of the bunked beds in a partitioned sleeping area in the Trade House.

As she was rolling out her bedding, it was to see a thick-set man pause as he passed, glance appreciatively at her, and then fix on her face. The man's eyes narrowed into a thoughtful and pinched expression as he studied her.

"Help you?" Night Shadow Star asked in Trade pidgin.

"You are Cahokian?"

"Been there. Came from up north," she lied. "You know the Illini River country?"

The Trader shrugged, something distasteful in his movement. He gave her a last look and passed from view.

"What was that all about?" she asked Winder in a whisper.

"You sure you didn't know him? Haven't seen him before? His tattoos were Casqui. From down south on the Father Water."

"Thousands of Traders pass through Cahokia."

"Probably just enjoying a nice-looking woman, but those Four Winds tattoos on your cheeks are a dead giveaway."

"And how many Four Winds women would be posing as Traders way up the Tenasee?"

"You know, Lady, I asked myself the same question."

Winder's expression had gone introspective, veiled as he stared after the Casqui.

Desperately tired, Night Shadow Star gave it no more thought until after they'd Traded for a meal of hominy, boiled freshwater clams, and roasted passenger pigeon stuffed with acorn bread.

She was in her blankets by full dark, almost asleep when three men crowded into the partitioned space. Winder had said something about looking up an old friend, his bed still empty.

Now, alone, she wished she'd set aside a knife, something, as the men's dark shapes loomed above her head.

"What do you want?" she asked in pidgin.

"Those tattoos, they're Four Winds," the big shambling Casqui Trader noted. "You know what we do to Cahokians in this country?"

"I told you, I'm not Cahokian. And you're Casqui. What would you care if I was a Cahokian or forest barbarian? Now, go away. I just want to sleep."

The three muttered back and forth in a language Night Shadow Star couldn't understand.

"You three deaf? Leave me to my peace, or I'll make you more trouble than you know what to do with."

"How's that, Four Winds?"

"The Power of Trade is enforced here. That includes not harassing women who don't want to be harassed. I don't want to be harassed."

Again, they conversed in the unknown language.

"Lady Night Shadow Star, how did you get this far on your own?" the big man asked in Cahokian.

She fought an uneasy chill. "Who? That's not my name. Now, get out or I'll scream. Shout out that you're trying to rape me. Steal my Trade."

Again, the conversation. The big man nodded in the dark, saying, "As you wish, but let me give you this. A token from a man who is looking forward to seeing you."

"Who?" She reached out as the man extended his arm.

The move was perfectly executed. He grabbed her by the extended wrist—jerked her clear of the bed and blankets with all his strength.

Night Shadow Star had no time to react, pain shooting through her wrenched shoulder. She was sucking a lungful of air to scream as a hard hand was clapped over her mouth. The other men had rushed forward to grab her, wrapping their arms around her. One had her around the chest, pinning her arms against her body. The third by the legs.

She was bodily lifted, fear running bright in her veins.

Twisting, jerking, throwing herself this way and that, she almost broke loose. Opening her mouth wide, she bit down on the muffling hand, tasting salt and old grease as she ground her teeth into the web of the man's hand.

He bottled his scream, the sound that of choked pain.

The blow he dealt her to the side of the head left her reeling, half stunned as they hurried her from the partitioned cubicle, through the dark and quiet Trade House, and out into the night, replete as it was with the sounds of chirping crickets. Somewhere, on the other side of town, someone was playing a flute.

Getting her wind, Night Shadow Star tasted blood, opened her jaws wide and took another bite, this time getting a thumb as it slipped past her lips. With all her might, she clamped down, willing her fear-charged strength into the bite. Bone crunched under her teeth, the man uttering a whimpered half-shriek.

Nevertheless, he kept her from shouting as she bellowed against the hand he tried to stuff deeper into her mouth. Which allowed her to get another bite, crushing a finger this time.

"I'm going to break your neck," the man whimpered through his pain. "You are going to die slowly, painfully, in ways that will make your souls wail. I swear it."

"Hush!" the man who had her arms pinned around her chest hissed. "You want to wake the whole town? What we're doing will get us killed."

Then he lapsed from Trade pidgin back into his native tongue.

The man who had her by the legs added his own whispered reprimand.

Night Shadow Star continued to work her teeth into her captor's hand. He shifted his grip enough to slam his free fist into the side of her head again and again. Stars blasted through her vision with each hollow impact.

Just keep your teeth locked.

She had images of the plaza off to the side, the *Tchkofa* in its center conjuring the memory of Snapping Turtle in the Underworld, shell-down in the mud. She was being carried through the shadows, headed out past the houses.

A dog barked from one of the ramadas, raising her hopes, but one of the men shouted at the beast, and it slunk away. No one, it seemed, was going to check. Maybe dogs barked all the time in Canyon Town.

She thrashed, energized by the rising fear. No one here knew her. No one but Winder would miss her. And were he to find her missing? What then? Would he simply bundle up her Trade, call it a square deal, and go back to his Yuchi wife a much richer man?

Some part of her desperate and terrified imagination pictured Fire Cat, picking that moment to emerge from the dark, his war club in hand.

Without a word, he'd begin laying about him, spreading death and mayhem as he shattered her captors' skulls.

But no such image emerged from the night. They were out past the last of the ramadas now, headed across the corn, bean, and squash fields for the woods.

They are going to take me out and kill me.

The terror lent renewed energy to her struggles. She got a lungful of air, tried screaming past the hand shoved into her mouth. The sound was a muffled squeal, nothing that would be heard beyond a couple of steps away.

And then the man carrying her legs jerked, his head flopping to one side accompanied by a loud crack.

In an instant, Night Shadow Star's legs were freed, which pulled the man holding her chest off balance. He, she, and the Casqui Trader whose hand was in her mouth tumbled.

Something tore through the air, the sound that of a swung club. The meaty impact could be felt through the man's arms that held her chest. He jerked, moaned, and fell away.

Night Shadow Star was turned loose; still she kept her teeth sunk into the man's bleeding hand. She held her bite as her assailant tried to rise, the timing such that something cut the air just over his head.

On the ground now, he balled a fist, smashed her hard in the side of the head. The blow blasted lightning behind Night Shadow Star's vision, shook her to the roots of her souls. Caused her to lose her grip.

Her assailant pulled his hand free, and then he was running, making whimpering sounds as he hunched over his wounded hand.

Night Shadow Star felt herself spin, blinked, trying to get the world to slow. She rolled to her hands and feet, tried to stand, but her head was still reeling, a ringing in her ears from the blow.

Some awareness of the dark form standing over her made her catch her breath, afraid that hard male hands were going to reach down out of the darkness, pick her up, and carry her off into the dark forest.

Instead a familiar voice said, "Lady? You all right?"

"Winder?" She spat the foul-tasting blood from her mouth.

"Here. Take my hand. Let's get you up."

She got a grip, almost fell as he pulled her to her feet. Was gasping for breath. Only to bend and vomit.

"Hit me in the head," she explained. "Hard. World's still spinning."

"Here. Lean on me. We've got to get out of here."

"They took me! Right out of the Trade House!"

"Yes, they did. And I think I've killed one, maybe two of them. Not the sort of thing that will make the good folk of Canyon Town think fondly of us. It will call down the kind of questions you don't want to answer. If they find out who you really are, it will mean more trouble than you've ever known."

"What do you mean?"

"Drop the pretense. Let's get back, get our packs. I've got a canoe lined out for us down at the landing. If we're on the water by first light, we can be upriver before the trouble really starts."

"But I don't—"

"Hold your tongue, Night Shadow Star. We'll talk when we're long gone from this place. Now, keep quiet and let's see if we can get out of here with our hides intact."

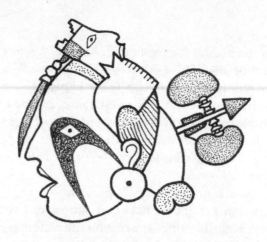

Fifty-nine

Flat Stone Pipe, being a dwarf, was used to small spaces. That he now huddled under the sleeping bench, a snoring warrior sagging the mattress straps over his head, was disconcerting. This was far from the only time the little man had had to crawl beneath bed frames. He'd learned the art of pushing boxes and pots out of the way by bracing his back against the wall and shoving.

That didn't mean he liked it. Too many critters lurked in the dark corners, especially spiders. Most were inoffensive creatures who were terrified when Flat Stone Pipe tore his way through their webs; they only wanted to get away without being crushed in the process.

But the occasional black widow or brown recluse was another story. Both were found in numbers in Cahokia, and longtime association meant that they received ample respect from the human population, which included dwarfs like Flat Stone Pipe.

And then there were mice. Not that they'd harm a person. But sticking his hand into one of their nests, having the squeaking and panicked little beasts run up his arms, sometimes scramble into his hair and scamper between his collar and shirt to scratch their way down his chest, back, or sides was always unsettling right down to the foundations of Flat Stone Pipe's shivering souls.

And snakes. They *loved* slithering through the dark recesses beneath sleeping benches. Most were harmless, but then the occasional copperhead or even more rare rattlesnake . . .

No, don't even think about it.

Flat Stone Pipe made a face.

Listened to the warrior snoring above his head. Then a break. The man shifted, the strapping that supported the cloth-and-straw mattress creaking and swaying over Flat Stone Pipe's head. The man was big, overweight for a warrior, and of obvious low status given that he was in this particular bed.

The strapping held.

Flat Stone Pipe used his leverage against the wall, pushed with his hands, and managed to ease a large brownware pot out far enough that he could crawl up to the wooden poles that blocked any further progress.

Shifting, the dwarf pulled out his long-bladed quartzite knife and began sawing on the dried leather bindings. As he did, he matched each stroke to the snoring warrior whose body hung just above him.

This would have to be done judiciously. Carefully.

As he worked his blade back and forth, he considered the irony of his situation. He had been trained as an engineer, particularly in the construction of mounds. His parents had considered it appropriate training, given that being a dwarf would never allow him to serve as a warrior, Trader, farmer, or craftsman. His acumen had been recognized within the engineers' society, which sent him all over burgeoning Cahokia as he learned the craft of mound building. Being the affable object of curiosity a dwarf usually was, he'd built an extensive network of contacts.

Contacts he had been able to develop after a fateful meeting with young Lady Columella. By chance he had been able to provide her with information that allowed her to cement her rise to the matronship of Evening Star House.

She had reciprocated with wealth and professional respect that had eventually led to her bed and a loving relationship that had spanned the years.

For most of that time, Flat Stone Pipe had spent his energies battling Blue Heron and the other Houses. At least until the abomination that was Walking Smoke had burst into their lives.

Now, in the aftermath of that disaster, here he was, an ally of the woman he'd spent most of his life trying to destroy, and beholden to a clanless, womanizing, and footloose thief.

The insanity of it brought a smile to his lips even as the first of the bindings parted. He shifted to the next and began sawing.

Only the intervention of Power could explain it. Blue Heron, who had spent her life keeping a lid on Evening Star House and blunting Columella's plots, scheming, and struggle for supremacy, had just cemented his matron's hold on her house. Coming through with more food stores than Columella had given out had silenced the critics.

But Blue Heron had pulled that coup off at her own expense. North Star House, Horned Serpent House, and River House knew who had forced them into giving out their dwindling stores and were fully aware of how that action had strengthened Evening Star House.

Granted, River House had called Blue Heron there, surrendered their stocks out of weakness, and in desperation. That was going to take some thought.

Three Fingers, especially if he ruled through Broken Stone, might not be an improvement on War Duck. Nor was he sure that Round Pot would fight War Duck's replacement; she was still smarting that her brother had voted for Slender Fox for clan matron. War Duck had been firmly behind his sister until Slender Fox lured him into her bed during the negotiations. That wasn't the kind of betrayal that could ever be atoned for.

One almost needed scoring sticks to keep track of the intricacies of Cahokian politics.

A second binding gave way. As it did, the hickory pole popped sideways with a thump.

Flat Stone Pipe held his breath. The warrior overhead didn't awaken.

Craning his neck, Flat Stone Pipe noted that neither did Seven Skull Shield, though the burly thief looked a lot worse for wear.

Was he even still alive?

Ah yes. The faint rising and falling of his bruised shoulders could be seen.

Across the room, one of the warriors climbed to his feet, yawned, and headed for the door. In the dim light of the fire, the man was a mere shadow.

Flat Stone Pipe used his knife to attack yet another of the bindings, asking himself, *Why in the name of pus am I here when I could be safely tucked away in Columella's warm bed?*

The answer, of course, was that if the situation were reversed and he were the one in a cage, being beaten and ultimately headed for the square, it would be Seven Skull Shield who would be risking his life.

So here he was, the whole world turned upside down. For the first time ever, Columella's position was secure because her friend Blue Heron had made it so. Flat Stone Pipe was hiding in the new Keeper's palace, sawing on Seven Skull Shield's cage. He did it not just because the miscreant had saved several of Flat Stone Pipe and Columella's children, but because the scurrilous thief was a friend. The kind of friend who would have put his own life second to Flat Stone Pipe's.

Talk about convolutions, twists, and turns in what should have been a smooth and straight path.

Flat Stone Pipe gave a sigh of relief as yet another rawhide binding gave way.

Sixty

Fire crackled and spat sparks up toward a night sky that dazzled with constellations. Stars, gleaming against a background of black, frosted the heavens in glittering waves. The familiar sight of Horned Serpent dominated the southern sky, the great winged serpent staring down with a beaming red eye.

Moonrise was still a couple of hands of time away, and the forest above Fire Cat and Blood Talon's camp was alive with night insects, frogs, and nightjars, though their symphony was partially masked by the roar of the Tenasee where it pounded and surged in the narrow canyon below.

Camp had been made on a restricted flat where the trail crossed an outcrop of bedrock. That it was often used for such was readily apparent, not just because the ground was beaten down to dirt, but when they'd arrived the firepit had still contained glowing embers from the previous night's campers.

All that had been necessary was to climb the steep-walled canyon, find wood, and descend back to the level spot to rekindle the flames.

Blood Talon sat with his back to a beech tree, the bark polished from hundreds of previous backs that had taken repose there. Across the fire, Fire Cat sat cross-legged, a frown marring his face as he used a chert flake to peel bark from a willow stem. He had cut a number of them in anticipation of the chance to make more arrows.

"I really appreciate that you didn't leave me in White Chief Town," Blood Talon told the man. Then he winced, shifting his position slightly to ease the burns on his left side. He had grown tired of the pain. Warrior he might have been, tough, inured. Didn't mean he wasn't on the point of tears for most of his waking hours. Not that sleep came easily, as he was limited to flat on his back to avoid irritating the burns.

Fire Cat glanced up from his arrow, eyes thoughtful. "I must be getting soft. That or so homesick I couldn't stand the thought of not hearing the occasional word in my own language. Besides, you were almost to the point of dropping to your knees and begging."

"Not to my knees. It would have hurt too much." Blood Talon glanced away. "I've hanged men in squares before. Led the festivities with the torch and knife. Laughed as they screamed. Pitied them as weak and cowardly when they pleaded for death. Always figured that if I was ever in their position, I'd bite my tongue off before I cried out. That down deep inside, at the core of my souls, I could take it."

"I didn't notice you screaming."

"No." Blood Talon glanced down at his hands, grimy from the trail and with dirt under the nails. "They'd just gotten started. Hadn't been at it for more than a finger of time, I suppose. It was just my sides and underarms. It wasn't like when a flaming brand is raised up under a man's shaft and stones, when he smells his hair down there burning. Or when they pry his mouth open, shovel in hardwood coals, and cook his tongue in his mouth."

Firelight was dancing in Fire Cat's eyes as he shot Blood Talon an evaluative look from across the flames.

The squadron first said, "I suspect I would have screamed. I would have pleaded for a quick and easy death."

"I prayed that myself the night my lady came and cut me down. Thought she was First Woman come for my souls."

Blood Talon flexed his hand, watching the fingers move, oddly touched at the complexity of the bones, tendons, and joints. "Why am I telling you this?"

"Because for the first time in your life, you don't know who you are."

"I'm Blood Talon, squadron first, of the Snapping Turtle Clan, and . . . and . . ."

"And you're in a distant land where no one gives a pebble for any of that. You saw the looks you were getting back there in White Chief Town. They saw a half-naked man dressed in a ragged breechcloth who they knew had been freshly tortured, his burns still peeling, weeping pus, and covered with grease.

"Worse, it was a man who barely speaks Trade tongue, who knows none of the local languages and nothing of the customs. You were afraid. Afraid of being left there. Alone." Fire Cat smiled. "And of all the things

I could have done to you, leaving you there to face that would have been the cruelest."

Blood Talon picked at his dirty fingernails, unable to meet Fire Cat's eyes. "I'm not a coward."

"Everyone has a place, time, or situation that terrifies them. Fortunately for most people, they manage to live their lives through to the end without finding themselves there, in that place or moment. But for Spotted Wrist sending you here, you might have been one of those lucky people."

"And you've faced that moment of terror?"

Fire Cat nodded, concentrating on the arrow as long slivers of bark were peeled from the shaft.

"Was it when we threw you into the canoe and sent you to Cahokia to die?"

Fire Cat smiled wistfully. "It was in the Sacred Cave, in the darkness. I stood, terrified, before Horned Serpent. Eye to eye with the creature. At the same time the fingers of the Dead kept pulling at my skin, hair, and face."

"That was when you and Night Shadow Star went after the living god's souls."

"She shared her courage with me."

Blood Talon took a deep breath, feeling his burns pull. "If I survive this, I will never put another human being in a square again."

Fire Cat gave him another of those probing glances.

Blood Talon grinned back humorlessly. "I want to go with you, Red Wing. For the time being anyway. Yes, yes, I was sent to kill you. And looking back, I don't blame you for what you did on the river. If I'd had the courage, been in your position, I'd have tried to do the same."

"So here you are. And the only familiar thing you have to cling to is me. A man whose family and clan you destroyed, and whom you would have murdered. Either here on the river or through treachery back in Cahokia. Not a ringing recommendation for trust, is it?"

"No, I suppose not."

Fire Cat gestured with his partially finished arrow. "There's a lot of blood and pain between us. My family. My children . . ."

Blood Talon pursed his lips, frowned. "I should have died back there with the rest of my friends and companions. Power saved me. Spat me out on the bank to be found by those barbaric weasels back in that village. And here I am. With you."

"Like I said, that remains to be seen."

"I see the concern in your eyes. You're almost soul sick with worry about her. You're not going to stop until you find her."

"What business is that of yours, unless you still think you're going to take her back to Spotted Wrist?"

"No. The two of you, you're too Powerful." Blood Talon looked up. "That's what we never understood. What they still don't understand. Spotted Wrist and Rising Flame, they can beat you and Night Shadow Star down, take away all that you think you are, and you just keep coming back, stronger, more Powerful. Night Shadow Star really is protected by the Underwater Panther. You serve her. Are part of her. Part of Power."

"I'm just a man who has given her my oath."

"The famous Red Wing honor?"

Fire Cat shrugged dismissively, attention back on his arrow.

"It's safer and faster, traveling with two. If you have my help, it will be that much sooner when you finally catch up with this Winder and your lady."

"What about your oath? The one you swore to Spotted Wrist?"

Blood Talon stared blankly at the fire where it crackled and shot another fountain of sparks toward the night sky. "That problem has me confused. Funny, isn't it? I've always followed orders. Served him with my heart and soul. I did it because I was expected to. In all those years I did things because I promised him I would. But it just hit me. I have no oath to serve him, never promised I'd bring Night Shadow Star back to him. He just ordered me to."

"So, what does that really mean, Squadron First?"

Blood Talon squinted into the flames, trying to see the truth of it. "That's what confuses me. I'm not sure."

"Then maybe you'd better be about finding out."

Sixty-one

The words "liquid with fear" meant something to Blue Heron. She was totally immersed in the meaning, feeling it as it ran through her veins, tickled her stomach, and shivered her bones.

This is taking too long!

She shifted from foot to foot, staring around in the night. They were going to be discovered. She kept expecting some shouted alarm, that warriors were going to come boiling out of Spotted Wrist's palace and seize them all.

Morning was just a half a hand of time away over the eastern horizon. Better were this the middle of the winter instead of nearing the summer solstice. Night was just too cursed short to get anything meaningful done.

An owl hooted from the roof of the Surveyors' Society building where it overlooked the Avenue of the Sun just east of the Great Plaza.

This was madness. She could think of a hundred things that might go wrong and get her, Flat Stone Pipe, and who knew who else hanged in squares.

"You sure this is the right building?" Wooden Doll asked as she strode up beside Blue Heron and squinted at the dark palace.

"Can't miss those guardian posts," Blue Heron told her, pointing to the two tall double-headed eagles atop their high poles on either side of the walkway leading up the low mound. "It's Sun Wing's palace. The one right behind it, between us and the Great Plaza? That's the Recorders' House. That next one down is the Men's House. This is some of the most prized ground in Cahokia."

"Shhh!" Wooden Doll reached out, dragging Blue Heron into a crouch at the side of the sloping earth.

From Spotted Wrist's palace, a man emerged, little more than a shadow in the darkness. He made his way around to the back of the mound, and, standing on the corner, undid his breechcloth.

The sound of spattering urine could be heard in the still air.

Blue Heron held her breath as the man retraced his steps to the palace veranda and stepped inside.

"Bet that has Flat Stone Pipe's attention."

"Hope he's the kind who can get right back to sleep after he pees." Wooden Doll rose to her feet again, eyes on the Keeper's palace. "I hate men like that. Especially the ones with dinky little bladders. Keep me up all night."

Movement by the door of Sun Wing's palace solidified into two young men dressed in breechcloths, their skin gleaming slightly from the grease and mosquito repellent they'd rubbed on their bodies.

On silent feet they skipped down the short stairway to the ground, and one said, "It's set, Lady. In fact, listen."

Blue Heron turned her right ear, the one that heard the best, toward the doorway. The faint crackle and popping was just audible over the keening of crickets and the slight breeze rustling through the thatch.

"We don't have much time."

"How did you know that Lady Sun Wing would be staying the night in Rides-the-Lightning's temple?" Wooden Doll asked as they retreated to where her litter sat in the shadows behind the Recorders' House.

"The Earth Clans shaman owes me. Not to mention that he really appreciated the whelk-shell cup I sent him when I asked if he'd invite Sun Wing to bring the Tortoise Bundle up for a pre-solstice Blessing ceremony and a cure."

"And Spotted Wrist?"

"What's the point of running a spy network if you can't use it? He's in Serpent Woman Town. House business. He won't be back until tomorrow morning."

Wooden Doll's shake of the head was barely visible in the darkness. "Can't believe that you would burn your niece's palace. It's a bit extreme if you ask me."

"Not a great loss. The place is a dump. It needs burning. Sun Wing's not the same these days. Walking Smoke broke something inside her when he tried to sacrifice her. Being the Keeper for the Tortoise Bundle?

It's given her a purpose, but she's living in the Spirit World where keeping a clean house doesn't seem to be a priority."

Wooden Doll studied her in the darkness. "You know what will happen if this goes wrong tonight?"

"I was just dwelling on that very fact."

"Me? I can just fade away. Spotted Wrist will be coming after you. You're the most logical one."

"I am."

"Why? Skull's a clanless thief. I can understand that he'd be an amusement, a novelty for a woman like you. But to attempt something like this?"

Blue Heron shot the woman a sidelong glance. "You've never really trusted me, have you?"

"Excuse me, Lady, but my associations with nobility haven't exactly taught me to believe they're the most trustworthy of humankind. Just the opposite, in fact."

Blue Heron took a deep breath. "Seven Skull Shield and I have a joke that we share. We agree to never let anyone know we're friends because it would disconcert people who think better of us. Yes, he's a pain in the ass. Absolutely irreverent, and he refuses to treat me like the high-ranking and exalted personage I am. A fact for which I dearly appreciate him. When I really needed him, Seven Skull Shield was there for me."

Wooden Doll turned her eyes to Sun Wing's palace. "This is it." She turned to the men crouched in the darkness. "Get ready."

Blue Heron fought to settle her pounding heart. "We'd better hope that Flat Stone Pipe has done his part."

"If not, here." Wooden Doll slipped a small jar stoppered with wax into Blue Heron's hand.

"What's this?"

"Concentrated essence of water hemlock. If we can't get him out of there, it's the kindest thing we can do for him."

"You think he'd drink poison?"

"Rather than hang in a square? I thought you said he was your friend, that you knew him?"

"You're right."

The first flames ate their way through the roof of Sun Wing's palace. Time.

Blue Heron, nerves jumping like scalded crickets, hurried across the avenue, climbed up the short stairs to Spotted Wrist's palace, crossed the veranda, and pushed the door open.

Into the dark room, she shouted, "Fire! Next door! Hurry! If you don't put it out, this whole section of Cahokia is going to burn! That happens,

Spotted Wrist will have your asses cooked and handed to you on a carved wooden platter!"

It took a couple of heartbeats as the warriors all sat up in their beds, glanced wide-eyed in her direction.

"Well, did you hear me? *Fire!*"

The beds erupted in a flurry as men clawed for their clothing.

Blue Heron stepped back, clearing the way as the warriors pelted out the door, calling to each other.

Across the narrow gap, Sun Wing's palace was now a burning torch in the night.

It took longer than it should have to peel Seven Skull Shield's comatose body out of the cage. Despite the bindings cut by Flat Stone Pipe, the cage had been very, very well built.

Nevertheless, not a finger's time later, Blue Heron was able to fade into the darkness as Wooden Doll's litter was borne off to the west, the thief's unconscious body sprawled in the seat.

All right, that's done. Now the fat's in the fire. Spotted Wrist will be coming, and he'll know exactly who to blame.

Sixty-two

This time the Traders were Chalakee. The four tall, muscular men with long streaming black hair they wore roached and tied with red and white cloth were the first of their nation Night Shadow Star had ever known. The eldest was Slinking Cat, an affable man in his early forties. Blue Wolf was his dry-witted friend. Cuts Hominy came across as sardonic and worldly for his late twenties. The youngest, Thorn, was in his teens, quiet, and still learning the river. The one woman, Pestle, was of medium stature with broad shoulders and had a round and pleasant face. She carried a war club hung from her belt, an accoutrement entirely in contrast to her good-natured and sunny personality.

In all her years, Night Shadow Star had never known a Chalakee, or Cherokee as they were sometimes called. Seemed that the rest of the world had trouble with the preferred pronunciation.

Like all good Trade canoes, the one Night Shadow Star now found herself in was thin-hulled, wide of beam, and carefully crafted. To build such a craft took just the right kind of wood: cypress or red cedar was preferred. It needed a straight grain that wouldn't warp as it seasoned, and as few knots as possible since they would loosen and leak. The process of burning out the interior required a master's skill and patience. The hull couldn't be too thin, or the wood would crack. Too thick and the craft would be sluggish; every bit of unnecessary wood not only took up space that could be filled with Trade but made the canoe ride lower in the water. All of it extra weight that had to be propelled by the paddlers.

As the Chalakee drove their canoe along the Tenasee's flower-speckled bank, Night Shadow Star tried to ignore her splitting headache and carefully probed her swollen and bruised lips. Her jaws ached, and nasty bruises had darkened on the side of her head. She was grateful that her cheek hadn't shattered under that last ringing blow.

Spit and blood, she wished she had some red willow bark tea.

Her shoulder felt as if it had been pulled out of its socket. She winced as she probed the swelling on the side of her head and stared out at the river, its waters taking on a silvered look in the morning light. Mist hung in the emerald-green growth along the banks, rising in thin streamers through the thick band of forest that grew down to the bank.

The morning smelled of the Tenasee's earthy musk, the rich odors of leaves and vegetation. Birdcall, in a riotous cacophony, echoed down from the high canopy and mixed with the chirring, whizzing, and clicking of myriad insects. Some sort of hatch was in progress, the air alive with the shimmering of diaphanous wings as insects by the thousands rose from the water and into the sunlight.

"I think the Casqui and his friends got the worst of it," Winder remarked from where he paddled behind her. He'd been watching her gentle probing of her wounds.

"Why did you wait so long?"

"Needed to have them out beyond anyone's hearing before I laid into them. Lady, you've got to understand, they take the Power of Trade and keeping the peace very seriously at Canyon Town. Doesn't matter that you were the victim. If you'd made a scene back there, people would have wanted to know why. It's better all the way around that we just slipped away. Especially if I killed either of the two I smacked in the head."

"It makes no sense," she cried. "I'd never seen that Casqui before in my life. How did he know who I was? How did you, for that matter?"

"As for me, you might have saved yourself the effort and shouted it out. A Four Winds lady possessed of Underworld Power, accompanied by a battle-scarred Red Wing? Who could they possibly be? The only question being why they might have hired White Mat and be traveling up the Tenasee.

"Beyond that, you know too much about the river, the country, the people. Tell me, how many minor Four Winds nobles know who the Timucua are? Let alone that they live down south in the peninsula? But Night Shadow Star was being trained for the Matron's chair. She would know. And after Fire Cat went back to take down those Cahokian warriors? You slipped, called him Fire Cat a couple of times when you weren't paying attention."

She turned far enough to give him a hard look. "So why play along?"

"It's the smartest way to travel. But that brings us back to the Casqui. You're right to ask how he'd know to be looking for you. That, in turn, leads me to ask, what's this all about? What's in Cofitachequi? And why are you, of all people, headed there? Last I heard, you and the Red Wing were the darling heroes of Cahokia. Or did the Morning Star turn on you after you saved his souls from the Underworld?"

"You think I should trust you?"

"Seven Skull Shield is really a friend of yours?"

"Why bring him into this?"

"Answer the question."

Her chuckle was filled with dry humor. "There are only two men alive whom I would trust with my life. Seven Skull Shield is one."

"It must be some story. By that I mean whatever absurd scheme he was involved in that brought him to your attention without getting his sorry carcass hanged in a square."

"It was Piasa who whispered his name into my ear. Seven Skull Shield has done me great service. Been there when I needed him. I owe him."

Winder was silent for a moment. "Three."

"What?"

"There are now three men whom you can trust with your life."

"That's a bit brazen, don't you think?" But Piasa was flitting through the corner of her vision, almost dancing with each throbbing of her headache. She barely caught the satisfied gleam in the creature's yellow eyes as they turned into a flare of sunlight on water. The effect was like a hot lance driven through her skull.

"Beautiful woman like you, I can guess how Skull looks at you. And a Four Winds noble? Sister to the Morning Star? Niece to that Keeper he's so fond of? You must be like nectar to a bee."

"If you think that, you don't know Seven Skull Shield. Or at least, you don't know the man he has become."

"You really mean that. Unbelievable."

"Then, like I say, you don't know him."

"Oh, I do. And yes, he cut me down from that square. I'm not sure how he avoided taking the blame for that."

"He bought your freedom with the Quiz Quiz War Medicine."

Winder almost missed a stroke with his paddle, then laughed bitterly. "Figures. He had it all the time, did he?"

"That's my understanding."

"Blue Heron knew?"

"Fire Cat told me that she was as surprised as anyone when Seven Skull Shield pulled the war medicine out of some canoe and slipped it over his shoulder after freeing you."

Winder shook his head. "Bet he hid it at Wooden Doll's. That it was right there, probably in the same room. I can be such a fool sometimes."

"Hiring yourself to the Quiz Quiz wasn't one of your brightest moments."

"It should have been simple."

"Nothing ever is."

"I guess not. Take the way he talked about the Keeper and you. I thought he'd been hit in the head too many times. That his souls were scrambled beyond any good sense. And then I watch you, traveling as a common Trader, paddling like an honest woman. I see the love you have for that Red Wing, watch him sacrifice himself for you. Watch you talking to the Spirits in your head. I begin to see what Skull sees in you. Why he trusts you."

"I'm just me."

"So why are you going to Cofitachequi, Lady?"

"To kill my brother, Walking Smoke."

"Haven't heard of Walking Smoke being in Cofitachequi. If your brother was there, I'd suspect that some word would have come down the river."

"He'll be calling himself something different. You've heard of some new chief? Perhaps a sorcerer or shaman? Someone using Power for selfish purposes, offering sinister services, probably involving human sacrifices?"

At Winder's silence, she turned, found him watching her with intent and dark eyes.

"If I had known that was who you were after, I would have turned you down back at Big Cane Town and stayed with my wife."

"So, still want to be that third man?"

"I'm having second thoughts, Lady. But I've had second thoughts before and never been smart enough to quit when I've been ahead." He gave her a humor-free smile. "I just hope I'm not being as stone-headed stupid as I was with the Quiz Quiz."

"Oh, you're not."

"Why's that?"

"Because I'm telling you right up front, this will not only be dangerous, but difficult. Anything but simple. In fact, I suspect that killing Walking Smoke is going to end with my death."

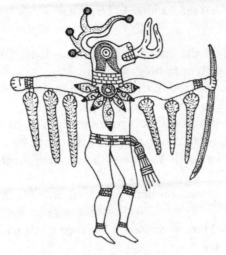

Sixty-three

The fact that it took three days spoke volumes about Spotted Wrist's abilities as Clan Keeper. But come he did, marching down the avenue that separated Blue Heron's palace mound from the base of Morning Star's great mound.

He strode purposefully forward, dressed in a gaudy eagle headdress, a flowing white cloak of finest dogbane fabric trailing in the breeze. A white, scalp lock–style apron hung to a point between his knees, a Spirit Bundle tied to its front.

At Night Shadow Star's he pointed, sending a detail of the troops who followed him up the stairs to hurry past Piasa and Horned Serpent and into the palace.

Sitting on her veranda, watching, Blue Heron could well imagine the tumult they were about to turn loose on her niece's palace. Green Stick wasn't the kind who took easily to strangers ransacking his lady's home.

As I am going to have to take to the ransacking of mine, she realized as Spotted Wrist continued on, his face grim. Behind him came a troop of ten remaining warriors. At the foot of her mound, five split off, trotting to encircle her mound, thereby cutting off any escape.

Blue Heron sat on a low bench, her back to the palace wall, shaded by the eave of her thatch roof. In her hands she held a ceramic cup filled with mint tea. Freshly brewed from leaves Smooth Pebble had Traded for that morning down in the Great Plaza.

"Trouble coming," she called through the door. "We're about to be searched. Cause the Keeper no grief."

Dancing Moon appeared in the doorway, saying, "Him? You're going to let that butcher into this house?"

"I know what he did to you and your family. You have to promise me. You'll leave dealing with him to me. And if anyone has to go to war with him, Fire Cat has first call. You hear me on this? And you'll keep your daughters out of it."

Dancing Moon chewed on her lips. Hard enough that it had to draw blood.

"I mean it," Blue Heron insisted. "He'll be dealt with. But this is not the time, nor the place."

"Yes, Lady," Dancing Moon said with reluctance. "Daughters. Come. I need you out here on the porch where the lady can remind us not to spit on the Cahokian trash about to defile our home."

"Our home?" Blue Heron wondered as the Red Wing women filed out and took their places along the wall beside her.

Smooth Pebble stood in the door, asking, "Lady?"

"You either. Don't cause me trouble."

The berdache lifted her hands in surrender. "Me? Wouldn't think of it."

Spotted Wrist appeared, having sprinted up the stairs. He bowed low as he passed the Eagle guardians at the head of the stairs and led his remaining warriors down the short walk. Drawing to a stop just shy of the veranda, he demanded, "Where is he?"

"Haven't a clue."

A keen delight mixed with the anger in Spotted Wrist's eyes. "Funny that you don't have to ask who. The fact that you know to whom I refer condemns you."

"Just because you are an idiot, you don't have to act like one. Given my networks, I was informed before first light the day he was rescued. You didn't find out until midafternoon. And even then, it was through one of your warriors. One who hadn't even been in your palace that night. The others were still stumbling around the plaza figuring they could find the thief and have him locked up again before you learned he was gone."

With a gesture, Spotted Wrist ordered, "Squadron Second, search this place."

"You'll rotted well stay out of my palace," Blue Heron protested. "I give you my word, as a noble and lady of the Morning Star House, of Black Tail's lineage, that the thief known as Seven Skull Shield is not in my palace. I give you my further word that I did not carry him out of your palace. And, beyond that, if he was rescued, it was by friends of his. The thief has associates in River Mounds City, Evening Star Town,

Horned Serpent Town, Serpent Woman Town, as well as in communities up on the bluff. While he could be anywhere, I'd suggest that you start at the canoe landing and work your way out from there."

"Your word?"

She nodded, looking back at his suddenly uneasy warriors. "You men, you heard me. I gave my word as a lady of my lineage, that the thief isn't here. If the war leader disregards my honor, it will be—"

"Search this palace," Spotted Wrist snapped. "Tear it apart if you have to."

"—an affront to the Morning Star House and my lineage," she finished. The words struck home—she could see it in the warriors' eyes as they hesitated.

"Well, go on!" Spotted Wrist snapped.

"War Leader, er, Keeper?" the squadron second began.

"Do it!"

Blue Heron narrowed her eyes to slits as the uneasy warriors pushed past Smooth Pebble, who remained defiantly in the doorway.

"You had better find him in there," Blue Heron said as the sound of a breaking pot could be heard from inside. "If you don't, it will be all over Morning Star House that you essentially called me a liar, and that you insulted my honor."

"Your honor? You were supposed to help me. Remember? Your deal with Rising Flame? That you would advise me on the duties of Clan Keeper in compensation for the right to stay in your palace here."

"You will recall that I tried. Did my best for a whole moon long after you made it clear that my advice not only wasn't wanted, but would be entirely ignored. You, after all, were the Hero of the North, and what need had a man of your *military* ability to listen to some old woman?"

Spotted Wrist glanced dismissively at Dancing Moon and her daughters. "If you ask me, you've been corrupted, tainted by heretics. You and that insolent niece of yours, your whole House. You forgot why we fought in the north. What it took to subdue those pus-licking Red Wings."

Blue Heron held up a restraining hand, adding, "Don't!" as Dancing Moon started forward with murder in her eyes.

"Well, I see you've got the pond scum trained to heel at least. Almost as good as you could do with a dog."

From inside, something else fell with a crash. She could hear the squadron second order, "Easy! You want to wind up in a square if this goes wrong?"

Blue Heron slitted her eyes. "You know, this means war between us."

"You declared that the day you stole the thief."

"And I give you my word that I didn't turn him loose. That I never laid eyes on that cage I heard you had him in. For that matter, I've never so much as set foot inside that palace of yours."

All of which was true. She'd just shouted through the door.

Spotted Wrist, of course, wasn't buying it.

Something else crashed inside, made Blue Heron grind her few teeth.

The squadron second appeared in the doorway. "Uh, Keeper, there's no one here. We've looked everywhere. Checked the floor for hidden chambers, searched all around the foundation and under all the beds. Even looked in all the storage boxes large enough to hold a man. He's not here."

"Search it again."

The squadron second shot Blue Heron an apologetic glance. As if he were in physical pain, the man turned and reentered the palace.

"You really don't know when to stop, do you?"

"Keeper, you said it yourself. There's no going back for either of us now."

"May *Hunga Ahuito* have mercy on your soul."

"I was thinking the same thing for you, Blue Heron. You and your heretic-loving kind have had it your own way for far too long."

"Find the Koroa copper yet?" she asked mildly.

And with that, Spotted Wrist followed his squadron second into the palace great room, where the sounds of smashing pottery and the crashing of chests grew louder.

Sixty-four

Fire Cat led the way out of the forest, nodding to people and calling greetings as he and Blood Talon passed through the fields and into the outskirts of Canyon Town.

Fire Cat took in the traditional Muskogean bent-pole structures around the square, then he noticed the chunkey court, rude thing that it was. So how ingrained was worship of the reincarnated god here?

Some sort of assembly seemed to be in progress at the *Tchkofa* in the center of the plaza.

"What's all that?" Fire Cat asked, gesturing toward the crowd around the Council House.

"Some excitement," a Koasati woman told him in Trade pidgin. "A man was murdered, another badly injured. Happened a couple of nights ago. It was a violation of the peace. The *mikko* and the clans are trying to work out what happened and who was responsible."

"Any ideas about who it was?"

"The man who survives says it was the River Fox and some Cahokian woman who were at the bottom of it. That he was hired by a Casqui Trader to abduct the woman and take her to Cofitachequi."

Fire Cat stopped short, staring at the Koasati woman. She looked to be about thirty, had that worn appearance that came from bearing and caring for too many children. "So, did the woman get away?"

"She did. The wounded man, a mixed-blood Trader with a bad reputation around here, says that a party of men attacked him and the Casqui in the darkness. Took the woman back and vanished into the night. They're still looking for the Casqui, but he seems to have disappeared."

"And what about the River Fox and the Cahokian woman?"

"Took their packs in the middle of the night, and they're gone. Maybe on the river with some Cherokee Traders, maybe on their own, or maybe down one of the forest trails that lead south."

"What is she saying?" Blood Talon asked.

The woman shot him a disdainful glance, taking in his wounds and tattered breechcloth.

Fire Cat relayed the woman's information.

"What do you think?" Blood Talon asked.

Before replying, Fire Cat thanked the woman and started into town. "Winder might be a scoundrel, but he is no one's fool. He thinks his best chance to lure Night Shadow Star into his bed and get all the Trade is to get her to Cofitachequi quickly and safely. He also has to prove his competence, be charming, and earn her gratitude."

"You're saying that a common Trader thinks he can seduce Night Shadow Star?"

"Well . . . he was Seven Skull Shield's best friend once upon a time. They grew up together, which means they're sort of like two halves of the same walnut. And you didn't see Winder when he thought I wasn't looking. So, yes, he thinks he has a chance."

"But she's a *lady*! A noble."

"Which means what?" Fire Cat gestured around. "You're in Canyon Town, and Cahokia is somewhere half a world away."

Blood Talon shook his head. "No wonder you're worried. Night Shadow Star is traveling with some lowly Trader? Alone? He could do anything he wanted with her. And there's nothing she could do about it."

"I already told you, Winder is no one's fool."

"I don't understand. You said he's a scoundrel, a common—"

"Just because he's a scoundrel doesn't mean he's not smart." Fire Cat waved a finger. "The man didn't become the renowned River Fox by acting impetuously. No, trust me, he's playing the long game, biding his time, winning her trust and affection."

"And that doesn't worry you?"

Fire Cat shrugged. "Squadron First, there's risk in everything, but after all we've been through, I'll put my trust in my lady."

Blood Talon had his hands on his hips, staring around Canyon Town. In terms of towns, it really wasn't much to look at. And the crowd at the *Tchkofa* looked about to break up.

"So, what do we do?"

"Find a canoe headed upriver and offer our labor as paddlers in return for passage. That, or steal one come dark."

Even as they watched a man was led out of the *Tchkofa*, a wrapping around his wounded head. The fellow wasn't going freely.

Within moments the locals had ripped his clothes off, tied him up in a square at the edge of the plaza, and began beating him with sticks.

"Who do you suppose he is?" Blood Talon asked nervously, his own recent torture on his mind given his expression.

"I'd say he's the fellow they were interrogating about Night Shadow Star's abduction. It's true, they really do take the Power of Trade and the peace seriously here. My guess is that if we end up having to steal a canoe, we should be most judicious in how we do it."

Walking to the edge of the terrace, Fire Cat stared out over the Tenasee's green waters, his eyes following the river's course upriver through the mountains until it vanished around a bend.

I'm coming, my love. It won't be long now.

Assuming he could figure out how to get a canoe with the little Trade he had from the sale of the dugout he'd taken at Black Clay Bank village.

Glancing back at the man in the square, hearing the shouts of the crowd, it wouldn't do to be caught crosswise with the locals. So how did an ex–Red Wing war chief, freed bound servant, and owner of weapons, armor, and chunkey gear manage to accumulate enough Trade to barter for a quality canoe when . . .

His gaze went once again to the crude chunkey court, and a slow smile bent his lips.

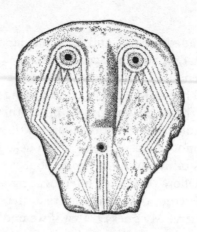

They Don't Understand

*I*t amazes me. One would think they would learn. Especially after all the times they've tried before. But they don't. It is a particularly baffling aspect of how their thoughts and souls work.

I come awake in darkness. I am in my bed, the fire burned down to low coals. I know it is the middle of the night, and we're in the dark of the moon. The only sound is the harmonic of a thousand crickets, then the plaintive call of an owl out in the forest.

I rise, my hand going instinctively to my war club. I can sense his presence. Call it an awareness of the proximity of a living being. It's the beating of his heart, the pulsing of blood in the veins. If I close my eyes I can almost hear the breath sucking in and pushing out of his lungs. Feel his building fear and desperation.

Turning, I stretch my senses, let them drift out and . . . yes, there. He's just on the other side of the wall, slipping along. I follow as he reaches the front corner, hesitates.

I imagine him peeking around the corner, searching the pitch-black veranda, afraid that I am hiding there. The image fills my souls of an insect who knows a wolf spider is lurking nearby, hidden in its den.

Oh, yes, come closer, my prey.

He rounds the corner, and cocking my head, I can hear his slow and fumbling approach as he feels his way along the veranda. Reaches the door.

I smile as I consider his problem. The door is closed. What does he do? Try to lift it out of the way? Is it latched from the inside? Will it make noise?

And if it does, will it bring me fully awake and cognizant of his stealthy approach?

I am aware of a fast, rhythmic thumping and am surprised to realize I'm hearing the sound of his frantic heart. He is scared half to death. Nevertheless, he demonstrates courage. His fingers give off the slightest rasp as they trace the planks, and he fastidiously lifts my door, swinging it to one side.

I see the faintest outline of his shape against the darkness beyond. He is a big man, thick-shouldered, and I just make out his hair style: Muskogean.

The faint movement of his arm is that of a man pulling a war club from its thong. Despite the darkness, I know he's got it raised, a bony fist gripping the handle.

He feels his way forward with a hesitant foot, the pounding of his heart ever more rapid, his breath loud now. I can almost feel the electric tingle of fear as it traces patterns across his skin. I can smell him, his odor thick with terror.

One step, two, and he's craning his neck, searching frantically in the faint glow from the hearth to discover which bunk I might be asleep in.

I let him take another step, then ghost up behind him.

As boys, my brother and I were trained in the war club by the best warriors in Cahokia. Being the sons of Red Warrior Mankiller, we had the benefit of learning where to strike by practicing on prisoners. Mostly those captured in war.

I position myself, get my feet just so. And swing with all my might.

My club makes a sodden and meaty sound as it thuds into the back of the man's spine just at the base of the neck. One heartbeat he's standing, the next he's on the ground with no feeling in the rest of his body.

Pulling his limp legs around, I quickly bind them, shove him onto his belly, and tie his hands behind his back. Only then do I throw wood on the fire. I study him as the flames rise around the knots of oak and hickory.

As the light flickers on my face, he gasps, and a whimper dies in his throat. I see tears begin to leak from his eyes. They trickle down around his nose like pearls of light and drip onto the matting beneath his head.

"I see by your tattoos that you are local," I tell him. "What possessed you to try to kill me? Let alone in the middle of the night?"

"My two little girls," he manages through sobs.

But how would he know that they ended up . . . ? Well, doesn't matter.

"Looks like Power just isn't on your side, but it does run in your blood. At least, as much as can be attributed to the father. Your little girls granted me the Power to see across a great distance. Though I would much rather have the girls' mother—more Power is transferred through the womb than from a drop of semen, you know—it will be an experiment. I'll be fascinated to discover how far your blood and entrails will allow me to see."

The fire is now leaping high enough to fill the room with light. More than enough to allow me to be about my work.

Following me with his panicked eyes, he throws his head back, a terrible scream almost ripping his vocal cords from his throat.

Yes, he's figured out what I'm going to do with my long, intricately flaked chert knife.

He screams again when I sever the thong that holds his breechcloth in place. Got to hand it to the man, I would have thought his vocal cords would have given out long before I finally got around to slicing the thin muscle of the diaphragm loose from his rib cage to expose his heart. The thing was beating so fast you'd have thought it was a terrified rodent huddling between those deflating lungs.

But that was at the end, after I'd studied the patterns in his living intestines as I lifted them from the man's gut cavity and spilled them on the matting.

Raising a burning brand from the fire, I then studied the blood pooling on either side of his spine, seeing the image they reflected in the dancing light.

I can see Night Shadow Star there. She is on the river. Coming closer by the day. The Casqui, the storm, both have failed me.

I consider the problem as I peel the Muskogee man's skin from his limbs; the firelight flickers on his still-twitching muscles. Remarkable things, muscles. Half of the duality of movement. The other being bone. Bones do no good without muscles, and muscles are worthless unless attached to bone.

There should be a lesson in that when it comes to my problem with Night Shadow Star, assuming I can figure it out.

I finish with my work as the first streaks of dawn find their way across the treetops and into Joara. The framework I have made of sticks isn't the best workmanship I am capable of, but it will do until I can craft something better.

I am out digging a hole as the full force of the sun finally illuminates the plaza and casts a long shadow from the mikko's pitch-roofed palace. That done, I lift my framework and set it in the hole. My Muskogee would-be assailant's skin hangs wet and loose, but it will tighten with the sunlight and breeze to dry it.

I look around, take in the town, hoping to share my sense of satisfaction. But for the small knot of warriors at the palace where Fire Light now dwells, I see no one. It strikes me that Joara is oddly quiet. I hear no calling children, no smacking of stone axes on wood or the thumping of pestles in log mortars. People should be out and about, calling greetings to each other.

Nor is the priest in his usual place down at the temple on the west side of town.

Only that one old woman without relations, who lives at the far end, too crippled to hardly move, is standing at the edge of the plaza, watching me with worried brown eyes.

She shouldn't. True Power lies in the blood of the young.

Have I missed something? Perhaps a holiday? Is it summer solstice? Surely it can't be the Green Corn Ceremony. And the lunar maximum was long ago.

So, where is everyone?

"Well, no matter," I tell myself. "I have plenty of firewood, the fields outside of town are full of growing corn, beans, and squash, and as of last night, there's plenty of fresh meat for breakfast."

I shall spend the rest of the day smoking my Muskogean friend for future meals. And who knows, perhaps his wife will come along, and I can see if her blood and body have more Power for clearer visions than her husband's did.

That would be most helpful as I plan my trap for Night Shadow Star.

"You just keep right on coming, sister," I whisper.

But next, I must talk with Fire Light.

Poor man.

Sixty-five

For a full quarter moon—seven unending and painful days—Seven Skull Shield had lain in bed. For most of that time, he'd had trouble with his souls—wandering in and out of his body. When they were out, he floated in a world of Dreams: times spent with Winder; golden days with Wooden Doll; or hearing amusement in the Keeper's voice as she berated him. Sometimes it was laughing and joking with the shell carvers or the cord spinners.

Once he was even in Mother Otter's bed, staring down at her as they shared the most wondrous coupling, her body undulating under his. That one, when he awakened, he knew to have only been a Dream. Some things, thank the Spirits, stretched credulity beyond the farthest reaches.

Then there were the other places to which his souls fled: dark, filled with death, terror, and angry men who pounded down narrow passageways blocked on either side by buildings—fire, pain, and agony shooting like lightning out of their fingers.

And through it all, fear filled him. The knowledge that he was about to be locked in a small cage, his body pierced with sharp sticks, burned, and beaten . . . and then would come the final agony of the square.

Other times he was awake, fully conscious of the ache in his body, the pained muscles and joints. It seemed that every inch of his hide hurt, either burned or punctured, bruised or battered. Knots covered his head.

But he knew where he was: Wooden Doll's. Not only was her fine bed with all its pillows and soft blankets reassuring, but the familiar setting proved a tonic for his soul.

He'd barely been conscious the first time she'd taken a damp cloth to sponge his wounds. Remembered the lines of worry in her fine brow as she'd lifted his leg to the side, stifled a gasp, and tenderly cleaned his abused genitals.

Given her reaction, he wasn't sure he wanted to look.

Helped upright by Whispering Dawn and Wooden Doll, his first urination into the pot they held had been dark with blood.

"Skull, so help me." Wooden Doll had shaken her head. "I always knew you'd come to grief."

"Not dead yet, girl," he'd told her. "Call it a success, huh?"

"A success? You can't even stand, every inch of you is hurt, and half the time you're out of your head."

"Got me back into your bed, didn't it?"

She'd thumped him playfully on the shoulder, which shot pain. At his wince, she'd winked and said, "You might have wiggled your way into my bed, but you're not worth much now that you're here."

"He never was much for planning," Whispering Dawn replied from the side where she bent awkwardly over her pregnant belly and stirred the stew.

On the seventh morning, he awakened with clarity he hadn't possessed since his rescue. He blinked up at Wooden Doll's ceiling. Shifted, which triggered the dull ache in his shoulders. His kidneys burned, but didn't throb, and the headache was gone.

Beside him, Wooden Doll rolled onto her side, pulled her hair back over her shoulder, and propped herself on an elbow, thoughtful eyes taking in his condition.

He tried to smile. Winced at the scabs on his lips. "I thought I was Dreaming that I was here."

"Oh, you did plenty of Dreaming. Some of it silent, some just mutterings, and some was loud and apparently most unpleasant. At those times either I or Whispering Dawn would usually lean close to your ear, tell you it was all right, and you'd drop back into deep sleep again."

"How did I get here?"

"On my litter."

"You got me out of there?"

"It was a combined effort." She arched an eyebrow in disbelief. "Had you asked me a couple of years back, I'd have said the chances that you, of all people, could have friends the likes of which you have would have been a head-struck delusion. Now, I wonder what I have missed in the seeing of you."

"Now you lost me."

"Have I just been blind? Or did I purposefully mislead myself about the kind of man you are?"

"I'm just me."

"That's my point. Maybe I've been so close to you, I've missed it."

"Missed what? Don't make me think. My head is still too beat up for it."

"A bunch of us planned and conducted your rescue. Blue Heron and I, along with Flat Stone Pipe and Matron Columella. We had to wait until the time was right and Spotted Wrist was in Serpent Woman Town, then we had to lure Sun Wing and the Tortoise Bundle away so we could set fire to her palace, clear out the guards. Flat Stone Pipe sneaked in early, got to work cutting the bindings that held your cage together. But it took Columella's warriors to break the last of the poles loose so we could get you out. Then they carried you to my litter. I had my porters bring you here."

"A quarter moon ago."

"That's right."

Seven Skull Shield reached up with a scabbed hand and rubbed his eyes. "I have to go."

"No, you don't."

"That pus-licking new Keeper will have people out looking for—"

"His warriors are all over. Had one loitering around here for a couple of days. Flat Stone Pipe anticipated that. He's had a series of his people show up one by one, be ushered inside for a hand of time or two, and then leave grinning. I had Whispering Dawn walk over to proposition the watcher. She asked him point-blank: How much Trade did he have, and that if he didn't have the copper, shell, or textile that it took to lock hips with me to move his silly carcass out of here because he was pathetic."

"He left?"

"Guess he figured I didn't have the half-dead Seven Skull Shield in my place if I was servicing men and willing to give him a milking."

"What about your regular clients?"

"Whispering Dawn tells them a Trader from up north dropped a sack of copper and a stack of white-fox hides on my floor to buy me for as long as his Trade will carry him. And that if they want to do the same, start piling up the Trade and I'll consider how much time I'll spend with them when I'm done."

Seven Skull Shield tried to grin, but it pulled the scabs on his face too much. "But you're still losing a pile of Trade while I'm laid up here."

"I am."

"So, I'd better find a place where my presence isn't—"

"You'll stay here."

"But I—"

"No argument. Couple of days back, Spotted Wrist tore Blue Heron's palace apart looking for you. Almost came to out-and-out war at Columella's, his warriors and Evening Star House's, but she let them search her palace anyway, each warrior accompanied the entire time. After you weren't found, she issued an ultimatum, that if her word as matron wasn't proven good enough, that from this point on, her cooperation with the Keeper was over. Finished. And that any of his people who were found in Evening Star Town would be captured, tied up, covered in hot pine pitch, and dropped on Spotted Wrist's doorstep by armed warriors."

"All of that? For *me*?"

"Well, partly. Let's be honest here. There's a struggle going on for control of the city. North Star House and Horned Serpent House against Evening Star House and Morning Star House, with River House in a sort of weakened and paralyzed neutrality. Rising Flame is on one side, *Tonka'tzi* Wind and Blue Heron on the other. You've become a symbolic pawn in the middle."

"Pus and muck. Why me?"

"That's what I've been trying to tell you. Blue Heron, Flat Stone Pipe, and Columella, not to mention Night Shadow Star, they all consider you a friend, think themselves in your debt. That's the part that amazes me, given how long I've known you. These are Four Winds nobility. When Spotted Wrist took you out of Night Shadow Star's palace? He took one of their own."

"One of their own?" Seven Skull Shield repeated, trying to fit that into his understanding of the world and how it worked.

"You risked your life for them on several occasions. Blue Heron would have died but for you getting her away from the Quiz Quiz last year."

"She's my friend."

Wooden Doll laughed, shook her head. "It amazes me. That's your greatest strength, Skull. And in the end, it will kill you."

"Having friends?"

"You know, you're not out of this yet. Spotted Wrist won't rest until he has you dead. Taking you like we did? That just raised the stakes in the game."

"And now you're a player. He will find out eventually, you know."

"Maybe. Maybe not. The only one I even half know is Blue Heron. In fact, she said I could take anything of hers I wanted in compensation for any Trade I might lose because of your stay here."

"She didn't stipulate? Set a limit?"

"No."

He felt a warming of his heart. "I'm not the only one who's 'one of them.' You impressed her somehow, probably over that trouble with Horn Lance, that ex-husband of hers."

"That was business."

"Watch yourself, you're going to end up as deep in this as I am." He took a moment, really studied her. Let his gaze trace the lines of her face, the perfect nose, high cheekbones, and the angle of her jaw. As he did, the question grew in her eyes, that slight lining of her brow as she tried to read him.

"What?"

"Thank you for bringing me here. That's all."

"You're stalling, trying to change the subject. What was that look?"

"I don't suppose there's any way you'd run away with me. Go somewhere where it isn't a constant fight."

The old familiar "I'm amused" eyebrow lifted. "We've had this conversation. You couldn't stand being someplace that wasn't here. Boredom would drive you insane, make you impossible to love, and I'd end up smacking you in the back of the head sometime when you weren't looking."

She paused. "But on a similar subject, what did you see in that woman? Willow Blossom? How did she mislead you, of all people?"

He took a deep breath, regretted it as his cracked ribs sent spears through his chest. "She lit up for me. Her eyes sparkled. That smile."

"Any woman can do that."

"You don't."

"That doesn't answer my question. How did she fool you? By Piasa's swinging balls, what were you thinking?"

"I was lonely. And, well, I thought that maybe she could be another you."

This time the pain in his heart came from a different kind of wound. Looking at Wooden Doll, he suddenly understood that there would never be another one like her.

Sixty-six

The *tonka'tzi*'s elevated palace dominated a large flat-topped mound on the western margin of the Great Plaza across from the World Tree pole that rose in the plaza's center. Larger in area, though not as tall as the Morning Star's palace, the *tonka'tzi*'s palace played host to visiting embassies, was an informal meeting place for different nations while in Cahokia, and served as the dwelling of the *tonka'tzi*. Here, Wind lived with her husband, Fine Catch, and her considerable household and professional staff.

Running the palace took effort and consumed time. Not only might Wind be required to offer the occasional unexpected feast to visiting nobility, but the mound staff and guests needed a constant supply of food, water, beds, storage, shelter for subordinates and slaves, not to mention the necessities of state such as recorders, messengers, a bevy of warriors on call for security, the occasional medical professional, surveyors, consultations with the Sky Priests, and who knew what else.

That entailed a steady supply of firewood, cooks, people who could sew, the servicing of chamber pots, washing, people who could help with hair, and a multitude of other skills that might be called upon at a moment's notice.

In addition to her duties up at the Council House, the running of Cahokia, as a city, fell in Wind's lap. She was the second-to-final arbiter of disputes, subject only to the Morning Star himself. Rarely, however, did the living god deign to involve himself in the mundane affairs of the city. Therefore, every squabble between settlements of dirt farmers, misunderstandings between the various petty chieftainships in the Earth Clans, Trade relations, boundary disputes, broken contracts, and even the occasional domestic disturbance ended up on Wind's doorstep.

Which brought Blue Heron and Columella to the *tonka'tzi*'s palace. They both sat in their litters, each having been brought up the steps of the *tonka'tzi*'s palace mound and between the two-headed eagle guardian posts that invoked *Hunga Ahuito*. They'd been carried into the great room, with its audience consisting of the occasional House lord, some of the Earth Clans chiefs and matrons. A smattering of lesser nobility was present; the ones who stayed as a show of status or in the hopes of cadging a free meal.

Now it was Blue Heron and Columella's turn. A chance to raise the stakes—not that Wind wasn't fully aware of the growing crisis in the Four Winds Clan, but this would make it official. Take the conflict out of the shadows, the next move in a calculated struggle that would eventually see one side or the other prevailing.

After the black drink had been brewed, and the pipe smoked with the appropriate prayers uttered to the Spirit World, Wind—seated atop her dais on the other side of the fire—asked, "What brings you to the *tonka'tzi*?"

"We come with grievances," Columella began. "As matron of Evening Star Town, I am here to declare that my House has been abused and belittled, and while I am hesitant to do so, I must inform you that as of this moment, Evening Star Town has been forced to withdraw its support of the current Clan Keeper. Neither Spotted Wrist nor his agents are welcome in Evening Star Town. A messenger has delivered our notice to the Keeper. I am here, *Tonka'tzi*, to inform you in person that should the Keeper's agents be found operating in Evening Star Town, they will be summarily removed. If they resist, they will be removed in an unpleasant fashion."

Wind's expression might have been cast from stone. "Lady Blue Heron?"

"I am here to file a complaint. My palace was torn apart by the Keeper after I had informed him—upon my honor as a Four Winds Clan noble— that a missing person he sought was not in my residence. Further, that the person he had taken, and then lost control of, was an agent of the Lady Night Shadow Star, and working in her service as a caretaker of her property while she is away on the Morning Star's business in the south."

"And what reason did the Keeper allege for taking this person in the first place?"

"The person known as Seven Skull Shield apparently embarrassed the Keeper in front of the Morning Star and assembled nobles by means of a remark about the Keeper's inability to get Night Shadow Star to marry him."

Snickers sounded around the room. The story had indeed made the rounds.

Blue Heron watched as the recorders in the back of the room sorted through their various colored beads, making a record of the charges.

Where she perched on cougar hides atop her dais, Wind shifted, thoughtfully, propped her chin with her fist. "This sounds like Four Winds Clan business; why was this not dealt with by the clan matron?"

"She apparently doesn't think the honor or integrity of Evening Star House is worth her time," Columella replied. "And, *Tonka'tzi*, this is an affront aimed specifically at my House. My agents have discovered that neither North Star House, Horned Serpent House, nor River House have been searched. To us, this smacks of a political vendetta. Therefore, in the interest of keeping the peace, we hope to bring this to you for a ruling."

"Very well." Wind snapped her fingers. "I need messengers to summon Clan Keeper Spotted Wrist and Four Winds Clan Matron Rising Flame. I need to hear their side of the dispute."

Along the back wall, two young men leapt to their feet. Each carried a staff of office as he raced from the room.

Wind arched an eyebrow. "It may be a while. Care for a cup of tea and some freshly roasted turkey?"

Given the formality of the session, Wind prudently allowed the staff, nobles, and busybodies to wait in the room. To Blue Heron's delight, as she sipped at her cup of tea, a constant trickle of people entered the great room, fully aware of the drama being played out. Excellent, couldn't be better. The more ears to hear, the more mouths to spread the tale.

The call, "Make way for Rising Flame, Four Winds Clan matron," announced the arrival. Rising Flame came striding into the room, followed by several of her attendants and an armored warrior from her security escort.

That latter fact amused Blue Heron. No one but Morning Star had ever wandered around with armed warriors until Night Shadow Star had taken to having Fire Cat constantly in her company during Walking Smoke's reign of terror. Once Rising Flame had adopted the practice, so had Slender Fox and some of the younger and aspiring nobles. So, too, had Three Fingers, a fact that annoyed War Duck and one that Blue Heron herself would probably have to deal with before eliminating the threat to her old rivals at River House.

"*Tonka'tzi*," Rising Flame greeted, striding up to the fire and between Blue Heron's and Columella's litters. She gave them both sidelong glances, immediately surmising the meaning of their presence. "I do hope that you have not been inconvenienced by a minor clan squabble that should have been taken care of in a less public manner."

"Both Evening Star House and Lady Blue Heron have made charges against the Four Winds Clan Keeper, both have stated that they applied to you for redress and were unsatisfied. Are you familiar with the merits of their case?"

"I am, *Tonka'tzi*. Though I must confess that while I find Lady Blue Heron's interest understandable given her previous associations with the miscreant, Lady Columella's concern for a clanless and shiftless thief is somewhat incomprehensible in this matter."

"What is at issue here," Blue Heron insisted, "is not the thief's character, but the way the Keeper is treating me and Evening Star House. The fact that our word of honor is cast aside as worthless, that my palace was torn apart, ceramics broken, statuary smashed, grain spilled, oil jars upended, and personal effects soiled goes beyond the Keeper's mandate. The job of the Keeper—"

"We know what the job of the Keeper is," Rising Flame interrupted. "The fact that a known criminal—"

"Do you know what the Keeper's job is?" Blue Heron shot back. "It's to keep harmony among the various Houses in the Four Winds Clan. To ensure that House doesn't rise against House. That—"

"And you were so good at that? Playing each House off against the others? Having them at a constant low boil? Each scheming against the others?"

"It's not even a year, Matron. And Evening Star House is on the verge of revolt."

"We are," Columella interjected. "If we find the Keeper or his people in Evening Star Town, he *will* be forcibly removed. If he comes with his squadron behind him, he will be met with force of arms."

"That is unacceptable," Rising Flame replied coldly.

"Unless you want to test the resolve of our squadrons, you'll find a way to accept it, Clan Matron."

"Enough!" Wind snapped from her dais. She leaned forward on her litter, a hard gaze fixing Rising Flame. "But for a last-minute miracle, we barely avoided open warfare between the Houses last fall. I will not see it come to that over a simple thief."

"He's not a 'simple thief,'" Blue Heron shot back. "He is the man Lady Night Shadow Star placed in charge of her affairs. He is a personally appointed representative of her authority."

"This is Seven Skull Shield we're talking about," Rising Flame cried. "He's a known thief, a womanizer, a slippery . . ." She made a face. "Are you sure you want to make a stand on a thief's behalf?"

"Why did Spotted Wrist's warriors enter Night Shadow Star's palace by stealth? Seize Seven Skull Shield and lock him in a cage to be tortured?"

"The man's a thief."

"What did he steal?" Blue Heron asked.

"I can name the Quiz Quiz War Medicine, for one."

"Ah, the War Medicine box that he acquired while recovering the sacred Bundle stolen from the Surveyors' Society? The one the Quiz Quiz brought to ensure their success in stealing *our* Bundle? The same War Medicine he Traded to you, honestly and up front, in exchange for the release of the Trader, Winder? Why didn't you order him seized on the spot?"

Rising Flame's glare was sharper than a freshly ground bone stiletto. "It is common knowledge that he was the assassin who threatened to cut Round Pot's throat at River House, the man who extinguished their sacred fire."

Columella dryly said, "To my knowledge, no one has ever had their throat cut with a potsherd. Beyond that, not even Round Pot can say for a fact that Seven Skull Shield was the man in her room that night searching for the Quiz Quiz, which means it is not common knowledge. But, for argument, let's say it was. What did Round Pot and War Duck declare stolen that night?"

Rising Flame's brow pinched. "I don't understand."

"It's an easy question."

"I haven't a clue as to what was missing."

"Some thief," Columella said, turning her attention back to Wind. "*Tonka'tzi,* you are fully aware—as many in this room are not—that Seven Skull Shield is and has been an agent for the Morning Star House. He was instrumental in ending Walking Smoke's murderous spree, saving countless lives. He provided us service when the Itza would have led us into disaster and was responsible for bringing the Quiz Quiz to justice. That he—"

"The man is a scoundrel!" Rising Flame barked.

"He embarrassed Spotted Wrist," Blue Heron insisted, "and that's why he was taken, caged, beaten, and abused. He—"

"The beast is a most loathsome and despicable creature!" Spotted Wrist bellowed as he forced his way through the now-packed doorway. "You should have heard the things he confessed to while he was in my custody. The rape of children, sacrilege, the man shouted insults against

Power, and that he walked the avenues of Cahokia for as long as he did? That is a disgrace to all of us!"

Blue Heron turned in her litter as she watched the Hero of the North stride forward. He stopped, a falcon-feather cloak thrown back over his shoulders; a beautifully dyed crimson war shirt hung down to his knees. His Four Winds tattoos had faded into the deep lines on his cheeks.

"The rape of children?" Columella almost spat the words. "Either you don't know Seven Skull Shield, or you're a foul-mouthed liar on top of being a complete incompetent."

"You don't speak to me in that tone, woman," Spotted Wrist declared, pointing a hard finger at her.

"You'll hear the truth in whatever tone I decide to put it in."

"*Enough!*" Wind thundered from her dais. She fixed hard eyes on Spotted Wrist. "War Leader, what is the purpose of the Four Winds Clan Keeper? I mean, just what is it that you are supposed to do?"

"*Tonka'tzi*, surely you jest. You know fully well what the Clan Keeper's responsibilities—"

"Do you know?"

"Of course. I am to discover and foil plots against the Four Winds Clan Houses, to ensure the safety of Morning Star and ensure harmony throughout—"

"What part of going to war with Evening Star House ensures harmony between the Houses?"

"I am not going to war with Evening Star House. If they have taken offense at my pursuit of my duties, I would respectfully suggest that the fault lies with the good Matron Columella and that old dried-up, so-called friend of hers." He made a face. "Oh, excuse me. That's your sister, isn't it?"

Rising Flame took a deep breath and rolled her eyes. The others in the room were silent as mist, eyes wide, taking in the spectacle.

"Make peace, Keeper," Wind snapped. "That's an order."

"I've made my peace, *Tonka'tzi*. I did it by flattening the Shawnee, by crushing the heretics at Red Wing Town, and by squashing the Houses that were on the verge of war here last fall. You deal with your enemies your way, and I will deal with mine in my own."

That old familiar tightening of Wind's eyes made Blue Heron flinch.

The *tonka'tzi* said, "The position of Keeper isn't a blunt instrument, War Leader. It's more like a fine obsidian blade that is to be used judiciously." To Rising Flame she added, "Clan Matron, please instruct your Clan Keeper on the proper conduct of his office. Please inform him of the value that the Four Winds Clan nobility place upon their word of honor. Explain to him that unless individuals can be proven to be working against the interests of peace and harmony within the Four Winds Clan, they are not to be seized, tortured, and harmed."

"But—"

"Matron Columella," Wind thundered, refusing to be interrupted, "you will assist the Clan Keeper in the pursuit of his official duties."

Then Wind extended a finger Blue Heron's way. "Lady Blue Heron, you will not harbor fugitives from Clan justice. As the old Clan Keeper, you will offer any assistance the new Keeper asks of you. You will give that assistance freely and without dissembling. Is that understood?"

"It is, *Tonka'tzi*."

"Then it is finished. I don't care what you have to do, make peace."

From where she sat in her litter, Blue Heron could hear Spotted Wrist's teeth as they ground in his clamped jaws. The man's eyes gleamed like fire. He turned, stomping his way back through the crowd that, showing uncommonly good sense, scrambled out of his way.

Rising Flame, her young face pinched, growled something too soft to hear. She fixed first on Columella, saying, "Don't do this to me again." And to Blue Heron, "We had a deal. You were supposed to help him."

"I tried. Clan Matron, in order to learn, a person must first listen. It doesn't matter how much water you have to pour into a vessel if the vessel already thinks it's full."

Rising Flame shook her head, as if in despair, and stalked out.

Wind had stepped down from her dais, waving the whispering and incredulous crowd away. She glanced back and forth between Columella and Blue Heron. "I hope that you both know what you're doing, because I know that man. He'll never forget what you did to him here tonight."

"It has already gone too far," Blue Heron told her. "From here on, he can't come directly at us. Not without embarrassing Rising Flame and the others."

Columella added, "He has to come at us from the shadows now, and, *Tonka'tzi*, if there's any chance we have of coming out of this alive, it's because in the shadows, we're on equal footing."

"Just don't let this thing burn out of control. I've invested too much in this city just to see you two burn it down over some clanless thief."

"Haven't lost one yet," Blue Heron muttered, but life had taught her, there was always a first time.

Sixty-seven

Did you hear what that old camp bitch said? Lectured me, did she? On my responsibilities as Four Winds Clan Keeper? Pus and blood, who does she think she is?" Spotted Wrist ranted as he strode back and forth before his palace fire.

He kept glaring stilettos of rage at the broken and empty cage along the south wall.

Rising Flame stood in the center of the room, her arms crossed. As she watched him pace, she said, "She's the *tonka'tzi*. Daughter of Black Tail and Magic Woman, aunt to Chunkey Boy, the young man who now hosts Morning Star's souls in his human body."

She had inspected the broken cage earlier, noticed the severed rawhide bindings. She'd been around long enough, had traveled through the southern lands, to know something about cages. The like were built for bears. Not easy to take apart. Someone had been sawing at the bindings for some time before enough had been cut to free the prisoner.

Did that mean Blue Heron or Columella had someone inside Spotted Wrist's palace? If so, who?

"I mean it," she told him. "You back off of those women. If you pursue this, it will end in a war between the Houses."

He shot her a sidelong glance. "North Star House and Horned Serpent House are already infuriated. Times were lean enough—and being forced by Blue Heron to send a portion of their stores to Columella was like sticking cactus thorns into an open wound. Now they're weaker.

Columella is stronger. She has actually sent messengers out to her squadrons, ordered them to prepare for an immediate callout should I march my squadrons on Evening Star Town."

He raised knotted fists. "Back in spring, had she made such an announcement, the Earth Clans in her area would have raised a merry howl, refused, backed that cousin of hers, um . . ."

"His name is Red Hail. You're supposed to know these things, keep track of these people. He's in the best position to ever depose her."

"Well, he'd have stopped this nonsense on the spot."

"You do remember why she loaned that food in the first place? Something about a burned warehouse for the Cofitachequi expedition?"

The look he gave her was full of rebuke. "What's past is past."

"There, finally! I agree. Now, leave this nonsense behind. Blue Heron, Columella, and the thief have won this round. Part of politics is knowing when to accept you've been bested and move on to the battles you can win."

"Can you believe Blue Heron? The hag ran to her sister?" He turned his voice falsetto: "*Sister, sister, the Keeper tore up my palace. Save me, save me.*"

Rising Flame cocked her head, studying the man. "Did you whine like this in front of Blood Talon, Nutcracker, and your squadrons?"

"No!" Spotted Wrist stepped close, thrust a clenched fist under her nose. "I gave them orders, we re-formed the ranks, and we marched on our enemies in order to destroy them. That's what you do, Matron. You *destroy* enemies."

"Do you also listen to orders from your superiors?"

"Don't be silly. That's what war leaders do."

"The *tonka'tzi* gave you an order."

"She's on her sister's side. One of them."

"Then I'm giving you an order: Leave this be."

"Thought you were tired of Black Tail's lineage having all the authority and prestige. Thought you wanted them cut down to size."

"I do." She gave him a smoky gaze of reprimand. "But you need to dig the wax out of your ears. The *tonka'tzi* gave you some very good advice. She told you that the Keeper's position was not a blunt weapon."

"Yes, yes, the thing about the keen obsidian blade."

"Can you learn that?"

"Of course."

"You didn't when Blue Heron tried to teach you last fall."

"The woman was full of lies. Jealous. You don't know. Cunning old sheath that she is, she was setting me up to fail."

"That's why you kicked her out?"

"Do you think I'm a fool?"

She just gave him a cold smile. "Forget this grudge match with Blue Heron, Columella, and the thief. Move on. You have a potential disaster looming in River House. Keep that from blowing up, and we'll talk some more."

He gave her a slight nod, a broken smile on his lips and some unspoken promise deep behind his eyes.

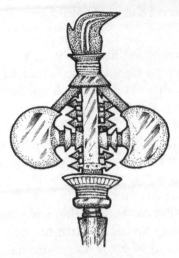

Sixty-eight

Where was Fire Cat? The question had begun to consume Night Shadow Star. Worse, as her worry about him increased, so, too, did the fleeting glimpses of Piasa as he flickered at the edge of her vision. And sometimes, at night, she'd see him stalking just beyond the light of the fires, or in the dim recesses when they stopped at one of the numerous villages that lined the upper Tenasee.

"We made a deal," she whispered to the shadows as she stood on a rise overlooking the clear-flowing Wide Fast River and Chestnut Place village, a muddled collection of huts a day's journey up from the confluence. The local Yuchi called the river the Wide Fast—a major tributary of the Tenasee that split off, headed southeast, deep into the mountains, and would eventually lead her to the final portage that would cross the divide into Cofitachequi.

"The price. He will come to you in Cofitachequi."

She knotted her fists, hearing the breeze in the towering branches of the chestnut tree overhead. She'd never seen such impressive trees, giants that dominated the long ridges and thickly forested valleys she now traveled. Mixed with mighty black oaks and beeches, there were places where she walked in the shadow of the forest, looking up through a perpetual twilight at a canopy that stretched so far above she could have fit her entire palace beneath. Even the vines, thick as a man's torso, defied her imagination with their dizzying heights as they rose to lofty branches above. Literally a Sky World.

Walking in their depths left her humbled, a mere midge in the presence of serene majesty. In Cahokia she might have been a force to be reckoned with. Here, she was nothing. A speck. A mote in an endless and incomprehensible realm of vast forest.

Ache as she did for Fire Cat. Dream of him, she might. But the forest, overwhelming in its Spiritual presence, made her needs seem small and petty. What was her love for a man compared to the Power of the land, to the evil that awaited her up the Wide Fast?

"*Yes,*" Piasa whispered from behind her ear.

She turned, expecting to see him there in the shadows cast by the great chestnut. Nothing moved, no form disturbed the thick carpet of leaf mat. Only the sound of birds and chirring insects filled the late afternoon.

In the village below, dogs barked; a child's laughter carried on the lazy breeze. She could hear the sound of a pestle thudding into a log mortar as corn was pounded into meal.

Just beyond the village, the Wide Fast stretched across to the tree line on the opposite bank; the clear waters roiled, welled, and sucked, having a different soul and Power than did the Tenasee. From this bend where the village was situated she could see the mountains rising to the east, tall, mightier than anything she'd seen so far.

"We'll have to take to the trails when we reach the narrows and the water runs fast," Winder had told her. "From there it's almost a straight shot east to the divide, and then down to Joara and Cofitachequi."

She took a deep breath, filling her lungs with the scent of chestnut, forest, and river.

Fire Cat, I wish you were with me.

If she closed her eyes, she could almost feel his presence, reliable as hickory, that calm strength radiating from his posture, that ironic smile tugging at his lips. In her imagination she reached out to run a finger down the Red Wing tattoos on his cheeks.

How could she have taken him so for granted, come to rely on him with all of her being? He had become her strength, and while she had discovered a new self-reliance in the days since he'd disappeared, his absence remained an ache in her souls.

"You all right?" Winder called, climbing up into view from the village trail.

"No."

"Want to explain?"

"The Spirit Beast that owns my soul is whispering in my ear. I broke a promise. The man I love may be lost to me forever. I am in a strange land, among strange people, headed for a confrontation with the most evil man I know. If I do not win it, I had better die in the process, because if he takes me alive . . ." She ended with a shiver.

Winder stopped just short of her, a serious expression on his square face, the directness of his gaze unnerving. "Then why are you rushing headlong? Slow down. We'll stay a while here, at Chestnut. If Fire Cat's coming, he's coming through here."

"You don't understand."

"What? That you're rushing to face the Lightning Shell witch? Now, me, I've never seen him. He showed up after my time in Cofitachequi. Doesn't mean I haven't heard the stories. If even half of them are true, you don't want anything to do with him."

"You've always changed the subject. Found a way to keep from telling me these stories that are supposedly passing from mouth to mouth along the river."

He shrugged dismissively. "You say he's your brother. I don't want to be gossiping about someone you're—"

"Tell me. There's nothing you could say that would enrage me. Well, unless you were to try to convince me that he's a kind, caring, and compassionate human being. Tell me he's the Spirit of light, a man whose souls draw butterflies and songbirds. That's about the only tale you could spin that would be beyond belief."

"Word is that he strips the flesh from living young girls. Consumes it in front of them. Uses them in the conjuring of some sort of terrible witchery. That he bathes himself in the blood of children. And that those who have tried to kill him are dead. Either by his hand, or lightning. That the Powers of the Sky World protect him."

She nodded, frowning.

He said, "You don't seem surprised."

"The last time I faced Walking Smoke, it was over the murdered, dismembered body of my sister, Lace, and pieces of the baby she'd been carrying in her womb. The flesh-eating is new. But certainly not out of the question. He has always been preoccupied by souls and how to possess them. Probably because of what happened to Chunkey Boy. Requickening—that is, reincarnating the Dead—obsesses him. Maybe he thinks that by eating and digesting people he can make them one with him."

Winder's gaze, if anything, had grown more intent.

She gave him a humorless smile. "What? Surprised that I'm not shocked, or are you just rethinking if you really want to be part of this madness? It's all right. Get me to Joara, or wherever my brother is in Cofitachequi, and you're free to flee as fast as you can back to that cute and willing wife you left in Big Cane Town."

He huffed a sigh, stepped up beside her, and turned his attention to the peaceful Yuchi village below. "All the more reason to stop here for a while. I can rent that hut we're in for a moon or two. Give you some time to wait for Fire Cat to catch up. And, who knows, in the meantime maybe news will come from the other side of the mountains informing us that the Lightning Shell witch has been killed. If he's as evil as they say, it wouldn't surprise me. I've been up and down the rivers, around plenty of places to know. Terrify enough people, and, well, it's pretty much guaranteed to get your head bashed in from behind when you least expect it."

"Not Walking Smoke."

"Even Walking Smoke."

Again, she gave him the humorless smile. "It's not some wild story: He *is* protected by Sky Power. I don't doubt that people have tried to take him down. That they've been struck down by lightning at the last moment when it seemed they would succeed."

"What possible use would Sky Power have to keep a monster like that alive? I mean, he's evil, right? Mucking around with souls and perversion and abomination. Are you trying to tell me that Sky Power is inherently evil?"

"It's not about good or evil. It's about balance, the eternal war between Sky and Underworld. Walking Smoke became a pawn in the game when he tried to open a portal to the Underworld, to free Piasa's soul into our world and allow it to devour his own. I took him to my master, sank Walking Smoke in the river for Piasa to destroy. The Thunderers took that opportunity to try to kill Piasa. Blasted the river with lightning. Piasa escaped, and the Thunderers saved Walking Smoke."

"So? What does that have to do with you?"

"Morning Star, Piasa, and I are in this together. Born into an unholy triangle. Morning Star is Sky Power living in Chunkey Boy's body. Because of that, Walking Smoke hates him. Enough so that eventually he *will* try and kill him again.

"Morning Star wants Walking Smoke dead. Piasa wants him destroyed because he's a threat to the Underworld. The Thunderers want him alive, committing atrocities, because doing so makes it even more important that I kill him."

Winder blinked, looking confused.

"Don't you see, Winder? He's bait to get me to Cofitachequi. Piasa devoured my souls, so we're linked. The Thunderers hope to get at Piasa through me. They're luring me to Cofitachequi so they can strike when he's vulnerable."

"That's . . ."

"Insane?" She laughed. "Welcome to my world."

"Pus in a bucket, Lady, why don't you run? Go back. If you can't find Fire Cat, I'll make you a place where—"

"You don't understand." She tapped the side of her head. "Piasa is in here, part of me. I *belong* to him. I can no more run away from him than you could run away from your arms, your testicles, or your liver."

"It seems that the Morning Star, if he really cared if you win or not, should have sent you with an army instead of all by yourself."

"He tried. Doesn't matter, it will still come down to just him and me. Face-to-face. And afterward, only one of us will walk away."

"But why you? Oh, I heard all that business about Power. Why you, personally?"

"Just as he is driven to murder the living god as a means of getting back at Chunkey Boy, he is obsessed with possessing me."

"By possessing . . . ?"

"Oh yes. In all the appallingly perverted and taboo ways you're thinking. But what he'd do to my body is nothing compared to what he'd do to my souls."

Sixty-nine

So this is what it meant to be a warrior. For the first time in his life, Blood Talon thought he finally understood. Since he was a boy, he had trained to learn the arts of war, the skills of battle, of tactics. He had survived the physical privations, wounds, and exigencies of life on battle walks, endured the endless training and the trials of soul-sapping boredom.

Now, for the first time in his life, he traveled with a true warrior. A man dedicated to a cause. Not just a unit, a leader, or a mission. Here was a warrior who had committed himself fully, without hesitation, to another human being.

Never in Blood Talon's life had he doubted he could match up to the challenge. He had been tested often enough in the past, pushed himself to be the best.

In all those instances he had known down in his core that he measured up. Now, glancing across the canoe, for the first time in his life, he wasn't sure.

Had it just been a physical challenge, a matter of endurance or will, he wouldn't have worried. But Fire Cat, from the beginning, had proven to be so much more. At times Blood Talon couldn't help but wonder if the man wasn't bigger than life.

Not only had Fire Cat rescued him from the torments of the locals who'd tied him in that accursed X, but he'd tended him. Never hinted that it wasn't more than just his duty to a fellow human being. Never used it to put Blood Talon in his place.

And then, back at Canyon Town, Blood Talon had been awed when Fire Cat innocently walked over to the chunkey court and began practicing.

"We need Trade," the Red Wing had said reasonably. "I can see only one way to get it that won't get us hanged in squares as thieves."

For two days, Blood Talon had watched Fire Cat play chunkey. The first day, Fire Cat won some and lost just as many. *This* was how the hero of Cahokia played chunkey? The mediocre games were always close. Won or lost by a point or two. And word passed. Additional players appeared, wanting to try their hand against the Trader. And again, Fire Cat won and lost, sometimes in circumstances that stretched Blood Talon's belief. The man *had* to be losing on purpose.

That night he had asked, "What were you thinking? That last cast was outside the bounds! A child could have won that match. *I* could have won that match."

"Of course you could," Fire Cat told him with a wink. "The goal isn't to win the match, it's to win us a canoe full of Trade."

"Well, I saw you lose half a canoe full of Trade on that last match. So, are you really the man who beat that Natchez and took his head to save the city?"

"Sometimes I wonder that myself," Fire Cat had mused before he rolled over to go to sleep.

The next morning, the crowd had grown. Yet more players brought their Trade and wagered it against the Red Wing Trader from up north.

And finally, in the late afternoon, Fire Cat had amassed enough wealth, learned his opponents, and in a final great match, played an epic game of chunkey, winning by two.

"I figured you could have won by ten," Blood Talon muttered. "And then you gave back fully *half* of what you won! We could have left here with *two* canoes full of Trade!"

"Think it through, warrior," Fire Cat had told him. "The people here think well of us. Those I beat in the game don't feel that they've been taken, tricked, or abused. We were given a marvelous feast afterward. And the canoe we Traded for, along with enough to hire six men to paddle it, is more than compensated for."

And the next day they had left at dawn, traveling mercilessly upriver.

Fire Cat was a driven man, never harsh but always firm, never angry but brooking no excuse, willing to drive himself even harder than he drove the men who worked for him.

And proceed they did. Past Hiawasee Island, ever northeast, up the broad valley of the Tenasee, to the fork of the Wide Fast, the main river that traveled east through the mountains to the divide that would take them to Cofitachequi.

Despite the time they'd lost on the lower river, they were gaining. As they passed the various Yuchi, Hiawasee, and Muskogean villages, they learned that Night Shadow Star and Winder were now only four days ahead of them.

That night they camped at the mouth of the canyon, in a mixed-ethnic village called The Flats for its level terrace above the river's flood stage. Here Fire Cat dismissed his paddlers and Traded his canoe to four strapping young men in return for their, and their pack dogs', services in making the trek along the riverside trails through the high mountains. Word was that there would be no canoe travel for days as the river carved its way through challenging terrain in a series of rapids, rough water, and cascades.

"From this point forward," Fire Cat told Blood Talon, "we're Traders. I'm even dickering for a staff, complete with white feathers."

"Traders? We're Cahokians, warriors. No, even more, you were a war chief, I was a squadron first. I can no more be a Trader than I can be a fish."

Fire Cat, firelight reflecting in his face, asked, "Have you learned so little, Blood Talon? If Power wanted you to remain a squadron first, would it have taken your warriors, lost you your weapons, and cast you alone on the river?"

He frowned, lines etching deeply into his forehead. "Do you find it so easy, Red Wing? Giving up who and what you are? Or are you so lost and without a heart and strong souls that you no longer know?"

Fire Cat had smiled wearily. "Just the opposite, Squadron First. I know who I am in ways I could never have comprehended back in Red Wing Town. It is you who is stumbling, blindly clinging to the man you used to be. Terrified to find out just who you really are."

Blood Talon's first response was anger, but somehow he stifled that. "What makes you think you know all this?"

"Because to fully find yourself, you must first completely lose yourself." The man arched an eyebrow in question. "The tricky part is, not everyone can survive the transition. Sometimes, Squadron First, the souls inside are just too fragile or too frightened to take the chance. If that's the case, you are condemned to fail. If you do fail, you will never completely recover but will be a half person, forever incomplete, for the rest of your life."

"You seem to know a lot for a slave." He hated the bitterness of his retort the moment he said it.

"How do you think I learned it in the first place? Now, get some sleep. Tomorrow, we're Traders."

As he rolled into his blanket beneath the ramada where they were staying, the thought kept echoing through Blood Talon's head: *What if I don't know how to be a Trader?*

Which wasn't nearly as frightening as the notion that he might ultimately be one of those fragile ones. The ones who broke and spent the rest of their lives incomplete.

Seventy

The scream of a cougar brought Night Shadow Star wide awake in her blankets. She'd heard it before on this trip, but at a distance, far back in the forest. That it was so close—her thought was that it had been at the foot of her bed—had her heart pounding in her throat, her every muscle tense.

She stared around the dark camp, seeing the porters and their dogs outlined by the glow of their fire not five paces from the one she and Winder shared. As the dogs barked their warnings, the porters, too, were sitting up, staring out at the inky forest that rose above their camp.

"She-cat," Winder told her from his blankets. "Probably with kittens. My guess? She was leading the young ones on a hunt. Some trick of the wind hid our scent until the last instant. That we were so close and so many, not to mention the smell of the fire and dogs, must have given her a real start."

"What do we do? How do we defend ourselves in the dark?"

"She's long gone, Lady."

"I didn't hear her leave. Remember those elk we spooked yesterday? You could hear them crash and bash all the way up the mountain."

"Those were elk, these are cougars. Nothing is as silent in the forest as a cougar. Well, maybe an owl. I've had them glide past my ear and not a sound. Nothing but silence."

"How do you know all this?"

"How do you not?"

At the other fire, the porters were talking and laughing, quieting their dogs and lying back down in their blankets, obviously relieved.

"I lived all my life in Cahokia." She felt like she was physically forcing her heart back down into her chest. "This whole trip has been a learning experience. The rivers, the forest, the camps and creatures. I almost got lost once back downriver where we camped at Maygrass Town. Went for a walk in the forest. Got turned around. Started to panic. And I remembered something one of the Traders said: 'Follow the water. It will always lead you to the river.'"

"Good advice."

"But I'll never forget that sense of panic, of being lost. Terrible feeling, suddenly having no idea where you are, which way to go. That you might lose everything, flounder about and starve alone."

"It is."

"What about you? You were raised in Cahokia. You came from the city. Where did you learn about cougars and owls?"

"That was part of becoming an 'influential' man. I was already rich, but being a big man? Depending upon which people you're living among out here that can mean a lot of things. For many it involves having some kind of skills in the forest. The forest, you see, is in their blood. Real men are hunters, warriors, people who can survive in the backcountry. Either I learned, or I would have been the subject of ridicule and derision."

She lay back in her blankets, listening to the crickets, heard the plaintive call of a nightjar. And in the far distance, high up the mountain, the eerie howl of a wolf carried over the rushing sounds of the river down below them.

I am, once again, becoming someone else.

Did it never stop? Was the woman called Night Shadow Star as shifting and impermanent as a sandbar on the river? Here one season, then washed away and re-formed somewhere else downstream in the river of life.

"How many peoples have you lived with?"

"A great many," he told her.

"How many women do you have?"

"A great many."

She laughed at that. "And you would still add me to your list?"

"Faster than a heartbeat."

"You're more of a scoundrel than Seven Skull Shield."

"Less, actually. The difference between us is that I try to keep mine."

"It would never work."

"Because you're a lady and I was an orphan? You never know. I might have been one of Black Tail's sons, stolen from birth by Spirit Raven to grow up as an orphan in the city, only to become a wealthy Trader who would be there for you to fall in love with. The ending of the story is that together we remake the world and unite Power. Or at least, that's how it will be told on down through the ages."

"Nice try."

"Stories have to begin somewhere. Come, slip over here to my blankets. It's a cool night, let me share my warmth. Two people, alone like this on a long journey, it might just be comfort, or perhaps, if we give it a try, we really can spin that magical story."

"Just like that?"

"It's only coupling, Lady. A man and a woman doing what men and women have done from the Beginning Times. And, just because we share moments of pleasure and delight, I'll make no claim on you."

"Indeed. Just a passing comfort?"

"A moment for the souls to enjoy the reassuring sensation of another caring body against yours. Just a hard shaft and a willing sheath. That burst of delight down in your hips, and then the security of being held close, warm, and safe."

"And if you plant a child?"

"I assume you know your body well enough to know when a man's seed might take root. I have no problem avoiding that quarter moon when your loins are fertile. Nor am I squeamish, given that you neglected to inform us of your flux a couple of days ago. By the way, that was admirably done. The porters hadn't a clue. Must have been a light discharge."

"Seems that way ever since I've been working as hard as I have paddling and packing. But that's beside the point. It really wouldn't work."

"How so?"

"Even if Fire Cat wasn't the one I will love forever, you're not the kind of man who can spend the rest of his life balancing precariously on the edge of darkness. You're the type who plots and plans for the future—the kind of future that's filled with smiles and hearty slaps on the back for a job well done. You see good times ahead, feasts, laughing, and frolicking with your women. Being honored and adored. Being—how did you put it? 'A big man.'"

"Is that so impossible for you?"

"No. But it is for Piasa and Power." She smiled wearily. "Your future is festive. Mine is tortured and dark. Suppose Fire Cat and I survive my confrontation with Walking Smoke, it will just be the beginning of another trial. Eventually, Piasa is going to pull me under for the last time. When he does, you don't want to be around."

"Maybe there's a way you can change that. Maybe I could change it for you."

She shifted in her blankets. "Don't even try. I mean it. Get that notion out of your head. I don't want to be the one to go back and tell Seven Skull Shield, 'I'm sorry, but when we were in Cofitachequi, I got your best friend killed.'"

"Bah, I'm hard to kill."

"Not when it comes to Walking Smoke. The last time he and I faced each other, he didn't understand who I'd become. This time he does, and you can bet he's planned for it."

Seventy-one

The knock came in the middle of the night. Insistent tapping at Wooden Doll's door.

Seven Skull Shield came immediately awake. Beside him, Wooden Doll shifted beneath the blankets, calling, "Dawn? See who that is."

"Yes, Lady."

". . . And tell them it's the middle of the night. I'll see them in the morning."

"Yes, Lady."

Seven Skull Shield rubbed his eyes and stared up at the dark roof overhead. Charred with soot as it was, it might have been an eternal blackness. Fact was, he'd been cursed lucky to get out of Spotted Wrist's cage with both of his eyes intact.

He wiggled onto his side, enduring the painful stitch from his barely healed ribs. Pus and blood, it took forever for ribs to heal. His deeper cuts and burns had barely started to mend.

Truth be told? He should have been on his feet days ago. He suspected that Wooden Doll knew it. Knew for a fact that Dawn did. He could see it in the Chickosi girl's suspicious dark eyes.

Didn't matter that he'd saved her, brought her here. If the young woman ever trusted a man again, it would take years, and most definitely the right kind of man.

He elevated his head enough to see her waddle to the door and ask, "Who comes?"

"Open the door. I need to see Wooden Doll and her, um, rich Trader. Now! It's an emergency. Tell them it's the little man."

Dawn turned, head cocked quizzically. "You know any little man?"

"Let him in," Skull said, feeling his hide pull as he sat up.

Dawn unlatched the door, lifting it to the side, peering out into the night and almost missing the dwarf who slipped in below her line of sight.

"Flat Stone Pipe," Seven Skull Shield greeted.

Wooden Doll forced herself upright, clawing back the thick tangle of her hair and turning her eyes on the dwarf.

"Sorry, but there's no time," Flat Stone Pipe said as he strolled over to the fire in his rollicking round-legged gait. "Spotted Wrist is calling up his squadrons. Quietly. Not even Rising Flame knows. He says it's for drills. But he's replaced several of his commanders with new people. His people. Cousins from North Star House. They've been meeting in his palace for the past two days. My call? They're moving on us."

"You sent word to Columella?" Seven Skull Shield asked.

Figuring this was more than a quick call, Dawn tossed wood onto the fire from the pile near the door. Flames began to lick at the pieces.

"Does the sun rise in the east? Of course my lady knows. If Spotted Wrist tries to cross the river, he'll be in for a surprise."

"Thanks for the warning, I'll—"

"If he's willing to move on Evening Star House, he's willing to move on Morning Star House as well. That's Blue Heron and Wind. Maybe he's doing it with Rising Flame's approval, or he's figuring that with Horned Serpent House in his pocket, and War Duck and Round Pot . . . What are you doing?"

Seven Skull Shield threw off the covers, sliding his legs around Wooden Doll.

"Skull? You're still hurt. What do you think—"

"I've got to get Blue Heron out."

Wooden Doll protested, "She's been playing this game since before you were born."

"Yeah, well, she's not as tough as she thinks she is."

"Neither are you," Wooden Doll snapped as she stepped up to stop him from yanking his breechcloth over his hips. "You're barely out of Spotted Wrist's cage, and you're headed right back to it? He won't leave you to linger if he catches you again. You understand that, don't you? You will die. Fast and hard."

Seven Skull Shield smiled into her eyes. "He has to catch me first."

He watched her facial muscles work as she sought to control her expression. Her voice dropped. "Don't. Please. Stay here. With me."

"She's my friend."

"So help me, if you leave here, don't come back."

He bent close, ran a finger down the gentle curve of her cheek, saw the panic in her eyes. "You know I love you. See you when I'm sure Blue Heron's safe."

He left her standing, looking desolate.

Dawn was giving him the same kind of look she'd give a lunatic, and Flat Stone Pipe had a wizened expression on his face, as if he'd known all along how this would turn out.

"Spit and piss," Seven Skull Shield muttered as he stepped out into the hot and muggy night. "Where's Farts when I need him?"

But as he wound his way through the dark workshops and warehouses to reach the Avenue of the Sun, it hit him that maybe Farts was the smarter of the two of them. Maybe the big brindle dog had found a new home, one where he was fed, played with by children, and could live to a great old age.

At least he hoped so, because Seven Skull Shield was rapidly coming to the conclusion that he had just walked away from the woman he longed for . . . and was headed toward a short and nasty end.

Seventy-two

The man's name was Splinter Branch. He had arrived in the middle of the night, just the latest in a constant stream of Blue Heron's spies. She had been getting reports for the last two days. Stories of runners arriving at all hours of the day as they shuttled between Spotted Wrist or Slender Fox's palaces, of their being secluded in private meetings in Horned Serpent House.

That something was being brokered between North Star House and Horned Serpent House was evident. An example of the rapidly shifting alliances given that the two Houses had been exchanging the vilest of insults and on the verge of war barely nine moons past.

Not all the messengers were streaming between the north and south. Others were beating feet from Spotted Wrist's palace to a Council House in River Mounds City. There, Blue Heron's spies reported, they were meeting with Three Fingers, Broken Stone, and Waving Reed. And from the Council House, so the spies reported, other runners were slipping back and forth among allied relatives who opposed War Duck and Round Pot, and most saliently, among the prominent Earth Clans chiefs under River House's governance.

In the midst of all this had come news that Spotted Wrist had removed some of his squadron firsts and seconds, replacing them with either trusted subordinates or, worse, relatives.

And for what possible reason would the Hero of the North be

reorganizing his veteran squadrons, helping North Star House to broker alliances, and talking to rebels in River House?

She'd been brooding on that through most of the night, unable to sleep, when Big Right, one of her guards, had answered a call at her door.

She was up and dressed, almost muzzy-headed from fatigue, as Splinter Branch was ushered into her great room. Blue Heron herself threw a couple faggots of wood onto the coals, watched them bloom into flame, and settled herself on her dais to ask, "What news?"

Splinter Branch bent low, touching his forehead to her mat, then straightened. "I thought you should know, Lady. Just at dusk most of a squadron moved out of Serpent Woman Town. It's like all those warriors just appeared out of nowhere. No one saw them assemble. They came marching into Serpent Woman Town a couple of hands of time before sunset. Ate a big meal that Slender Fox had had prepared in the Men's House, and then marched out again. They were on the river trail, headed south. My guess would be that they'll be in River Mounds City by morning."

At that she'd straightened, seeing it all in her mind.

"What do you think?" Smooth Pebble asked, having risen from her bed.

"You can bet that's not the only squadron on the move," Dancing Sky said from where she'd sat up in her blankets. "The change in command structure? The secret call-up of the squadrons? This is Spotted Wrist. He learned his lesson in the north when he surprised Red Wing Town. This is all about surprise."

Blue Heron closed her eyes, felt that sick sensation in her gut. "He's going to take River Mounds City," she said. "Depose War Duck and Round Pot. With Three Fingers either controlling Broken Stone or taking the high chair himself, River House will back him in a move against Columella. There's old animosity between River House and Evening Star House. Spotted Wrist and Three Fingers? It's a natural fit."

"What can you do about it?" Smooth Pebble asked. "Alert Morning Star? Get him to intervene?"

She rubbed her face, trying to sort it through. "Might be too late. And there's no telling where Rising Flame is in all this. Spotted Wrist is her chosen. Wouldn't put it past her that she's egging the Keeper on, hoping to remake Cahokia in her image."

Dancing Sky added, "If the squadron left Serpent Woman Town at sunset, they're making a night march. Along the river, that's tough travel given the swamps, the marshes."

"They're moving along the levee. It will be slow going, especially in the dark," Blue Heron agreed. "There still might be time. Splinter Branch, I know you're tired. I need you to get word to War Duck and Round Pot. Fast. I'd hire you a litter, but it's the middle of the night. You'll have to run. Can you do that?"

"Yes, Keeper!" The young man stood, a grim set to his wide mouth. He tapped a fist to his forehead and turned, headed for the door.

"Wait." Blue Heron reached down and plucked up her staff of office. "You'll need this. It will get you right in to War Duck and Round Pot. Tell them what you just told me. Then tell them I think their lives are on the line. That I don't think it would be beyond Three Fingers and Spotted Wrist to have them and their supporters murdered on the spot."

"Yes, Keeper!" Splinter Branch took the staff of office, a look of wonder in his eyes as if the thing were a magical talisman.

Blue Heron watched him disappear through the door and into the night.

"So much for sleep," Smooth Pebble announced as she crossed to the fire. From a basket she took a handful of toasted yaupon and tossed it into a pot of water. This she placed on the now-snapping flames. "It'll take a hand of time to boil."

"Made it a bit strong, don't you think?" Blue Heron muttered, rubbing the meaty part of her palm into her weary eyes.

"I think you're going to need all your wits, Lady."

"White Rain? I need you to get dressed, take word of this to Wind. The sooner she knows, the better prepared she'll be. Soft Moon?"

"Yes, Lady?" The young woman was already dressing.

"Go find my porters. Have them carry you to Evening Star Town. Alert Columella."

"Yes, Lady."

"Dancing Sky?"

"Lady?"

"Grab a cloak, I'm counting on you to get word to Five Fists. Tell him that Spotted Wrist is moving his army. I doubt Spotted Wrist would move on the living god, but Five Fists needs to be ready for any eventuality."

Dancing Sky took no longer than needed, an amused look on her face as she prepared. At the door she turned, looking back. "So, Old Enemy, it has come to this?"

With that she inclined her head and touched her forehead, then vanished into the darkness.

Blue Heron considered the woman's departure, surprised by the irony of it. How odd that Cahokia's fate once again rested in the hands of the Red Wing heretics. Once her most despised of enemies, those women—who still considered Morning Star a hoax—were now off to serve the best interests of the city. She tried to recall the exact moment when she had won their loyalty.

Couldn't.

"What next?" Smooth Pebble asked as she bustled about the fire, tossing cornmeal, squash blossoms, mint, and dried cubes of venison into the stewpot. The black drink was boiling now, starting to foam, the rich scent filling the room.

"It will all hinge on how Wind reacts. She's the *tonka'tzi*. I need to be there, to back her up. She'll need to coordinate with Five Fists, decide whether to take it straight to Morning Star, or whether to call up the Morning Star squadron. If she does that, it puts her in direct conflict with Rising Flame. In essence, she's overriding the clan matron's authority."

"That would be a bitter and burning stone for the clan matron to swallow."

"If Wind does call up the Morning Star squadron, and if she can sustain the authority to do so over Rising Flame's objection, what does she do with them? It's one thing to order War Claw to maintain order and security around the great mound, another if she asks them to march on Spotted Wrist's squadrons. One is a police action, the other is civil war."

"Morning Star *has* to intervene."

"Does he?"

"If he doesn't, what's he going to do? Just sit up there atop his high mound and watch the city burn itself down to ashes?"

Blue Heron pulled at the wattle under her chin. "He might. Morning Star always plays a deep game. Layers within layers. And lest we forget, he's a Spirit Being. A living god. What's important to us mere humans, to the Houses, the Earth Clans, and the dirt farmers, isn't always what's important to him. For all I know, he's seeing some mystical future where Cahokia no longer fulfills his or Power's purpose."

She paused. "And if that's the case, well, who knows?"

Where she stirred the pot, the berdache frowned. "He's acted before. When Walking Smoke was wreaking havoc, when his souls returned from the Underworld."

"Those times it was about Power. And don't forget, he let the Itza run roughshod over the city when Horn Lance brought that despicable Thirteen Sacred Jaguar and his warriors here to unleash chaos." She pointed a hard finger. "*Don't* ever try and second-guess the living god. His priorities are usually different than ours. Pus in a bucket, he was actually *looking forward* to being dead when that Chickosi girl poisoned him."

The sound of something thumping out on the veranda distracted her from her dire thoughts. By Piasa's swinging balls, what was Big Right doing out there? Dancing?

"There's got to be a way out of this. It's probably right under my nose."

Smooth Pebble handed her a cup of the stew. "Here, eat this. Food helps you think."

As Blue Heron used her horn to spoon the hot stew from her bowl, she said, "You'd think that Spotted Wrist would have learned his lesson that night at the *tonka'tzi*'s. Columella and I completely outflanked him. Even Rising Flame was taken by surprise. Doesn't the man ever learn? She *ordered* him to make peace. And here he's moving a squadron on River House?"

"So, what happens if he succeeds?" Smooth Pebble asked. "Backed by his warriors, Three Fingers deposes War Duck and Round Pot. Maybe he puts Broken Stone on the dais, maybe he caves his head in and takes the high chair for his own. Let's say that they consolidate Three Fingers' authority, and he calls up the River House squadrons. All the Earth Clans supply their warriors. Then what? Does he think he can march on Evening Star Town? Columella will have her squadrons watching and waiting on the other side of the river. Not to mention the dwarf's spy network keeping tabs. Any element of surprise is gone."

"That means . . ." Blue Heron glanced up at the movement at her door. Two warriors stood there, dressed in battle armor, bows strung and hanging over their backs, war clubs protruding from behind the shields they held.

A terrible sense of foreboding ran through her as she asked, "Who are you?"

"New security, Lady," the first said. He might have been in his forties, Deer Clan tattoos on his cheeks. "Compliments of the Hero of the North, we're here to ensure your safety."

Blue Heron's heart stuttered in her chest, her stomach going tight. She set her bowl to the side and stood. "The last thing I need is Spotted Wrist's protection. Where's Big Right?"

"I think he's taking a nap." The warrior gestured with his war club. "Now, we're going to close the door, make sure that no one else bothers you tonight. So, you be a good lady, eat your stew there, and get a good night's rest, yes?"

She gaped as they pulled her plank door closed.

"Lady?" Smooth Pebble asked, rising to stand by Blue Heron's side. "They can't do this!"

That sensation of falling kept expanding through her gut. "I think they just did."

"This is . . . is *unthinkable*! You're Red Warrior Mankiller's daughter! Descended from Black Tail! Sister to the *tonka'tzi*!"

Blue Heron staggered back, sank onto her dais, blinking in disbelief. "He must think that doesn't matter anymore. And that means he's moving on the Morning Star House as well as River House. The stupid fool! Doesn't he understand that this will split the city in two? He's gone too far. There's nothing left now. Wind, Five Fists, Columella, and I have to fight. We have no choice."

"You're locked in here," Smooth Pebble reminded. "Held prisoner by his warriors."

"I'm not the thief. He can't take me prisoner. Not for long. I'm too high in the . . ."

She and Smooth Pebble stared at the door, hearing the sound of something liquid splashing against the planks.

"Someone empty a chamber pot?" Blue Heron muttered. "Do they seriously think that I'm going to worry about a little insult when I'm faced with the potential destruction of the city?"

Smooth Pebble crossed to the door. Fingered some of the liquid that seeped through the cracks in the planks. "Hickory oil."

She tried the door, finding it tied off and blocked from outside. "Hey! Open this!"

The warrior outside called back, "We learned this from you. Remember how you got us away from the Keeper's so you could get what was left of that thief?"

"What's he talking about?" Smooth Pebble asked, still pushing with all her might against the door.

"Piss in a pot!" Blue Heron cried, leaping to her feet and racing to the door. "You open this! That's an order. I'm *Lady* Blue Heron. Daughter of—"

"We know," came the harsh answer. "Too bad it's the middle of the night. Wonder how long it will take before someone notices? Huh, too bad. Maybe if you lived in a place with fewer society houses and more neighbors, you'd have a chance of being heard, but yell all you like."

Pushing on the door, she found it tightly secured. Didn't matter that she and Smooth Pebble both were straining as hard as they could. However the warriors had secured them, the planks didn't budge.

She heard the crackle of the flames heartbeats before she smelled the first of the smoke.

"Too bad there's no way out the back," the warrior called. "But we checked that day we ransacked your house. One way in, one way out." A pause. "Oh, my. The thatch on your roof just caught fire. I wonder how that happened?"

Blue Heron stepped back, staring up. She could hear the characteristic sound of fire in thatch, had heard it too often before. The first wisps of smoke worked their way through the bundles over the door.

"Let us out!" Smooth Pebble bellowed, pounding on the planks.

Above the flames, all Blue Heron could hear was the combined laughter of the watching warriors.

Seventy-three

Herosihachi—in Muskogean, it meant Beautiful River. It flowed into the Wide Fast from the north, following a long valley hemmed by the Blue Mountains on the west and a rounded line of thickly forested hills on the east. While some of the Herosihachi's course was navigable, enough shallows, shoals, and fast water made the long-distance travel by canoe unfeasible.

"We're better off to walk," Winder had said, gesturing to the remaining porters and their big-boned pack dogs.

Night Shadow Star had always been athletic. First there was her passion for stickball. As a girl she'd spent her life running, wrestling, shooting bows, throwing stones, and even—to the horror of her parents and clan—playing the occasional men's game of chunkey.

After all these moons of paddling, packing, hiking, and hard work, her body was solid with muscle, thews like rock. Now she stepped out on the trail, the final one. This was the route east, the ancient trail followed by Traders, war parties, and people moving across the divide that separated the interior from the plain leading down to the eastern ocean. A couple of days of travel and she could cross through that gap, follow the headwaters down to Joara, the westernmost town in the Cofitachequi colony. There, she would, hopefully, hear word of her brother's whereabouts.

And then it's only a matter of running him down.

The question was: Did he have any idea how close she was?

Or would Power warn him?

She was, after all, the hunter. The moment to strike was hers to decide.

At her request, Winder had said nothing about the Lightning Shell witch in the towns and villages they had passed through on the Wide Fast, and now on the Herosihachi.

But as they'd traveled, they'd heard plenty. It had started with the occasional mention of a witch in Joara. As they'd progressed, the assertions became more frequent, more dire. In the beginning the Lightning Shell witch had been referenced with an amused awe that had given way to more serious assertions, and by the time they'd left Cane Town at the confluence of the Herosihachi and the Wide Fast, the name was barely whispered, its utterance accompanied by averted eyes and warding signs made by nervous fingers.

"Makes you suspect that we're getting close, doesn't it?" Winder had asked.

It did. Night Shadow Star could feel it. As she looked east up the valley toward the low hills that formed the gap, she sensed her brother. Like a dark and threatening cloud that hung just past those innocent-looking slopes.

They followed a path along the south bank, there being fewer, and smaller, creeks for the trail to ford. The way was forested, the trail meandering around the great hickory, oak, sweet gum, and maple trees. She had grown used to the forest, feeling at home, almost embraced by its shadowy depths, by the chatter of the squirrels, the trilling of the hundreds of birds in the canopy above.

And her feet were quicker, used to picking their way where webs of roots twisted their way across the beaten path. The musty smell of the leaf mat was now a familiar perfume, a comforting pungency.

Her pack on her back, she was following the porters and their dogs, only slightly aware as a bachelor flock of turkeys called to one another somewhere just out of sight on the slope to her right.

At the front, the lead pack dog, called Hawk, slowed. His ears were pricked forward, a low growl sounding in his chest. The other dogs followed suit.

"Someone comes," the lead Chalakee called back in soft pidgin. Then he said something to the dogs. They immediately quieted.

Night Shadow Star craned her head. "We're Traders, right?"

Winder, following behind, said, "They should recognize the Power of Trade. We're on the main trail. But it wouldn't hurt to have that war club you keep hidden in your pack handy. Don't brandish it but have it available."

"We are deep in the forest. Unlike the river, there's no one to see."

"That's why you keep that club within reach." He paused, stepping up beside her as the Chalakee stopped short, shifting their own packs, untying weapons. "I assume you know how to use it?"

"Odd that you should ask. The last time I used it was in a fight against Walking Smoke's Tula warriors. Haft got burned up. I had to have it rebuilt after I recovered the pieces from what was left of Columella's palace."

"Good," Winder muttered, pulling his hafted stone ax from his pack and slipping the thong onto his belt. "Me? I'm not much for clubs and such. I'm a lot happier in a knock-down brawl. You know, eye gouging, kicking them in the stones, whacking them in the head with a rock, that sort of thing."

"You and Seven Skull Shield."

"Better than brothers."

The first of the people appeared out from behind the trees. Within heartbeats he was followed by others.

Night Shadow Star took a breath, her heart slowing from its worried beat.

The man in the lead bore a heavy pack; the wooden poles protruding above his head were tool handles, not weapons. Probably hoes and the like.

Behind him came two women, each bent under a tumpline that ran back to heavy packs balanced on their hips. Then children appeared, one after another until seven, ranging in age from ten or eleven on down. In the end came an old gray-haired woman, and finally a young woman with a cradleboard-bound infant on her back.

The man—hardly a model of forest acumen—finally looked up from the trail, his eyes going wide.

In Cahokian, he cried, "Wait! We're friendly. Don't shoot."

Winder stepped forward, his pack at a jaunty angle. "Do you notice any drawn bows? We're Traders. Headed to Cofitachequi. Notice the dogs? The packs?"

The man grinned sheepishly, looked back at the women and children who'd come to a stop and crowded around him. They were taking Winder, the Chalakee, the dogs, and finally Night Shadow Star's measure.

"Me? I mean, us? We're just farmers. We're no threat."

"Where are you headed?" Winder asked.

"Away. Anywhere." He shot a thumb over his shoulder at the young woman with the infant. "That's Pretty Root. My third wife. She's Muskogee. From down at Cane Town. I'm going to go see if her family will take us in. Married-into kin, you see."

Night Shadow Star stepped forward. "Bit late in the year for farmers to be leaving their fields, isn't it? You're just a couple of moons from harvest."

"He can have it," the man muttered.

"Who?"

He pursed his lips, seemed to be thinking it through. "The witch."

"The Lightning Shell witch?" Winder asked casually.

"Don't use that name!" one of the women, maybe in her midthirties, cried. "You'll call him. Bring bad luck down on your heads."

"You're leaving because of a witch?" Winder said. More of a statement than question.

"You don't know," the farmer said, becoming more agitated. "Most of Joara has fled. We didn't want to. Like you said, the fields are full. It's a remarkable harvest coming: corn, beans, squash, maygrass, goosefoot. Then he took Cattail Down's daughters. Stole them in the night from their bed." He indicated the second woman. "She's my brother's wife. Was. The girls were my nieces. The witch, he did . . . did . . ."

The farmer swallowed hard, looked away. Face averted, he said, "My brother went to kill him. In the middle of the night. He . . ."

"Go ahead," Night Shadow Star urged.

The man took three tries before he said, "The witch hung his skin on a frame out in front of his house. Now, excuse us. We're leaving. We're not a threat. Just farmers."

"You don't want to go there," Cattail Down told them in broken Cahokian as she passed. "Turn back. Leave Joara to the witch. There's nothing but trouble back there. And Death. And . . . and terror."

Night Shadow Star stood by Winder's side as the farmers shuffled past, their feet rustling on the leaf mat.

They never looked back, just kept plodding down the trail.

"Left the brother's skin hanging on a frame?" Winder wondered.

"Sounds like Walking Smoke."

"Nice fellow, this brother of yours."

"You don't know the half of it."

Winder rubbed the back of his neck before refastening his pack. "Well, at least we know where he is. Joara."

"And people with a bumper crop in the field are leaving it all behind. Good. Means there are fewer people to get in my way."

Winder was giving her that now familiar I'm-really-concerned-about-you look. "You sure you want to go through with this?"

"This is why you don't want anything to do with me. I told you I was headed toward a dark fate."

His voice was filled with unease as he reshouldered his pack. "I guess I'll take my chances."

"Get me to Joara. Then you leave. I told you, I don't want to have to tell Seven Skull Shield that I got you killed. Especially by Walking Smoke. It would hurt something deep in the thief's soul if your skin was hung on a frame."

"I'll keep that in mind."

"Good. How far to Joara?"

"Maybe three days."

"Let's get about it, then." And as they started up the trail again, she mused, "Hung his skin on a frame? Wonder what my charming brother did with the rest of the poor man?"

But she thought she knew.

Seventy-four

"War Leader?" The words brought Five Fists to full wakefulness. He opened his eyes to the faint glow of the eternal fire; it illuminated the high ceiling of Morning Star's palace with its reddish glow.

He sat up in his bed, feeling Foxweed stir beside him. The Panther Clan woman—perhaps to the surprise of both of them—had been in Five Fists' bed now for more than a year. As if, different though they might be, some long-hidden parts of their souls had fit together.

"War Claw?" Five Fists placed the dimly lit shape standing at attention. He tossed the blankets to the side, swinging his legs out of bed. "What's wrong?"

He kept his voice low so as not to disturb the others who slept on the ornate benches surrounding the walls.

"Warriors are moving in the Great Plaza, War Leader. Small squads. The guards at the bottom of the Great Staircase just sent me word. I came straight here. What do you want to do?"

"Call up the Morning Star squadron? No, I need more information. Who they are? What are they doing? Could just be one of the Earth Clans running a training drill they forgot to tell us about." Five Fists rubbed his face, feeling his crooked jaw. "That's all you know? Just small squads of warriors?"

"That's all the guards reported, they . . ."

The palace door was set aside, one of the guards from the Morning Star Gate hurrying into the great room. He came straight for Five Fists' bed, tapping his chin in salute. "War Leader? There's a fire. Lady Blue Heron's palace."

"What?" War Claw cried.

"Let's go look," Five Fists growled. To the guard, he said, "I want you back on the gate. Something rotten is afoot."

Pulling his breechcloth on and grabbing up his old war ax, Five Fists got to his feet. He hated the feeling of stiffness from old bones and injuries. War Claw close on his heels, he hurried out the double doors and into the palace courtyard.

The night was warm and humid, the sky washed with patterns of stars. Picking his way past some of the litters, he hurried to the southwest bastion, quickly climbing the ladder. Poking his head through the access hole, he stopped short.

"Lord? Is that . . ." Yes. He knew Morning Star's silhouette where it blotted the stars. "Excuse me, Lord. Something's—"

"Tell War Claw to have the Morning Star squadron stand down."

"Yes, Lord." Bending his head to peer down the ladder, he asked, "You heard?"

"Yes, War Leader." War Claw banged out a formal salute. "Any other instructions?"

"Tell your warriors that I don't want them starting trouble. They are not to interfere," Morning Star's voice called down. "Tell them to be patient, and to follow orders."

"Yes, Lord!" War Claw called, bowing his head low and touching his forehead respectfully. Then he whirled, leaving for the gate at a run.

Five Fists hesitated. "Lord? A guard reports that Lady Blue Heron's—"

"Step up here, War Leader. We must talk."

Five Fists, warily, climbed the rest of the way up into the bastion. His heart hammered as he stared down at Blue Heron's palace, the roof a fountain of flame. He could see warriors, in battle armor, standing in a semicircle at the foot of the old Keeper's stairs.

"We should get someone down there to see—"

"Too late," Morning Star said softly, his face given a reddish cast by the burning palace. "Events will unfold as they must."

"Lord?"

Morning Star turned, his attention to the distant southeast as if he could see beyond the horizon. "When Power employs a human, it is always a gamble. Will they succeed, or fail? Most are never strong enough to win. And, ultimately, they are so fragile. Death being what it is, humans are at best a short-term and unreliable resource."

Five Fists experienced an unusual churning in his stomach as he cast another glance at the burning palace below. "Lord, those warriors down at Blue Heron's aren't even trying to help. They're just standing there, more like they're ensuring the place burns along with anyone inside."

"Power is shifting. The game—if you will—is about to change. Some players sacrificed, new ones added to the play. Everything is about to be different."

"Lord?"

"Your job in the coming days, War Leader, is to follow my orders without question. Nothing more, nothing less."

"Yes, Lord. But what if these warriors try and take the palace? You could be in great—"

"All of existence, Cahokia itself, is a gamble. The gaming pieces are cast. Let them fall where they will." Morning Star's eyes remained focused on the southeast. "One could almost pity them, you know. It's not going to work out like any of them anticipate."

"Who, Lord? You mean Lady Night Shadow Star and her party? The expedition?"

"I mean for any of them," Morning Star said with a curious resignation, as if awaiting some—

The flash of light burned out of the southeastern night, brilliant to the point of blinding. Trailing yellow-green fire, it streaked across the sky like a bizarre flaming arrow as it hurtled toward Cahokia.

Five Fists experienced that old queasiness that came at the launch of an enemy attack. Almost ducked out of instinct, and watched the light flicker out as it passed directly overhead.

"So, it begins," Morning Star whispered. "I'm so sorry."

Five Fists stared down at the fire consuming Blue Heron's palace, wondered at the distress in his gut, disturbed that she was burning alive in there.

Warriors on the move, orders to stand down, Blue Heron's palace burning, the meteor streaking the skies—he placed a hand to his suddenly sick stomach.

"Lord, can't you give me something to hope for?"

Morning Star continued to gaze off toward the southeast as he said, "Chaos and death."

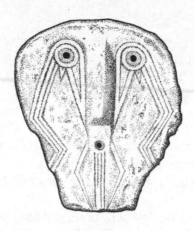

Final Steps

The Casqui is back. I have just listened to his story. Of how he carefully abducted Night Shadow Star from Canyon Town. Was pushing out onto the river in his canoe when he was attacked at the last minute by a band of heavily armed warriors.

How he struggled to get away, clamping his hand over Night Shadow Star's mouth. How he couldn't fight off the last of the attackers, while his "war hand" was on her mouth.

So, he tells me, he has hurried upriver, waited at Cane Town, and upon the arrival of Night Shadow Star's imposing party, has hastened here to warn me. Hopes that in some small way, that will entice me to reward him.

Oh, staggering joy.

I yawn.

Instead of beating his head in on the spot, I smile, telling him, "These things happen."

And oh yes, I will "reward" him. One should always get due compensation for being an idiot.

And knowing she was in Cane Town? That tells me which direction she is coming from.

I knew it had to be through Joara. The only question was which trail she would arrive on. West or north?

West it is.

I glance around my little "palace," see it for what it is: a Clan House filled with shrines I have built from people's bones, the Power designs I have painted on the walls with their blood. My sleeping bench in the back.

Nothing here to save.

And it will serve its purpose.

Night Shadow Star will have heard of it. People talk. And I am thrilled down to my bones to be one of their most-discussed topics. My doings passing from lip to lip. She expects to find me here. At the center of my Power. In my lair.

If all my other measures fail, she will come to this final place, step through that door.

If all my other measures fail.

Time to go see Fire Light. Tell him that the wait is over. Now he will have to step up. Earn his way back to Cahokia. Not that he has much to do. Just lend me some of his warriors.

Traps must have layers within layers. Snap. Snap. Snap.

So, if one doesn't work and seems to have been avoided, the next is ready to be sprung.

She must be led to think she's winning.

And, who knows? Perhaps Fire Light's warriors will ambush her party on the trail, kill her protector, and bring her to me all trussed up, ready for our Blessed reunion?

Seventy-five

Cane Town stood on the Wide Fast's south bank, a collection of bent-pole dwellings around a square with its *Tchkofa*. Behind the town, the forest rose like a majestic wall to roll up the sides of the hills like a lumpy green blanket. From the open ground in town, Fire Cat could see west toward the bulk of the mountains, great heaves of rock and soil that rose in successive waves, each bluer and fainter as they receded into the distance.

He had ceased to be amazed that the surface of the world could be mounded so high, or that there seemingly was no end to it.

"Thoughts?" Blood Talon asked, stepping up beside him.

Fire Cat smiled wearily. "Just thinking about what a fool I've been."

"How's that, War Leader?"

"War leader?"

"I think it's time I address you as such. Especially since I haven't seen you act like much of a fool since you pulled me off that scaffold back downriver. So, what exactly do you refer to?"

Fire Cat gestured toward the distant mountains, and then at the world around them. "As a young man I considered Red Wing Town the center of the world. Then the world expanded to Cahokia, which humbled me. Surely that was all the people in the world. And now I have traveled this far, past the Blue Mountains, and still the world continues. I was arrogant in my knowledge of my place and my city's place at the center of things.

Now, considering the vastness, I understand just how insignificant I really am."

Blood Talon squinted up at the high peaks, nodded. "I think we both have learned. I have Traded for dried corn, pawpaws, and mulberries. I also found a fisherman down at the canoe landing who will carry us across the river to the Herosihachi trail that will take us to the divide."

"Even better than that," Fire Cat told him, "I talked with a family of farmers who just arrived from Joara. My lady and Winder are just over a day ahead of us. Now, let's go find your fisherman. It might be a hard run, and we might have to eat those supplies of yours cold, but I think we can catch them before they reach the divide."

Blood Talon tapped his chin in salute. "Then let's be about it. It will be my chance to show you just how far and fast a Snapping Turtle Clan squadron first can run."

Fire Cat grinned. Gave him a slap on the back. "Faster and farther than a fat, lazy Red Wing, no doubt. But, Blood Talon. Once we catch up with Night Shadow Star and discover where Walking Smoke is, I don't want you involved. You've heard the stories about the Lightning Shell witch? It's him. I know it."

"I owe you my life." Blood Talon looked down at his tanned, callused hands. "Even more so since I destroyed so much of yours. What do I care about some witch?"

"Look at me. Yes, right in the eyes. You still don't understand about the Power—that this is Piasa against the Thunderers. Sky Power opposed to Underworld Power. Something terrible is going to happen when Night Shadow Star faces Walking Smoke. Last time she almost died."

"Doesn't matter, I'll be at your side and—"

"Whoever goes into that final confrontation, they're not coming out of it alive."

Blood Talon shifted, stubbornly scuffed his foot on the hard-packed soil. "The way you put it? Sounds like the kind of fight a true warrior was born for. Maintaining the balance of Power? Me, I'm born of Snapping Turtle Clan, we're earth people. This Lightning Shell witch we've been hearing about? A warrior could find no better death than helping to end such a thing."

Blood Talon extended his arm in the direction of the canoe landing. "Lead forth. Let's go catch the lady and kill the witch."

"You do my lady and me honor."

"Funny you'd say that. Most everything I've learned of honor, it seems, I've learned from you."

Fire Cat kept his expression blank, turned on his heel, and led the way to the canoe landing.

In his head he kept seeing the inside of Columella's palace that day Night Shadow Star had interrupted Walking Smoke's abominable ceremony. The severed body parts, arms, legs, torsos, arranged in such a precise pattern on the blood-soaked matting.

My friend, you don't know the depths of his depravity. Or how cunning and clever he is.

Seventy-six

Fire roared up the angle of the roof, consuming the thatch, dropping sparks and bits of burning grass that landed on the sleeping benches. There, within moments, they set fire to the blankets, the folded fabrics. The same with the beautifully dyed textiles that hung from the front walls. Flames now curled up their colorful patterns, turning them black.

Blue Heron kept a grip on Smooth Pebble's arm, pulled her backward, past the fire, and then past her dais.

"I don't want to die like this," Smooth Pebble told her, a tremble running through her body.

"Wasn't exactly my plan, either," Blue Heron admitted.

Still, it was masterfully done. Of course, everyone would suspect she'd been murdered, but there was always doubt. She'd relied on that herself over the years as she'd eliminated rivals, destroyed opposition. That was how politics worked.

Tomorrow, while Wind and her people sorted through the ashes, assuming she had the time to do so, Spotted Wrist would present himself to offer his most solemn condolences. "Such a terrible accident. If only it hadn't happened in the middle of the night! Poor Blue Heron and Smooth Pebble. Must have been sound asleep. From where their burned remains were found, they'd awakened, tried to fight their way to the door, but, alas, it was too late!"

"You are a vindictive bit of walking vomit," she said, addressing Spotted

Wrist as if he were in the room. "If I could go back? My first act would be to poison you the day you returned from Red Wing Town."

"Bit late for that," Smooth Pebble said. Then she caught a lungful of smoke and started coughing.

"Getting a bit warm in here," Blue Heron said, retreating to the door to her personal quarters. "You really want to burn to death?"

"Have your souls taken leave of your senses?"

"There's a way, you know."

"What way?"

"A way to turn this back on Spotted Wrist. A way where you and I don't die in agony. A quick way that will drive a thorn right through Spotted Wrist's heart."

Smooth Pebble gave in to a fit of coughing again as a portion of the thatch over the door collapsed into the room to leave a blizzard of twirling and angry sparks in its wake. Open to the outside now, the fire drafted hotter as it burned its way up past the ridgepole.

"What way?" Smooth Pebble asked.

Blue Heron beckoned her. "We'll do it back here."

"What are we doing?"

Blue Heron found the old stone-headed war club. Lifted it in the gaudy firelight that shone through her door. Over the roaring fire, she shouted, "Suppose they found you at the foot of my bed with your head smashed in? And suppose they found me in my bed, with a long chert blade sticking out of my ribs?"

"They'd think someone burned the place to cover your murder."

"They would, wouldn't they?"

"And who's going to do this?" Smooth Pebble bellowed over the increasing roar of the fire.

"I'll kill you," Blue Heron shouted back. "It'll be quick. I promise. You won't feel a thing."

"And then what?"

Blue Heron reached into the box where she kept the long brown chert blade, the one Walking Smoke's assassin had once tried to cut her throat with. "I drive this in." She pointed. "Right here, under my breast. I can cut the lung and slice the heart. Won't take me but a few heartbeats to die."

Smooth Pebble's eyes were wide with disbelief, her breath coming in panicked gasps. "You're insane!"

Blue Heron gestured at the fire. "Describe insane."

Smooth Pebble was having trouble swallowing, sweat beading on her skin. She was shaking now, the rising fear gleaming in her eyes as she stared out at the great room. More burning roof thatch fell in a cascade of fire.

"I guess . . . I guess . . ." Smooth Pebble blinked, tears streaking down her cheeks. "Just . . . Yes. Do it." And so saying, she dropped to her knees, bending her head down to give Blue Heron a clean strike at the back of her skull.

"You have been a good and dear friend to me," Blue Heron told her as she tightened her grip on the club. "I will see you on the other side."

She tried to steady her arms and hands. She'd never done anything like this. At least, not the cold-blooded execution of a beloved friend.

"Will you hurry!" Smooth Pebble pleaded, her hands clenched at her sides.

Blue Heron gritted her few teeth, took a breath, and . . .

"Hey!" the bellowed cry came from the corner of her room. "What in Piasa's name are you doing?"

Blue Heron glanced up, peered through the smoke. Could barely make out the face staring at her from the thatch at the top of her wall.

"Thief?"

"Hurry up. Both of you! It's still dark on this side, but it won't be for long. Climb up on the box there. Come on!"

Blue Heron dragged Smooth Pebble to her feet, and together they staggered, coughing, gasping for breath, to climb up onto an ornately carved storage box.

Seven Skull Shield reached a bruised and battered arm into the room, barely managed to pull Blue Heron up far enough that she could scramble over the mud-daubed wall, her ribs, belly, and hips complaining.

Then she was out in the clear night air, the cool drafts filling her lungs. She broke into a coughing fit as Seven Skull Shield helped her down off a wooden stump and went back to reach inside for Smooth Pebble.

She looked up, seeing the section of thatch drop like a trap door, as the thief literally yanked Smooth Pebble out of the room, thick curls of smoke billowing as she came.

"There's a hole in my roof," she said through a fit of coughing.

"Yeah. How did you think I always managed to show up in your bedroom without anyone seeing me?"

"But I checked it. The wind would have lifted it."

"That's why you tie these things down, Keeper." He reached for her hand. "Come on. We've got to be out of sight by sunrise."

"The tonka'tzi's, we've got to get to Wind."

"Not a chance. The Great Plaza's crawling with warriors. Now, careful.

Don't want to fall getting down the mound side. There's warriors out front. They catch sight of us, and it's all over."

Blue Heron fought to keep from coughing. "Where do you think we should go?"

"As far from here as we can get. We've only got until your palace burns down before they figure out you're not in it."

Halfway across Four Winds Plaza, Blue Heron cried, "Wait!"

She turned, watching the fountain of fire that rose from inside the walls of her palace. She felt as if something inside her had torn apart, and it hurt. It really hurt.

"Keeper, you all right?" Seven Skull Shield had turned, his face concerned where it reflected the fire's orange glow.

"That's my life," she told him, eyes on the inferno. "The men I married, the ones I threw out. The place where I laughed. Where I plotted. That's where I was most myself. Blood and spit, don't you understand? *I'm* in there. *I'm* burning. Or, at least, a part of me is."

"You'll build again," Smooth Pebble said softly. "You'll rise again."

Blue Heron closed her eyes. Nodded. *But part of me is dying back there. That part of the soul that seeps into prized possessions, that becomes part of the floor, the walls, the benches.*

"Gone," she whispered. "All . . . gone."

Seventy-seven

They crossed the divide, dropping down the eastern side, following the tree-lined trail where it wound around stony outcrops; a trickling of stream led them downhill for more than a hand of time.

Then the trail wove its way up a rocky slope, the outcrops lichen-covered and poking through the leaf mat, across a narrow ridge, and down to a small spring in a covelike hollow. Water trickled from cracks in moss-covered rocks and came welling up, clear and cool.

The camp had been used for generations, as could be seen from the charcoal-rich soil, the occasional potsherd, glinting flakes of tool stone, and bits of soapstone that lay about on the trampled vegetation.

Winder called a halt as dark clouds came rolling in from around the peaks to the west. Flickers of lightning, still so distant they remained silent, flashed in the western sky.

Supper consisted of a quickly cooked corn gruel, sunflower seeds, and an unlucky box turtle they'd happened upon.

Winder tied a couple of hides between the trees for a rain fly. At their fire, the Chalakee were also battening down for a wet and miserable night.

"You can have the shelter," Winder told her. "I'll make do. There's a good-sized pine back there with low-hanging branches."

She gave him a "you've-got-to-be-kidding" look. "There's room for both of us. I think I know you well enough now that we understand each other." She grinned. "Besides, if I discover your shaft trying to wiggle in where it shouldn't I'll whack it with my war club."

He erupted into entertained laughter, adding, "You know, Lady, I could really get to like you."

As the first gust of wind tore through the treetops, they took to the shelter.

Lightning flashed, thunder boomed. As Night Shadow Star drifted off to sleep, the sound of rain filled the night around her. Part of her considered it a betrayal, another part of her felt relief that Winder's big, warm, muscular body was pressed next to hers, reassurance that she wasn't alone in the darkness, storm, and torment.

And the Dream came . . .

In a pale darkness, Night Shadow Star sat beside the small spring, watching the water trickle up from the earth. She perched on her knees, hands forward and palms out. Movement down in the shadowed depths caught her attention. Bits of slithering color that shifted beneath the water's surface.

Of course they would be here. Springs were openings, portals to the Underworld. Recessed springs like this were among the favorite lairs of the Tie Snakes. These were the denizens of the Underworld. Servants to Old-Woman-Who-Never-Dies, guardians of springs, creeks, and the deep pools where rivers ran slowly.

She could sense them here, in this place, their Power beginning to pulse. The triangular shape of a Tie Snake's head could barely be made out as the creature swam its way up from below, broke the surface, and slipped across the rock in eerie silence. Scales in colorful diamond patterns gleamed as if lit from within. The Spirit creature gave her a knowing inspection, the forked tongue flicking as it tasted the air.

Flowing out of the spring as if from a womb, the great snake might have been smoke, so quietly and effortlessly did it follow a circle around where she sat. Only when its triangular head reached the gourd-shaped rattles on the beast's tail did it stop. The head rose, slitted black pupils in yellow-green eyes fixed on her. The tongue flicked and whipped.

"Where's your master?" Night Shadow Star asked.

"He comes."

"And why are you here?"

"Protection."

"He hardly needs protection from me," she told him and added a derisive snort.

"No. Protection for you."

And at that moment lightning flashed above, streaked down, blasted one of the oaks that spread its branches over the little cove.

She glanced up, watched flames begin to dance along the bark where the bolt had struck.

"Come." Piasa's voice took her by surprise.

She turned, seeing her Lord where he perched at the edge of the spring. Not even a drop of water slicked his furred hide or beaded at the tips of his barred and spotted wings, let alone on the scarlet antlers rising from his cougar's head.

The hard yellow eyes watched her with curious intent as the beast extended a yellow eagle-clawed foot in her direction.

She rose, felt her heart begin to hammer, and stepped forward. The Tie Snake pulled back both head and tail, creating an opening for her to pass.

Reluctantly she placed her hand in Piasa's taloned grip. Time seemed to smear, slowing, stretching. A haze blurred the edges of her vision while it sharpened to minute detail in the middle where Piasa's depthless black pupils seemed to expand in their yellow irises. Her souls were being sucked into those stygian depths, drawn relentlessly into oblivion.

She felt herself lifted, turned, and had but a fleeting sensation of being drawn down into the darkness. Water streamed around her, rushing along her skin, slipping through her long hair as she was pulled down, ever deeper into the Underworld. Her gaze remained locked with the Underwater Panther's, the effect paralyzing, terrifying.

It might have been eternity. It might have been an instant.

Her thoughts, fears, longings, and desires rushed up, turned themselves inside out. Memories of her most private moments with Fire Cat, the physical sensations of his shaft moving inside her, the taste of catfish in White Chief village, her whimpering fear as the Casqui carried her from the Trade House, sunlight on the Tenasee, the aching in her souls for Fire Cat, everything, exposed, right down to the roots of her being.

As quickly, it changed direction, shot back inside her, like vomit reversing in midstream and snapping back into place with a physical pain.

Night Shadow Star staggered, suddenly turned loose of Piasa's grasp, her gaze freed of his.

"Why do you do that?" She gasped, sank down to the soft mud, disturbing a crawfish in the process. The little creature shot away, claws and antennae pointing to the rear.

"To know who you are."

"You're in my head all the time."

"Not like that. Not to know the depths of who you are, what you will do. On occasion, you still surprise me."

She glared up at him, watched the bristling whiskers spread on either side of the pink nose. She could just see the beast's fangs, slightly exposed by what might have been a smile. Could remember the feel of them piercing her scalp, how they punched through her skull, into her brain, before the sharp molars sheared through bone to crush her head.

"What did you find that you didn't already know?"

Piasa studied her, the eagle feet depressing the moss and silty sand. The beast's serpent tail flipped back and forth, the rattles clacking hollowly. She saw no give in those stony yellow eyes as Piasa said, "I needed to know that you would still destroy your brother. That that, too, wasn't a hollow promise."

"Fire Cat and I—"

"Yes. Love. It was Old-Woman-Who-Never-Dies' notion. Back in the Beginning Times. A way to give people passion, keep you together long enough to conceive and ultimately raise your young because you're not responsible enough to complete the task on your own. The fear was that you would be far too concerned with your own selfish desires. That you'd birth the little animals and wander off to look for nuts in the forest or some such."

"What would you know about love?"

"Nothing. A fact for which I'm eternally thankful, since it leaves me with a clear sense of purpose and the ability to concentrate on what must be done. A hope I'd had when it came to you and that abomination of a brother of yours."

"I'm here, aren't I? Where's Fire Cat?"

"Not yet. After your brother is destroyed. I just had to endure a taste of your longing for him. I can't take the risk."

"Risk of what?"

"This *love* of yours. The knowledge that you would do anything for Fire Cat turns him into a weakness, a potential gaming piece Sky Power could use to manipulate you."

"Not true."

"Oh? If it came down to a choice between Fire Cat and sparing your brother's life? Just walking away?"

She ground her teeth, felt the tearing in her breast.

Piasa laughed. "Yes, as I suspected."

"If I destroy Walking Smoke, I essentially change the balance in favor of the Underworld. But in the beginning, *Hunga Ahuito* created the worlds and Powers to be in constant struggle, while at the same time maintaining balance. You claimed me the moment Walking Smoke arrived in Cahokia. If I kill him, I become the imbalance. What happens to me?"

Piasa's black pupils expanded against the background of yellow. "You, too, would have to be destroyed."

As her heart skipped and her tongue knotted, he added, "Or I could release you. Set you free, Powerless, to become just another of these foolish breeders. Leave you be to mindlessly grow corn, cook food, worry about the weather, and grow old as your body wears out and your children have to assume the bother of caring for you until you die and are turned into fertilizer in the fields."

She closed her eyes. *Fire Cat, do you hear? We have a chance.*

"I'll take that option."

"You will no longer be Lady Night Shadow Star. You'll have to give that up, be no one. What do you call them? A dirt farmer? A fitting if not flattering title."

She laughed, daring to be amused. "Master, sometimes you even trick yourself."

The question lay behind his midnight stare.

She told him, "I have spent this entire trip learning to be no one. Learning to be a woman. Just . . . a woman. And all that means."

"If you destroy your brother."

"The story being told is that he is in Joara. It's what? A day's travel from here?"

"It is."

"They say that most of the town has fled, that he's become so terrifying that only some chief and his warriors are left."

"And?"

She considered. "The last time I faced him, he didn't understand. Thought I was the same woman he raped that day he was exiled. When I rolled that canoe on him, he was caught by total surprise. But for Sky Power rescuing him, he would have been yours. He's not near water this time."

"And even if he were, the Thunderers wouldn't allow me to get close. That is why this is up to you. He cannot die by water."

"Sneak close? Use a club?"

"Risky. He is guarded by Power. The Thunderers watch over him."

"Word on the trail is that lightning has killed several who have tried to sneak up in the middle of the night and murder him." She considered. "He knows I am coming. He won't want the Thunderers to kill me. No, just the opposite. He wants me alive. *Needs* me alive. He will set his ambush inside his lair. Up close, so he can look me in the eyes as he springs his trap."

"I can grant you one gift, empower whatever weapon you decide to use to destroy him. Made lethal so that with one strike it can release Underworld Power. Perhaps your knife? Your war club? Some poison? You need only dip it in the spring water before leaving this place."

She considered, frowned, stared at the gnarled roots that clung to the cavern walls. Thought she saw Snapping Turtle back in the shadows of a stony gallery that emptied off the main passageway.

Why in the shadows? But then, Snapping Turtle had never approved of her. Wouldn't be here if there wasn't a chance . . .

She felt her heart sink. "That charming tale about just being a woman when this is all over. That was a lie, wasn't it? Separating me from Fire Cat, that wasn't just because of love, was it? You didn't have to let that Cahokian canoe catch us. They were on the river, your domain. You could have delayed them by any of several means. You *wanted* them to catch up. Knew that Fire Cat would do anything to keep me out of their clutches."

Piasa hissed, the sound chilling to her souls.

Night Shadow Star closed her eyes, the sinking sensation filling her. "That's why I know he's not dead. He's following, closely. You want him here to make sure, don't you?"

Piasa's yellow eyes had narrowed to slits, a low growl deep in the beast's throat.

Night Shadow Star put the pieces together. "When Walking Smoke kills me, the balance will change. The Thunderers will have no use for anyone as disruptive and violent as my brother. They'll withdraw their protection."

She laughed aloud at the audacity of it. "You never thought I'd kill Walking Smoke. But you knew Fire Cat would do whatever it took, just as he's always done. Like with the Itza, and Morning Star's souls in the Underworld. After Walking Smoke kills me, if Fire Cat has to use his last breath to do it, he will end his days standing over my brother's dead body."

She felt herself lifted, the force of it compacting her body, but she was hurled upward and out. Her vision blurred, and in an instant, she . . .

. . . Awakened in the night as rain pelted down and thunder boomed and echoed from the high mountains.

Fragments of Dream filled her head. And through them, she could see Walking Smoke's dark eyes, hear his laughter, mocking and hollow.

He was behind her, his penis, hard and insistent, prodding her from the rear.

She blinked, coming fully awake. Fear, liquid and paralyzing, shot through her. His arm was around her, heavy, restraining.

He moved, his pressing penis causing her anus to tighten.

"No!" she screamed. Batted the arm to one side. Felt him jerk, gasp. And then she was out of the blankets, scrambling out into the rain and mud.

"What the . . . What's wrong?" The voice wasn't Walking Smoke's but deeper, familiar.

"Winder?" She gasped, still trying to catch her breath.

"Lady?" She could see his dark head poke out past the rain fly. "You all right?"

"Your . . ." She swallowed. "Your . . . What were you trying to do?"

He hesitated, head cocked. "Well, I was absolutely sound asleep, and having the most delicious Dream about Amber Flower. Not that you need to know the details, but she was bent over, casting enticing glances over her shoulder as I . . . Well, she has the most charming and rounded . . . Oh, you know."

"Who is Amber Flower?"

"I married her down among the Pacaha. Charming young thing with the most incredible appetite for just about any kind of activity a man might care to indulge in when it comes to . . . well, you know."

She sucked the cold damp air into her lungs, finally managing to slow her heart.

"Nightmare?" he asked gently.

"Let's just say that your most pleasant Dream and my most horrible one fit together in a most uncomfortable way."

"My most sincere apologies." A beat. "Not that I mind Dreaming of you in that most pleasant of ways. But I think perhaps I should make my way up to that pine we discussed earlier so you can sleep in peace."

"No." She thrust an arm out to stop him. "The storm's mostly passed. I'm going to sit by the spring for a time. I need to think. Go back to sleep. I'll be back to my blankets soon. Maybe a finger of time."

"You're sure?"

"Go. Sleep, my friend. In the morning, well, it will be a new day. We can plan over breakfast."

She watched his head disappear back into the rain fly's shadows, heard him sigh as he resettled himself.

She couldn't hold such a thing against a man who was Dreaming about his wife. Assuming she could really believe that's who he was Dreaming of. Winder being Winder and all.

A weary smile crossed her lips.

She shook the misty rain from her hair. Walked over to her packs. She was surprised to see that a couple of coals still glowed in the firepit despite the rain. Several of the porters' pack dogs were watching her where they lay curled by their masters.

She took only her personal pack, shaking the water from it before removing her slender-handled copper-bitted ax.

Mindful of Piasa's words, she dipped it in the spring, thought she saw the copper take on a blue glow, and stared at it in the darkness.

"Lord, you expect me to die?"

The feeling of loneliness and abandonment enveloped her. At the same time, she found it liberating.

If she was killed in the process of destroying Walking Smoke, Fire Cat would be truly free. He would have the rest of his life to find a good woman who would bear his children, have his farmstead, and perhaps die an old man, his head full of memories of Night Shadow Star, the lady he had loved, and Cahokia, and the accolades that had been showered upon his head.

"As if you'd know the first pus-rotted thing about love," she told the Spirit Beast.

As she took to the trail, the last thing she heard was Piasa's hollow laughter.

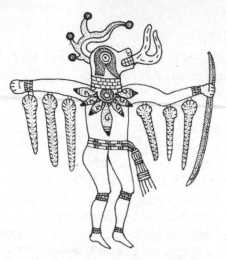

Seventy-eight

Tonka'tzi Wind sat in her great room, atop her litter where it perched on her dais, and studied her visitors through slitted eyes. Spotted Wrist had a look of triumphant joy. He wore a scarlet cloak over his shoulders, a striking white apron embroidered in black that fell to a point between his knees, and a gleaming copper headpiece, worthy of the Morning Star.

Rising Flame had a painted bunting–feather cape over her shoulders, shell necklaces around her neck that hung down between her full round breasts, and a calf elk–skin skirt, finely tanned and scraped, that clung to her hips. Her hair was up in a matron's bun, pinned with eagle feathers.

How did this happen?

Looking back, she couldn't think of a more ironic way to wake up. Over the years, she had awakened to tragedy, to every type of bad news imaginable, to the loss of friends and family, to news of defeat, even catastrophe.

She had never awakened to the reality of being a hostage in her own palace and that her enemies had not only dared to invade her sanctuary but had done so with impunity. The action had been so well handled that she had slept right through her own downfall, and only found out when she'd rolled out of bed, called for her head of household, and saw Spotted Wrist himself come striding through her door, saying, "Ah, up at last, I see. Good. I thought you needed a good night's sleep."

"Where is Wild Rose? What are you doing here?"

"Your head of household has the rest of your people preparing breakfast for me and a select few of my warriors. Oh, and don't bother calling for your guard. They're currently huddled down on the avenue, trying to figure out what to do with themselves."

So she'd dressed, surprised that they'd let her mount her dais and adopt the trappings of her office.

Now she sat, the remains of the breakfast she'd forced herself to eat like a stone in her stomach as she considered Spotted Wrist and Rising Flame. She found it ominous that they were the only two allowed in the room.

The Keeper was saying, ". . . nothing changes. This afternoon, escorted by my warriors, you will be transported to the Council House to conduct the city's business with the Pacaha, Tunica, and Quigualtam embassies. There are also messengers who have arrived from several of the colonies. I suspect you'll get an update from the Cofitachequi expedition, perhaps even word on the progress of your niece." He paused. "If you hear anything about Squadron First Blood Talon and my warriors, please alert me first thing.

"Other than that," he continued, stepping close to fix her with his hard stare, "be careful. You do understand *careful*, don't you? It means that for the moment you are useful. I need you here, doing what you do. It's called creating the illusion of stability and continuity."

Rising Flame had stood with her arms crossed, one slim leg forward. Periodically she cast emotionless glances at Spotted Wrist, and then at Wind. Whatever was going on behind her expressionless face, Wind couldn't tell.

Spotted Wrist added, "Actually, the transition should come as a relief. Your life just got a whole lot easier. You can sleep late, don't have to worry yourself sick about House or Clan politics. All you need to do is show up when asked and do as you are told. Simple, really."

He paused. "So simple that if you fail to do as I'm requesting, if I discover that you're unable to follow instructions, or are working against me, you will be replaced. No matter how inconvenient it would be for me. You see, Green Chunkey, down at Horned Serpent Town, is hoping that you fail. If you do, if you give me the slightest reason, he's the next *tonka'tzi*."

So that was what you promised him? But then, it would have had to have been something good to overcome the bitterness between the two Houses after the near bloodshed they'd teetered on late last fall.

"That should just about cover it." Spotted Wrist turned to go, hesitated, and looked back. "Oh, and one more thing. My people detained one of those pesky Red Wing women last night. The ones your sister took in. She showed up at a most unimaginable time. Middle of the night. I thought about hanging her in a square, but I'm offering her to you. Consider it a peace offering of sorts."

"I'll take her."

"Odd how your lineage has this predilection for heretics. I'll have the section first in charge of your palace send her in to you."

Purposefully, he strode across the large room and out into the day.

"I find myself moderately surprised that I woke up alive this morning," Wind told Rising Flame. "Is the Hero of the North slipping?"

"He let you live at my request," Rising Flame told her, face still emotionless. "I made the point that when Blue Heron and Columella brought their grievances to you, you could have condemned him, sided entirely with your sister. Instead, despite family, you ordered each side to settle it. I emphasized that despite family ties, you were acting for the good of the city." The first flicker of emotion crossed her brow. "Please don't prove me wrong."

"What's happening out there? I'm cut off. Essentially a prisoner. My recorders, messengers, household staff, everyone's missing."

"For a couple of days now, Spotted Wrist has been assembling his squadrons. I was informed late yesterday. He moved on River House last night. By this morning, if all went according to plan, Three Fingers is sitting on the high chief's chair at the River Mounds City palace. I haven't a clue what they decided to do about War Duck, Round Pot, and their children.

"Another of his squadrons marched all night to take positions around the Great Plaza; some, as you know, control your palace. Others are occupying the Council House and courtyard, which controls access to Morning Star's palace. They also took control of the Four Winds Clan House, the Men's House, and the Recorders' Society."

"What about Morning Star?"

"They're leaving him alone for the time being. Spotted Wrist isn't sure what Morning Star's relationship is with Five Fists. Until he knows for certain, he's not going to move on the war leader. He is, however, monitoring who goes up and down from Morning Star's palace. Ensuring that orders aren't given to the Morning Star squadron that would end in an unfortunate effusion of blood."

"I see."

"The bulk of Spotted Wrist's forces, however, are headed to River Mounds to control the canoe landing and to build strength before moving on Evening Star House."

Wind closed her eyes, struggled for breath. "You heard Columella. She'll make a fight of it. Is that what you want?"

Rising Flame's full mouth narrowed to a distasteful pucker. "Cahokia needs new blood. The old Houses were in a constant state of chaos. The Keeper says he can bring harmony."

"He *took* the city!"

"Why are you surprised? He worked out exactly how to do it at Red Wing Town."

"And you just let him?"

"Life was a great deal simpler back when you were clan matron. You never had to face the question: What do you do when a charismatic and much too ambitious war leader returns from the field with three fanatically loyal squadrons who will follow his every order? My first concern was to ensure that Serpent Woman House and Horned Serpent House didn't go to war. Appointing him Keeper, with his warriors to back him up, ensured that."

"But you created a monster."

Rising Flame shrugged, a calculating look behind her eyes. "I spent most of my youth among the Nations in the south. Those who are unified, who don't fight among themselves, are great and lasting. When Black Tail founded the Houses, he seeded dry rot into our system. My first challenge as clan matron was stopping a war between the Houses. Spotted Wrist was my tool to do that. I didn't expect he'd take things nearly this far. Whether it was right or wrong, I'll just have to see. But for the time being, with the exception of Evening Star House, the Four Winds Clan is at peace. And as for Columella, if I have to turn Spotted Wrist loose to crush her House, I'll do it."

"I'll be interested to see if you can control this cougar you have on your leash."

Rising Flame shrugged. "Time, and perhaps the Morning Star, will tell. In the meantime, I very sincerely suggest that you heed the Keeper's warning and do as he says. I won't be able to save you a second time. As it is, there's been a fire at Blue Heron's palace. It's still too hot to see if she was inside or not. When it cools we'll be able to search for bodies. I wouldn't get my hopes up, however. If she had made it out, one would think she'd have raised the alarm, be on the avenue, giving orders. But no one reports seeing her."

Wind sat stunned as the woman turned on her heel and left. For what seemed an eternity she remained motionless on her litter, her stare vacant as she tried to absorb the enormity of her loss.

Seventy-nine

The years of training brought Blood Talon awake, his head clear, alert, as a light nudge to his thigh broke his fragmented Dreams.

"What?" he asked softly, blinked in the half-light of predawn. Birds were chirping morning song in the trees; the last of the crickets were singing and the croaking of a tree frog was somewhere close.

The storm had passed; fortunately the ancient chestnut he had slept beneath had shed most of the water. Didn't matter that it had sent the occasional drop to splatter on his blanket or that the lightning had done its best to shred the sky—he'd slept straight through.

Fire Cat told him, "We're close. Let's go find them. Maybe we can enjoy a cooked breakfast at my lady's fire."

Blood Talon slipped out of his blanket, crouched to roll it. The morning felt cool, the world damp with the heavy dew that followed rain. Streamers of mist were rising. "And if not, we can gobble a couple of handfuls of ground corn and some of those pawpaws as soon as we find water to wash them down."

He packed quickly and efficiently, feeling the tight pull of his leg muscles. Despite his bragging, by the time they'd reached the divide last night, he'd been stumbling in fatigue. The only solace was that Fire Cat hadn't exactly been the image of grace either as they'd panted and sweated their way along the trail.

Only when it had grown too dark to see, and knowing they'd reached the divide that crossed into Cofitachequi, did they finally surrender to the inevitable.

Blood Talon stepped to the side, emptied his bladder, and wished for a drink. He and Fire Cat had split what remained of their water last night. The good news about the country they traveled was that water was never scarce.

Taking the trail, they found it slippery with last night's mud, and set their steps to the leaf mat beside it.

Fire Cat allowed them a stop just long enough to fill their bellies with water at the first trickle of a creek. As the light strengthened and they could see better footing, their pace picked up.

A pileated woodpecker was hammering at one of the hardwoods. The sound brought a smile to Blood Talon's lips. Woodpecker, the warrior, a Power bird. Among some of the clans, the rapid staccato of sound was considered a call to combat.

The trail split off from the creek where it disappeared into a tangle of raspberry and briar. The way climbed up a low and rock-studded ridge, topped out onto—

Fire Cat raised a knotted fist. Stopped short. Blood Talon cocked his head, listening.

Voices. Sounding angry. Definitely speaking Cahokian.

On silent feet, Fire Cat led the way down the trail where it snaked into a small cove surrounded by pines, a couple of giant beech trees, oaks, and hickory.

The small spring at the back dribbled water down moss-covered rocks. A camp had been laid out. Two fires, both smoking.

Pack dogs were held back by what looked like locals, given their dress. The men sat in a line to the side, arms around their growling and bristling dogs. Five warriors, in Cahokian-style dress, North Star House designs on their aprons, stood in a ring. One was poking through Trade packs.

"I'm a Trader," the sixth, a big man, insisted, thumping his chest with a fist. "This is an open trail. Under the Power of Trade, I deserve free passage."

"Second?" the warrior picking through the packs called. He straightened, lifting a copper plate. It was molded into the shape of Morning Star with his head adorned with a split-cloud emblem, feathers spreading from his arms as he danced his way into the sky.

"Where is she?" the second asked, facing the big Trader. "We're looking for Lady Night Shadow Star."

"I don't know what you're talking about," the Trader almost growled back. "I'm here on the Power of Trade. You just proved it from the packs."

"Second?" The warrior fingering through the packs lifted a beautiful black dress decorated by white chevrons and the Morning Star House insignia atop the Four Winds Clan spirals.

"A Trader? And I suppose you Traded for that on Morning Star's mound. Maybe it was a gift from Clan Matron Rising Flame?"

Fire Cat shifted his pack, slipped his bow and quiver free, handing them to Blood Talon. His copper-bitted war club he kept for himself as he lowered the rest to the ground.

Then the Red Wing started down the trail. The way he moved reminded Blood Talon of how a panther closed on a herd of unwary deer.

Stringing the bow, Blood Talon flipped the quiver onto his back and drew a shaft. Good. War arrow with a keen Cahokian point at its tip.

Blood Talon followed as quickly and silently as he could, took a commanding position at the foot of the trail, nocked, and waited.

To his amazement, Fire Cat stalked into the middle of the camp, placed himself in front of the amazed Trader, and said to the squadron second, "You will stand down. You will turn around, and you will leave. This man is protected under the Power of Trade."

"Who do you think you are?" the second was looking Fire Cat up and down, seeing a sun-blackened muscular man in a simple brown hunting shirt who wore his long hair in a Trader's braid.

"I am a bound man, in service—"

"A *bound* man? You're a slave." The second broke out in laughter. "I guess this isn't your lucky day. You're about to change masters. Hope your last one treated you better than Fire Light will. Now, be a good fellow. Hand me your master's war club. Piss on a rock, the thing's copperbitted!"

The second's expression changed, hardened. "No bound man would be allowed to touch a thing like that. Why am I starting to think you're all a bunch of thieves? Copper, Four Winds fabrics? Or are you all in service to Lady Night Shadow Star? And just where is she? Speak."

"I told you to leave."

Blood Talon felt that old familiar tingle as he tested the bow's pull. He wasn't familiar with the weapon, not that he could miss at this distance.

The second stuck out his left hand. "Give it here."

"Leave. Last chance." Fire Cat's feet were positioned. Didn't the second see that? But he seemed fixed on Fire Cat's face.

"That's it." The second flipped his war club back to strike.

He never got the chance. With a flash of copper, Fire Cat's keen edge slashed across the second's throat. Skipping left, Fire Cat's return stroke caught the next warrior in the ribs. Before the man could bend in response, Fire Cat had leaped at the third. Still surprised, the warrior barely managed to parry the blow. He staggered back, off balance. Fire Cat was on him, hammered past his defense, and caved in the side of his head.

Ripping the war club free of the man's skull, Fire Cat skipped back as the fourth warrior charged forward, screaming his rage, and swung with all his might.

Fire Cat ducked the blow, closed, used the handle of the reversed club to drive into the man's throat at the base of the tongue.

The fellow dropped his club, grabbed at his throat, eyes wide. Fire Cat turned on the fifth warrior, the young man so stunned that he still crouched over the pack.

"Wait! Don't!" The youth toppled backward on his butt in his desperate scramble to get away.

The fourth, finally catching a breath, bent over double. Threw up. But as he straightened, he drew a deer-bone stiletto from his waist.

Blood Talon drew, set the tip of the war arrow on the man's chest, and released. The hiss-and-hollow thump of a solid hit filled the now-silent air.

Blood Talon instinctively stripped another arrow from the quiver, nocked it, and made his way into the camp.

The porters, still holding their growling and snapping dogs, stared with horror-filled eyes. No doubt they'd never seen the like.

Now, as a group, they rose, barking orders at their dogs, and fled. "Stop them?" Blood Talon asked.

"Let them go," Fire Cat returned, staring down at the terrified young warrior. "Something tells me they'd be more trouble than they're worth."

Meanwhile, the Trader stood rooted, a disbelieving look on his blocky face with its sideways-mashed nose. Now he reached up, ran anxious fingers along his jaw. "Good to see you again, Red Wing. I think."

"Where's Lady White Willow?" Fire Cat asked.

White Willow?

"That farce lasted only as far as Canyon Town," the Trader said. "Not that I didn't know all along. She's not here. Left in the middle of the night. Said she had a Dream. Me? I should have known she'd pull something like this. Just didn't think she'd try to skip away until we were closer."

"Joara's how far?" Fire Cat asked, still glaring down at the young warrior.

"F-full day's run," the young man stammered.

"Why are you here? Who sent you?" Fire Cat slapped his bloody war club into his palm.

"Lord Fire Light."

"How did he know Night Shadow Star was coming?" Blood Talon wondered. "As hard as we've been traveling, it would have taken a falcon on the wing to beat us upriver."

"It's the witch!" the youth cried. "Lightning speaks to him. Gives him messages. He sees things in the pooled blood of infants. He asked my lord to send us here. We were supposed to find the lady, destroy the man who accompanied her, and bring her and her possessions back to Lightning Shell."

"In return for what?" the big Trader demanded, stepping forward. His scarred fists were clenched, the kind of fists that had been damaged on too many human skulls.

"I don't . . . Wait, something about a way for Fire Light to get back to Cahokia. Somehow the witch can fix it. Make it happen."

"Long way from Cahokia to be making those kinds of promises," Blood Talon mused.

The big Trader asked, "The witch responsible for sending that Casqui to abduct the lady back at Canyon Town?"

The young warrior gave a worried shrug. "I guess. He doesn't exactly tell us everything. Not that we'd want to know. Do you know what it's like? Living in Joara? Hearing the screams? We don't sleep. None of us. And the lord, he's half possessed, but he'll do anything for a pardon. Especially now that his sister's clan matron."

"Well," Fire Cat mused. "At least that news has made it this far."

"What do we do with him?" the Trader asked, indicating the warrior.

Fire Cat glanced around. "Winder, Night Shadow Star's on her way to Joara, right? Is that a safe assumption?"

"That's where her brother is."

"We'll take her box and Trade, leave the rest."

"What about him?" Winder asked. "He was sent here to murder me and the porters."

"He's carrying part of the load." Fire Cat bent down, peering into the young warrior's frightened eyes. "You understand, don't you? The moment you're any kind of a problem? If you're not working your heart out? You're as dead as they are."

"Or worse," Winder bellowed, bending down to glare into the young warrior's face. "I won't leave you dead, you weak-shafted little shit. I'll leave you alive *after* I rip your balls off your body and shove them down your throat."

Blood Talon, as a squadron first, figured he'd seen threats before. From the boiling anger blackening Winder's face, this was a lot more of a promise.

"Let's go," Fire Cat barked. "We've got to get there before she can get herself killed."

"She won't just go rushing in, will she?" Blood Talon asked as he tried the dead warriors' war clubs out, one by one, swinging them, checking the feel. He'd have liked the one with the greenstone celt set into the end, but the balance was wrong. He settled on a fire-cured hickory club with crosshatches engraved along its length.

"She did last time," Fire Cat growled as he tossed items back into the box that the warrior had pulled out in his search.

"Not this time," Winder said, packing his own things. "She's been telling me that she needs time to plan. That he almost killed her last time."

"Sounds like you've been talking to her a great deal, Trader. I would hope that talk is *all* you've been doing."

Blood Talon lifted an eyebrow at the tone.

Winder pulled his pack strings tight, turned. "Not that I'd have minded doing a little more than talking, Red Wing. And not that I didn't give it my best, but you and I had better get one thing set straight right here and now. You're the luckiest pus-sucker alive. That woman loves you in a way I've never seen a woman love a man. Not even the way women love me. And if you ever muck it up for her by being an idiot, I'll hunt you down and gleefully choke the life out of you."

"You're as bad as Seven Skull Shield."

"Who? Skull? You think he's tough? Compared to me, he's cottonwood down on the wind."

"What about these bodies?" Blood Talon asked.

"Might make people shy away from camping here in the future," Winder noted. "Leaving them to rot right next to the water, pretty as this place is? That's a bit rude."

Fire Cat, practically vibrating to be after Night Shadow Star, hesitated. Blood Talon watched his face work. Then he snapped, "Yes, yes, let's drag them out of here. Maybe down there, onto that rock outcrop. But nothing fancy."

The look on the young warrior's face, now that the immediate violence was over and he was helping drag the bodies of his friends, was a study in hatred, revulsion, and growing anger.

Wonder if it wouldn't be smarter to just sneak up and smack him on the back of the head?

But carrying what they had would be strain enough. And they were already too far behind.

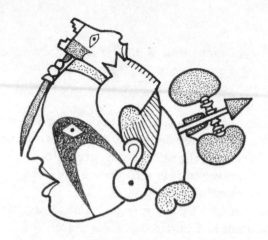

Eighty

Joara had been easy to find. The trails were deeply worn, the occasional farmsteads occupied by helpful people, some of whom spoke a smattering of the colonial tongue: Cahokian.

Just ask, "Joara?" And they'd point to the right trail.

The town itself was a crossroads located in the midst of a web of creeks that ran down from the eastern slope of the Blue Mountains. To the immediate west was the gap that led to Beautiful River and the Wide Fast. To the northwest lay a more precipitous pass through the mountains where a trail descended to one of the many headwaters of the Tenasee. East was, of course, Cofitachequi proper and the trail that led to the great Eastern Ocean.

Joara should have been bustling. The fields—all on fertile soil up and down the creek—were lush, the ears of corn full enough the locals should have been preparing for the Busk: the sacred Green Corn Ceremony. Instead of people preparing for games, fasting, ritual purification, and finally, the feast that would celebrate the relighting of the sacred fires and the cooking of the first green corn, the place was occupied by a few skinny dogs that wandered about the houses.

And of course, there was the palace on the east end of town atop its low mound.

Night Shadow Star had arrived just before dusk after a hard day's travel, most of it done at a trot.

Rather than rush right in, she'd kept to the forest, eased from tree to tree, taking her time, learning the layout of the town.

As night fell, she slipped in among the buildings, finding ample cover. She prowled from house to house, finding many left as if the people had just walked away. One had a hunting bow still standing in the corner next to a quiver of arrows. Others had jars of tea, bowls of shelled corn, a pot of pitch, blankets and bedding untouched. Weaving on looms left as if the owner had stepped away for but a moment.

A whole town, abandoned.

From dark doorways she could survey the plaza. Watched as warriors— there appeared to only be five—loitered on the palace veranda. The chief—a Cahokian who wore North Star House designs on his apron— was a small man, wiry. Despite the darkness and distance, she immediately recognized the exiled Fire Light. Why would he be here? And since he was, what was his deal with Walking Smoke?

Across from her, the Clan House couldn't be missed given the flayed human skin hanging from a framework built of sticks standing out front. Two human skulls, missing the lower jaws, had been impaled upon poles at either corner of the building. An inverted elk skull was resting on its heavy rack of antlers, the bone white in the gathering night.

Her heart jumped a beat as she saw movement at the door. Watched the figure of a man emerge from the shadowed veranda.

"*Yes!*" Piasa's harsh whisper sounded just behind her right ear.

She eased farther back into the darkness, letting the doorway mask her outline. A cool tingle of fear danced lightly through her as Walking Smoke stepped out, head cocked in that old inquisitive manner. Lightning flashed in the night, and Walking Smoke raised his hands, throwing his head back.

In another white flash, she could see the bent smile, realized something was wrong with the side of his face.

"I know you're out there!" he called. "I can *feel* you! Like I felt you last night. You know. I had you by the waist. Held you tight. I was just about to drive my shaft all the way into that warm and soft sheath of yours!"

He laughed, almost cackled.

The warriors on the chief's palace veranda had stepped out, watching in curious silence.

Night Shadow Star took a deep breath. Tried to still the pounding inside her. What kind of magic was that? Had he really been there?

Once again lightning flashed across the sky.

"I need you to come to me," Walking Smoke called. "It's this Power. Playing us. Sky Power, Underworld Power. They expect us to kill each other."

He circled around, staring this way and that. "Where are you?"

Well, at least he wasn't headed her way at a run. She shifted the copper-bitted ax. She'd shoved the slim hickory handle through the rope belted at her waist. Ensured it would be easy to rip free at a moment's notice.

"*Think* about it," Walking Smoke cried into the darkening night. "We're gaming pieces. But what happens if we change the game? Underworld crossed with Sky World. Male and female. White and red. Brother and sister. Not just any brother and sister, but the most important ones in the world!"

She made a face.

"You want to end this?" He lifted his hands in the gloom. "Come to me, sister. What if instead of killing each other, we melted your Power into mine? You and me. In union. Our Power mixing, becoming stronger and stronger. Together."

"You're still a twisted and abhorrent excuse for a human being," she whispered under her breath.

"I've just given you the key," Walking Smoke bellowed. "The reason they *fear* us so much. The reason they want us to murder each other. The moment we merge our Power, we destroy them!"

The warriors in front of the palace looked uncomfortable as they shifted back and forth.

"I'll be inside," Walking Smoke told her. "I have roast meat and black drink on the fire. However you want to do this, I am ready. Let's finish this once and for all."

With that, he turned, walked back into the building, leaving the door open so that the glow from the fire inside could be seen.

Night Shadow Star sagged back into the darkness.

Now that she was here, faced with his madness, her courage had fled.

She dropped her face into her hands, wishing Fire Cat was with her. She'd always been brave when Fire Cat was at her side.

Remember? That's who Piasa thinks is going to finish this.

"Just walk across the plaza. Walk in the door, and all I have to do is drive my ax through his skull."

She flexed the muscles in her right arm, ran her fingers down them. She'd never been stronger. Day after day, she'd paddled, carried a pack, climbed up and down tortuous trails in mountain country.

Walking Smoke would have been here, playing the part of a witch. Lounging, eating well, being lazy. Of her two brothers, Walking Smoke had always been the one to take the easy route.

"He won't be expecting my strength. My agility."

"*Come to me,*" his words echoed in her memory.

And in that instant, a slow smile crossed her lips.

That's what Walking Smoke, the Thunderers, and Piasa were counting on.

Eighty-one

Night was falling, and the trail, pointed out by the captive warrior, whose name was Field Snake, kept climbing, the way more treacherous as it wound along a ridge. Given the thick canopy of intermixed oaks, hickory, maples, beech, and the few giant isolated pines, there was no way to orient, barely enough sunlight through the occasional hole in the canopy to so much as get a hint of which way was which.

"Just a little farther," Field Snake kept insisting. He was panting, sweat running down his hide, trickling down his back and skinny ribs. He'd done a solid job, Fire Cat thought. Pitching in, carrying his end of the box. And he'd insisted that taking this trail, across the ridge rather than down the creek to its confluence with Joara Creek and then back north, would save a couple of hands of time.

As the light was now fading, Fire Cat wondered. He could see the growing skepticism on Winder's and Blood Talon's faces as they labored up the steepening trail. The footing was tougher, and they had to clamber over roots, lift and snake the packs and Night Shadow Star's box around the dangling vines.

"If this isn't the right way . . ." Winder told Field Snake.

"Do you think I want to die?" Field Snake retorted. "If I lied, you'll make my death miserable. So, yes, this is the short way. 'Cause the sooner we're there, the sooner you'll let me go."

Which, Fire Cat, had to admit, was sound reasoning.

A half a hand of time later, with the light failing, he wasn't so sure.

W. Michael Gear and Kathleen O'Neal Gear

Darkness came fast in the deep forest. The way was even steeper than before. They were clambering over outcrops of worn sandstone now, the roots and vines thicker.

The only sound was the call of the evening birds and the occasional late chattering of the squirrels.

At a steep ascent, the slope falling off at the edge of the trail, the gloom so deep it was almost dark, they slowed, Field Snake at the front.

Fire Cat didn't see the details. Just the shadowy blur of motion. Field Snake set the box down, turned. Looked like he was moving a fallen branch out of the way. Bent as he was, slightly elevated on the trail, he put all of his body weight into the swing.

Winder barely had warning, but got an arm up. The section of awkwardly balanced branch skipped off his forearm, knocked him on the skull, and whistled off into the dark.

With that, Field Snake leaped off the trail, sliding and kicking his way down into the darkness.

Blood Talon went after him, crashing down through the leaf mat.

"Pus and blood!" Winder cried as Fire Cat leaned over him.

"Let me see."

"Little pus-sucking maggot smacked me a good one. Piss in a pot, it's bleeding like a throat-cut turkey."

Down the slope more thrashing could be heard. Fire Cat peered over the side, seeing nothing but dark shadows.

Fire Cat made a pad from a square of cloth, used it as a compress to stanch the blood as the world around them turned from gloom to dark.

"Where are you?" Blood Talon called from below.

"Here," Fire Cat bellowed, his rage building. "You find him?"

"Can't find my spitting hand in front of my face!"

The thrashing of distant leaves could be heard.

"I think we've been tricked," Winder muttered. "I'm hunting that little shit down and tearing him apart, slowly and surely."

"Tricked in the worst way," Fire Cat said through gritted teeth.

Somewhere out there, Night Shadow Star was on her own.

Eighty-two

Seven Skull Shield had to admit, Blue Heron had taken to her new circumstances with a great deal more aplomb than he had imagined she would. And, if ever a person's circumstances were reversed, it was now. The woman beside him looked anything but like the onetime Four Winds Clan Keeper.

No, indeed, the Blue Heron walking down the avenue that separated Morning Star's great mound from Night Shadow Star's, the various society houses, and finally the mound upon which she used to live wore an old hemp-fabric skirt. A square flat-bark sun hat perched atop her gray locks, and a cape made of woven cedar bark hung on her shoulders. She bore a light load of sticks held together with a leather strap; the sort of kindling used to start fires.

For his part, Seven Skull Shield was fine in his usual hunting shirt, a rope belt around his waist with the pouches he favored for carrying this and that. That was the great thing about being Seven Skull Shield. He was used to looking like nine out of ten of the men he passed on the avenue.

Blue Heron stopped short at the base of her mound and looked up. The stairs—squared logs set into the ramp—still led up to the eagle-post guardians. But beyond that, there was nothing. No imposing roof rising toward the sere sky.

She took a step toward the stairs.

"Don't," Seven Skull Shield told her. "Put one foot on that step, and anyone watching will know you're no dirt farmer come to Trade firewood. Such a thing would never cross a low-status woman's mind."

"You're right, of course." She continued to stare longingly up past the top of the staircase. "Word is that they found only one body, mostly charred, on the veranda just outside the door. Had to be Big Right. That rot-balled warrior told me he was 'napping.' Must have really hurt him if he didn't wake up when they started the fire."

"Good thing you sent everyone else away."

She nodded thoughtfully, turned, eyes seeking the high bastion that stood on the southwest corner of Morning Star's palisade.

Seven Skull Shield followed her gaze, saw the single figure who peered over the bastion's clay-covered wall. Sunlight glinted on polished copper, shone through an eagle-feather splay on either shoulder. Only one person would be atop that bastion and dressed like that: Morning Star.

The living god raised a hand, seemed to make a salute, touching his chin and extending the gesture Blue Heron's way. Then he turned, vanishing from the high aerie.

"Think he knew who you were?"

"He's Morning Star. How should I know?"

She turned. "Come, I want to go see what's happening in the Great Plaza. Hear the gossip."

"You already know. *Tonka'tzi* Wind is a virtual prisoner. Doesn't go anywhere unless she's escorted by Spotted Wrist's warriors. If she so much as sneezes, Green Chunkey replaces her as *tonka'tzi*. Your warning got to War Duck and Round Pot in just enough time that they're safely hidden away, using their connections to keep Three Fingers from claiming control of River House. Columella's squadrons are fortifying the west bank of the river."

"Impasse. At least for the moment. But it won't last."

"Nope. All Spotted Wrist has to do is bring his army across. Win or lose, it will be bloody."

They picked their way through the throng of people flocking along the Avenue of the Sun, past the crowd of vendors, Traders, and hawkers who'd lined the sides of the Great Plaza, some in stalls, others with tables, and the most modest having spread a blanket on the ground to display their wares.

"The squabble at the top of the Four Winds Clan doesn't seem to have discouraged Trade," Blue Heron noted as they meandered their way through the press. Out in the plaza, the midsummer sun shone on the World Tree pole. A stickball game was being waged on the south end— literally for blood as a limp player was carried from a battling knot of young men. Hawk Clan, dressed in blue, was playing a Panther Clan team, wearing white.

At the foot of the *tonka'tzi*'s mound, evenly spaced as pickets, stood no fewer than ten warriors, each dressed in armor, bows strung, looking serious and deadly in the hot light.

"More of them around the sides," Seven Skull Shield noted. "But not unreasonable. I could get past them."

"One of these days, thief . . ." Then she chuckled.

"What? You're on my side now. Every meal you and Smooth Pebble have eaten since the night they burned your palace has been stolen."

"It's humbling."

"Well"—he gestured at the palace—"you're not getting in there. At least not in bright daylight, and certainly not without help. Besides, your sister is up at the Council House. Saw her litter sitting at the bottom of the Great Staircase."

Blue Heron made a face, reached up with her free hand to pull at the wattle of skin under her chin. "If I just knew there was some sort of hope. That we weren't in this alone. Sure, there's Columella, but her first responsibility is Evening Star Town, and that's been a closely run thing. War Duck and Round Pot? How long can they run resistance from inside Crazy Frog's storehouse? Eventually Three Fingers' people are going to figure that out. And Wind"—she gestured—"is living like a turtle in a wicker cage. Me? I can't even get word to my spies, and I have nothing left to pay them with if I do."

"We're not beat yet, you know."

She gave him that old "Are-you-insane-or-just-head-struck?" look. "Maybe not right now, today, as we speak, but in the long run? Time is on their side. Spotted Wrist and Rising Flame control the clan. Have the authority to win over the long term. In the end, thief, we're too weak to prevail."

"Hey!" a voice called. "You!"

Seven Skull Shield turned, dropped to a crouch, ready to leap into whatever trouble this was.

Pus and blood, this was going to be bad. Two warriors. Each in Morning Star House armor. The fancy stuff, like Morning Star's guard wore up at the high palace. Maybe, back before he was beaten and starved in Spotted Wrist's cage, he could have knocked them sideways, gotten away in the crowd. But with Blue Heron to look after, he didn't have a chance.

"So, Keeper," he muttered out the side of his mouth, "when I jump them, you run. Got it? Just get far enough to get out of their view, toss the firewood, and mingle with the crowd."

"I said you." The lead warrior was pointing now, not more than three paces away.

This isn't going to end well.

But, piss in a pot, it had been a good life. He'd had some great times, enjoyed . . .

"That firewood," the warrior said. "We need that. Will you Trade?"

Blue Heron was gaping, seemed to be lost for words.

"Why, of course, good Squadron First!" Seven Skull Shield beamed as he stepped forward. "And this is the finest kindling in Cahokia. Taken dry in the uplands a full ten days' travel upriver. Good stuff. Look, it's hickory and ash, the kind that will burn hot at the merest hint of a spark."

The warriors had stopped, their eyes oddly wary. Now the second shifted, his gaze roving as he took in Spotted Wrist's men at the base of the *tonka'tzi*'s mound and then began searching the crowd. Seven Skull Shield knew a lookout when he saw one.

Every nerve in his body was tingling, but so was his curiosity.

"What'll you Trade?" the first warrior asked.

"You from Morning Star's mound?"

"It's for the living god's fire," the warrior told him, keen eyes trying to convey some deeper message. "In fact, it was he who saw you from the wall. Told War Leader Five Fists you had wood. Good man, the war leader. Sent me to find you. Make a Trade."

"Can't find a better sort than that Five Fists," Blue Heron agreed. "Hope he's doing well, what with the changes going on."

The warrior gave her a wary smile. "Morning Star has mentioned to the war leader that he hopes the changes aren't permanent. Told Five Fists that for his own reasons, the living god can't interfere. At least, not directly."

Seven Skull Shield's heart began to quicken.

Blue Heron was grinning. "As the living god wills."

"Careful," the second warrior said, eyes on several of Spotted Wrist's warriors who'd fixed on Morning Star warriors being so close.

"I'll Trade this," the first warrior said loudly, offering a sack of something that dangled from his fist.

"Done!" Seven Skull Shield cried, handing over the bundle of kindling from Blue Heron's back. "You need more? Got plenty where that came from."

"If it's good, we'll need more tomorrow. Say around a hand's time after dawn. Maybe you could have someone waiting on the Avenue of the Sun just out from the chunkey courts."

And with that the warriors turned, pacing off, the bundle of kindling hanging from one's shoulder.

Spotted Wrist's warriors had retreated to their positions along the base of the mound.

Seven Skull Shield, one hand to Blue Heron's shoulder, led her back the way they'd come. "How's that for a stroke of good fortune?"

Blue Heron, meanwhile, had taken the sack. Now she opened it, glanced inside, and grinned. "It's got a string of beads. It's a message."

"What's it say?"

"How do I know, thief? We need a recorder to read it." She stopped, staring up at Morning Star's high mound. Again, just visible against the summer sky, that lone figure stood atop the bastion, sunlight glinting off polished copper and eagle splays.

Eighty-three

The singing of crickets, the distant call of the whippoorwill, an owl hooting in the forest to her south. The sounds filled the night, helped to cover Night Shadow Star's steps as she crept around the corner of a society house until she could see Walking Smoke's front door, the fire's glow still visible inside.

Her preparations had taken a couple of hands of time. She had thought it all through.

Walking Smoke was guarded by Sky Power. If she tried to approach with her copper-bitted club, dripping of Underworld Power as it was, her brother would know. Understand immediately the source and nature of the threat.

He wanted her to come to him?

That meant he had taken precautions. Walking Smoke would never allow her to approach unless he held all the advantages. Who knew what sort of traps he might have constructed—falling nets, deadfalls, pits, snares, something noxious like tossing poison ivy into the fire?

A knot had pulled tight in Night Shadow Star's throat. Now that she teetered on the precipice, she was frightened down to her marrow.

She resettled her war club, slanting it sideways across her belly where it wouldn't impede movement.

From her shoulder, she took the hunting bow she'd found. Were it not for her current strength, she would have never managed the pull. Each of the arrows in the quiver had been serviceable, most with stone hunting points. She had soaked strips of cloth in pine pitch, then wound them around foreshafts and tied them. The fire she'd had to start; then she'd allowed it to burn down to the coals. Those she put in a small jar of sand that she hung around her neck with a thong.

Stepping back out of sight, she pulled an arrow. Lifted the pot of coals and inserted the pitch-soaked cloth. Blowing on it, she coaxed a flame. Pulled three more arrows, used the lit arrow to set fire to the rest.

Committed, she ducked around the back of the society house. Fear lent her strength and speed. The first arrow she drove into the thatch, shooting it up at the same angle as the roof so that it slipped into the dry grass with barely a sound. At the far corner, she did the same. Circled to the front of the house. Shot into the roof. Crossed in front of the door at a run and shot the last arrow into the fourth corner of the roof.

Panting, she ducked back behind the society house wall, craned her neck out only far enough that she could see the first flickering flames in the thatch.

Pus and blood, she wished she had something to drink. Night Shadow Star swallowed hard, pulled another arrow, stepped out, and nocked it. Maybe he wouldn't hear the growing flames, maybe he'd fallen asleep.

Or, as she expected, he'd realize his situation, charge out into the light of the fire, where she'd be able to step close and drive her next arrow right through his heart.

It took longer than she would have thought. The roof had turned into a roaring tower of flame. The entire time she quivered, half in fear, half in anxiety. Surely the man had to realize. Or, could it be? Was she really lucky enough that he was going to awaken to his situation too late?

Then she heard the curse, barely loud enough to carry over the flames.

He charged out from the burning building, head down, arms raised and crossed above as if for protection against the searing heat.

Panting, muscles pumping, she sprinted out, drawing as she did.

No more than five paces from him, she stopped, held her draw, and fixed on his chest.

Only to have him turn.

"You!" she cried.

He gaped at her, firelight glaring yellow on the side of his face. In horror he lifted his hands, the mangled thumb and finger on his right forever etched in her memory. "Lady, don't! By the Spirits, I was just hired. He's . . ."

Her shaft took him through the chest, stopped just short of the fletching. The Casqui's eyes bugged, his mouth dropping into a silent O. He staggered, fingers pulling weakly at the fletching. Stumbled sideways.

She watched as he dropped to his knees. A whimpering sound could barely be heard over the roar of the flames.

"You," she repeated, struggling to understand. She blinked, looking back at the roaring inferno. She could see inside the door, had a view of the room. Pots, jars, sleeping benches, weird frameworks made of human bones. Blood had been smeared in designs over the walls. She'd seen the like before. In Cahokia. During Walking Smoke's murderous rampage.

She had no warning. Arms wrapped around her from behind. Took her by complete surprise. Lifted her.

She struck out, lost the bow. Screamed her fear.

"Good. So very good. See, I told you I'd take you from behind. But we'll have plenty of time for that."

Walking Smoke wasn't ready for her strength, with all the whipcord muscle she'd built on the river. She managed to jerk her arm free. Ripped the ax from her belt.

She got half turned, could only make an awkward strike. Swinging low and back between his legs. Felt it connect with a solid thump.

Walking Smoke uttered a high-pitched scream. But his hold on her didn't break.

She hammered an elbow into his ribs. Heard his explosion of breath. Jerked her head back violently, slammed it into his face. Managed to twist free. All it would take was one good strike with her . . .

She barely had a glimpse, a body coming in from the side. Something hit her head. Knocked it sideways. Blasted yellow dots of light through her vision.

She felt herself falling, knew she'd hit the ground.

Her senses were swimming. Her souls seemed disconnected from her body. She couldn't control her arms or legs.

"Shit in a pot!" Walking Smoke screamed. "She hit me right in the stones!"

In her swimming vision, she saw him pick up her ax, fling it toward the burning building where it missed the door, hit the wall, and bounced back into the trampled grass.

"Good thing it wasn't the sharp edge that hit you, isn't it?" the voice said. "Come on. We've got her. She would have killed you but for me. I've fulfilled my part of the bargain. Now, let's get out of here so you can fulfill yours."

"Tomorrow. In the morning."

"Before first light."

Night Shadow Star blinked, trying to steady her blurry vision. Her cousin, Fire Light, was illuminated by the burning Clan House. Several of his warriors were standing in the background, alternately glancing at her, then at Walking Smoke as, weeping, he cupped his genitals, and then at the burning building.

She lurched forward, threw up, then again, and again.

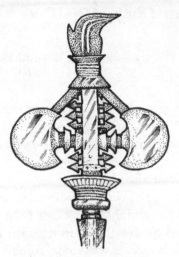

Eighty-four

Trade had been about as good as it got. That was the thing about having the warriors from two squadrons encamped in the vicinity of River Mounds City. Not that Robin Feather cared about the politics. In the end it wouldn't matter if it was War Duck, Broken Stone, or Three Fingers, he would still have to surrender a percentage of his Trade. That's what chiefs did, they took a piece.

The sack on Robin Feather's back rattled reassuringly as the clamshells in the bottom shifted. The rest of it was stuffed full of hanging moss from way down south. Not that he depended upon either for his rope making, but he could Trade them for things he did need.

Yes, it had been a good day.

He wound his way through the warehouses, past Gray Mouse's arrow-making shop, rounded the stone grinder's, and stopped short. The dog was missing. The heavy stake he'd driven into the ground still stood there, and a rope lay abandoned on the dirt beside his spinning jig.

He hurried forward, growling under his breath. Which was when he noticed that the door to his workshop had been set to one side.

"Piss in a pot, that was part of what the dog was for. Keeping people out of my workshop!"

He glanced around, seeing old Flat-and-Wide where he sat on a stool beside a pile of cattail leaves that he was plaiting into matting. The old man had a small shop where he Traded matting for the few things he needed now that his wife had died and his children had traveled off to some colony up north.

"Hey! You seen my dog?"

The old man, hard of hearing, didn't react until Robin Feather was standing over him. "Where's my dog?"

Flat-and-Wide blinked his rheumy eyes, squinted over. "Oh, yes. I see your dog's missing."

"Did you see who took him?"

"No. No. I had to go to the canoe landing. Needed to Trade for a loaf of acorn bread. You want some? Got enough for a couple of days."

Robin Feather lifted his free hand in despair, turned, and plodded back to his shop. The building was long, roofed with split cane, and oriented to the same celestial direction as the rest of the buildings in River Mounds City.

He stepped inside; the late-afternoon light was streaming through the gap between the walls and roof. The first thing he noticed was his latest basswood rope, still on his spinning jig. If anyone was going to take anything, it would have been that.

He set his sack of Trade to one side—and caught movement as the big brindle dog dropped onto its butt and scratched, its ears flopping. "There you are! I ought to bash your thick-skulled head in. I swear, I'll throw you in the stewpot as soon as look at you. How'd you get loose, anyway?"

The dog ambled up, lifted its leg, and peed on the pole that supported his spinning jig.

"Hey! Piasa curse you!"

He grabbed up one of the wooden blocks he used to separate fibers, cocked his arm, and took aim to throw it when a voice in the back said, "I wouldn't do that if I were you."

"Well, it's my shop. My dog."

"Farts, come here," the voice called.

The big dog bounded to the rear, leaping into the shadowed man's arms. What looked like a wrestling match ensued. The big man laughing, growling playfully with the dog, and finally ordering, "Down, beast. Down."

Then he rose and stepped into the shaft of sunlight.

"You!" Robin Feather turned, dropped the block, and grabbed up a thick wooden mallet he used to beat raw stock into fibers.

"Whoa!" Seven Skull Shield thrust his arms out, hands wide. "Hear me out. Look." He pointed.

Robin Feather followed the finger to see three thick coils of rope about midway down his floor.

"I heard you offered three fine coils of basswood rope to anyone who could find me. Well, you made all three of them. That's the price, right? So, I'm Trading for myself."

"That wasn't the point. But I'll take them. Still doesn't mean I'm not beating you to death for what you did with Willow Blossom. Do you know what that did to me?"

"Stop it! In the first place, you're not a kind, loving, and caring husband. You're a narrow-minded, self-concerned, walking piece of human dung who can't see past the latest piece of rope he's making and what it will get you. I'm surprised you didn't kill Farts just to get back at me."

"Bah! That was the idea. I needed him alive. Want you to see me smack him in the head before I throw him in the stewpot. As refreshing as it would have been to pay you back by eating him first thing, it will be so much better if you're watching while I do it."

"Maybe I'll take those ropes with me when I go."

"You're not going anywhere."

Seven Skull Shield's grin had an evil twist, a gleaming promise in his eyes as he stepped close. "You want to take a try with that hammer? Now, me, I've been beat up, burned, poked, kept in a cage, watched a lot of bad things happen to people I like. So, I come here. Figure I'm going to make amends. Tell you I'm sorry. Let you know that the woman you took into your bed is a spider. One of them kind that eats the men she lets into her sheath. She's trouble, Robin Feather. For whoever is in her bed at the moment."

"She was mine!" He thumped his chest.

"She would have eaten you alive! She played you like a fine eagle-bone flute. She played me. Now she's playing Spotted Wrist." He paused, looking thoughtful. "Not that I mind her milking him for everything he's got. But for once, she might have bit off more than a mouthful."

"She's with him?"

Seven Skull Shield nodded, lips pursed. "You were a stepping stone to get her away from Moon Mounds. I was another stone to get her from you to Night Shadow Star's, and she gave me up to get into Spotted Wrist's bed. If she talks the war leader into getting her into Morning Star's blankets . . . well, that will be a whole new angle of impossible."

Robin Feather took a deep breath. "I should still beat the spit out of you. Just on principle."

Seven Skull Shield grinned. "How about we let that be our secret. There's your rope. Tell people you and I got even. That you're no longer after my scarred and bruised hide."

"You do look a bit beat up."

"Thanks to Willow Blossom. Do we have a Trade? Me for the ropes?"

"Where'd you get them?"

"Do you know how hard it is to steal one of your ropes? Took all my skill. People really value them."

"You're giving me stolen ropes?"

"Are you telling me you can't Trade them for just as much as you got the first time? Oh, but don't tell anybody where you got them. That's got to be part of the deal."

"I must be out of my head."

"Come on, Farts. We've got work to do. And, at least for a while, we don't need to be looking over our shoulder all the time while we're doing it."

Robin Feather shook his head, watched the big man amble out of his doorway, the brindle flop-eared dog leaping and cavorting at his side.

Seven Skull Shield threw his head back, singing, *"She gives lots of hugs, her breasts big as jugs. I up and laughed as she grabbed at my shaft."*

And then he was gone.

Eighty-five

Fire Cat led the way into Joara as the first light of dawn spread across the eastern sky and left the tops of the trees a black silhouette against the sky.

He, Winder, and Blood Talon looked like they'd spent the night falling down the side of a mountain. Off and on during the dark hours, they had. Somehow, feeling their way, they'd managed to retrace the tortuous path back to the main trail, stumbled onto the occasional farmstead where they evaded dogs, pounded on doors to get people out of bed, and got directions to Joara. Several of the worried locals had repeatedly told them to go elsewhere, anywhere, away from the witch.

"Hope it doesn't come down to a fight," Blood Talon said through a yawn. "I can barely walk."

Fire Cat saw the leaves and twigs in Blood Talon's hair, the smudges on his face.

Not that he or Winder looked any better. The big Trader's head was matted with dried blood, a streak of it now visible in the growing light.

"Not sure I like that smell of smoke," the Trader said as they walked through abandoned houses, the doorways dark, the ramadas curiously empty.

The palace was plain to see, a high peak-roofed building atop a low mound. "On your toes, my friends. That should be where Fire Light and his warriors are."

"Circle around," Blood Talon said. "Come in from the side so we can see what's what before we blunder into something."

"Having already been tricked like fools, I can agree to that, Squadron First. Let's hide Night Shadow Star's box. There, in that field shed."

Fire Cat let Blood Talon take the lead as he snaked his way through the houses lining the square, though this one was more elongated than the usual *talwa* style. And, as they finally got a look at it from between dwellings, it had a World Tree pole in its center. Definitely felt more Cahokian.

"That would have been the Clan House." Blood Talon pointed to the smoking ruin on the opposite side of the plaza.

"That's Walking Smoke's, all right," Fire Cat agreed, his heart beginning to hammer in his chest. "That's a skinned human hanging out front."

Grinding his teeth, fighting sudden tears, he started forward.

"Get back here!" Blood Talon gritted through his teeth. "They'll shoot you dead!"

Heedless, Fire Cat broke into a run, pulled up, stared at the smoking wreckage. Not only the roof, but the walls had burned through, the clay daub on the outside apparently not thick enough to stop the flames. The fallen roof poles were still burning. What was left of the thatch was now just hot powdery ash. Some sort of altar could be made out in the back.

As the first rays of sunlight cleared the forest to the east, a golden light spread across the plaza. Turned the rising smoke a curious orange and pink. The smell was of incinerated wood.

Fire Cat closed his eyes, inhaled, moderately relieved to realize that he wasn't catching a scent of cooked human.

Winder had appeared at his side, staring at the wreckage.

"I don't see a body. There's bones, but they're burned white and cracked in those checked patterns the way old dry bone burns."

"She could still be under one of the thicker piles of ash."

But he didn't think so.

Blood Talon approached at a trot, his war club held ready. "Palace is empty. Packed up. You ask me? They're gone."

"When?" Fire Cat asked, his souls reeling and tumbling.

"Not long. Last night. Fires are down to coals, but they're still hot enough to cook on."

Fire Cat turned, saw the gleam of copper. Stooped and picked Night Shadow Star's war club from the beaten grass.

That welling sense of emptiness and impotence rose in his gut like vomit, sucking away any thought, any strength.

Something terrible has happened to her.

"War Leader?" Blood Talon said cautiously. "Look."

Fire Cat turned, saw an old woman appear from the west end of the plaza, plodding out into the open past the temple.

Back bent, she hobbled along, each step supported by a cane.

Fire Cat turned, ran, willing . . . anything into his tortured souls.

"Hello! Do you speak Cahokian?"

The old woman waved a weary hand, stopped short. She cocked her head at him, dark eyes like pits sunk into the wrinkly folds of her face. Her nose stuck out, a fleshy hook. The lips were sucked in around toothless gums.

"Who're you?"

"Friends. Looking for a woman. Young. Would have carried this war club." Fire Cat lifted it.

The old woman stared at it, nodded.

"The witch got her."

Fire Cat swallowed hard. Ground his teeth to keep his jaw from trembling.

"Oh, she gave him a good whack with it first. Would have killed the witch if that chief hadn't sent his warriors in to grab her."

"Where is she?"

"Gone." The old woman waved in a circle. "All of them. Wish I was, too. This place is ruined now. Would have been gone, but I got no family. Can barely make it to the creek for water. How can I get all the way to Cofitachequi?"

"When did they leave?" Winder asked kindly.

"Middle of the night. That nasty kid warrior came stumbling in just after all the excitement. Said a Cahokian army was coming. That they killed four of Chief Fire Light's warriors. Were coming for the witch."

"Which way did they go?" Blood Talon asked.

The old woman gave the ghost of a shrug. "Away. Cofitachequi . . . maybe. That's the closest big town. That's where the *mikko* went. Don't know. There was something about the witch getting a pardon for that snotty chief. A pardon in Cahokia. He hated it here. Heard his sister was some important person now."

"Middle of the night?" Fire Cat wondered. "Surely we'd have passed them on the trail."

"If they went that way," Winder reminded. "There's a reason Joara is where it is. It's a crossroads. Trails run east, north, west, and south."

Blood Talon laid a hand on Fire Cat's arm. "We'll get her back. We know she's alive. First we have to eat something. Rest. And then we'll go get her."

Fire Cat blinked, wanting to drop to his knees and cry.

Yes, we'll get her back.

In his head, stuffed full of fatigued fog as it was, he could hear Night Shadow Star's words: *"But you know there will be a price."*

Of course. Nothing he wouldn't pay.

As soon as they'd eaten, caught a little sleep.

Just a matter of time.

Eighty-six

The crickets were making a racket, as loud in the hot and muggy night as Willow Blossom had ever heard them. She rode in splendor on her litter, lounging as her porters trotted up the avenue that ran along the base of Morning Star's mound. She wore an intricate lace veil—the delicate crochet made from finely combed cottonwood fluff. The thing was a masterwork, had taken years of detailed craftsmanship and could have been Traded for a fortune at the canoe landing.

Fortunately, it had been a gift from Spotted Wrist. One she particularly valued because from here on, appearance was everything. "And it keeps me from being pestered by these hideous mosquitoes."

That was the thing about traveling at night. The nasty little bloodsuckers weren't as bad in the heat of the day—then it was the flies that were the nuisance—but at night? When it was cool, they came in swarming clouds.

Knowing the way, her porters veered off, passing between the Panther Clan Council House and a copper workshop, winding their way back through a section of smaller Four Winds palaces belonging to a not-so-well-to-do lineage—distant cousins to the *tonka'tzi*—and finally to her own modest dwelling.

She was carefully lowered to the ground, rose on her own, and said, "That will be all."

"Thank you, lady," her head porter replied, touching his chin. She reveled in the gesture, usually reserved only for nobility.

As they vanished into the night, she stepped up onto her veranda: a sign of her newfound fortune, constructed as it was with split planks. She undid her door and entered the dark house, stepping down to the subterranean floor.

It wasn't much, just a single room, earth-banked trench-wall construction with wall-bench beds and a split-cane roof. But it was hers. And it would do for the time being.

Some things, however, still had to be dealt with personally. She wasn't wealthy enough to Trade for a good slave. That, like all things, would come.

She bent down, fished for the stick she kept by the hearth, and used it to dig around in the ash until she found a glowing coal. Then another.

Using shredded juniper bark as tinder, she blew, watched it catch, and added kindling until the fire was a leaping tongue of flame. Adding a bundle of twigs ensured it would ignite the two short sections of oak branch she placed on top.

Clapping her hands to clean them of ash, she straightened, and froze. Her heart skipped, breath caught with sudden fear.

"Who are you?"

"A visitor," the woman said.

She was seated in the dark corner, back to the wall. In the growing light, Willow Blossom could make out that she was tall, very well formed, her hair up in a bun and pinned with polished copper skewers in the form of feathers. The fire barely did justice to the colored lines of feathers that ran down the back of her exquisite cape. The woman's skirt was a gauzy thing, intricately embroidered, and worth a fortune in Trade.

"You're in my house."

"So, you're observant as well as talented."

"Who are you?"

"I'm a businesswoman, as are you. I work in the same profession. Men pay me for my body's talents. They pay me very well."

"I am *not* a paid woman!" She felt the hot flush of anger overcome her fear.

"Indeed? Your litter just dropped you off from an evening of servicing the Keeper. I've been through your little jar, found the herbs you use to keep from conceiving, the menstrual blood–covered knot you sleep over. You don't have much, but what you do is quality. The bedding—for those instances should he ever come here—is kept separate from what you normally sleep in, the oversized sleeping bench, even the fact that he gave you this house for your service is pretty much a dead give-away."

"If you think Spotted Wrist would give a woman a house just for milking his shaft, you don't know a thing about him."

"Ah, that was for turning the thief over to him, wasn't it?"

"Who *are* you? What do you want?"

The fire was leaping now, filling the room with light. Willow Blossom watched the woman rise, the action stately, somehow reminiscent of smoke lifting, so fluid was she.

She stepped over, head cocked.

Willow Blossom drew herself up to her full height, still having to look up into the woman's midnight eyes. "I said, what do you want?"

"Yes, I see," the woman mused. "You are very beautiful, good breasts, that narrow waist. Given your background, I'll bet you're still learning the arts your sheath is capable of. But the thief would have taught you a lot about that."

"Why do you keep going back to that thief? What do you want from me?"

"I have a professional question. When you work them, do you feel anything for them? Any fondness, any delight in their company?"

"What are you talking about?"

"He's just a means to an end, isn't he? A job. Like shucking corn. I'll bet you even consider it something that has to be endured. An unpleasant reality. No love, no hate, no human connection. Men are just objects to be manipulated."

"Oh, I get it. Is that a paid woman thing? Listen, it's the only way to the finer things in life."

"Along with the occasional betrayal of someone who makes the mistake of caring for you." She gestured at the surrounding walls. "Especially if it will get you a house. I should have been so lucky."

"Maybe I'm just better at this than you are."

"Maybe you are. Tell me, would you assassinate the Keeper? For the right price, of course."

"Are you crazy?"

"I'll give you a stack of copper plate as high as your knee."

Willow Blossom hesitated, tried to understand if the woman was serious, sensing some trap. Pus and blood, Spotted Wrist hadn't sent her, had he? Best to be safe. "No."

"Is it because you care for the Keeper?"

At that she laughed. "He's old enough to be my grandfather. Did he send you?"

"He would be most upset to know that I, of all people, was talking to you."

And then it made sense. *She* had been in his bed, too. "Oh, jealous, huh? Afraid I'll take your precious Keeper? Well, you'd better be very good with that sheath of yours, because I'm going to be the perfect woman. Wind him up tight and make him think I'm the end of his Dreams."

She enlarged her eyes, adopted her adoring expression, parted her lips in anticipation, and expanded her chest so her breasts rose as she took small breaths to make them rise and fall.

The woman's smile was knowing, somehow sad. "A stack of copper plate, and I'll even throw in an Itza blanket. You do know who the Itza are, right? All you have to do is drop a potion into the Keeper's tea."

"Get out of here. You don't have anything I'd want. But something tells me Spotted Wrist is going to be very interested in knowing you're trying to kill him."

"Seriously? You don't care about the man. All you want him for is what you can use him to get. And I'll make you rich."

"Not as rich as he will." Willow Blossom walked to the door. "You want to give me your name so it's easy for the Keeper's warriors to run you down, or do you want to make it hard for them?"

"I'm all for easy," the woman said, starting to step past her for the door.

The movement was low, quick, barely caught from the corner of Willow Blossom's eye. The sting, lancing deep and up just under her ribs, could be felt right through her lungs, excruciating. She could *feel* the thing as it speared her heart, felt her chest quiver as each heartbeat wiggled it in her flesh.

She tried to scream, her mouth agape. Pain filled her chest, heavy, pulsing. Breath wouldn't come.

She was staring into the woman's eyes. Practiced, the woman caught Willow Blossom's weight, turned her, eased her onto the closest bench.

"You could have made a fortune," the woman told her. "You had the body, the raw talent. You even had the heartless part right, but to be a success in this business, you have to be smart enough to know when a better offer comes along. Had you, I might have forgiven what you did to Skull."

The smile was back, somewhat wistful this time, and then she said, "Or perhaps not."

Willow Blossom's body twitched and shivered as the long deer-bone stiletto was pulled out of her chest. The eeriest feeling she'd ever known, that bone sliding out.

She blinked.

The woman had disappeared.

She ran a hand to the wound, felt the hot blood bubbling out as she struggled to catch her breath.

The room kept growing darker and darker, her fire now dim, fading. A final spot of light in an encompassing . . .

Eighty-seven

The fact that she was dressed as a dirt farmer, with her starburst tattoos covered by a thin brown smear of paint, had begun to wear on Blue Heron. All of her years, she had been trained in the reality of politics. This wasn't the first struggle for political control that she'd ever found herself in. Only the most dangerous and deadly.

She missed her palace, the prestige, good food, and fine clothes. Someone would pay for this.

Spotted Wrist had cunningly taken most of Cahokia without anyone being the wiser. At least not until his squadrons were dispatched and strategically placed. Military messengers were trotting back and forth, providing the Keeper with intelligence on what each of the Houses was doing.

Well, all but Evening Star House. There the central plaza was being fortified, squadrons called up, every precaution being taken prior to Spotted Wrist's inevitable invasion. That would happen in a matter of days given that two of Spotted Wrist's squadrons were camped at the canoe landing. All they were waiting for was the requisite number of heavy canoes to be assembled to allow the individual sections to make the crossing in sufficient force to take the town.

With all that hanging in the balance, Blue Heron had come here, to the Recorders' Society House where it stood atop its mound facing the Great Plaza on the west and overlooking the Avenue of the Sun on the north.

She had been accorded a rather disdainful welcome by a fresh-faced and way-too-young apprentice, forced to sit for a couple of hands of time in the sun, and finally ushered up the steps to the society house. She hadn't been allowed past the veranda. But, to her surprise, when she requested to see Master Lotus Leaf, the old man himself had appeared, asking, "Yes?"

She handed him the string of beads.

Taking them, Lotus Leaf thoughtfully ran them over his gnarled old fingers. A curious frown crossed his brow. "Where did you get these?"

"Traded them. For firewood from Morning Star House. Had to. We were right under Spotted Wrist's nose."

"This is Mallard's work. He's Morning Star's recorder." Only then did he really look at her, a sudden light coming to his eyes. "You're supposed to be dead."

"Good. And you haven't seen me alive, either. What did Morning Star want me to know?"

"The beads say this: 'All is not lost. Work from the shadows.'"

Lotus Leaf pointed. "You see this single copper bead? The way it is positioned in the string, it can mean either, 'The southern copper is the last solution' or 'Save the southern copper until the last.' Mallard wouldn't have strung them this way if he hadn't meant both."

The southern copper? Did he mean the Koroa copper?

"And this final section: 'You do not fight alone.'"

Blue Heron took a deep breath. For the first time since the fire, she felt a sense of relief.

Turned.

From her position on the Recorder's veranda, she could just make out someone standing on the southeastern bastion atop Morning Star's palace wall. Across the distance and elevation, she could see the glint of sunlight on a copper headpiece.

Even her old eyes saw the living god incline his head, and most uncharacteristically, touch his forehead in salute.

"I guess we've got a chance after all," she mused.

"They will kill you if they find you," Lotus Leaf noted.

She gave him a knowing grin. "They already tried. Time for me to get even."

"I wish you luck, Keeper."

She took the string of beads, stood, and said, "Thanks, I'm going to need it."

And with that she descended the stairs to the Avenue of the Sun and its crowds of Traders, hawkers, pilgrims, and farmers. No one looked twice at her. She was faceless, invisible.

And this was Cahokia.

Where she knew how to wage war in the shadows.

Eighty-eight

The terrible headache had slowly receded as Night Shadow Star's bound body was borne with haste along the shadowed forest trail. Overhead the interwoven branches had precluded any glimpse of the sky, but she knew her litter was being carried northwest, along Joara Creek, and then up the old Trade and war trail that led to the mountain pass.

As her suffering head healed and blurred vision cleared, the periodic bouts of vertigo and nausea diminished. She was able to finally assess her situation. They kept her carefully bound, two warriors in constant attendance. She was fed three times a day, and to her disgust, "assisted" when she needed to relieve herself.

Fire Light had made it clear that he would take no chances. The man had told her straight: "One way or another, you and your brother are going to see me home to what is rightfully mine."

Trussed up like a turtle bound for the roasting pit, she nevertheless seemed to be in better condition than Walking Smoke. That underhanded blow she'd delivered to his crotch had him bent double and moaning. Made her wonder at the Power that dip in Piasa's spring had given to her war club.

They were camped that night at the top of the pass. She'd been taken from her litter, fed, and given tea to drink. Now she was bound to a beech sapling.

Chief Fire Light walked over, his face partly illuminated by the flickering flames of the central fire. He crouched, studied her thoughtfully. "Are you well, Lady?"

"Better than my brother." She inclined her head in Walking Smoke's direction. "Given the damage I did to his manhood, I was really wishing I could have hit him in the head."

"He says that the moment he's healed enough, he's going to make you his. Mix your Power and his in some grand ritual mating."

"Word among your warriors is that he can barely make water, let alone harden his rod."

"Me, I don't care. I want to go home."

"Untie these ropes. Let me have the use of your war club for a couple of heartbeats, and I'll see you get your palace."

"I could almost believe you, Lady. But he's a Powerful witch. The things I've seen him do?" The man shivered.

She took a deep breath. "He's obsessed with incest. Doesn't that bother you?"

"Everything about the both of you bothers me."

"Listen, Chief: After the death of my first husband, I sent my souls to the Underworld. Piasa found me, devoured me, and made me his. I came within a whisker, literally, of dragging Walking Smoke down to my master. Then the lightning saved him. Old-Woman-Who-Never-Dies tasked me with the destruction of my second husband, the Itza. And in the end, he hanged himself. When Morning Star's souls were carried to the Underworld by Humming Moth, I was the one who descended into the depths of the Sacred Cave to bring him back. Now I have pursued Walking Smoke here, to Cofitachequi. But for your interference, I would have killed him. As it is, I just neutered him. So, do you really want to stand against me?"

"But you didn't kill him."

She hardened her glare, watched him glance away. "You couldn't have known what you were doing. Now you do. You have a choice. You can let me loose to finish my task, or I will have to destroy you. Your choice."

"Destroy me?" An amused smile played on Fire Light's lips. "Brave words from a young woman tied to a tree."

"Walking Smoke was going to rape me the moment he had me as his own. How's that working out for him? He can't even touch himself without howling, let alone consummate this magical mixing of Power he's obsessed with." A pause. "Your choice, Chief. Home in triumph, or left broken in humiliation and defeat?"

She watched Fire Light wrestle with the offer, as if he really wanted to believe her. Then he shook his head. "Sorry. If I let you free, and you tried to kill him . . . No. He's too Powerful. As soon as he finished with you, he'd turn on me. I can't take that chance."

He stood then, turning away.

"Then you leave me no choice," she told him. "I'm sorry, cousin. After tonight, I can't save you."

"As if you ever could have in the first place." He snorted derisively as he stalked off for the warriors' fire.

How is this going to end? she wondered, eyes searching the star-strewn night sky.

Somewhere, behind her, Fire Cat was already searching for her. Would he know where to follow? Could he figure out this latest twist?

"In the end," Piasa whispered, *"it will just be you and Walking Smoke. Locked in a deadly Dance. Then Power will decide. Yours. And his. Whichever is stronger."*

"Just promise me, Lord. Whatever the cost I must pay, Fire Cat not only survives, but lives happily to a ripe old age. Grant me that, and I'll do anything you ask."

From the corner of her eye, she saw a flicker of blue out under the night-shadowed trees.

Followed by Piasa's mocking laughter.

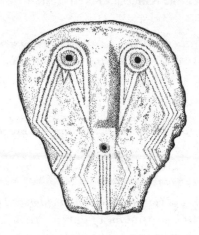

Pain

*I*t is three days now. What did she do to me?

The pain in my testicles remains debilitating. I can barely walk, can hardly straighten. Truly, the feeling is like she'd caught me with the edge of her blade instead of the blunt back of it.

Fire Light, however, is more than happy to have his men carry my litter as well as Night Shadow Star's. He is headed home, and nothing is going to stand in his way or slow him down.

Especially given that he has me and Night Shadow Star.

In his Dreams, he is already a lord atop a high palace mound overlooking the Great Plaza.

Our way has been north-northwest, following Joara Creek up into the mountains, then along the narrow canyon where the trail has been rutted into the soil by generations of Traders and war parties.

Fire Light is no fool. After that incompetent dolt, Field Snake, stumbled in out of the night almost shrieking that a Cahokian war party was hot on his heels, Fire Light used every trick in the book to hide his trail. Figured any pursuit would be less likely to tackle this route over the pass and down to one of the tributary headwaters of the Tenasee.

If only it weren't for the constant burning ache in my testicles, I would be enjoying this: borne like the lord I am through this majestic, breathtaking scenery. I had no idea mountains could be so high, or so beautiful.

But the throbbing ache won't go away. The mere act of standing is agony.

And when I have to drain my water, it hurts like I'm urinating little shards of obsidian, and my piss comes in fits and dribbles. The warriors helping me look away, not daring to so much as make a face, lest I inflict some curse on them.

This isn't funny.

My soul is aching to take Night Shadow Star, but my shaft and stones refuse.

This night we make camp at the summit of the steep pass; here people have camped for generations. A central fire is built, the warriors' rations of hominy are being boiled.

The air is cool, the breeze blowing through the high saddle carries the scents of the forest, and overhead a hoary frosting of stars is glowing on the soot black of the night. I can hear the hooting of a great horned owl in the distance, and then the curious calls of a herd of elk deep in the woods.

This is not how I imagined I would celebrate my victory. But my day will come. As soon as I am healed, I will fulfill my Dream. I will have a special lodge prepared, have Night Shadow Star stripped and tied.

I will purify my body, paint designs of rebirth on my flesh to invoke vigor, and filled with the Power of the lightning I will mount Night Shadow Star. I will drive my shaft into her—a merging of Sky Power and Underworld Power. In that glorious moment, when my hot semen jets into her, I will possess her Lord's Power and mine. Piasa and Thunderer, combined. Opposites crossed.

I will become the most Powerful man in the world.

When I do, not even Morning Star can stand against me.

I stare up at the sky, see a streak of yellow fire as a meteor burns its way from east to west. A sign that the Sky World has heard and approves of my thoughts.

Painfully I stand. Hobbling, I make my way to where Night Shadow Star is bound, her back to a sapling. She is dark against the white bark.

I try to bend down, to stare into her hard eyes, illuminated by the dancing firelight as they are. Can't. Hurts too much. Her remarkably muscular arms are straining against the bonds, and I know that if she could get free, she'd strangle me in a moment.

Wounded as I am, she might even be able to do it. Fair, I guess. Once, in a wild rage, I tried to kill her that way.

I smile, savoring my victory. It will, after all, only be a matter of time before I am healed.

I say, "Hello, Sister."

And then I proceed to tell her all the things I am going to do to her when I am well.

She listens, her eyes gleaming. Is that fear or anticipation?

To my surprise, she says, "Before I die, I will stand over your dead body. I swear it before the Powers of Sky and Underworld."

She says it like she believes it.

As she does, I see a flicker of blue at the edge of my vision, and lightning streaks the cloudless skies.

Acknowledgments

From the beginning, Tom Doherty and Linda Quinton have supported our efforts to bring the story of North America's first peoples to life. Without their belief, encouragement, and commitment to our nation's cultural heritage, these novels would never have existed.

To Theresa Hulongbayan and the Facebook Gear Fan Club: Book Series First North Americans go our eternal thanks.

We particularly want to thank the great staff at the Cahokia Mounds State Historic Site. Mark Esarey, Matt Migala, Bill Iseminger, their staff, and the volunteers keep this remarkable World Heritage Site open to the public. To learn more, contact www.cahokiamounds.org. Better yet, when you're in the St. Louis area, experience Cahokia yourself.

And finally, a special thanks to Jen, Cyle, Ashley, and the wonderful staff at the One Eyed Buffalo in Thermopolis for brewing Michael's stout and Kathleen's Sessions IPA. OEB is our haven for brainstorming plot, story, and character.

Authors' Note

Great story lines, character arcs, and epic tales often exceed the scope of a single book. Night Shadow Star, Seven Skull Shield, Fire Cat, Blue Heron, and of course Farts will return in *Lightning Shell,* book five of the People of Cahokia series. Coming to you soon from Forge Books!